King's Gold

Michael Jecks gave up a career in the computer industry to concentrate on writing and the study of medieval history. A regular speaker at library and literary events, he is a past Chairman of the Crime Writers' Association. He lives with his wife, children and dogs on northern Dartmoor.

Also by Michael Jecks

The Last Templar
The Merchant's Partner
A Moorland Hanging
The Crediton Killings
The Abbot's Gibbet
The Leper's Return
Squire Throwleigh's Heir
Belladonna at Belstone
The Traitor of St Giles
The Boy Bishop's Glovemaker
The Tournament of Blood
The Sticklepath Strangler
The Devil's Acolyte
The Mad Monk of Gidleigh
The Templar's Penance
The Outlaws of Ennor
The Tolls of Death
The Chapel of Bones
The Butcher of St Peter's
A Friar's Bloodfeud
The Death Ship of Dartmouth
The Malice of Unnatural Death
Dispensation of Death
The Templar, the Queen and Her Lover
The Prophecy of Death
The King of Thieves
The Bishop Must Die
The Oath

MICHAEL JECKS

**SIMON &
SCHUSTER**

London · New York · Sydney · Toronto

A CBS COMPANY

First published in Great Britain by Simon & Schuster UK Ltd, 2011
A CBS Company

1 3 5 7 9 10 8 6 4 2

Simon & Schuster UK Ltd
1st Floor
222 Gray's Inn Road
London WC1X 8HB

www.simonandschuster.co.uk

www.michaeljecks.co.uk

Simon & Schuster Australia
Sydney

A CIP catalogue record for this book is available from the British Library

Hardback ISBN 978-1-84737-902-3
Trade Paperback ISBN 978-0-85720-111-9

Typeset by Hewer Text UK Ltd, Edinburgh
Printed and bound in Great Britain by CPI Mackays, Chatham ME5 8TD

This book is for the Marvellous Marvins
with thanks for Fnob Cheese!

GLOSSARY

Abjure   felons who claimed sanctuary in a church
                      were sometimes offered the chance to abjure
                      the realm i.e. accepting voluntary exile in
                      preference to being executed. They must
                      confess to their crime, after which their prop-
                      erty was all forfeit, even if subsequently they
                      were pardoned or shown to be innocent.

Alaunt   a ferocious hunting dog, built like a grey-
                      hound but much larger.

Black bread   the bread of poorer folk, used especially for
                      making trenchers, was made from flour which
                      was not so carefully sieved and prepared as
                      white flour.

Braies   underclothes consisting of linen or loose
                      woollen material that was full in the bottom
                      and reached sometimes to the calves. The
                      waist was often curled over and over to form a
                      sort of belt, sometimes with strings to tie it up.

Fuller
a channel running along the length of a sword blade, sometimes called a 'blood gutter', it was intended to reduce the weight of the blade without weakening it.

Half-staff
a staff held with hands apart over the middle so that roughly half the staff was between the hands. As a weapon, it could be used to jab with either end, or to block another fighter's weapon with the mass of the centre.

Host
in medieval England the King could call on men of a certain age to serve in his levy. The word army came from *armée*, a French term that would not come into common use in English until the Hundred Years War.

Kennel
central gulley or gutter in a medieval street.

Lampreys
a primitive, eel-like fish that was prized as a delicacy in medieval times. Henry I was said to have died from 'a surfeit of lampreys'.

Maslin
mixture of rye and wheat, used for breadmaking.

Niddicock
fool, idiot.

Pandemaigne
special, creamy white bread made with the highest grade of flour, from which much of the bran (but not wheatgerm) had been removed by sieving through cloth.

Peine Forte et Dure
torture in England was illegal before the 1300s, but if an accused man refused to plead, he could be forced to lie on the floor, shackled to rings, and to have weights set upon his chest until he complied. Many died, unable to breathe (another 'natural' death for a prisoner).

Perry   drink made from fermenting pears – similar to cider, but sweeter.

Quarter-staff   (see **Half-staff**) the manner of holding a staff with one quarter of the stave between the hands, both hands nearer one tip, leaving three-quarters of the weapon pointing at the enemy like a lance.

Rache   a running dog, like a greyhound but smaller than an **Alaunt**.

Rifflers   bands of men who looted and robbed at will when King Edward II left London.

Rounsey   general purpose horse of a good size, used by men-at-arms for a warhorse, or a packhorse.

Scavengers   workers who cleansed a town's streets of faeces and rubbish.

Sumpter   a baggage horse.

Verderer   the official responsible for the law in the King's forest.

CAST OF CHARACTERS

Sir Baldwin de Furnshill   Keeper of the King's Peace, known for his astute investigation of crimes.

Jeanne de Furnshill   wife to Sir Baldwin.

Edgar   Baldwin's servant and chief man-at-arms.

Simon Puttock   Once a bailiff on Dartmoor, now a local farmer and freeman, Simon has been associated with the new government because of his hatred of the Despenser regime.

Margaret Puttock   'Meg' is Simon's wife.

Edith   Simon and Meg's daughter.

Hugh   Simon's servant.

Sir Richard de Welles   friend to Simon and Baldwin, Coroner to the Hundred of Lifton.

Sir Ralph of Evesham   a knight loyal to the old King.

Willersey

Father Luke	vicar of St Peter's, Willersey.
Ham	a farmer in Willersey.
Agatha	wife of Ham.
Jen	daughter to Ham and Agatha.

London

Bardi	family of Florentine bankers who helped fund the King of England, based in Florence, but with a house in London.
Manuele di Bardi	the oldest of the brothers and head of the Bardi family in London.
Benedetto di Bardi	second-in-command of the bank.
Matteo di Bardi	youngest brother of the family.
Sebastian & Francisco	two merchants from the House of Bardi.
Dolwyn of Guildford	bodyguard; supporter of Edward II.
Alured the Cooper	a law officer.

Camp of Sir Edward of Caernarfon

Sir Edward of Caernarfon	once King Edward II of England, he has been forced to abdicate the realm and pass it on to his son.
John of Shulton	a man-at-arms from the Despenser estates.
Paul of Bircheston	John's best friend; also a Despenser vassal.
Harry le Cur	one of the men-at-arms who had been besieged at Caerphilly.
Senchet Garcie	another member of the Caerphilly garrison.

Stephen Dunheved	an instigator of the plots to rescue the former King.
Frere Thomas Dunheved	brother of Stephen, and a Dominican Friar, Thomas had been a confidential agent for King Edward II and remained intensely loyal to him.
Brother Michael	a monk at the Augustinian Priory of Llantony-next-Gloucester.
William atte Hull	nephew to Brother Michael.
Sir Edmund Gascelin	ally to the Dunheveds and involved in their plots.
Donald, Earl of Mar	a Scottish earl who was intensely loyal to Sir Edward of Caernarfon and involved in many plots to release him.

Camp of King Edward III

King Edward III	the young son of Edward of Caernarfon, he rules only with the approval and consent of Sir Roger Mortimer, his Regent. Also known as the Duke of Aquitaine.
Sir Roger Mortimer	for many years Sir Roger was King Edward II's favourite general, but now he is Edward of Caernarfon's most hated enemy.
Earl Henry of Lancaster	one of the most powerful noblemen in England, who inherited his title when his brother Thomas was executed by Edward II for rebellion.
Sir Jevan de Bromfield	a knight in the service of Henry, Earl of Lancaster at Kenilworth.

Lord Thomas de Berkeley   son-in-law to Sir Roger Mortimer.

Sir John Maltravers   a close friend to Lord Thomas.

Gilbert   chief guard of Edward of Caernarfon.

Squire Bernard   porter at the gate of Kenilworth Castle.

AUTHOR'S NOTE

In trying to write a book about the gaoling of Sir Edward of Caernarfon, lately King Edward II of England, I have been forced to study a large number of documents to make sense of the crazy politics of that era.

Scholars have argued about the poor King's end. The general story, that he was captured, his friend and adviser Sir Hugh le Despenser executed, and the King himself forced to go under guard to Kenilworth, is not disputed. The wretched fellow must have passed a miserable Christmas in 1326, held captive by a man who sought to take the kingdom for himself – Earl Henry of Lancaster – but Edward's problems went deeper than one aristocratic enemy.

Earl Henry was not alone in desiring power. Sir Roger Mortimer was shrewd, ruthless, and well-connected. It was he who had raised the army that captured King Edward II. Earl Henry schemed and achieved some political success, but Mortimer had the ear of the Queen. Soon he took control and forced the King to abdicate. King Edward II became Sir Edward of Caenarfon.

However, many were determined to see him released ... which begs the question: *why?*

After all, this man had presided over a catastrophic period. There had been famine, war and disease, and through it all, King Edward II had sought to maintain and reward only those for whom he had the strongest affection. Others were treated as convenient sources of funding. Many were robbed, seeing their lands, wealth and authority stripped away by a King who sought to pass them to his favourites: first to Sir Piers Gaveston, then to Sir Hugh le Despenser. And these two were not averse to grabbing what they desired – with or without the King's help.

Yet many did try to rescue the King and return him to his throne. There were three attempts to free him in 1327. Prominent in these plots were the Dunheved brothers and their gang.

I am sure that some who risked their lives to free Sir Edward of Caernarfon were motivated by fealty, by love, and by simple loyalty. Others were acting from a desire for reward: power or money. What is certain is that most of them lost their lives.

This was a particularly brutal time. At the turn of the fourteenth century, King Edward I had been forced to throw aside the usual system of courts, and replace them with a process designed specifically to curb the depredations of a new breed of felon, the 'trailbastons' or 'club-men'. These bands of outlaws would set upon travellers or farmers, killing, raping, looting, and then moving on. The courts of trailbaston were designed to enforce the King's Peace, as were the Keepers of the King's Peace – men like Sir Baldwin de Furnshill.

These knights were given warrants to hunt down murderers and other felons, actually chasing them from hundred to hundred, shire to shire. Their job was to to capture criminals, unlike the coroners, who existed mostly as tax-gatherers:

coroners went from body to body, noting all salient facts about each corpse on their great scrolls, so that when the Justices arrived up to ten years later, they would be able to see all the facts and impose whatever fines were relevant.

From the look of the writs I have seen, the Dunheved gang had been keeping Keepers busy in recent years. Stephen Dunheved himself had been forced to leave the country in 1321, having abjured the realm (see *Glossary*). It is interesting to speculate on his crime. Presumably it was murder – but the fact of it did not prevent his brother from acting as confessor to King Edward II. That may seem odd to us now, but the taint of a crime did not adhere to a family name in the 1300s. If it had, there would have been few men qualified to remain in the King's household.

Noted criminals of the time were routinely found amongst the King's companions. Sir Gilbert de Middleton is one example.

Irritated by the manner in which the King treated his relation, Adam de Swinburne, who was thrown into gaol when he criticised certain of Edward's policies, Sir Gilbert took Adam's case into his own hands. But not for him the usual method of presenting his case in court. In preference, he attacked a delegation heading to Scotland to negotiate a peace with those troublesome Scots. The fact that among the men he kidnapped were two papal envoys did not endear him to his King, and he was captured in fairly short order and taken to London in chains before being executed.

Middleton was by no means alone. There was Sir Peter de Lymesey who stole a woman's lands, and when she tried to take the matter to court, he prevented her by threatening all her witnesses with maiming, burning or death. In 1311 it was said of Sir John de Somery that no one could win justice in Staffordshire due to his control of the area. He was a man of 'considerable notoriety'[1]. And not only knights were keen to use their positions in the King's household for their own advantage. Robert Lewer, 'an out-and-out thug in household employment'[2], was only an archer when he threatened to 'dismember some sergeants sent to arrest him, either in the presence or the absence of the King'. His violent life came to an end two years later, when he suffered the *peine forte et dure* (see *Glossary*) because he refused to plead in court.

This was a time of powerful young men who were certain of their status and their authority. And many had cause to be grateful to the King.

Knights were made Coroners, Sherrifs, Keepers, Justices of Gaol Delivery; they were asked to go to Parliament; some few served in the King's household among other duties. All these positions gave opportunities for the unscrupulous, and all too often the knights proved themselves perfectly content to make profit. As shown above, they could resort to extreme violence when it suited them.

And that points to another possible motivation for a number of the men involved in the schemes to spring the King from gaol: some may well have realised that the crimes they had committed were so heinous that it was likely a new administration would come down heavily on them. They had enjoyed their freedom before King Edward III took the throne from his father, and they sought to return King Edward II, his father, to the throne in order that they might gain pardons for more recent crimes they had committed. Or so that they could continue their lawless way of life.

1 'The Unreliablity of Royal Household Knights', by Michael Prestwich, in Fourteenth Century England II, edited by Chris Given-Wilson, Boydell Press, 2002.
2 Ibid.

Whatever their reasons, it is clear that many men were prepared to risk their lives in rescuing Sir Edward of Caernarfon from whichever gaol he currently inhabited.

Once again, I am hugely indebted to Ian Mortimer, who very generously gave me an early sight of his latest book, *Medieval Intrigue*, which was published in September 2010. I am also glad to acknowledge the great help I've received from Jules Frusher and Kathryn Warner, and from their excellent Edward II and Despenser sites on the internet.

Many other books have been of great assistance. There is a list of them on my website at www.michaeljecks.co.uk – please see the *Bibliography* button on the left.

For now, I hope you enjoy the story as you slip back into the past and into a period in which life was more brutal and more dangerous than it is today, and when the people of England felt little compunction about rebelling against injustice.

Michael Jecks
North Dartmoor
July 2010

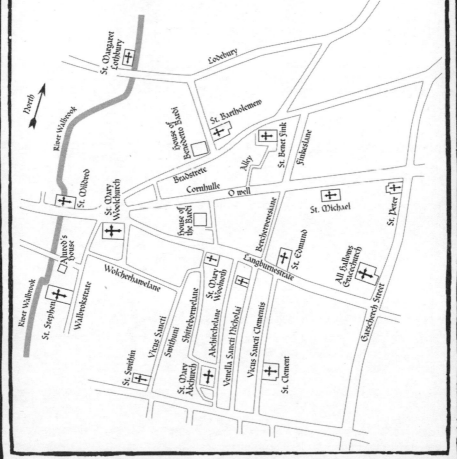

London around the House of the Bardi

North

River Wallbrook

St. Margaret Lothbury

Lodebury

House of Benedetto Bardi

St. Bartholemew

St. Benet Fink

Finkeslane

Bradstrete

Alley

St. Oilberd

St. Mary Woolchurch

Cornhulle

O well

St. Michael

St. Peter

House of the Bardi

Brchernerslane

St. Edmund

River Wallbrook

Alured's House

Langburnestrate

All Hallows Gracechurch

Wolcherhawelane

Walbrokstrate

Gracechurch Street

St. Stephen

Vicus Sancti

Swithuni

Shitteborwelane

St. Mary Woolnoth

River Wallbrook

Abchirchelane

Venella Sancti Nicholai

Vicus Sancti Clementis

St. Swithin

St. Mary Abchurch

St. Clement

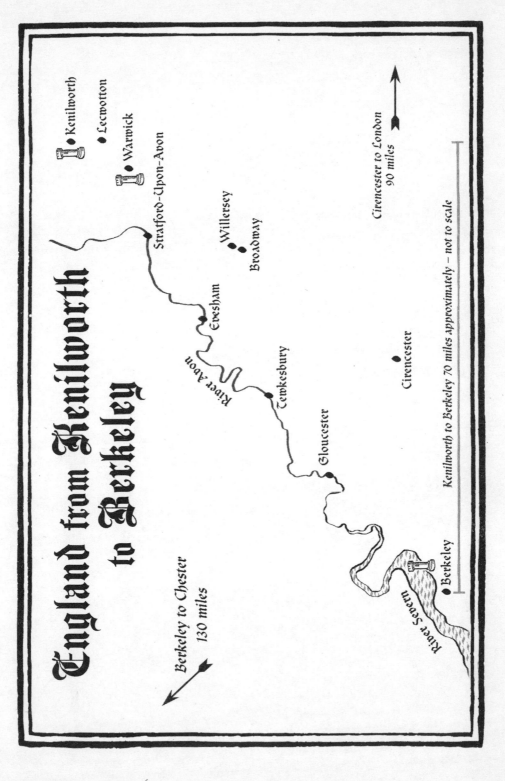

England from Kenilworth to Berkeley

Kenilworth

Leewotton

Warwick

Stratford-Upon-Avon

Willersey

Broadway

Evesham

River Avon

Tewkesbury

Cirencester

Gloucester

Cirencester to London
90 miles

Berkeley

River Severn

Berkeley to Chester
130 miles

Kenilworth to Berkeley 70 miles approximately – not to scale

CHAPTER ONE

Third Wednesday after the Feast of St Michael,
twentieth year of the reign of King Edward II[1]

Abchirchelane, London

Matteo di Bardi hurried up the lane. His bodyguard, Dolwyn, was beside him; two more men behind – all anxious. At times they broke into a brisk trot, for it was impossible to saunter along when the city was in flames. Matteo must get to the meeting.

The smell of charred embers was everywhere. He had heard that the houses of the Bishop of Exeter were all aflame, that the homes of other bishops were besieged or broken open, that men of prestige and authority were lying slain in the streets. It was lunacy!

The third, and youngest brother of the House of Bardi, Matteo could have had a magnificent career in Florence, but

1 15 October 1326

the lure of the court of King Edward II had tempted him to join Manuele and Benedetto. He was shrewd and well-informed: with these talents, he reckoned he must soon rise in the family's bank. Instead, he was witness to the destruction of the kingdom's greatest city.

Ahead lay Langburnestrate[1], the great road that led from Garscherch Street to St Mary Woolchurch, and he knew that when he reached it, he must head west along it for a few yards before turning north.

Usually Langburnestrate was full of vendors hoping to snare some fool into buying their maggoty pies and mouldy bread, but not today. The street was deserted. This eerie silence, Matteo knew, was the brief calm before the 'rifflers' arrived and began to torch, rape and murder. There was nothing those barbarians would not sink to. Truly, the only cure for them was to put them to the sword or hang the bastards.

Matteo di Bardi was a small man, with thin, pallid features on which his black beard and dark, dilated eyes stood out like those on a fever patient. However, Matteo was not unwell: his was the pallor of the scriptorium. He spent his days assessing, calculating and carefully researching. And in his purse now he had the results of his labours.

There was more smoke. He could practically *taste* it – along with the stench of death. At the end of the street he stopped, his heart pounding, as Dolwyn edged forward and peered around the corner. Nothing. He beckoned, and Matteo made haste to follow him.

Here in Langburnestrate there was no one to be seen, only an occasional movement at an unshuttered window. Farther along the road, where it widened at the door of St Mary

---

1 Lombard Street

Woolchurch, there was a large bonfire, but apart from that, the area was deserted. That was not a good sign, since the men who had constructed this bonfire would not have left it without reason.

The four hastened along the road until they reached the church, at which point they could turn along the narrow northern lane. At last Matteo saw the great stone house that was the London residence of the Bardi and pounded on the timbers with his gloved fist, his men behind him.

The house of the Bardi was old. Over the door was a stone lintel in which the arms of King Edward II had been deeply carved, a proof of the bankers' status in the city. The house gave him a feeling of safety – at least for now, he thought as he glanced nervously about him.

The door opened and Matteo Bardi slipped inside with two of his men. However, Dolwyn remained outside; then, at a signal from his master, Dolwyn made his way back into the lane.

St Peter's Willersey

Father Luke was kneeling at his little altar when he heard the rumble and clink of men and a cart in the lane outside. He was quick to finish his prayers and stride to the door.

This last summer had been a good one, but rumours of impending disaster had abounded. Everyone in the country knew about the Queen's treachery, and tales were flying around about how her mercenaries would despoil the kingdom. It was enough to make Father Luke consider pulling out his father's old sword to defend himself, but he knew he'd be more likely to incite an attack than protect his church.

Outside he found two men-at-arms on horseback, seven reluctant-looking peasants on foot, and a cart with a strongbox on it.

MICHAEL JECKS

'Father, I've heard you have a secure storeroom?' one of the riders asked. He was a swarthy fellow with a bushy red and brown beard, and brown eyes in a square face.

'Yes, of course,' Father Luke said. Churches were the best places for men to store valuable items. They would trust a priest not to rob them, and even if a church were to be broken into, it was rare for thieves to get into a strongroom within. Until recently, even the King himself had stored his crown jewels and gold in the church at Westminster Abbey.

The man introduced himself as Hob of Gloucester. 'We have a box to deposit with you, for my lord, Sir Hugh le Despenser. He cannot fetch it, and we cannot carry it with us, since it's too heavy. Will you keep it for him?'

'Oh, well, yes, of course,' Father Luke said, flustered. Sir Hugh le Despenser was the King's right-hand man. Some considered him to be more a brother than a friend, they were so close. In fact, he had become the second most powerful man in the kingdom. Sir Hugh was detested by many, including the Queen. It was due to him that she had run off to France, it was said.

The chest was lifted from the wagon, which creaked in gratitude to be relieved of its heavy load. Then the men carried it into the nave, across to the doorway, down the staircase and into the undercroft. There it would be safe.

'Thank you, Father,' Hob panted.

'Where are you going?' Father Luke asked, as Hob pulled on his gloves before remounting his horse.

His face grim, he replied, 'I go to join Sir Hugh and the King. They are making their way west – fleeing from their enemies.'

'God speed you, my friend, and bless you.'

'Thank you, Father,' Hob said. 'Please – pray for us. Especially if we do not return.'

'I will.'

'And pray for the kingdom too. I foretell a time of war and murder, Father, and only the Devil and his own will flourish.'

House of the Bardi, Cornhulle, London

'Matteo, you are most welcome,' his brother Manuele greeted him as Matteo strode into the hall, still trying to calm his urgently beating heart. The men in this room were the most powerful in the family, and if they saw his weakness they would despise him.

The other men present gave him a nod or a thin smile. Benedetto, the middle brother, appeared fretful, while Sebastian and Francisco, who worked with Manuele, looked haggard and exhausted. These were the men who controlled the untold wealth of the Bardi family here in England, but today disaster faced them.

It was a massive chamber, Manuele's hall, as befitted the master of the most important bank in London. A great fire roared in the hearth against the chilly air outside, but the breath of the five men was still misting before them. Matteo could see the steam rising from his clothes, and felt filthy compared with them. They must see the dirt on his hosen and boots – well, damn their souls if they did. He was past caring. They would soon know the same terror. The rioting crowds outside were full of dreadful hatred.

And most of all they hated bankers.

'Did you not bring your horse?' Manuele asked, glancing pointedly at his soiled boots.

'Men on horses are targets,' Matteo said. He added, 'I saw the Bishop of Exeter pulled from his horse today.'

'Pulled?'

'They beheaded him with a knife,' Matteo said without emotion. 'His body they threw in a ditch.'

5

Manuele's smile became a grimace of shock. 'Bishop Walter? He's dead?' He rubbed a hand over his face. 'There will be a terrible retribution for this when the King hears.'

Matteo eyed him with disbelief. 'Manuele, the King is running for his life. He won't come back here!'

'Nonsense!'

'You have to accept the facts,' Matteo said steadily. 'You think the King is all-powerful. I tell you he is not. He is weak – and all those who would have sought his protection are fleeing. There is no safety here in London. We need to have a thought for our own survival!'

'You are our intelligencer. What intelligence do you bring?' Benedetto asked. Younger than Manuele and more intellectual, he was also taller, a wiry man with the darker skin of one who had only recently returned from Florence. He had spent much of the last year there, and was more used to the Byzantine intrigues of that city. Matteo knew he was much more competent than Manuele, who was grown fat and lazy here in this cold climate. Benedetto was *hungry*.

'You know it already,' Matteo snapped. 'The Queen has returned to the kingdom, and at no point was she turned back. We know she could have been repelled at sea, but King Edward's navy refused his orders to stop her. She could also have been prevented from landing, but of the men King Edward sent to capture her, all went over to her side. As she progresses across the kingdom, the King flies before her, losing men-at-arms like a bucket leaking water, while every day her followers grow in number. She will eventually catch her husband – and when she does, who can say what will happen?'

'She may catch the King, but the King has the authority of the coronation behind him. No one has ever killed a crowned King except those whom God favours.' Manuele sipped from his wine, eyeing the others as though daring them to argue.

'It is true. But the Queen has the support of the people. And her son is with her; who would dare to stand in *his* way? To dispute with her would be to dispute with the future King.' Matteo was keen to convince them. This could be the end of their house if he failed, and he had no intention of seeing it destroyed. 'London has declared for her.'

'*London*,' Manuele sneered. 'The city is only one of many in the realm. It is not like Florence.'

'True, it is not independent like Florence,' Matteo said earnestly, 'but in many ways it is more influential. It helps govern the whole kingdom. The King of this fractious and intolerant people has to be strong to hold their allegiance, and they perceive Edward as weak because of his attachment to Despenser. So they will overthrow him.'

'In London they will, possibly,' Benedetto said. 'But, little brother, I agree with Manuele: there is more to this kingdom than just one city.'

'Yes,' Matteo agreed. 'Men flock to the Queen from *all* over the realm.'

'The King has friends elsewhere. What of the Welsh?'

'My spies tell me some may rise in his support, but there is no sign of it as yet. If they do not hurry to his aid . . .'

'For the King to be saved, they will have to declare for him soon, yes,' Benedetto put in.

Matteo shook his head impatiently. 'Do you not see, the King has already lost?'

Benedetto glanced at Manuele. 'I know it is alarming, but the city can soon be brought back under control.'

'And if you are wrong?'

'Matteo, you grow strident,' Benedetto said with a conde-scending smile. 'You bring us intelligence and we adapt our policies to suit. There is no need to become upset.'

'Brother, the Queen will almost certainly defeat the King. The question is, what then? Will she kill those who caused trouble between her and her husband, but then return the King to the throne?'

'Of course,' Benedetto said. 'She can do nothing else.'

'She has made her husband wear the cuckold's hat, brother. She shares a bed with Sir Roger Mortimer. So, tell me, do you think it likely she would return her husband to the throne, knowing he could charge her with treason and have her lover hanged, drawn and quartered? Or would she prefer to see King Edward imprisoned while she rules in his place?'

Benedetto stared at him for a moment, and Matteo saw a shrewd calculation flare in his eyes.

Manuele held up a hand. 'No! The Queen would of course return her husband to the throne. He has been anointed by God.'

Benedetto kept his eyes on Matteo as he said, 'I am begin-ning to think we need to reconsider this.'

'You have been in Florence too long, Benedetto,' Manuele scoffed. 'I have lived here many years. The people may be angry and argumentative, but they believe in the law, and the law does not give them the right to evict their King. They will come to the brink and then surrender, as they have done before. That is why our investment must remain with the King.'

'And if they don't?' Matteo asked pointedly. 'If you are wrong, and all our money is with him, we shall be ruined, because I do not think the Queen has any liking for our House. She wanted us to help her last year in France and she was snubbed, if you remember?'

Manuele pulled a face, a tacit admission that his decision at that time had been wrong. 'We thought that she was only there for a little while, and would return to her husband. How was I to know that she would leave him and form a liaison with a traitor? It was only logical to continue to support King Edward.'

'You took the decision for the best of reasons,' Matteo concurred, 'but events have overtaken us.'

Manuele had lost his way, Matteo thought privately. Benedetto was stronger, and he possessed a certain crafty slyness, but he was too concerned with the Queen. It was enough to make a man despair. The bank needed strong leadership now, more than ever, and his brothers were so hidebound.

Matteo wanted to groan. He knew best how to guide the bank because of the flood of reports that swamped his table daily. Armed with that information, he could ensure the security of their money better than either of his brothers.

He tried a persuasive tone: 'The Queen is back, and we must consider how this changes things for us. We should attempt to win her favour – offer her our support. We must gain her respect and that of her advisers. I have held discussions—'

'Yes. It is as I have argued,' Benedetto interrupted smoothly. 'I have connections with Queen Isabella's advisers – influential men. They can see that, with our support, she is more likely to succeed in deposing her husband.'

Matteo threw him a suspicious look. He had not expected Benedetto to be persuaded so easily.

'This is nonsense,' Manuele snapped. 'The Queen? Pfft! She is nothing.'

'We have to retain our position at the heart of the government,' Benedetto said. 'It is the source of all our profits. With our money behind her, the Queen can win the realm, and she will have reason to be grateful to us.'

Manuele frowned with exasperation. 'What risk would there be to our investment in the King if he should return to power?'

'His reign will soon end,' Matteo said. 'The people detest him and his advisers, especially Sir Hugh le Despenser. If Despenser fails to escape, he will be executed, and all the money which we have earned from his investments will be gone.'

'Despenser's funds are already gone,' Benedetto said. 'He has withdrawn his money, and I doubt that he will return it to us if he flies abroad. I am inclined to the opinion that we should throw our weight behind the Queen. The King is a broken straw.'

'A broken straw will support cob or daub and make a strong wall,' Manuele argued. 'The man will recover his authority. He has done so before.'

'He may, but I fail to see how,' Matteo stated. 'He has so alienated his barons that the country supports his Queen, not him.'

'So that is why we should give our support to her now,' Benedetto said. 'That is your proposal.'

'I say no!' Manuele said heatedly. 'We have invested too much in him.'

'I do not say we ignore him,' Matteo said, then paused. From the window, he could hear angry chanting in the street. 'We should also bear in mind that the King is in need of friends.'

'But if you are right, he will be insignificant shortly,' Benedetto protested.

Matteo took a deep breath. He had hoped that Benedetto would understand.

'Yes. But if he loses all for now, he may yet regain influence in years to come. He may tutor his son, he may again command the respect of some barons, perhaps win back the love of his Queen . . . who can tell? If he ever returned to power, he would richly reward those friends who had provided support or finance to him in his hours of deepest need, would he not?'

10

Benedetto smiled. 'I think you grow confused. We should support only the Queen. She is the source of power now that she controls the heir.'

'*No!*' Matteo growled. 'You still don't understand!'

London Bridge

The bridge was closed. At the road leading to it, Sir Jevan de Bromfield studied the closed and barred gates, the men standing about with polearms and axes. There would be no escape there.

All in good time. There were other gates by which a man could leave this cursed city. For now he had to hurry to his meeting. He had an urgent mission – the first serious business since his return to England.

With the force led by Sir Roger Mortimer and the Queen, Sir Jevan had spent his time in idle meandering about the countryside. That was all it had been, an amiable wandering, while the populace turned out to cheer and applaud. The mercenaries could have been liberators instead of invaders.

But that would soon change if there was no money.

The Queen had used the little wealth she had stored in maintaining herself in France. Sir Roger Mortimer had nothing, because his estates and belongings had been confiscated when he was declared a traitor and imprisoned. As soon as his death warrant had been signed, he had lost all. So now their men, mercenaries from Hainault and the Low Countries, with some adventurers from France and a few English fighters determined to take back what they had lost, were marching with empty pockets. Money was desperately needed.

That was why Sir Jevan was here, in London, to ensure that a deal was struck. If it would hasten the end of Edward's obnoxious reign, he would treat with the Devil himself.

CHAPTER TWO

House of the Bardi, London

There was a crash outside the hall, and the men in the room spun around to stare at the window as though they expected to see the mob spilling into the hall.

'What do you suggest, then?' Manuele demanded of Matteo. 'You speak of supporting first the Queen, then the King – I don't follow your reasoning.'

'An offer to the King. Of gold, or influence. Anything he needs. A letter couched in careful terms, that would give him hope, if nothing else. Money to help him in his prison. We can tell him that he can always count upon our support, that whenever he has need of us, we will aid him. If we can get that to him, he will gain confidence from it, and reward us if he ever does return to his throne.'

'And if the Queen or Sir Roger Mortimer found it, we should be ruined,' Benedetto snapped.

'Brother, hear him first,' Manuele said, his dark eyes remaining fixed on Matteo.

'The letter would remain a secret known only to him and us. We would have a trusted messenger take it to him. And as I said, if we couch the letter in careful terms,' Matteo explained patiently, 'the Queen would not seek to harm us. Especially if any doubts were already assuaged by our support for her and her son. If we advance her money, she will believe us when we state our allegiance to her. We gain the friendship of both sides, and thereby assure our continued profits no matter who wins.'

There was another crash outside. 'Matteo, can you write such a letter?' Manuele asked.

In answer Matteo pulled the carefully written note from his purse and passed it to him. Manuele took it warily, as though touching it conferred guilt.

There was a shriek in the street, a clattering of weapons, and the men all started.

Manuele read the parchment, then, taking up a reed, he slowly wrote his name at the bottom in ink. 'For the House of Bardi,' he muttered to himself as he sprinkled some sand over the wet ink. Removing his seal ring, he melted a little wax in a candle-flame, and sealed the document, setting it aside to cool on the table.

'I will see that it reaches the King's friends,' Matteo said, feeling the warm glow of success. With this letter the House was safe again, and with fortune, he would soon control it.

A sudden pounding on the front door interrupted their discussions. Matteo was relieved. He had feared that the visitors might have been waylaid. 'Let them in,' he called.

There were four men-at-arms in the party, all wearing mail and coats of plates and, from the way that they held themselves, it was clear that they had been expecting trouble on their way here.

13

Matteo introduced the men. 'Stephen Dunheved, John of Shulton, Harry le Cur, and Senchet Garcie. These gentlemen are here to listen to our position regarding the King.'

'Not only that,' Stephen Dunheved said, 'we are here to have your absolute declaration of loyalty to the King of England, my lord Edward II. He demands your obedience, else he will have all your House closed in England, your funds sequestered and all loans cancelled.'

Matteo reached for the signed document, but before his hand could touch it, Manuele had removed it. 'Brother?'

'Quiet, Matteo.' Manuele stood slowly, the parchment in his hand. 'You come to my house to threaten me?' he demanded of Dunheved. 'Do you know who I am?'

Matteo swore under his breath. He had won the day already, and if these men would only show a little respect due to Manuele, they would win all they wanted. But he could see Manuele was having second thoughts: if one of these men were a traitor who had already turned his coat to support the Queen, he dared not talk of the parchment nor ask any of these to take it to the King. The risk of betrayal was too great.

Dunheved, a weatherbeaten man with the build of a fighter, took a step forward, his hand on his sword, but before he could pull it more than half-free, there was a rush and clatter of steel, and Manuele's servants had their own weapons drawn and ready. Three held swords at Dunheved's throat.

'So this is your answer, then? Betrayal and deceit?' Dunheved hissed.

Manuele walked to him and studied him for a moment. 'No, it is not. I will consider how best to aid your master, but I will not be treated as a churl in my own home. You will leave, and we shall speak no more of this. When I am ready, I will invite you back to discuss this with me. Perhaps.'

'It will be too late! The Queen knows you have maintained the King. And remember that you denied her money when she was in Paris. You think she will forget that and reward you? She will ruin your House, and impoverish you!'

'She may try,' Manuele said suavely. He walked to his sideboard, the parchment still in his hand, and picked up a goblet of wine. Sipping, he gazed at the rich gold and enamel about the bowl. 'You realise that my House is more wealthy than your King's? I have more money at my disposal than he – which is why he sends to me to beg for gold. Well, I am of a mind to answer his call. But not yet.'

As though to emphasise his words, just then a rock the size of a man's fist flew through the window, narrowly missing Benedetto. '*Stronzi*,'[1] he snarled, his hand on his sword.

Manuele walked to the stone and peered at it. 'It would seem that your mob is interested in meeting with us, too.' he said. Then, more seriously: 'Your King will have my answer in a few days. But this city is dangerous just now. You may leave.'

Dunheved set his jaw and would have spoken further, but the man called Senchet called quietly, 'Stephen, you escaped death once before, my friend. I think we should depart while it is still a possibility.'

'Very well,' Dunheved said. 'You will find us at the House of the Lion near the Black Friars.'

He turned, jerked his head to his companions, and they were gone. The servants of the house walked with them, and soon there was a bellowing from the front of the hall.

'I think,' Manuele said with a small smile, 'that the people there wish to talk to our friends.'

'And what of the letter?' Matteo demanded.

---

1 pieces of shit; lit. 'turds'

'Your letter is good. It will suffice,' Manuele said. 'Send it as we agreed, by a safe messenger.'

'We should leave,' Benedetto said urgently. 'The mob is enraged, and they may well attack us. Let us go by the back gates!'

'Very well,' Manuele said absently.

Matteo led the way to the rear of the house, past the kitchen and gawping servants, and out to the gate at the back. There was a short alley here, which gave onto Cornhulle. When sure that the road was safe, he called the others to follow.

Manuele was last to leave. He insisted on his taking his palfrey, and stood tapping his toe until his groom brought the beast.

Matteo protested, 'There are gangs all about the city – a man on horseback is an easy target for their rage and enmity.'

'I am not slim like you. If I meet with a mob, I need a means to escape,' Manuele said with a smile. 'At least on a horse I am more fleet than the London mob.'

As Manuele trotted off into the distance, his two henchmen with him, Matteo watched anxiously. He saw a mass of men erupt from the side streets and envelop his elder brother. A thin scream of terror came from Manuele, and then Matteo too was running away, pounding for his life up a side street with his own two remaining guards.

He only managed a few paces when his legs were knocked from beneath him, and he fell on the cobbles. Something clubbed the back of his head, before the blade slid into his flesh and he toppled into a vast emptiness.

Cornhulle, London

Sir Jevan de Bromfield ran along the roadway at full tilt, and seeing an alleyway, he hurtled into it, hiding in a little corner and gripping his sword tightly.

The mass of feet went thundering on along the main road, and he slowly began to relax. Risking a glance around the corner, he saw the alley was clear.

But then there was a step behind him. He knew that it must be one of his pursuers who had outflanked him to get behind and slip a knife between his shoulderblades while he stared back towards the road like a fool.

He would not die like this!

Whirling like a berserker from a Viking ship, he slashed with his sword and felt it slither into soft flesh. The dragging of meat on his blade was enough to slow his movement, and he had time to gaze upon the young woman's face as his blade sliced deep into her neck. And then his blade was through the bone, and with a gush of blood, her head flew away.

Behind her, the young man who was her swain stood with his mouth wide in horror, so shocked that even as her torso collapsed and the blood besmottered his face and shirt, he could not speak or cry out.

Without hesitation, Sir Jevan reversed his blade and stabbed twice quickly before the lad could call, both wounds in the fellow's breast. One at least punctured his heart, for he died without speaking, the two bodies entangled in death.

Sir Jevan cursed quietly under his breath, then wiped his blade on the young woman's skirts. Her face was pretty, he thought, studying her dispassionately. He regretted their deaths, but for him, a man who had been declared outlaw and exiled by the King, it was better to take no chances. The couple should not have crept up behind him like that.

He moved up the alley away from the road, hoping to avoid any other embarrassments. All he wanted now was to get away from this God-forsaken city and out to the safe, open country-side. But first he had to attend to the Queen's business.

Reaching the end of the alley, he made his way westwards again until he saw the building he sought. Heavy stone walls and small, slit-like windows gave it a grim appearance, but in times like this, it was a welcome sight. Sir Jevan rapped smartly on the door.

A small peephole snapped open and he saw an eye peer at him, then behind and around him.

'You know me,' he said. 'I am here to see *him*.'

The bolts were drawn back, and the door pulled open to reveal a narrow passage.

Sir Jevan walked inside, but was pulled up short by the sight of two swords pointed at his throat and belly: one held by Benedetto, one by a servant. 'What is this? You mean to betray us and our cause? Your deaths will be sealed if you harm me!' he hissed.

Benedetto's sword wavered. 'I'm not betraying you,' he whispered. 'I'm betraying my family . . . and the King.'

'A pox on your family, and the King. He betrayed us all,' Sir Jevan sneered. 'He'd sell the kingdom if he thought it a pretty enough bauble for his darling Despenser!'

'It is agreed, then?'

'You keep up your side of the bargain, Master Benedetto, and yes, Her Royal Highness will be pleased to make use of your money.' Sir Jevan moved forwards, slapping away both swords. 'I have details with me of where to deliver it. You are sure you can provide it? Your brothers won't cause trouble?'

'I can promise it,' Benedetto said. There was an edge in his voice that did not go unnoticed.

'Good,' Sir Jevan said. 'Don't fail us. The Queen may be forgiving, but by the Gospel, I swear Sir Roger Mortimer is not – and neither am I.' He turned with a feline grace, drawing his dagger and pulling the banker off-balance. His blade rested on Benedetto's throat as he warned, 'And next time you hold a sword to my guts, man, you had best be ready to use it. I don't take kindly to such a reception!'

Alured the cooper had never known a time like this.

He was a hoary old man now, almost fifty years old, and he'd seen enough of death in his life. Clad in a strong leather jerkin over a padded jack, wearing the three items he considered most essential for his office – a dagger, a horn and a heavy oaken staff – he listened carefully for danger as he patrolled the streets.

London was his home. As a boy he had run about these streets, breaking windows, banging on doors, almost turning to crime himself, but then something happened to change his whole outlook on life. He had killed a man who was trying to rob him, out near the Austin Friars, and for the first time, Alured discovered what it was to wish to protect his own property from those who would steal it. When later he was elected as a constable for his parish, he took to the role with relish.

The law had to be upheld, that was his belief. But no one was bothering to serve the law today.

There were more than enough men in the Tower to calm the mob – so where were they? It wasn't the whole city on the rampage, in God's name, just some foolish hotheads – apprentices, clerks and the like. There may have been some bad apples in among them, but most were simple, harmless folk who saw that with the King gone, the city was theirs for a while. Well, Alured would exert what authority he could – alone, if need be.

He came across small groups as he did his rounds. For the most part they were content to make way for him. Only a few hundred yards from Cornhulle he met three lads, and sent them packing. Then there were two more boys gawping at a fire,

19

who cleared off quickly enough, and finally he saw a mob of twelve, rampaging along one of the streets that led south from Cornhulle itself, all of them drunk and full of the courage that comes from ale. Observing them from the protection of a doorway, Alured soon identified the two troublemakers amongst them, and nodded grimly to himself. Christ alive, not one of them was more than eighteen years. If he couldn't cow lads of that sort of age, he didn't deserve to see his fiftieth birthday.

The two ringleaders were hurling missiles at the windows of a large house, and when Alured could see it clearly through the smoke of a bonfire that raged somewhere nearby, he recognised it as the Bardis' place.

He himself didn't care for bankers. To his mind, they were a shameful bunch, lining their pockets at the expense of decent men who laboured long hours, afraid to get their own hands dirty. Still, they were not lawbreakers, so far as he knew, and he was an officer of the law.

When the two had flung their stones, and had set to prising cobbles from the road as missiles, Alured stepped out from the doorway. Wearing an amiable smile, he nodded at the youths about him until he reached the two ringleaders. Once a little behind and between them both, he moved his staff in his hands, holding it half-staff, and struck both men smartly on the back of the head: one-two, right first, then left. The two collapsed like pole-axed cattle.

'You've had your fun, boys. Now bugger off,' he said, facing the others.

There was one on the left who scowled belligerently and took a half-pace forward. 'What'd you wanna do that for? They're only lads. You shouldn't have hit them!'

From the others there came some expressions of agreement, but as yet no one else moved forward. Alured was tempted to take up a defensive stance, but instead he set his staff on the ground and leaned on it. 'They may only be boys, but if you don't clear off, and take this heap of garbage with you, I'll break your pate too. Understand me?'

'Your mother was a whore, and your father—'

The fellow choked off as the staff's tip struck his Adam's apple. It was not a hard blow, not enough to break his neck, but it was firm enough to make him fall back, clutching at his throat, and now Alured held the staff like a lance, quarter-staff, the tip waving gently from side to side.

'Lads, I've been to war. I've killed. You don't scare me, because I've got a staff, and you can't reach me without I hurt you. Now pick up these three dog turds and go home. If anyone else tries something stupid, I'll stick this pole right up your arse!'

As he had thought, the three on the ground were the leaders; the nine remaining were the sheep who followed. There were some muttered oaths, and more comments on his parentage, but he stood by with his affable smile fixed to his face and waited. Soon they had gone. Alured watched them leave with satisfaction. He felt he'd handled them well.

There was another shout from up at Cornhulle, and then screams and cries for help. Gripping his horn in one hand, his staff in the other, Alured pelted up the road towards the noise.

This was no gang of drunken youths. As he reached Cornhulle, Alured saw a large group over near a big fire outside St Mary Woolchurch, and in the opposite direction there were a few men gathered together too. He recognised two of the men in that smaller band. They weren't rioters and felons, he knew, and he bent his steps to join them.

'Hello, Bill,' he said to a short man with a thick, grizzled beard and bright brown eyes. 'What's all this?'

'Those arses,' Bill responded, pointing with his chin at the group near the fire.

Alured nodded, but his attention was already on the body lying on the ground behind Bill and the others. 'Who was he?'

'Don't know. The poor follow was already dead when we got here.'

'You saw him die?'

'No. I was watching that lot and tripped over his body. See them?' Bill was a sturdy fellow, Alured knew, but even he was visibly shocked by the violence he had witnessed. 'I saw them kill three men a while ago – one man on a good horse with a couple of guards riding at his side. No reason: all three dragged from their horses and then beaten on the ground. Kicking and battering at them . . . I saw that and ran back up here, before they had a chance to start on me. I'd guess this poor soul was felled here just before that. They killed him, then went back to their bonfire and attacked the other three.' He lifted a shaking hand to his eyes.

'Calm yourself!' Alured said sharply. 'Keep your wits about you, Bill.'

He looked back towards the main group of rioters – but it was a mob of drunken men, women and even children – who already had their eye on him, Bill and the others.

Before they came running up the road, Alured went to the body and rolled it over. The clothing was expensive, he saw from the fine wool tunic and linen chemise under the warm, felted cloak. Pulling the hood to one side, he saw a young, somewhat pale-faced man. His eyes were closed, and when Alured prised one open, he saw that they were green. There was blood on his chin and about his mouth, and some trickled from a deep gouge over his right ear. Alured studied the body for other wounds.

'Stabbed in the back,' he stated.

'Yes – and clubbed about the head. Poor devil wouldn't have stood a chance.' There was a short cry, and Bill narrowed his eyes. 'Look!'

Alured went to his side and stared. He could make out a fellow being taunted by the rest of the crowd. Luckily, this fresh target appeared to have distracted them from attacking Alured and Bill.

Hitching up his belt, Alured grunted, 'Let's hope there's someone in among them who's got a swyving brain,' and drawing a deep breath, he began to stride towards the mob – but even as he set off, it was too late. The crush of people had begun to cheer as they poured up the road, and then into the back of the Bardi house.

There was no point trying to prevent the mob's entry. There were too many.

'Come on, Bill,' Alured sighed. 'Let's get the coroner.'

Just then, there was a noise from up an alleyway – footsteps running – and Alured glanced along it. The alley led to St Benet Fink, he knew, and he threw a quick look over his shoulder at the fire again, before telling Bill, 'Wait here a moment.'

He darted up the alleyway, his staff in his fist, ready to slam the iron tip into the head of any man who dared obstruct or challenge him, but he reached the first dogleg corner without trouble. And then he saw the two bodies.

The head of the girl was on the ground a matter of feet away, but the lad was still alive, just. Alured touched him, and rolled him over, and the lad's mouth moved, but he could not speak. Only blood came from his mouth, making his face a ghastly mask.

'Hold on, boy,' Alured murmured, but even as he spoke, the dying lad gave a sigh and was still. There came a rattle farther up the alley.

23

He took his staff and slipped quietly along, his back close to the wall, staff outstretched.

'You won't kill me, will you?'

The cackling voice made him jump, and he almost brained the fool. 'What are you doing there?'

'Sitting!'

It was a little, wizened old fellow who had the better part of a gallon of ale in him, from the way he belched and grinned, sprawled on the ground at the foot of the wall.

'How long have you been here?'

Bleary eyes peered up at him. 'Me? Since I left the Boar's Head.'

'Did you see a man come this way a little while ago?'

'Someone. Yes. A knight, I think. I din't interrupt him. He was in a hurry.'

'What did he look like?'

'Oh, tall. Big.' His companion smiled. 'And he had a long tunic. I remember that.'

'What colour?'

'I don't know.'

'Come with me.' Alured grabbed the old man's arm and pulled him up. He hauled the fellow along until they came to the two youngsters' bodies.

'Oh, God's cods!' the man bleated.

'That's why you'd best come with me,' Alured said. He pulled him along the alley until they were back with Bill again.

'Thanks be to God you're back. I thought you'd been killed too,' Bill said nervously, eyeing the drunk without pleasure.

'There are two more up there,' Alured said. 'This man saw their killer. Come on, have you sent for the coroner?'

'No,' Bill said.

But the drunk had dropped to his rump by the body. He stared at the man lying there with an expression of curiosity on his old, wrinkled face. 'Why's *he* here?'

'Someone killed him,' Bill said shortly.

'But he's not dead.'

And Matteo Bardi coughed weakly, retched, and closed his eyes from the pain, as he muttered in his native tongue: *'The King's Gold . . . He'll take the King's Gold . . .'*

'Christ's ballocks!' Bill sprang away as though the man was a ghost.

'What did he say?' Alured asked.

'He's raving,' Bill said. 'He needs a physician.'

CHAPTER THREE

Fourth Friday after the Feast of St Michael[1]

Newgate Prison

The mob had taken over the prison. All those accused of supporting the King or his friends were thrown in here, and as Dolwyn was servant to a banker, he too was incarcerated.

Another man had died in the night, Dolwyn saw, glancing at the men huddled in the filth below the long shaft of light. There was a window twenty, thirty feet above them, and the prisoners clung to each other beneath it as though it offered escape. It didn't.

They had thrown the body to lie in the shadow towards the middle of the room, only a scrap of linen about his groin. All his other clothes were gone. Not that he had been dressed for a night here when he came. Dolwyn remembered thinking that his thin clothing would be no protection against the

1 24 October 1326

chill and the foul miasma that pervaded this place. Even those who squeezed together for warmth against the cold and damp suffered. That man wouldn't be the last to die here.

They would all die soon enough.

The dank cell was fifteen feet square, with curved ceilings like an abbey's undercroft. Blackened stone glistened in the darkness, running with moisture, and in the gloom the only sound was a constant, maddening dripping. It went on at the same slow rate all through the day and night. If water could tear at a man's soul, this did.

There were plenty of other noises vying to drown it out, but without success: screams from those demented enough to think their voices could interest the gaoler; the low mumble of the utterly lunatic; the sudden shrieks of a man being beaten by his cell-mate; the sobbing; the pathetic wailing of the boy in a chamber farther along the passageway; the scurrying of rats' paws . . .

Dolwyn had been in gaol before and the thought of death did not frighten him: rather, it was the manner of death that concerned him.

Hunger and thirst were the two constants of his exixtence here in Newgate Prison, but at least he could slake his thirst with a sip at the brackish, water-soaked walls. It tasted foul from the urine of the men in the chamber above them – but he didn't care; not now. The hunger was much worse.

Newgate Prison. It was hard to believe that he was in the foulest gaol in London because of a misunderstanding. He had escaped the rope before, only to come to London and be caught in the same predicament!

Only a few feet or yards up there was the sunlight. Out in the world, men lived, laughed, rutted on their women, ate, walked in the open air, free. How many would even give a thought to the poor devils incarcerated, justifiably or not, down here in the cells? All too few.

He could see the gate in his mind's eye. The great age-black-ened timbers, the square stone towers rising up on either side. And beyond the gate: *life*. A short roadway that gave out to the shacks and rough buildings thrown up towards Holeburnstrete[1], where those who worked in the city but couldn't afford a room congregated. These were no great mansions like the houses on the road to Westminster where he'd been caught: these were shabby hovels for workers and beggars, sprawling out on either side of the street all higgledy-piggledy, to the Fleet River and beyond.

And beyond were trees, he remembered. For a while he could almost taste the clean air, and his lungs seemed cleansed of the filth that encompassed this city of fools and fiends.

It was on La Straunde[2] that he'd been taken, hard by St Clement Danes. The mob was sacking a rich man's house – someone said it was the Bishop of Exeter's, but Dolwyn couldn't give a clipped farthing for that. All he knew was that there were bodies in the street, and behind them, men savaging the building. There were flames in the window, and three men came from the house's main entrance dragging a huge tapes-try. Behind them was a churl with a leather jug, from which he refreshed himself regularly. Catching sight of Dolwyn, he started to point and shout.

In a moment Dolwyn was surrounded by scruffy youths, the raggle-taggle of London's streets, all of them armed with knives, cleavers and hatchets.

'What's your name?'

1 Holborn.
2 The Strand.

'Dolwyn of Guildford.'

'Well, "Dolwyn", only spies and traitors come past here.'

'I am travelling home to Guildford – nothing more.'

'I think you're a spy.'

'No. I've nothing to do with this.'

'You're spying on us!'

Dolwyn looked at the place. 'My master is richer than this. You're welcome to it. I am with the Bardi . . .' And then he could have cursed his stupidity.

'You are a Bardi man!' one of them snarled. 'A pox on you and your money-lenders!'

The crowd gave an approving growl and edged nearer.

He said, 'I'm only a servant.'

'Just a servant, eh? God's faith! Those usurers helped the old King 'against our city,' the leader said, and spat into the street. 'King's gone now, though, and the Bardi won't be coming back. The city's ours!'

'You treat your property with care,' Dolwyn said, gazing at pillars of smoke rising into the sky.

'The King's running like a hare before the dogs. Him and Despenser.'

'He can rot in hell,' a voice muttered.

'I have no business with you, or the King,' Dolwyn said. 'I'm just a traveller.'

'I don't believe you!'

'I piss on you,' he snapped. 'I tell the truth!'

His words enraged someone, because in a moment he was on his knees, being struck repeatedly over the back with a stick. He endured it for a while, but then seized the stick and thrashed his assailant twice, but before he could climb to his feet, he felt a boot slam into his chin, and then fists and feet kept him down.

And he woke up here in the gaol, along with others the mob disliked.

There was a new noise. He could just hear it over the sobbing of the boy up the way and the constant drip-drip of water: a rumbling and thundering from overhead. There was a shout, and the sound of a door slamming. Rattles of iron, a quick scream, and then a crashing roar, as of the sea breaking on the shore. But he recognised it. It was the steady pounding of many booted feet.

Dolwyn moved away from the door warily, like the deer he had once pursued, until he was concealed inside a hollow in the wall. The group about the shaft stayed still, faces tight with renewed fear.

A party of guards might mean they were to be taken on the short march to Tyburn to dance their last, or perhaps London was on the rampage again. It was common enough in this changing world: there might be a new King, new advisers, a new council – but the mob was the mob.

There was a short cry, then cheering. Suddenly the noise was all around, as men poured into the passage between the cells. Faces appeared at the grille, lit by the fitful orange glare of torches, eyes flashing with disgust and horror as they stared into the cell, some dulled with ale, and all the while there was a cry of some sort, demanding to know where a man was held.

It was 'Bardi', he realised. It was plain enough why. No one liked Italian bankers, and now the mob had power in London, they were seeking those whom they most detested. And then he realised: to them, *he* was the Bardi man! Someone must have told of his capture, and the mob was here to kill him.

In the shaft's dusty sunlight one prisoner gibbered and drooled, begging piteously as each new face appeared. Another was portly, rich-looking. He stared back at the faces with contempt, sitting uncomfortably like one unused to a stone floor under his buttocks.

Dolwyn pressed himself against the wall, his mind working furiously. The Bardi were the richest bankers in London. And these fellows were after a Bardi. They would expect a wealthy merchant, not him . . . and in an instant he saw a way to save himself. He pointed at the fat man staring resentfully at the door and yelled, 'Here's the bastard! He's in here!'

As a torch was held to the grille, Dolwyn saw the poor soul start. His clothes held something of their past magnificence: rich scarlet woollens and emeralds showed beneath layers of muck. The fellow blenched and made the sign of the cross as keys rattled and bolts shot back, and then the door burst wide, slamming into the wall, and a ragged group rushed inside. Dolwyn had already hauled his cellmate to his feet. The fellow was shivering, but not from cold. He gazed into Dolwyn's eyes, hoping for pity, his mouth mumbling, but then he was grabbed by a dozen hands and pulled out, appealing for mercy, for compassion.

His answer was laughter as men kicked and punched him, and then he was gone. Dolwyn heard his pleas fading into the distance along the passageway and up the stairs. The others in the cell needed no encouragement, and raced out after them. In moments he was alone.

Dolwyn stayed, listening intently, until he was certain they had all gone. Only then did he peer around the open doorway, trembling with excitement. There was nobody in the darkened hallway. Only a pale light at the far end of the corridor, where the door remained open. With his legs stiff and hunger gnawing his belly, he would find it difficult to escape if the gaoler appeared. Grabbing his victim had exhausted him. But up there, perhaps he could find some bread, a lump of cheese or something – and a gulp of clean water or ale. From the sight of the mob, he guessed it was unlikely that the gaoler was still in the prison. He had taken flight – or had been killed.

'Take me with you!'

At the third door along the corridor, a pale face was staring through the grille at him. Two small fists gripped the bars. It was the boy who had cried so piteously for the last few nights. Dolwyn stood for a long moment, contemplating the lad. Then he went back to his cell and felt around the door. He was sure that the keys must still be here. A great steel ring hung from the lock, with keys strung along it, and he picked it up. The fourth key fitted the boy's lock, and he turned it, pulling back the two bolts to open the door.

'Thank you!' the boy wept, falling through the door as soon as it was opened wide.

Dolwyn pushed the child before him, along the passage and out up the stairs, keeping him in front of all the way.

He had no other defence. If there was danger, this boy would be his shield.

CHAPTER FOUR

House of Bardi, London

Alured had returned here two days ago to see how bad the damage was, and the sight was chilling.

The door had been broken in, and hung from the lower hinge only. Shards of pottery and splinters of wood lay underfoot. Some were from goblets and mazers, and when he sifted a handful, he saw the gleam of gold. The wood about it was marked with a knife's blade, and he assumed that here a decorative band of gold had been hacked from a mazer.

It was enough to make a man weep, he thought. This had been a great house, filled with glorious items of beauty, and now the rifflers had been through it like rats through a larder, destroying all they couldn't eat or carry away.

He entered, carefully stepping over the leaning door. In the passageway was a mess of broken barrels and pottery. Staves poked up like the breastbones of some strange beast, and there was a thick blanket of tapestry that had been dropped in a foul heap. He would have opened it out to view the pictures, but a warning odour of faeces deterred him. Instead he walked into the hall itself. It was a scene of destruction. The rifflers had not known the value of the items they carelessly tossed aside to smash on the ground. Glass crunched beneath his boots as he made his way to the middle of the room and stared about him.

A huge table had been overturned, and one leg wrenched from it, probably to build a fire to destroy the building, but for some reason the rest of the table was intact. Alured assumed that the strength of the timbers had deterred the rifflers. They had gone in search of easier fuel. Chairs had been thrown over, their legs snapped away. Cushions had been disembowelled, while men had pissed and vomited everywhere as a sign of their contempt for those who lived here.

All the doors had been tested, and those that were locked, broken open. If there had been money or gold here, it was gone, he saw as he investigated further into the house. They had enjoyed their time here, obviously, from the smell of sour ale and wine about the place. It was a relief that there were no bodies. By now, they would have grown smelly, he reckoned.

Alured walked from the house and stared at the door. He would have liked to shut up the house before leaving. He tried to lift it, but it was heavy oak and would not budge. He was standing, scratching at his head, his hat in his hand, when he heard steps.

'What has happened here?' Dolwyn asked, staring about him with horror in his eyes.

'The rifflers came to visit,' Alured said shortly. This fellow had the look of a felon himself, from his filthy clothes and lack of a weapon. He could well be another draw latch come here to try his fortune at a despoiled house. 'Do you know who used to live here?'

'I worked for them – the Bardi. My master was the youngest brother, a man called Matteo. But I left him here some days ago . . . Were they all killed?'

'No, not all.' Alured eyed Dolwyn with a speculative eye. 'Where were you?'

'I was sent away with a message.'

'Where? In London?'

'Yes, over towards the River,' Dolwyn lied. 'Why?'

Alured looked away. 'Nothing. There were so many murders that day, and afterwards.'

'I wasn't here,' Dolwyn said firmly. He glanced about the ravaged hall. 'They did this place well, didn't they?'

'This man you worked for,' Alured said. 'What did he look like?'

'A thin man, pale,' Dolwyn said, and went on to describe his master, including the clothes he had been wearing on the last day Dolwyn saw him.

'I think you may be in luck,' Alured said. He had tested the man, and it seemed that he was genuine. 'Here, help me with this door and we can stop any more pillagers.'

With Dolwyn's help, they managed to lift the door, the remaining hinge protesting loudly, and lean it against the frame.

'It will take a good blacksmith to mend those hinges,' Alured panted. 'I know a man not far from here can do it.'

'You said I may be in luck?' Dolwyn asked cautiously. He had no liking for bailiffs and constables, and feared recapture.

Alured looked him up and down, then nodded to himself. 'Come with me, friend,' he said.

Dolwyn did as he was bid, trailing after Alured as the man led him along narrow alleyways and streets until they came to a small house near St Stephen, almost beside the River Walbrook. Here Alured glanced at him again. 'Seemed safer to bring your master here to my own home than leave him behind,' he said, half-apologetically, and threw the door wide.

On a low palliasse on the floor near a hearth in the middle of the room lay a pallid, unhealthful figure.

'Master Matteo!' Dolwyn exclaimed.

Monday after the Feast of St Martin[1]

Woods near Caerphilly Castle

He had run as soon as it happened, and by a miracle none had seen him.

Thomas Dunheved panted wildly, his eyes staring back the way he had come. There were still occasional screams, the rattle of weapons beating on shields or armour, panicked neighing and whinnying from injured horses as the battle continued elsewhere.

He fell to his knees, a black-clad figure clutching his hands together, and bowed his tonsured head, his words tumbling out like water thundering over rocks, the tears falling and tracking through the grime on his cheeks, until he could speak no more, and instead his throat was clogged with sobs.

Frere Thomas Dunheved, Dominican Friar and Confessor to the King, could not beg for help from God. God Himself had betrayed King Edward. He had allowed His anointed King to be captured by his enemies – how could He have permitted that to happen?

The blackfriar rose to his feet, still weeping. After so many years working to protect and serve his King, reconciling him with the Pope, doing all he might to aid the King's projects in

1 17 November 1326

the hope that by so doing His purpose would be supported, now all was in vain. The King was captured by his enemies.

There was nothing more for him here. If he was found, he could be slain out of hand by those who despised him. No, rather than wait and be caught, he would make his way home. Perhaps there he could find some peace.

For others there would be little enough of that, now that the King was taken.

Second Tuesday after the Feast of St Martin[1]

Approaching Worcester

The prisoner rode like a man who had drunk mandrake, almost in a stupor.

Sergeant Gilbert le Sadler, a cheerful, large-bellied man with the red face of a committed ale-drinker, was worried about him. On this journey, while his lord the Earl of Lancaster saw to business of his own, it fell to Gilbert to take charge of his valuable captive. The sergeant had never been given such an awesome task before. To be responsible for King Edward II of England!

They had many more miles to ride, but from the appearance of the King, he would not manage half the distance. He lolled, swaying with every lurch of the beast beneath him, and several times Gilbert had been convinced that the King would topple from his horse.

'My lord,' he said again, 'would you like to stop and rest a little? I have wine, food . . . Come now, wouldn't a break do you good?'

1 25 November 1326

The King made no sign that he had heard him. He was still handsome, a tall, strongly-built man with long fair hair that framed his face perfectly. With his prowess in the lists and with his sword, it was easy to see how so many had fallen under his spell.

'My lord?' Gilbert tried again.

There was no response. The King was prisoner in his own country, and his manner was pitiable. After the shocks and disasters of the last year it was no surprise he had lost his mind. He had lost everything else.

Gilbert shook his head. He was only a sergeant, when all was said and done. This was the sort of job that should have been given to a lord, not to him. He had his own score of men, but today he was in command of a further hundred, just to guard this King.

'My lord, soon we shall rest – at the next village where there is an inn suitable for a man of your status,' he promised.

There was no flicker of emotion on the King's face. His hollow-eyed stare continued to study something far distant that obviously filled him with horror. Gilbert wondered: did he see his wife in the arms of her lover, Sir Roger Mortimer; or Sir Hugh Le Despenser, his closest companion, writhing and choking as he was hanged, then disembowelled . . . Or did he see his son, the figurehead of those who had come to humiliate him? Gilbert could not tell, but the expression on King Edward's face was enough to tell him that the man was all too aware of his precarious position.

No matter. Gilbert would safely convey this noble prisoner, to whom he still felt enormous loyalty, to Kenilworth, the Earl of Lancaster's great stronghold. Once there, King Edward would be passed on to another from the Earl's entourage, and Gilbert could relax.

He looked at the King again, and his heart was clutched with pity. Gilbert remembered a man who had lost his wife and children in the floods eleven years ago. He had worn the same air of confused distress as this King.

Gilbert had done all he could. Perhaps the kindest thing to do was to get the King to Kenilworth as quickly as possible.

He would be glad for this task to come to an end.

St Benet Fink

The old church was quiet as Alured approached it from the little alley. He came along here often now, as though hoping that something might leap into his imagination as he walked; perhaps some little detail of the alley that might help him discover who had killed the young couple.

It had been a simple task to learn who they were. The dead youth was apprentice to a leatherworker, while his girl was the daughter of a groom. Both families were happy for the two, and hoped that they would marry when they had a little money saved. The groom in particular was devastated to see his daughter killed. He had no other family, since the girl's mother had died giving birth to her. When Alured saw him at the inquest, the man had fallen in a dead swoon, and it took three men to carry his body to a tavern to recover.

The young couple were only two out of the many who had been killed that day, but there was something about their bodies that had wrenched at Alured's heart. Others had been attacked by the mob, and their bodies slashed and hacked with abandon as though killed by raving demons; this couple was different, though. They had been slain with precision. One slash to the girl beheaded her, while the boy had two thrusts to his breast. It was as clean as an execution.

39

The drunk had consumed too much to be able to recall anything in detail, but he was convinced that the murderer was a knight. A middling-years man, with dark hair and a white tunic. He had good Cordova boots, he remembered. From his angle, lying on the ground, that was the most definite thing he could see under the long tunic. Good Cordova leather boots with a red tassel at the top.

That description would match half of the King's two thousand knights. As for the boots, any man's tunic would conceal them. Alured had little or no chance of finding the killer among the teaming thousands of London.

He would have to forget the two dead lovers. There were other, more important matters to occupy him.

Reluctantly he turned his steps homeward.

Alured's house, London

Matteo Bardi woke when Alured returned.

He was still as weak as a puppy. He had recovered from the terrible fever that had nearly killed him – a result of the stab wound in his back – and thanks to the constant care of Alured and his wife, he was feeling much improved. In recent days he had even begun to read one or two messages from other merchants and bankers.

Matteo had become petrified of strangers. It was natural after being attacked by the mob, who hated those of his profession, and it made him want to return home to Florence by the swiftest means. He hated this cold, wet, miserable, uncouth land.

Only one man could he entirely trust. 'I am glad of your help,' he said to Alured.

'It was nothing. I hope someone would do the same for me,' Alured said gruffly. 'You were lucky I was near to hand.'

'Very lucky,' Dolwyn agreed. He brought a cup of watered wine to his master and passed it to him.

'I just wish I'd been there earlier,' Alured added. He told the banker and his henchman about the two youngsters murdered in the nearby alley. 'Perhaps the same man stabbed you as killed them,' he wondered, but it didn't seem likely. They had been so efficiently slain, while Matteo was still alive.

Matteo took a sip of his wine and peered at Dolwyn. 'Tell me,' he said, 'did you see anything of a man near me on the day I was attacked?'

'No, master. I was away from you, you remember?'

'Yes. And I was running from that mob,' Matteo said, feeling at his scalp. The hair had been clipped away. After prodding his skull and checking his urine, the physician declared he should live: his injuries were superficial. 'You have a hard head, master,' he had declared.

The day was creeping on as Dolwyn looked down at him, and Matteo felt uneasy. The growing shadows gave him an oddly evil appearance.

'There are messages for you,' Alured said, stepping over to the bed. Then: 'Are you well, master?'

Matteo gestured irritably. 'Just a little tired, no more.'

It was a firm belief of Alured that work was a great healer. 'These have all arrived in the last few days.'

Matteo eyed the pile of sealed notes without enthusiasm. 'So many?'

'Your clerk brings more every day.'

Matteo sighed and held out his hand. For the rest of the day, he lay back, absorbing snippets of information from the messages: one from the servant of Sir Roger Mortimer, one from the Abbot of Winchester, three from a merchant who traded between London and York, and then, after thirty or more

41

notes of minor importance, he came across a little scrawled parchment. It was from a disreputable coroner in Bristol whom he had engaged some years before. He had never liked the man, but an intelligencer did not need to like his contacts. It was enough that they were reliable.

A comment at the bottom took his attention. He sat up in his bed, frowning.

'Something wrong, master?' Alured enquired.

'I don't know,' Matteo muttered.

The note told him that the servants of the Queen were delighted to have had confirmation of the Bardi brothers' support. It was still more gratifying, he read, that the Bardis had sworn not to have any dealings with the King – that in future, all their efforts would be concentrated on the Queen, her son the Duke of Aquitaine, and their supporters.

Matteo stared at it. During the meeting with his brothers, they had agreed that they would make an offer of financial assistance to the Queen, but also send a similar letter to the King. This stated that the Bardis had sworn *not* to aid him. If news of this were to get out and the King heard, it would be impossible to recover, were Edward II to return to his throne.

That fool Benedetto had over-reached himself! Matteo swore under his breath at the thought of his carefully nuanced work, all ruined by this one act. Unless he could somehow retrieve the situation . . .

Then Matteo accepted that he had been here for a month now, lying in his bed, wracked by fever. Perhaps he was not so well-informed as Benedetto. The position could have changed.

And then the memory of Benedetto's shrewd face came to mind. Benedetto was schooled in Florentine politics and business, where it was desirable always to remove a competitor. Now that Manuele was dead, Matteo was Benedetto's sole competitor for running the bank. And since his stabbing, Benedetto had been quick to take over the reins of power. Very quick.

Almost like a man who had planned for the eventuality.

'Dolwyn,' he said, 'I have a task for you. I need you to go to Bristol and learn what you may from this man. But you must be very careful that you are not followed. You understand me?'

Matteo felt enormous thankfulness as Dolwyn nodded once, listened to his instructions, and then left.

Staring down at the parchments before him, Matteo rose with a grunt of pain, and shuffled to the fire. There he took out the letter which Manuele had signed just before his death. He read it, and was about to hold it to the flames when he hesitated. This letter could still be useful. It could be shown to the King, if he ever did return to authority, to prove that the Bardi *had* been on his side. He may not have received this letter, but its existence demonstrated that the bank had been willing to help him.

After a moment's thought, he shoved the letter into his chemise, next to his flesh, before going back to the bed and lying down with a grunt.

He fell asleep, hoping that Dolwyn would bring useful news from Bristol.

CHAPTER FIVE

Third Wednesday after the Feast of St Martin[1]

St Peter's, Willersey

Panic did not fully overwhelm him until later, when he heard of the death of Sir Hugh le Despenser, and went to open the chest hidden in his undercroft. Only then did he comprehend the full horror of his situation, and Father Luke cried out, gazing about him as though all the fiends of hell were encircling him, lurid in the gloomy light, watching to tempt him.

Because inside the chest, gleaming in the candlelight, was more gold coin than he had ever seen before.

Before the men appeared, that day had been much like any other. Calm, orderly, unexceptional.

Father Luke of St Peter's Church, Willersey, was unaccustomed to shocks. His had been an exemplary life. He had lived

1 26 November 1326

here in Willersey for eleven happy years, and now, in his middle thirties, his paunch attested to the wealth of the area. The crow's feet at his smiling blue eyes showed him for what he was, a contented, affable priest. His living was good, the tithes more than adequate for his limited needs, and the local peasants were willing to supplement his resources when he needed more food or wine. There was no doubt about it: since he had first arrived and seen the great church of St Peter's with its tall spire, he had thought he was privileged to serve God here.

He was a man of learning, who had early discovered that there was a lot of sense in the stern injunctions against amatory adventures. All too often he had seen his peers humbled as their little misdemeanours came to light. For Father Luke, it was better by far to accept his position and enjoy serving the souls of his vill than to indulge his natural desires with the women of the area.

His was a round, ruddy-complexioned face, with full lips and heavy jowls – a face made for smiling, while slightly protuberant eyes viewed the world with an amiable fascina-tion. He was that rare creature: a priest who genuinely liked his fellows. His slight pomposity made him human, in the eyes of the folks about him, and endeared him to them, while his irritation at their gambling in his churchyard on Sundays did not make them angry, only bemused when he railed at them for their ungodly behaviour. His was a figure designed to inspire jollity and companionship, rather than stern respect.

It had been an unexpected interruption when the horses arrived this morning – and a disturbing reminder of Despenser's men's appearance almost six weeks ago.

Earlier today, Father Luke had been at the base of the tower, idly studying the tympanum within the arch. The stone held a series of rich carvings: circles on either side with a flower inside them, a chequerboard strip beneath with a cross at either side, also set inside circles. In the middle, between the two flower shapes, was another circle, with four more set within, and a fifth as a hub between them all.

A strange design, this, which had always intrigued him. He wondered who the mason was, and what had urged him to make these patterns. Father Luke would have expected simpler devices, perhaps an angel's face, rather than these long-forgotten symbols that had been here for perhaps two hundred years.

The sound of hooves pulled him back from his reverie, and he walked to his door and peered out, watching as two men reined in weary-looking beasts. The men were sodden, from their hoods and cowls to their booted feet. One wore a russet woollen cloak drawn about him, but the fabric was so soaked that the water dripped steadily from the dangling corner. The other had a leather cloak that had once been waxed, but this too had given up under the rain's assault.

They wore no armour, but both had the stolid appearance of fighting men. Luke had to fight the compulsion to step away from them – there were too many stories of churches broken into and their priests knocked down for him to be entirely at his ease. For all that, he did not get the impression that they were dangerous, only desperate.

'God be with you,' he said firmly, making the sign of the cross.

'Father, God bless you and your vill,' said the taller one as they swung stiffly from their saddles.

'You look exhausted, my sons. Would you stop a while and take a little refreshment? Wherever you are going, you will be more likely to reach it with a full belly and rested head.'

The two men exchanged a glance. In both faces there was a desire to ease tired limbs, if only for a short while.

'Gentles, those brutes are as tired as you. They should be rested. Come, I have spiced cider and oatcakes.'

At the mention of hot cider both wavered, but oatcakes as well was too much temptation for men drenched by rain and mud. Before long they were sitting at Father Luke's little fire, while the horses were rubbed down and fed by Peter, the smith's son. Luke saw Jen, Ham and Agatha's girl, and asked her to fetch her mother. Agatha often cooked for Luke. It got her out of her house and that was always a relief to her, Luke knew. She was unhappy in her marriage to Ham.

'You've ridden far?' Luke asked as Agatha bustled about preparing drinks and tearing at a plump, cooked pigeon.

The taller man nodded. He was named Paul of Bircheston, he said. He had a well-featured face, although his dark eyes met Father Luke's unwillingly, as if he harboured a secret shame. The other, John of Shulton, was more confident, and more warlike, from the way that he settled and immediately drew his sword to dry it and smear grease over it to protect it from the rain.

He gave a grin and lifted an eyebrow as he glanced at the priest. 'News is slow around here, eh? It must be good to see strangers ride past.'

'Better to see them stop and talk,' Father Luke chuckled, leaning aside to allow Agatha to reach the fire.

'Aye, we've ridden far. And there are evil tidings and to spare,' Paul said, staring into the fire gloomily.

'Why, my friend?'

'The King is captured. That whining cur Lancaster has him, and is taking King Edward to Kenilworth.'

'Good God!' Father Luke exclaimed, clutching at the cross about his neck. 'But how? There was no news . . . Are you sure, my friend? Surely God would not see His crowned King brought so low?'

'We were there,' Paul stated baldly. 'The King was captured near Caerphilly with all those who remained loyal to him. There were few enough of them.'

'What will become of him?'

'He'll be at the mercy of Mortimer and the Queen. What they will do . . .' He broke off, clenching his jaw.

'Come, Paul,' John said. 'There's no need to torment yourself. We've done our duty.'

'You shock me,' Father Luke muttered. 'This is dreadful news. If a man raises his hand against God's anointed, He must punish the kingdom, surely.'

'Our King must be freed.'

It was John of Shulton who spoke, stroking a hone along his sword's edge. There was a faraway look in his eyes, but Father Luke saw the glitter in them, and the sight made him shudder.

Agatha sat beside Luke's fire and took up his old stone, setting it on the fire while she mixed the oatmeal. Luke had done this when he was young, when he was a boy near Durham. Oat was a staple still in the north, as it was here, but many considered it suitable only for horses and cattle. More fool them – for it made a good, solid base in the belly for a cold man, Father Luke reckoned. The action of mixing it and forming a paste with a little milk and water had always been enough to distract him. Now, he saw that Agatha was listening, open-mouthed to their tale, the cakes forgotten. Luke gave a click of his tongue, and she renewed her mixing.

The men drank deeply of their cider, and while their cloaks and jacks dripped on the floor, they watched Agatha dropping rounds onto the hot stone, moving them deftly with her fingers before they could stick. Soon there were fifteen little cakes, and while they cooled on the priest's single wooden trencher, Luke himself fetched a little cheese and some leaves from his garden. They had been badly attacked by slugs, and this late in the year they were tough, but any salad was good.

'Are you well, Father?' John of Shulton said, sucking a pigeon bone.

'I suppose I am . . . distracted by this news.'

Paul said, 'We were servants of Sir Hugh le Despenser. To think our lord could be . . . But while I have breath in my body and strength in my arm, I won't accept my King being held.'

'Paul,' John said warningly.

'I will do all in my power to release the King,' Paul said firmly. 'I don't care who hears it.'

'Oh?' Luke said.

It was then that he had the thought: if these two were Despenser's men, then perhaps they could take his chest with them. But dare he entrust it to two such desperate men? No, he decided reluctantly. Whatever was inside must be valuable. Maybe he should open it and take a look inside.

By early afternoon they were gone, and he was beneath the tower staring with terror at the money.

'Despenser's dead,' he muttered.

'What, Father?'

'Nothing, Agatha,' he said.

She had returned after the evening service to bring him some bread. Now she set her mouth into a prim line, as she turned to leave.

'I know,' Luke said. 'It is shocking to think that our King—'

'It was his wife saw to it,' she said grimly, 'That's treason of the worst sort.'

'Er, well, yes,' he agreed, watching as she made her way from his house. Women were beyond him, but he thought he could detect a hint of jealousy. Perhaps she was thinking of her own marriage.

He walked along the grassy path to his church, and crossed himself with a little water from the stoup, before kneeling on the hard tiles before the altar.

He could not keep it. That was certain. Those coins would be a magnet for every outlaw and drawlatch in Gloucestershire.

He took a deep sigh and gazed at the cross, seeking answers. Yes, he must send the money away . . . but to whom? The owner was dead, his heir held with his father's remaining retainers in a Welsh castle from which he might never escape. There must be someone who could take it, but at least it was safe here for now. No one knew of it but him.

He wished he had asked those two for advice, at least. They might have known what to do with it.

CHAPTER SIX

Dunchurch Manor, Warwickshire

Frere Thomas rose to his feet in the little chapel and crossed himself fervently. In the last days he had managed to avoid capture, largely because he had been aided by his brothers, but also God was preserving him too, naturally.

Ever since the Pope had made him a papal chaplain some years ago, this assurance of God's protection had given him the peace he needed to reflect on the actions he had taken, the actions of others, and to contemplate how he could have acted otherwise. However, no inspiration came. He had done all he ought. The King had been captured *despite* his best efforts, and that was surely a sign that God intended the disaster. Nothing could happen without His approval. It was merely infuriating that he, Thomas, one of the most senior Dominicans in his Order, could not understand His scheme. But that was, so often, the way of God's mystery. It was not for humans to comprehend the Almighty's intentions.

He had returned here only after great hardship. On the way he had heard of the death of Despenser, the ravaging of all Despenser's lands and estates, and the impudence of the Hainaulters and other mercenaries, wandering the land as though they were the saviours of the country. It was maddening! God had assuredly deserted England. He was leaving it at the mercy of the forces of evil.

A door at the rear of the chapel opened, and Frere Thomas turned to see his brother, Stephen.

'What is it?' Thomas demanded, his eyes going to the windows. 'Are they here to take me?'

'No! No, Tom, it's the King! He is here! Well, not here, but at Kenilworth. That's where he's being held – at the castle.'

Thomas gaped, and then felt the thrill of holy joy pass through him like lightning, and he turned to face the altar, arms outspread.

Now he understood. God had been teaching him patience, and now that he had learned his lesson, God was giving him an opportunity to rescue the King. Of course, he would need men. His brother Stephen could help there, but they should have enough to storm the castle by wiles, rather than by great numbers. A small fighting force, infiltrating the castle and then bringing the King to freedom. There were many who would want to join in on that!

'Dear Father, I shall not fail You a second time!' he prayed fervently.

Morrow of the Feast of Candlemas[1]

Kenilworth

In his chamber, Sir Edward of Caernarfon, no longer King, now merely a knight, sat at his table and stared at the silver plate and goblet placed before him.

1 3 February 1327

When he looked in his mirror, he still possessed the fair good looks for which he had been renowned. His long hair was rich and lustrous yet, his blue eyes clear, but where once laughter lines had illuminated his features, now it was the creases of care and fretfulness that showed themselves.

To think that Mortimer had once been his most revered and respected general! Edward closed his eyes as the memories flooded back. Those happy times. From childhood Mortimer had been one of his closest, most trusted companions. It was to Mortimer he turned when the Scots invaded Ireland.

Sir Edward pulled apart the loaf of paindemaigne and rolled a piece into a small ball, pushing it into his mouth and chewing listlessly. Life had lost all savour. A king separated from his kingdom was less than a man. Less even than a peasant, since no peasant could suffer such a loss.

When the emissaries arrived at Kenilworth's great hall, that was one day Sir Edward would never forget.

He had been warned of the delegation's arrival, and had thought they were come for a discussion of terms. After all, he was their King. He whom God had placed upon the throne could not be removed by rebels. God's anointment protected him. And so King Edward II had leaned back in his chair as the men filtered into the hall.

There were many: two bishops, Orleton and Stafford, two Justices, four barons, two barons of the Cinque Ports, four knights, Londoners, representatives of other cities and towns, and abbots, priors and friars aplenty.

'I am honoured to see so many,' the King observed drily. 'Will you enjoy the hospitality of the castle? I fear it is a little depleted of late, but I am sure that my gaoler would not wish you to leave here hungry or thirsty. Command him as you will . . . as you already do.'

His sarcasm hit the mark with several, he noted with grim satisfaction. He would show them how a real King should behave, he told himself. 'Well? Is there someone here with authority to treat with me?'

It was Orleton who spoke, the slug, but King Edward averted his head and gestured with his hand. 'I will not hear *you*, vile deceiver! It was you who preached sedition against me – I have heard. You do not rate amongst this gathering.'

'My lord,' Orleton said with that oleaginous manner Edward recalled so well. He had inveigled his way into the Queen's affections, but that did not make him any more appealing to Edward.

'I fear you *must* hear me, sire,' Orleton said, 'and you must listen to these honourable men, and the whole community of your realm. There has been a parliament in Westminster, and there were conclusions formed during it.'

'I will not hear you.'

'Sire, you have ruled poorly. You have been commanded by vile traitors and wicked advisers. You elevated some, but destroyed many of the peers of your realm. Your decisions have caused bloodshed on a scale not seen for many years, and you have broken up your father's lands in order to give them to your friends. You have shamed your inheritance, this proud land, and the people you swore to protect!'

'You dare accuse me?' the King had roared, and half-rose from his seat. To hear this litany of accusations – as though he was a common serf! There was no need for him to respond. He was the *King*! 'God *Himself* placed me upon this throne, and I'll be damned if some upstart felon like Mortimer will evict me, with or without your help, my lord Bishop!'

'You think it is only me, sire?' Orleton sneered. 'The whole community of the realm accuses you. Whence the prelates, the peers and the knighthood all wish you to resign and to pass the kingdom to your son, for him to reign in your stead.'

Edward stared at the bishop with a curious feeling of dislocation, as though none of this affected him personally. This was not truly happening. It did not matter what others thought: *he was King*. It was not a mantle a man donned and doffed, it was his heart, his blood. His *soul*.

He made a gesture of dismissal. 'My son cannot reign. *I* rule here.'

'Sire, Parliament has unanimously declared itself for your son.'

'Ludicrous! I do not agree. What of the boy – does he dare to shame me himself?'

There was a swimming in his head; his mind was befogged. Oh, if only Hugh were here, darling Hugh, to lighten his mood, to take away some of the sting of this appalling litany of complaints! If only . . .

'Your son refuses to accept the conclusion of the Parliament unless you agree. If you will pass on the Crown to your son, my lord, he will take it. But if you do not agree . . .'

'I remain King. I *am* King!'

'In name only. The realm will find a new leader.'

'You threaten me?' King Edward spat. 'You think to suggest you can remove me and install some puppet in my place?'

'Not I, my lord. Parliament,' Bishop Orleton said.

King Edward was stilled. The swirling sensation returned with renewed force, and it was only by a supreme effort of will that he managed to keep himself upright in the chair.

At first he dared not trust his voice because his speech must reflect the turmoil of emotions that crowded his heart. This was indeed a threat, without even a silken glove in which to conceal it. Parliament was a distraction: someone was influencing it behind the scenes. Only two men wielded enough power to control it: Earl Lancaster or Sir Roger Mortimer. They could protect Edward, or his son, or could see both father and son destroyed. Of the two, Edward knew who had dared already to remove his King: Sir Roger Mortimer. He would scarcely balk at doing the same to Edward's son.

'You . . .' He had to swallow and take a firm grip on himself. 'You threaten my son's safety if I refuse to acquiesce?'

'I threaten nothing, my lord. I merely warn you of the consequences. You must abdicate.'

Edward could remember that day so well – how his mind had cleared and he was able to think objectively about his boy, Edward, Duke of Aquitaine.

He owed his son little. Although he had sworn not to, the Duke became betrothed without the King's permission. While in France with his mother, he had refused to return home when King Edward wrote and ordered him to do so, claiming he could not leave while his mother remained. Perhaps he told the truth: maybe in France the Duke had already been under Mortimer's control. The traitor was there: all knew he had cuckolded King Edward in France.

When he was free he would have Mortimer tortured. He would have the churl put to the *peine forte et dure* to plead his guilt, and then see him executed in the same manner in which the bastard had tortured poor Hugh to death. *Damn Mortimer to hell for eternity*!

Yes, he owed the Duke little. Adam, his illegitimate son, would never have dreamed of such disloyalty. He, God bless him, was too kind, too gentle and grateful for anything his father offered.

But Adam had died five years ago during the campaign against the Scots. The lad had joined the host as a page, but died of fever on that horrible return march, as had so many others. He would never know what it was to be a grown man. He died so young – only fourteen years old.

Duke Edward was also fourteen, the King realised with a jolt. It sent a shiver down his spine to think that his oldest son was as old as his firstborn had been when he died. The two boys were so very different, it had never occurred to him before.

Edward wondered whether the Duke realised the danger he was in. He was under-age to be King. Mortimer would control him ruthlessly, and the kingdom. To agree to abdication would mean that the Duke would inherit his kingdom. Did he deserve it? Edward set his jaw. He would not willingly deprive his second son. His firstborn was already dead because he had followed him. He could not condemn his first legitimate son too.

He looked at the men in silence. But even then, back in January, Sir Edward of Caernarfon knew that the decision had already been made for him.

House of Bardi, London

Matteo had five messengers arrive that morning. The pile of different-sized parchments was daunting to him as he sat sipping wine, eyeing them.

It had taken time and a great deal of money to have the house tidied once more, but he did not begrudge Benedetto's expenditure. This house was a symbol and a statement of the Bardis' position at the pinnacle of English society.

Since Christmas, when they had advanced loans to the Queen and Sir Roger Mortimer, the bank had shifted to the centre of political authority and the House of Bardi was as secure as it had been throughout King Edward II's late, unlamented reign.

It meant stability, and that made Matteo reconsider his plan to leave the country. There was money to be made here.

Matteo was still wary of his brother. Every time they met, he felt a crawling sensation. He never turned his back on Benedetto. Instead he had spies watch him. Matteo also abandoned all outward manifestations of ambition. He wanted others to believe that his brush with death had scared him.

But he was not scared. He was hungry for more: more money, more control, more information with which to achieve what he wanted.

There was a knock, then the door opened and Dolwyn walked in.

'You have news?' Matteo demanded.

'Some. I met your informant,' Dolwyn said. 'He is dead now.'

'What?'

'He was hanged for murder.'

Matteo shook his head. 'A shame – he was useful. I shall have to find another man in that area. Did you learn anything from him before he died?'

'That Sir Edward of Caernarfon is not so weak as some would believe.'

'He has been deprived of his crown,' Matteo observed.

'But many would see him return to his throne. Plots are already being formed to bring him back.'

Matteo studied the man. Dolwyn was a useful henchman, certainly, mostly because of his brawn, not his brains. His skills lay with knives and daggers, not with the tools Matteo was happier to employ: words and information. The attack had made Matteo appreciate how different were their two worlds. 'Who?'

'All about Bristol and South Wales I heard the same: every-where the people had relied on the Despensers, there is a clamour for the return of Edward of Caernarfon.'

Matteo considered. There was merit in telling Mortimer this news, but the latter had his own spies so it would not be news to him. No, the only man who might not be aware of this, secluded as he was, was Sir Edward of Caernarfon himself. In the event of a coup, he would be very grateful to those who had aided him . . .

Matteo glanced at his reeds and inks, thinking that he could write to Sir Edward himself, offering the same as the letter from Manuele. The man would surely appreciate that. But if the letter were discovered, after the King's abdication from the throne, the author could rightly be suspected of treason against the new King and be sentenced to die a painful death. It was a shame that the original had not been sent.

And then he had an inspiration. 'I have a letter,' he informed Dolwyn. 'I need you to take it to Sir Edward of Caernarfon and deliver it to him, and him alone.'

It was perfect, he thought. The letter had been written and signed by Manuele before his death. The delay in sending it was explicable by the kingdom's upset in recent months, and if it was discovered, it was clear that the man who wrote it was now dead and could not be punished – and nor could those who had arranged for it to be sent on to the recipient in good faith.

In short, if Sir Edward received it, he would be assured of the bank's efforts to aid him, but if it was found by Mortimer's men, Matteo could explain the mistake.

*Two Saturdays before the Feast of the Annunciation,
first year of the reign of King Edward III[1]*

Willersey

Matins was over for another day. Father Luke smiled at young Jen and her mother Agatha as he wiped the chalice clean and began to tidy away the silver.

It was easy to smile at Jen. Small, like so many of the children after the winter, she had the fair hair and blue eyes of her mother, and the quick alertness of a hawk. The way that she set her head to one side and considered the priest while he spoke was utterly entrancing. If he had not taken the vow of chastity, he could have wished for no more appealing child as his own.

'I didn't see your husband here today,' he remarked to Agatha.

'The fool took a job delivering ale and food to the castle,' she said. 'A purveyor arrived last night demanding a cart, and Ham agreed a good price for his time.'

'Warwick Castle?'

'No. The farther one: Kenilworth.'

'Ouch!' Father Luke said. Warwick itself was more than twenty miles, and Kenilworth must be a deal further. 'That is a long way. I have never been that far since I came to the parish myself. Has he already left?'

'Fat chance of that!' Agatha sneered. 'You think my Ham would be up at this time of day and out on the road?'

'Father is seeing to the animals,' Jen said.

'There is always much for a man to do,' Father Luke agreed. 'Who will look after the beasts when he is gone?'

1 14 March 1327

'I think I will,' said Jen. For all that she was a child of only seven summers, she sometimes had the manner of a mature woman. The effect of living with her parents, Luke told himself sadly. She shot a look at her mother now, he saw, as though nervous of a buffet about the head for speaking out of turn.

Father Luke gave her a reassuring smile as he set all the church valuables inside the chest and locked it. Agatha was already sweeping the floor while Jen watched.

The priest knew Ham quite well. Ham was a happy-go-lucky fellow who enjoyed his ale and cider, as did Father Luke. However, he did suffer from his wife's nagging. She was convinced he could improve their lot by working harder, although he was already up before the dawn to feed his animals, weeding and toiling at his garden, and generally keeping out from under his wife's feet.

In her opinion, she should have married a man with better prospects. One of her friends, so Luke had heard, had wed a man from Warwick who went on to become one of the richest merchants in that great city. Whereas Ham remained a farmer. The idea that she should be stuck here in this vill, while her friend led the life of a wealthy burgess, had soured her. She was peevish, no matter how often Luke tried to show her she had plenty to be grateful for.

'Why would he be taking food so far?' Luke wondered. 'Surely there are suppliers nearer the castle?'

Agatha shrugged. 'The purveyor said there was a guest who had a liking for lampreys and good perry, so I suppose it's for him.'

'So your husband will be taking his cart to Kenilworth?' Father Luke said, and suddenly he had an idea so brilliant it took his breath away.

'Yes. The useless prickle will have a week's holiday, while Jen and me have to work double. Not that it'll make much difference – he's so idle. We usually have to feed the beasts and all, while he lays on the mattress snoring. He'd best bring back some coin for his effort, that's all I can say,' Agatha grumbled as she swept.

Father Luke paid her no heed. He was busy thinking. The money was Despenser's, and the person who should receive it was his heir; however, the Despenser family was from the Welsh Marches, which was a terrible long way away. But at Kenilworth, as everyone knew, was the old King, Sir Edward of Caernarfon.

If he were to take the money there, Luke would have fulfilled his responsibility by passing the money on to the correct person, and no one could complain. The priest was delighted at the thought of disposing of the money at long last. It was such a burden on his soul. And it would be up to Sir Edward, what he did with it.

CHAPTER SEVEN

Willersey

It was dry, and that was good, Stephen Dunheved thought to himself as he waited at the inn. It was a relief to see so much clear blue sky. Not that you could depend on it. In his experience, the weather in these parts could change too quickly for comfort.

Seeing the woman and her child approaching, he nodded courteously enough. That Agatha was a vicious witch, he reckoned. Fair, blue-eyed, but with the tongue of a snake. Stephen himself would not have married her for all the gold in the Tower – but then, when she was younger and less twisted by fate, perhaps she had been more comely. Trouble was, like everyone else in the kingdom, she had suffered: wars, disease and famine had all taken their toll.

It was enough to make a man weep, to think of the devastation which had been visited upon the realm in the last decade. The King had done all he might for his impoverished little kingdom, but there was never enough treasure for so many people.

And with that oafish stupidity so common to the peasant, the people of the country blamed him – as though it was *his* fault that the crops couldn't grow!

The barons were more culpable than their King. Their avarice and jealousy of each other meant that they were forever battling for personal advantage. Men stole their neighbours' cattle and flocks, they bickered, and rode out with their retainers to fight over the smallest dispute. Such matters were better suited to lawyers. At least in court, these disputes rarely led to bloodshed.

He watched the woman and her daughter pass by. She did look better when viewed in a more kindly spirit, he told himself, as he enquired, 'Mistress, is your man ready yet?'

'What do you think?' Agatha said rudely. 'Do you see him with me?'

Stephen's opinion of her returned to simple contempt. 'Where do you think he may be?'

'At home.'

Jen called out, 'Seeing to the pigs.'

'Thank you, maid.'

It was already an hour past daybreak, and Stephen was keen to be off. There were many long miles to cover. Ten leagues or more, in fact. With a cart, that would take at least two days, what with rivers to cross and the poor state of the roads. A cart would rarely manage ten miles in a day. Still, he was paying for fifteen miles a day, and he would make it, come what may.

A shiver ran through his frame, and he gave a little grin, thinking that his brother Thomas would have said it was someone walking over his grave. Stephen reckoned that was being overly optimistic. The prospect of his dying naturally and being placed in a coffin with weeping maids and children all about was nice to dream of, but highly unlikely.

He gave the sky another look, and tipped the drinking horn upwards, emptying it, before crossing to the wall where his horse was tethered to a large ring. Pulling the reins free, he led his pony along the road towards Ham's house.

Time to go.

'My friend, please!' called Father Lukc. He had seen the man rise and walk from the inn even as he himself hurried towards Ham's house.

'Father?' The man stopped and waited for the priest.

The fellow had the clear features and open, bright eyes of a man in his prime – but as Luke drew nearer, he saw that he had the wrinkles of someone ten years older. What's more, his dark eyes were watchful, as though he did not entirely trust even a priest.

'My son, I have heard that you are a purveyor, and that you have asked our Ham to accompany you to Kenilworth?'

'What of it?'

'Nothing, except I have a chest I need to take there and wondered if I could join you.'

'Why would you want to join me?'

Father Luke blinked. 'I would not wish to travel so far alone, that is all. It is a great distance to Kenilworth, and such journeys can prove hazardous.'

'That's true enough.'

To Father Luke's dismay, the man demonstrated little enthusiasm. It was discourteous in the extreme, the way that he was frowning at his priestly robes. 'Very well. If you do not want company—' he began, hurt.

'No, Father, I would be happy with your companionship for the journey. I was only wondering whether you would not prefer to find a more comfortable means of travelling.'

65

'I am perfectly capable of walking that distance!'

'Then I should be most glad to have your company,' Stephen said.

'How many carts are there?'

'Only the one.'

'All that way, and there's only one cart?'

Stephen said nothing, but merely stood with a thin smile on his face.

'Oh,' Father Luke said.

'We leave shortly. You need to bring food and drink for the journey.'

'Not only that. I have a chest, as I said. Ham will need to come to my church to collect it. It is very heavy,' Father Luke fretted.

'Then get him to go with you to fetch it,' the purveyor said. '*And hurry.*'

CHAPTER EIGHT

Exeter

Many miles to the south, Sir Baldwin de Furnshill walked amidst the din and smoke of the local smithies.

Sir Baldwin was a tall knight, strong in the arm, with a neck thick and muscled from long years of wearing a heavy steel helmet. The neat beard that traced the edge of his jaw had less black in it now, and was thickly salted with white, while the hair on his head was turning grey all over.

His was a face marked by experience. At his cheek was a long scar from the Siege of Acre in the Holy Land, but that was less prominent than the creases that passed over his brow and down at either side of his mouth, showing the pain he had endured in his long life.

He was tired. The last year had seen such unrivalled madness that he was weary to remember it. From the invasion of the Queen and her lover, their swift progress across the kingdom, snapping up towns as they went, the revolt in London, the slaughter of Bishop Walter II of Blessed Memory, the King's capture, the executions . . . All had happened in so short a space of time it was a miracle the realm had not collapsed.

To have forced the King to resign was a deplorable act. Baldwin had done his duty: he had remained at the King's side through those long weeks when Edward was forced to ride from Bristol ever farther into the Welsh countryside. Not until the day that the King's party was captured did Baldwin leave him. It was a matter of honour.

But honour was dead. The kingdom had once been God-fearing, with knights who believed in the chivalric ideals of piety and honour. He had himself proved his own religious dedication by joining the pilgrims who sailed to the Holy Land to fight in its defence. The Fall of Acre nearly saw his own death. It was the Templars who rescued him.

In gratitude, Baldwin had joined the *Poor Fellow Soldiers of Christ and the Temple of Solomon*, the Knights Templar, and served them until the dreadful day of Friday, 13 October 1307, when all were arrested by King Philippe IV of France.

The King, who coveted the Templars' wealth, had set in motion a plot to deprive them of their riches, their properties, and ultimately their lives. He laid at their feet accusations so appalling that all over France, men and women viewed them with horror. The Order was disbanded, the Knights harried and tortured. Baldwin himself escaped, and he made his way gradually to Devon, to his family's lands, where he had hoped to live peacefully as a rural knight.

Baldwin had been happy here. He had won a reputation as a fair judge of character, and been given the job of Keeper of the King's Peace, and his life had continued in its orderly manner until the recent civil strife.

Good God, he was tired. The kingdom was in a state of chaos, and men like him – those who were supposed to enforce the King's Peace – had been overwhelmed with work. In times of trouble, lawlessness increased – which was why he was here, in this place. Sir Baldwin needed a more reliable sword.

In Exeter there were many smiths and armourers of varying quality, but Baldwin knew one man who was capable of producing the very finest work.

Years of swinging heavy hammers had given David Smith's fingers a grip which rivalled that of the metal he bent and twisted to his will. He had a brown beard shot through with silver, and dark brows hooding suspicious grey eyes. His skin was like old leather, worn and blackened by his work. By nature, he was rude, morose, and prone to flashes of anger. He was also the most expensive of all the smiths in Exeter – and the best.

Until the last summer Baldwin had owned a beautiful sword. Its blade was as blue as a peacock's feathers, and although moderately short, it had a perfect balance. But during a skirmish at sea, he had lost it and ever since had been forced to rely on a cheap weapon that had all the balance of a sack of turnips. It was high time to replace it.

'Sir,' the smith grunted as Baldwin entered his little chamber. He was bent over a curving bar of glowing metal, beating it with his hammer.

'Master Smith, I hope I find you well?'

'Well as any man can be when he's been fleeced by the taxman again,' David Smith said angrily. 'They take all our money and then expect us to thank them! Thieving scrotes.'

'Is my weapon ready?'

'I said it would be, didn't I? Have you known me lie before?'

'Master Smith, I am keen to see it,' Baldwin said testily. This politeness in response to the gruff smith was wearing, no matter how good the man was.

David Smith gazed at him. 'You want to take over this?' he demanded, thrusting his curved metal into the forge. He watched as the metal began to glow, then gradually spit little sparks, before pulling it out and placing it carefully on his anvil once more, this time beating the curve down until it was almost flat again.

Baldwin had seen this process often enough before. Drawing out the metal took an age. Only when the shape was roughly formed would the smith begin to put some definition into his work.

He waited patiently. It was always the same when he came here. David was ever crotchety and difficult – but he could afford to be, knowing he was the best.

'Look over there, in the wrapping,' David said at last, thrusting the blank into a quench. The hissing and bubbling was deafening.

Baldwin walked to the table at which the smith had pointed, and found the package. Slowly, with care, he unwrapped the waxed material to reveal a new sword.

He held it joyfully. It was a perfect blue, polished to a mirror-like perfection, with a fuller that ran for some two thirds of the blade. 'You have created a marvel, David. This is beautiful.'

The smith had joined him, rubbing his hands on the old leather apron that covered the front of his body. It was blackened and scarred in many places, where sparks had caught and flared. The mere sight was enough to make Baldwin feel queasy. In the last days of Acre, when he was young, fires had been started by the Moorish siege engines, hurling boulders and flaming bales designed to cause infernos all over the city. He could recall the screams of people burning. Some ran to rescue those trapped in buildings, and their clothes were pocked and marked like this.

Baldwin swallowed and turned away. Death by fire was hideous.

'I've not had time to finish the surface as I'd have liked,' David said grimly. 'I need another few weeks for that.'

Baldwin hefted the sword in his hand. He had ordered this in December, when he first returned to Exeter after the trials of the last year. The smith had made the blade, while an armourer Baldwin knew, who worked with David quite often, had provided the cross and the grip, and had wound the fine leather about the hilts, fitting them together with the sword and then riveting the heavy round pommel in place.

'This is proof that you are a master of your art.' Inset into the blade on one side, Baldwin saw the letters picked out in fine gold script: *BOAC* (*Beate Omnipotensque Angeli Christi*: Blessed and Omnipotent are the Angels of Christ). On the reverse, in memory of his friends in the Order, he had a small circle, and within it was a Templar cross.

'Not perfect. I missed a little dint down there – see? I had my apprentice polish it up, and he failed there.'

'No, I do not see,' Baldwin said, smiling. 'You are a man who is determined upon perfection, my friend.'

'I don't know why you were in such a hurry for it, anyway,' the smith complained. He took the sword back and began to wipe a cloth smeared in fat all over it, rubbing quickly, and peering along its length to make sure that it was all uniformly covered. 'The land should be calming, now we have a new King.'

Baldwin took his sword. He would buy a scabbard from a shop farther along the street. It would be easy to find one that fitted.

'The land should be calmer,' he agreed. But as he left the smithy, he knew very well that the kingdom's troubles were far from over.

71

The King had been deposed and the Crown had passed on, but although many sought to uphold the succession, even if it was unorthodox, there were others who preferred to make as much profit as they could from the situation. Sir Roger Mortimer, his lover the Queen, and the under-age King Edward III ruling in a three-way council, was no recipe for peace. Baldwin suspected that the realm would suffer more dramatic shocks before long.

He was determined to be prepared for them.

CHAPTER NINE

Two Sundays before the Feast of the Annunciation[1]

Kenilworth

It was the middle of his second day in the town before Dolwyn managed to enter the castle. He had not expected it to be so easy.

The sun shone brightly, and without rain to wash away the ordure, the streets were becoming more noisome by the day.

He sat outside an inn and enjoyed a strong ale while he watched passers-by: men-at-arms, women with baskets offering flowers or trinkets, urchins calling for coins, pestering any who looked wealthy until sent on their way with a cuff about the ear. It was hours until the scavengers would come to clean the street of dung, scraping up dog mess for the tanners, that of the horse and cattle for the dungheaps, sweeping away piles of shit where the butchers voided the bowels of their carcasses.

1 15 March 1327

It was the same in all vills and towns up and down the kingdom, he thought. Wherever men lived, there was filth to be cleaned. In a way, he was a scavenger too, tidying up the unpleasant little problems the Bardi family preferred to keep hidden. Once he had worked for Matteo alone, but now he was henchman to the bank itself.

He couldn't complain. His post was well paid, and he needed the job. Since losing his wife and daughter, working was the only thing that kept him moderately sane.

In the yard behind the tavern, a cockfight was about to start, and the audience was gathering. At one side of the pit were men-at-arms from the castle, while a sprinkling of locals watched sullenly from the other side.

'There is bad feeling,' Dolwyn commented to a neighbour.

'What do you expect? Those prickles take everything they can, even our women. Whatever we do, they elbow their way in.'

'It must be difficult when they're all over the town,' Dolwyn said sympathetically.

There was a bellow of laughter from the yard, and Dolwyn turned to see one of the castle's men grabbing at a cockerel in the pit, and wringing its neck. The body he flung carelessly to one side, while another pair of birds were brought and armed with the vicious spurs, teased and tormented by their handlers to the point where they could not be held. Then, in a flash of feathers the two sprang into the air, trying to rake each other with spurs and talons.

'See that squire? He's porter of the castle, he is. A right devil. All he cares about is money.' Dolwyn's neighbour indicated the man who had killed the cock.

Dolwyn studied the fellow. Thick-set, short in the neck, but with an impressive breadth of shoulder, he was dark-skinned, and wore a thin beard with plenty of ginger in it. His dark eyebrows almost met over his nose, and his equally dark eyes seemed very knowing. He looked across and met Dolwyn's stare without interest, as a man might survey a slug, before returning to the contest.

'What money?' Dolwyn asked.

'He'll take anything he can,' the man said.

Dolwyn nodded, and finished his ale. He bought another and wandered back out to the yard, watching the men at the pit. He enjoyed cockfighting.

Feathers were flying about, and one cockerel was weakening, his head hanging a little, while blood dripped from his comb and beak. An eye was gone, and his left wing was twisted and useless. Enfeebled, he watched from his good eye as his opponent circled closer, and waited for the final assault.

There was a loud squawking. The fresher cock leaped up high, and it seemed impossible for the other to defend himself . . . but then he darted to the side, and as the other came down, in a somewhat ungainly manner, he jumped just high enough, and a barb caught the other cockerel in the back of the neck. There was a sudden spit of blood, and the one-eyed bird was the victor.

Both birds were soon dead, their bodies thrown to a boy, who sat plucking them. The porter stood, wiping his hands on a cloth, but when he saw Dolwyn again, his eyes narrowed. Dolwyn was about to walk away when the porter accosted him.

'Hey, you. You're a stranger,' he said.

'Yes. I am a traveller.'

'Where are you going, *traveller*?'

'I am on my way to Warwick from Leeds for my lord, the Earl of Chester,' Dolwyn said mildly. Earl of Chester was King Edward III's first title, granted long before he was made Duke.

The man studied him with his head on one side. 'And what do you want at Warwick?'

'The message I carry is secret,' Dolwyn said. He did not make a move toward his sword, but was ready to defend himself. Although he had no idea what was in the message, he daren't display it. He suspected that it would be dangerous.

It appeared that his confidence was enough to convince. 'So you say. That is good. Is there news from the north?'

Dolwyn did not relax his posture, but nodded slightly. 'That which all know. The Scots are attacking again, and their armies are ravaging the north. Lord Percy . . . I can tell you this: he has been negotiating with the Bruce for the last month or more, but the Scots won't listen to reason. There will be war.'

'I see.' It was evident that the man was persuaded by Dolwyn's story. 'So, you have a safe conduct?'

Dolwyn opened his purse and took out the parchment with its seal, but he did not pass it to the porter. 'You are?'

'I am Bernard of Oxford, Esquire. And you are?'

Dolwyn pushed the note back into his purse. 'Travelling without attracting attention, Squire. Now, I require food enough to last me to Warwick.'

'If you have a safe conduct, I would see it.' Squire Bernard snapped.

'Then you will have to kill me. This document was given to me by Lord Percy's own man.'

'Oh.' The squire looked askance at Dolwyn.

'Yes. You know what happened to Andrew Harclay when his negotiations went awry with the Scottish. He was executed. I have secret communications here which I must take urgently, or our business with the Scots may fail. Delay me, and incur the King's displeasure. So, will you aid me, or defy me?'

In less time than it had taken for the second cock-fight to finish, Dolwyn was in the castle's hall. He looked about him with interest as a page fetched meats and cheese and a loaf of bread. He was given a well-carved bread trencher, and a thickened stew was doled into a bowl. With the bread he soaked up as much of the gravy as possible, before attacking the meats on the trencher. The hard cheese he stuffed into his satchel, along with half the loaf.

The room was all but deserted – the men would be arriving later for their second meal of the day – and he took advantage of the quiet to look about the place. It was a newer chamber, but the fire was still placed in the middle of the floor, to his relief. He did not like fires set at the wall. They never seemed as effective, and in any case he missed the smell of the smoke.

'This is a quiet castle,' he commented, 'for so many men in the garrison.'

'The knight doesn't like noise,' the page said.

'What knight?'

'There's only one here we call that – Sir Edward of Caernarfon. The King's father.'

Dolwyn pretended astonishment. 'Him? You say *he* is here?'

'Aye, sir. And a more kindly gentleman you could never meet.'

Dolwyn said nothing, but scraped at his trencher and sucked the juicy bread from his spoon. 'I've heard he is that,' he lied. He licked the back of his spoon clean before carefully stowing it away in his satchel. 'It must be an honour to have him in the castle.'

'It's a lot of work,' the boy said.

'But he's held in a room here, not a cell?'

'We couldn't keep the King's father in gaol like some common churl!' the boy scoffed.

'I would hope not! A man of his estate should be treated with all respect,' Dolwyn said fervently. 'Tell me, boy, would you like a penny?'

'Why?'

'Just to know where Sir Edward is held. Nothing more. I am carrying a message for his son, and I'm sure the young King would like to know his father was being held without discomfort.'

'Twopence?' the page demanded, and then, when Dolwyn nodded, he considered and then nodded. 'Follow me.'

They walked over to the door, and the boy pointed across the ward to a small block of rooms. Inside, said the page, the King had two chambers, one above the other and both well-appointed. 'And he can ride and hunt whenever he wishes. You can tell the King we see to all his father desires – even the stranger foods he wishes. In fact, we have purveyors riding all over Warwickshire for his delight.'

Dolwyn studied the building. He watched as a middle-aged woman left a chamber by the gates: from the baskets she bore on a yoke about her neck, and the steam that emanated from the room she had left, he guessed that this must be a laundress. There would be few women allowed in a castle, but she was one of the exceptions.

His eyes took in the layout of the place, and when he was satisfied that he had committed the yard to memory, he passed two pennies to the page, before striding back to the hall and fetching his satchel. He must plan how to get the message to Sir Edward. After all, there might be a reward for making contact with the old King. With luck, just the act of taking messages from him could mean a purse of gold in gratitude.

He walked outside, and stared once more at the building across the castle yard. Yes, there must be guards, but there was no obvious activity.

It was worth a chance.

He took a quick look about the court, and then marched firmly over the hard-packed earth to the room where Sir Edward was held.

House of Bardi, London

Matteo Bardi stood stiffly and stretched. The chamber was chilly today, and he wore a heavy coat against the cold. At his fireplace, he held out his hands to the flames, idly dreaming of Florence. At this time of year, all his friends would be starting to eat outside in the bright sunshine, not cowering indoors. This land truly was abominable.

His back had healed. The scar would remain, proof of his part in the overthrow of King Edward II, and already a prostitute had commented upon it, as though he was a bold warrior, rather than a clever sifter of information. All he knew was, he was fortunate to be alive.

He could not speak to anyone about Benedetto. The idea that his own brother could have given him that blow was appalling. Such ruthlessness was unforgivable, but his brother had spent so much time in Florence learning the ways of politics and banking, that a little of the more forthright methods there of ensuring mercantile success must have rubbed off on him.

There was one thought uppermost in Matteo's mind: whether Dolwyn could have been bought by Benedetto. It was possible. Dolwyn was willing to take a life for money, he knew, but his henchman had been too far away by the time Matteo was stabbed. And if Dolwyn had wished to kill him, Matteo knew he would be dead. If not in the road, then later at Alured's home.

No, surely Dolwyn was innocent of that crime. He would not kill his own master.

At a knock on his door, Matteo turned, still holding his hands to the flames, and a messenger entered.

'You want the summaries for Benedetto? I will have them shortly,' Matteo told him.

Benedetto had travelled west to discuss matters with Sir Roger Mortimer, who was presently near Bristol. It was hard to keep track of the man. He was always out and about on horse-back, quelling opposition by his mere presence.

'No, sir, it is a message for you.'

'Me?' Matteo said with surprise. He took the parchment and glanced at the seal briefly, feeling his face grow pale at the sight of Sir Roger Mortimer's mark. Carefully he broke the seal.

'He wants me to join him – why?' he muttered. The thought of riding all that way across this accursed country to join the man, apparently now in Wales, was daunting.

'You are a banker. Perhaps he needs money,' the other man said curtly, secure in the protection of his King's messenger's uniform.

Matteo dismissed him and slumped down in his chair. This was a most unwelcome development. He was needed here, at the heart of his network of men, where he was most valuable. To redirect all his messages would take an age, and there was no apparent reason . . .

He took up the note once more, reading it carefully. There was no implied threat in it, but he was forced to wonder nonetheless.

If the note Dolwyn had been instructed to deliver to Sir Edward of Caernarfon had been intercepted . . . But no. If it had been, Sir Roger would have demanded to see Benedetto, the head of the House of Bardi, not him. So this couldn't be anything to do with that.

He rang the bell that stood on his table and told his serv-ants to prepare for a journey, and then asked a man to go and find Alured. If the latter could be prevailed upon to join him, Matteo would feel safer, since the local constable was strong and reliable. And if Alured was reluctant, Matteo could petition members of the Freedom of the City to prevail upon him.

His commands given, he gave himself up to reading through the notes and compiling his report for Benedetto, but all the while his mind would kcep returning to Sir Roger Mortimer.

What was so urgent that it required Matteo's presence?

CHAPTER TEN

Kenilworth

'What is it?' Gilbert said. The chief guard of Sir Edward of Caernarfon had eaten his lunch, and was sitting with his legs up on the bench beside him as Squire Bernard strode in.

Gilbert was in a foul mood, but there was nothing new in that. Since arriving here and being told that he was to remain with the King until he was relieved, he had been bitterly resentful. His duties should have ended four months ago when he deposited the King here in Kenilworth. That was what he had been promised. Yet here he was, still waiting, and with no one to relieve him. He would probably be stuck here until he died – or until the King did, he told himself gloomily.

'There's been a man here asking about Sir Edward and how well he's guarded,' Squire Bernard said. 'He told me he was a messenger for the King.'

'And?' Gilbert snapped.

'Well, I feel there was something wrong about him.'

' "*Wrong*", eh?' Gilbert snorted. 'I know all about "wrong". I'm still here, and that's wrong! Four months – and here I am, still kicking my sodding heels!' He hated this place. He hated being a gaoler, he hated waking every morning with a view of the land about here that was as different from London and his little estate near Eltham as it could be. In his opinion, this whole damned place was *wrong*!

He glanced up at the man standing before him, looking bemused. The fool obviously expected him to do something.

'So what is the problem?' Gilbert demanded, shooting a look over his shoulder at the door to the King's chamber. It was closed as usual.

'He would not show me his letter of safe conduct.'

'So you arrested him?'

'He told me he had safe passage, but that he was on an urgent journey carrying information about negotiations with the Scots,' Bernard said. 'I couldn't ignore him.'

Gilbert grunted and swung his legs from the bench, rubbing his eyes. 'Very well,' he yawned. 'But if this is all a noise about nothing, I'll make you regret it. Right – you go to the gate and check it. I want the guards doubled, and when it's curfew, the gate is to be locked no matter what, you understand?'

'Yes.'

'And Squire?'

Squire Bernard was surprised by the voice behind him. He turned to find himself staring into the square face of a tall man with green, brooding eyes. He had been leaning against the wall behind the door, but now he stepped forward. It was Sir Jevan de Bromfield, and Bernard's heart sank. The man's reputation for savagery was widely acknowledged.

'If you find a stranger, Squire, don't believe him when he tells you he's a messenger. The King's messengers go about in uniform. Spies are those who hide their loyalty.'

Second Monday before the Feast of the Annunciation[1]

Warwick

The road which passed by Warwick was a heavily used path, and after some days of warm weather, the ruts had hardened and a mis-step threatened a strained or broken ankle. It seemed to Father Luke, as he stumbled along as best he could, that the purveyor, Stephen Dunheved, appeared to be on his guard, riding on his horse like a merchant fearful of attack.

Father Luke assumed that this suspicion was a natural part of a purveyor's life. No one liked a taxman, and a purveyor was not dissimilar: he would enforce the prices he chose, and no peasant had the option of arguing. There were many who might wish to take a shot at him with an arrow.

Here, though, it was very unlikely that someone might try to assault them. The kingdom was more or less at peace now, and this was one of the quieter backwaters of the nation. After the past turbulent years and the constant threat of war, everyone was subdued. The fear had been so overwhelming, its removal was startling. Luke thought it was like a man about to dive into a dangerous lake, who took a deep breath in preparation, only to be commanded to turn away from the water.

However, it was good to find that they were approaching a small tavern. After walking all of yesterday, until it was dark and difficult to gather firewood, Luke's legs were weary by noon, and the purveyor – who had a high opinion of his own importance which Father Luke considered unwarranted – had refused to allow them to pause in Warwick. He did not want them to be delayed. That was enough to make Father Luke protest bitterly. The carter and he must walk almost all the way,

1 16 March 1327

for the horse could not manage any speed whilst bearing a man as well as hauling the cart.

Ham's beast was large, with a splash of white like a fist on his breast, and a star of white on his rump, while on the left foreleg he had a white band about his ankle. In his youth, Ham said, he had been a spirited beast, but now, after many years of hauling loads up and down hills, the poor fellow was no longer at his best. It was a miracle, Luke thought, that the animal had survived this long. And it would be a miracle indeed, if he made it all the way to Kenilworth.

Instead of halting here, Dunheved proposed to allow them to rest when they reached the little village of Lecwotten[1], a few miles north of Warwick. Ham and Luke exchanged a glance. Picking a fight with a senior official was foolish when the delay would be but a matter of an hour or so. What's more ale in a small place like Lecwotten would be considerably cheaper than in a town like Warwick.

So they agreed to continue and soon reached the inn, which was little more than a tatty ale-house designed to service the small local community.

The purveyor and Ham went inside, Dunheved loudly demanding drink and food, but Luke chose to wait outside, to keep an eye on the cart and his metal-bound chest.

He detested the very sight of that box, and could not wait for the moment when he could pass it on to someone else. At times, he had thought to give it to this purveyor, but at the last moment he had always resisted the temptation. Dunheved seemed a hard man, and Luke would not be surprised if he didn't just take the money for himself. Purveyors had a reputation for theft and shameless rapacity, often fleecing the populace and selling

1 present name Leek Wootton

the excess goods at a profit. There were regular stories of such men being arrested for their corruption. This man was almost certainly formed from that mould. The only reason Luke was safe was due to the presence of Ham. The fellow might have the brain of an ox, but an ox can intimidate, and Ham was loyal to his priest.

Luke wandered over to the cart. In the bed were the sacks of provisions which the purveyor had bought, and Luke had carefully installed the chest in the middle, between two small barrels of perry, and behind the sack of lampreys, to stop it moving about too much. Now he pulled the sack aside, separated the folds of some blankets, and reached in to touch his chest. It was there, but very well wedged, and he must tug hard until he felt it move. Soon it was at the edge of the cart, and he raised the lid and peered inside. All was well. The coins were in little sacks of soft leather, and he counted them: none was missing. He would not put it past the purveyor to open it and steal a purse, but so far as Luke had seen, the man had shown no interest in it. He had other things on his mind.

Taking a purse, Father Luke opened it and marvelled again. The coins were gold, with a lily on one side, the image of St John on the other. He knew it was called a 'Florin'. The Florentines minted them, and they were worth some shillings each. If they were valued at three shillings, he thought, with twenty purses of fifty coins in each, there were one thousand gold coins here: that must mean at least three thousand shillings – a hundred and fifty pounds! It made him weak to think of such wealth. He was about to shove the chest back into the gap, when he heard a cheerful voice calling to him.

'Father Luke? You're far from home!'

Luke spun on his heel and found himself staring into the face of John of Shulton, the man who had told him of Despenser's death. 'Why, good day to you, sir! And what are you doing here?'

'Riding to Kenilworth. What of you?'

After days with the sullen purveyor, Luke felt something akin to affection for this man. He forgot how nervous he had been when he first met John.

'Isn't that the mark of my lord Despenser?' John added, peering at the chest.

'Yes. It is his,' Luke whispered with a glance at the inn. 'He gave it to me for safekeeping, and I am taking it to Kenilworth for the King.'

'You mean Sir Edward,' John corrected. He eyed the chest with some interest. 'They call him Sir Edward of Caernarfon now, you know, Father.'

'Hey! Who are you, and what are you gawping at?' Dunheved shouted from the door. He was walking from the ale-house with a pair of jugs in his hands, and passed one to Luke. 'This load is all for the garrison at Kenilworth.'

'It is no matter to me,' said John, and nodded his head to Luke. 'I would have joined you on your journey, Father, but I think your grumpy friend here has no wish for company. Godspeed you on your way!'

Luke muttered his own farewell, but the man was already riding away at a smart trot.

The purveyor said nothing, but his eyes were on the man, and he wore a strange expression, almost a smile, as John disappeared into the distance. And then he shook himself and said bluntly, 'Food is on the way.'

Luke could not help but notice that the man's eyes turned now to the cart, and suddenly he squinted. And when Luke turned, he saw the edge of the chest protruding from the blankets, which he had inadequately arranged to cover it.

Lecwotton

Stephen Dunheved was eager for a drink. As soon as he had finished his first quart of ale, staring thoughtfully up the road in the direction John had taken, he went back inside the ale-house for another.

It was one thing to be assured of acting for the general good, but when it came to a situation like this, knowing that men would soon die, and that he himself could be one of them, that was a different matter. Not that he was scared, just tense, because he knew what lay ahead. A fight, certainly, and possibly the release of their rightful king, along with the glory that would ensue. It was a wonderful ambition – and yet he felt weary and fretful, and couldn't shake off a sense of impending doom.

He had been in difficult situations before, of course. Six years ago he had been forced to abjure the realm for killing a man, and didn't return until the King pardoned him. Within the year he was Valet of the King's Chamber, and soon afterwards, Edward made him custodian of Lyonshall Castle, then appointed him to hold an inquisition. Stephen's future had seemed assured. He had not conceived of the King losing his throne.

This wretched tavern seemed to emphasise just how far he had fallen. Once, he had moved in the best circles – not that you would think it, to look at him now. To all he was a scruffy acquirer of goods, little better than a churl, and everyone knew that purveyors had a bad reputation.

He grimaced. The fire was smoking profusely in the middle of the room, and there was a loud hissing as moisture bubbled from the ends of the green logs. It was typical of the landlord that he hadn't the foresight to cut wood earlier in the year so it could dry.

Going outside, he sat on a log near the door. Soon a wench came out with a tray on which there was a large round loaf and a lump of cheese, as well as two more jugs of ale.

'Thank you, maid,' he said, eyeing the loaf hungrily.

She set it on the ground, and wiped her hands before leaving them to their meal.

'Ham, come and eat,' Luke called.

Stephen was already cutting into the bread with his knife. He took a quarter of the loaf and studied the lump of grit-infested, blackened crust. He, who had eaten the best painde-maigne with the King's household, forced now to subsist on this! It was enough to make a man weep, he thought, washing a piece down with a mouthful of ale. At least the liquid made it soften.

The carter joined them at the table, sitting and reaching over for the cheese. 'I don't know that the horse'll make it much further today.'

'He won't have to go very much further,' Stephen said. 'It's only a league or more to the castle. We are halfway there, from Warwick.'

'Good.'

Luke glanced over at the horse. 'He has done well to bring us here so swiftly.' He saw the old beast droop his head towards the grass. He seemed hardly able to rip the grass from the verge.

Stephen looked at the sun. 'Don't worry. You can rest him a while here. We don't have to move off again yet.'

Wycombe

They had set off late the previous afternoon, and Alured still resented the way that he had been imperiously called into service. It was not the sort of job he had ever considered for himself, being a personal bodyguard to a banker.

It was lunchtime when they saw the little bush bound to a pole over a cottage's door, denoting an ale-house, and Alured went in to ask about food and drink while Matteo Bardi and the three servants with him waited outside. The old woman inside was content to let them share her food when she was promised payment, but even now, with food in his belly, Alured continued to eye his new master with suspicion.

He knew that Matteo was hiding something. The man had regularly thrashed around and cried out in his sleep during the time when he was at Alured's house, and the constable had a shrewd suspicion that he was petrified of someone close to him.

There were many who looked at Alured askance when he mentioned his intuitions, but he had been involved with people all his life, and knew how to read a man's thoughts. Fear was easy to spot; and he was getting the distinct impression of fear from Matteo Bardi.

When they were riding on again, he broached the subject while out of earshot of the other henchmen.

'Master, do you have reason to be fearful about this journey?'

Matteo turned to him with such a startled look that Alured had to stifle a grin. 'Scared? Me?'

'Look, I was ordered by the city to come with you whether I like it or not, and I will do as I'm told. But if there's some reason for your alarm, I'd like to know it. Then at least I can prepare for it.'

'There is nothing. Nothing!'

'All right,' Alured said, and jogged onwards.

'Why do you ask?'

'Because you're on edge, master. It's to do with your dreams, I reckon.' Alured snorted, hawked and spat into the roadway. 'When you were in your fever, you kept calling out to your brother – the one who died.'

'Yes.'

'You knew he was going to die that day.'

Matteo shot him a look with wide, alarmed eyes. 'I told him not to ride his horse. The mob were grabbing anyone on horseback. He didn't have a chance!'

'Then there was nothing you could do. It wasn't your fault he died, master. He was a grown man, and too cocky, that's all. He went off up there, assuming that everyone would back down when they saw him – that's what Bill told me. And he was proved wrong. Not your fault.'

'Perhaps not.'

'And then they got you too.'

Matteo nodded, then muttered, 'But I have my own suspicions about that.'

Alured heard him. 'What do you mean?'

In a low, conspiratorial voice, Matteo confided how scared he was of Benedetto. The brother who, he thought, had tried to kill him.

'He will try again,' he finished.

'Your own brother?' Alured said. But he knew there were many in London who had gained advancement by stepping into a dead man's shoes. And often a man would hate his own brother far more than any other enemy.

'He was there when it happened. He lives up towards Saint Benet Fink.'

Alured felt as though his heart had stopped. 'Where?'

'Saint Benet Fink. Why?'

Alured said nothing. But in his mind he saw again that alleyway with the two young bodies lying in it. The very same alley that led to St Benet Fink and Benedetto's house.

CHAPTER ELEVEN

Woods near Kenilworth

Father Luke was relieved to be moving again when they left the tavern. Soon he would see the castle in which the King was held, and so could pass over the box of florins. He wanted nothing more to do with any of it. But he also longed to reach the castle, simply so he could sit at a hot fire and drink spiced cider or ale.

Not many men would so willingly relinquish such wealth, but for Father Luke the trepidation which he had felt since hearing of Despenser's death had steadily increased over time, as if the weight of the cash was dragging on his very soul. A hundred and fifty pounds! The box contained more than the value of Father Luke's entire parish.

He wondered what reception he could expect at the castle. The men there would naturally be suspicious and might not let him see Sir Edward – in which case it was possible that someone there might actually steal the box. And if they did, what could he do to stop them? It was unlikely they'd take it and

say, 'Thanks, this will help pay for our garrison's Easter feast!'
More probably they'd take it, promise to pass it on, and then the
poor imprisoned King would never get to see it.

He was mulling this over, when there came a low whistle
from ahead.

The purveyor turned and said brusquely: 'Don't worry,
carter. These are friends of mine.'

Luke shot a look at Ham, and saw he was concerned. Ham
cast an eye over his shoulder as though estimating the chances
of turning his cart and fleeing, but of course it was too late.
Luke gazed ahead and felt a sudden surprise on seeing John of
Shulton and Paul of Bircheston.

The two men were on large horses, and as Dunheved came
closer to them, they rode forward and slapped him on the back,
laughing and chattering.

'Thought you'd got lost until I saw you in that tavern,' John
was saying. 'I was trying to find you.'

'I didn't want us to stand there chatting.' The purveyor
appeared to be less enthusiastic than the other two. 'I need to
be off out of here as soon as I can.'

'Don't worry yourself,' John said. 'This won't take long.'
His grin was infectious, and the priest found himself smiling in
return. The fellow really was attractive in a roguish way, and
Luke felt he would be an excellent companion in a tavern. He
would be the first to begin to sing or tell saucy jokes, and generally make any evening an event to remember.

As if reading his mind, the fellow began to whistle and then
sing, a silly tale about a woman who was trying to sue a man
for the paternity of her child, while the man refused to listen,
and instead boasted about the other women he had bedded, and
why he wouldn't touch an old trout like her. Which was amus-
ing enough – but the last verse told of how she was, unknown

to him, the wealthiest woman in the county, and since he had rejected her and caused her son to be known as a bastard, she would marry the man's servant instead, and elevate him to a position of significance in the land.

A fine song it was, and John managed to use different voices as he sang, with occasional lewd and bawdy gestures. It was all Luke could do not to laugh aloud at his antics.

But the joy in his heart was stopped when Paul and John moved to the back of the cart, and began to move things about.

Ham was the first to protest. 'Hoi, don't meddle with that stuff! It's the purveyor's, and I don't want it—'

Paul stopped and stood before Ham, smiling, but with his hand on his sword's hilt. 'Shut up, carter.'

The purveyor called, 'Carter, this is all right. There's nothing to worry about. They are making room for additional stores, that's all.'

Luke was watching John, though, as he peered at the casket on the bed of the cart. He pulled it towards him, then tested the lid. Seeing it was locked, he tried to pick it up, then made a face at the weight.

Luke felt as though the blood was rushing to his face. John of Shulton had the look of a fellow who would slit a priest's throat for twenty shillings, and in that box, as Luke knew, there were many pounds. He swallowed, anxious, but even as he did so, Paul walked over to John and began passing him the new cargo for the cart. Luke's eyes widened.

They were all weapons.

Near Kenilworth Castle

Dolwyn did not dare to stay in the town that night. Instead he left the castle, and then set off in an easterly direction until he came to a small farming hamlet, where he bought some ale and eggs fried with a spot of grease from a pot of bacon fat. It was delicious, and when he asked, he was permitted to make use of their little hayloft, where he slept the night in warm comfort, unworried by the rats and beetles that scurried about him.

All was well; better than well. He had seen the contents of the letter – and had hoped for some small reward for delivering it to Sir Edward. How naïve he had been! For now he saw how much more he could make by helping the man. While Edward's position was not as good as once it had been, at least Dolwyn had won his confidence. And if the grateful Sir Edward of Caernarfon was ever brought back to power, Dolwyn knew that he would personally be granted a good posting himself. Perhaps become a sergeant in a royal castle, or land some cushy job in the Tower of London – something like that, something without hard work. Ideally in a place like Barnard Castle, where there wouldn't be too many others to keep an eye on him. Then he could copy Jack the Irishman, and cream as much money as he liked off the local peasants. As a King's official, they would have no way to refuse any demands he made.

Life, he reflected, could be sweet.

Now that Edward knew that he had the support of the Bardi, he had said he must think about how to effect his escape from this prison. It was terrible, to think that all Dolwyn's future dreams depended upon the former King's escape, but better that than for Edward to remain in gaol and for Dolwyn never to see the fruits of his efforts.

He would help Edward escape, he swore to himself now, and as a result, he would be elevated to a position of importance.

All that remained was to work out *how* this escape could be effected. That, he knew, would take some thought.

Kenilworth

They were close now. Stephen Dunheved could feel his excitement growing as they passed up the road near to Kenilworth, his eyes roving about the trees that lay at either side of the road watching for any signs of ambush – a half-concealed figure, a glint of steel.

He was riding his own sturdy pony, but his urgency to reach the castle was such that even his mount was behaving like a destrier, prancing skittishly as they proceeded over the rough roadway.

This was not the first time he had set out on a journey that would end in danger. In the last months he and his companions had forged a reputation for ruthless determination. Only two weeks ago, he and others with Sir Edmund Gascelin had stolen horses, oxen and cows, as well as a thousand sheep, from villages in Gloucester, and then they had gone on to Shilton near Coventry and taken more. The beasts were good for barter, but also for food, and the men needed food, God knew.

At the castle approached, he offered up a short prayer for success. They would need all God's help if they were to succeed. It was a fool's errand, this. They could only summon a tiny number of their men at such short notice, and the plan depended upon their arrival as the gates were being closed. That was when the whole castle would be thinking of rest and not the possibility of attack. He prayed again that he was not too late. The light would be fading soon, and he knew that the gates would be closed as soon as the bells rang for the curfew. He wouldn't want to be stuck out here in the dark, easy prey, while the others all remained inside.

'Can't you hurry the beast?' he shot at Ham.

Ham threw him an anxious look. 'I'm sorry, master. The poor old nag can't go any faster, not with this load.' He was worried by Stephen's snappishness, and by John and Paul riding along behind them all.

Stephen cursed to himself under his breath, avoiding the eye of the damned priest. Luke had not been overly troublesome on the way here, but he had a habit of pursing his lips every time he heard even a mild curse that was intensely irritating to a man like Stephen. Since they had collected the weapons, he had pursed his lips more and more often, and he had a wild look in his eye; he could be a risk – he could give their plot away. Perhaps he ought to be left here, and not taken on. But the trouble was, Stephen daren't leave him unguarded, and the mere fact of his presence at the gates would reduce suspicion, surely. That was how his brother had got inside – hopefully. The others were supposed to have infiltrated the castle with the stores over the day, and with luck were in there waiting even now for Stephen and the weapons to arrive.

Until today they had made good time. Damn his stupidity! He'd thought that they would be too early, so it had been his choice to rest a while at that inn, the decision that had left them so late. He had underestimated the amount of time it would take to get here after meeting John and Paul, and that complacency could mean disaster. The others would all be ready, waiting in position. While it would have been hazardous to arrive too early, to be too late could be catastrophic.

He fretted, chewing at his lip. The cart was rolling along at a steady pace, but up ahead there was the castle, a red, square keep with a fearsome glow about it now in the light of the sinking sun, and it was still too far. They wouldn't make it in time.

Stephen felt the excitement and frustration growing at the same time, anxious that he might make another poor decision. Should he carry on here, hoping to make it in time, or . . .

'The pox on them!' he suddenly blurted out. 'John, Paul, I'm going to ride on and make sure they don't shut the gates. You stay with the cart!'

He set his face at the castle, then, taking his rein-end, he lashed hard at his beast's rump while raking at the animal's flanks with his spurs. Stung into action, the beast jolted, startled, and then sprang forward. Stephen urged it on, kicking and swearing at the brute, but the pony was already gaining speed. At a gallop, his mount bore him past the little cemetery of a chapel, past the fringes of a tiny village, and up to the bridge over the lakes. At the far end of this was the gatehouse to the castle itself, a great building in its own right, with a small tower at either side of the causeway.

It was the most imposing castle he had ever seen. All about it lay the water, an enormous lake of a hundred acres, maybe three quarters of a mile long, with one great loop to the west of the castle and second, smaller one to the south. Attack was all but impossible. The last siege here took nine months, and then it was only illness and starvation that caused the inmates to beg for terms. The best machines in the land could not harm the walls, and no one could mine them, not so close to the lakes. Miners would have drowned.

At the far side of the bridge as he rode onto the timbers, the wood echoing hollowly beneath him, he could see the Norman keep, a massive fortress in its own right built from the reddish stone of the area. It was here to subdue as well as defend, and the square, rugged outline against the sky was fearful.

Two sentries were there at the gates, and they crossed their polearms before he could pass, but he didn't get the impression that they were serious. 'I have food,' he gasped, jerking his thumb behind him to point at the cart. 'I'm purveyor – special foods for your—'

'Get in, then. Gate's to be shut soon,' one of the men said, and hawked and spat.

'Will you leave the gates until they arrive, then?' he asked, and received a noncommittal grunt in response.

'These your friends?'

There, behind him, he saw John and Paul riding at a trot towards the gate. It was enough to make him grit his teeth. 'Yes.'

'They're bloody late!'

Stephen turned, his hooves clattering over the stone cobbles, and trotted on, reining in a little beyond the gatehouse, peering about him. Here he was in the outer ward, a wide area that narrowed to his left. There before him were soaring walls. Inside them, he knew, lay his target, on the left, at the nearer side of the ward, near the great hall in the rooms he had heard called the White Hall. Out here there were still piles of rubble about the place, and areas of wall which had been extensively patched with new stone, and he was surprised that the castle was still being renovated after the siege. That had been forty or fifty years ago, after all. From the look of the place, the catapults had done their work, even if the castle had held. After nine months, the garrison must have been starving.

A man was striding across the court towards him, a moderately tall fellow with clean-shaven face and military haircut. 'You have food, the porter said?'

Stephen nodded as he sprang lightly from his mount. He saw a black habit behind the man's shoulder, and breathed a sigh of relief, just as the bell began to ring for curfew.

'Yes, the cart will be here soon.'

'Too late. It'll have to return tomorrow.' Squire Bernard shouted and waved at the sentries at the entranceway.

'But he's on the bridge already!'

'Then he won't have far to come tomorrow.'

'Why not let him in now?' Stephen demanded.

'We have rules, and as porter of the gates, I will abide by them. He can come back tomorrow.' He turned and bellowed a command.

The men came in from the gates, and there was a deep rumbling as the gates were closed, a rattling as the drawbridge chains were pulled in on the windlass, and men moved about in a desultory fashion before making their way to the bar to find ale.

'Well?' the porter said. 'What are you waiting for?'

The cart rattled abominably. Father Luke walked alongside, his mind whirling, while the two warriors rode easily behind.

'Keep your eyes on the road ahead,' John said with an encouraging chuckle.

His voice made Father Luke's stomach lurch. The humour and attractiveness he had seen earlier was gone now. This man was nothing more than a killer, he was sure, and the idea that he was here, with the cart loaded full of weapons, was alarming. What on earth was the man intending to do with them?

They passed under a little spinney of young saplings, around a series of strip fields, and then confronted the enormous lake.

'Dear God!' Father Luke drew to a halt with his mouth gaping wide.

It was easily the largest lake he had ever seen. Acres were inundated, and it made the priest marvel to see the result of so much labour. Only after he had absorbed the sight did he turn his gaze upward and gasp again. That was indeed a wonderful castle! He wondered how old it was. From an early age he had been dedicated to his studies in the Church, and he had little knowledge or understanding of castles and their history, but Kenilworth was one of those of which even he had heard as a child. It was a fortress extended and strengthened by King

John, added to by the local baron. And it had been attacked years ago in a great siege.

The cart continued on, the horse patiently clopping forwards, and the priest hurried to catch up again, studying the walls, the keep, the bridge. They were passing into a little stand of trees when there came, clear in the evening air, the slow clanging of a bell. For an instant he did not realise what it portended, but then he heard Ham swear under his breath.

'You will have to come to confess that, Ham,' Father Luke said sternly.

'Sorry, Father.'

John trotted up, and this time there was no humour in his eyes as he said tersely, 'Paul, if we don't hurry we're going to miss the gates.'

'I know, but . . .' Paul said nothing more, but it was clear that he was thinking of Luke and Ham.

'They'll be all right, won't you, Father?' John said. Father Luke nodded, and John continued, 'You come as quickly as you can, Ham. They may ignore the purveyor, but they won't ignore me. And if Father Luke can hurry, so much the better: a priest in God's service? They won't lock him out. I'll make sure they keep the gates open until you both arrive!'

And then he and Paul were off, cantering up the road to the causeway.

Father Luke was unhappy. He didn't understand what was happening. All he wanted to do was get inside the castle and divest himself of Despenser's gold, but he was anxious about the weapons and what they portended. He didn't think that the garrison of the castle would need so many more. There were swords, axes, maces, and even a crossbow, he thought – not that he'd had much time to stare. He had caught Paul's eye on him as he peered over, and looked away hurriedly. Paul was a fearsome man.

Too fearsome to ignore.

The bell was tolling again. Luke sighed and threw a fretful glance back the way he had come. It was tempting to make a run for it.

'Best keep on,' Ham grunted.

Luke nodded reluctantly. They could never hope to escape. If they turned, John and Paul would only have to trot to catch them within a mile. They were still some distance from the causeway, and he gave a short 'Tchah!' of disgust at his irresolution. His decision was made: night was coming on. He would have to stay in the castle, no matter what the possible danger from John. It was safer in there than out here in the wilds.

'I'll run on ahead, Ham. They won't keep the gates shut if they see me, I'm sure. You hurry on as you may!'

He picked up the skirts of his robe, winked at Ham, and then began to trot up the road. The last days had been tedious, rather than tiring, and he was not tired. Soon he felt his muscles begin to ease, and he could pick up the pace a little, and actually run. It felt marvellous! The air was cool in his lungs, like a draught of clear water, and he felt his legs come alive. At the gates, he could see Paul and John arguing, demanding that the bridge be lowered, and the gates opened . . . and then, as he reached the wooden causeway himself, he heard a hideous shriek that turned his blood to ice.

The shriek was followed by shouts of alarm, bellowed orders . . . and then he heard the unmistakable clamour of battle: the rattle and clatter of steel on steel, the clash of blade against blade, the *whoosh* of arrows, like a formation of geese close overhead.

'No! *No!*' he shouted, and forgetting his own safety, he ran all the faster, making his way to the gates.

CHAPTER TWELVE

Kenilworth

There was a loud shout from outside the gate as John saw the entrance closing. 'Hoi! Hoi! Wait for us, you slugs!'

'Keep back!' one of the sentries at the gate bellowed.

'What is going on?' Squire Bernard the porter demanded. 'I won't have that gate kept open any longer than I need to, damn your souls!' He was staring at the gates, and then, as John and Paul began expostulating from outside, and the porter gesticulated wildly to have the gates shut, Stephen saw the other men from his group. Fifteen of them, all looking to him for guidance. Two up near the main hall, another sidling nearer from the stables, others dotted all about the yard, expectantly watching, waiting for their weapons.

Their weapons that were in the cart.

A second man appeared, clad in a pale cream tunic. 'Squire, your gate is still open,' he called. 'What is the reason for this?'

'Sir Jevan, these men want to keep it open until their cart is inside.'

'Do they look like messengers, then? *Or spies*? Close the gates!'

Stephen met his brother's eyes, and then, muttering, 'Oh, *God's ballocks*!' grabbed at his dagger's hilt, shoving it deep into the squire's back.

Squire Bernard span on his heel and stared at Stephen, his hand scrabbling for his own dagger, then reaching up to scratch at Stephen's eyes. Stephen stabbed again, twisting the dagger in the porter's breast, the man's blood running freely, hot and revolting on his hand, along his wrist to the elbow. He pulled the blade free and stabbed twice more, remembering the old lesson: *Never let a man loose, who could still have life and strength to attack you.*

His brother Thomas Dunheved smiled. 'I am glad to see you. We wondered whether you would be here in time.'

And then there was a shout, the bell began to ring in earnest, and arrows began to slam into the ground all about them.

Luke saw the drawbridge fall, and he could make out figures struggling in the courtyard beyond in a hideous scene of slaughter.

John and Paul were hacking with their swords, trying to enter, but a lance was thrust out, and Paul gave a hoarse cry, all but toppling from his horse. John went to him, but then he too roared in pain, put his hand to his flank, and moved away, stabbing down with his sword. Another man appeared with a bill, and swung it at John, who only just managed to evade it, before he and Paul wheeled and began to ride away. As they passed Luke, he saw that Paul had a great spreading rose of blood on the front of his tunic beneath his throat, and his eyes were already half-closed. He was dying. John had his hand at his side, and there was more blood there, and then they were past him, and Luke felt sick. He stopped, fighting for breath, as another man staggered towards him on the bridge, his mouth wide in a soundless scream, and fell to his knees as though in supplication.

Luke heard that hideous bird's feather flight, and saw the two barbed heads spring from the man's breast. Two arrows, each a good yard long, and the man's mouth closed slowly as blood trickled from the corners, and he fell to his side even as Luke ran forward to give him the *viaticum* and hear his final confession, if he were able.

Behind him, Luke heard the cart approach, and he turned and gestured wildly. 'No, Ham – get away, you fool! Get away!'

Stephen gave a grunt of pain. The arrow had glanced off his belt, by a miracle, but then slid in under his skin at his hip and remained there, quivering.

The two were in the narrow gap between a storeroom and the outer curtain wall of the castle, a nasty, piss-ridden little space that had only one benefit: it was hard for the guards to see them to shoot them. It was the merest bad fortune that had led the arrow to strike Stephen here.

Thomas saw his brother's pain and darted to his side, breaking off the fletchings, and tugging the arrow through quickly. He glanced at the wound. 'You'll live,' he grinned.

Stephen gritted his teeth and tried to smile in return, but the suddenness of the attack had made his belly roil. He hadn't expected this. 'Our first battle together, eh, little brother?'

'Let us hope it will not be our last, Stephen.'

'Shit!' Arrows were hissing through the air and clattering on the cobbles of the ward. 'Thomas, this is madness. We cannot hope to make it to the hall's doors, let alone inside.'

'I will not leave without my lord.'

'What good will it do him to see you slain?'

Thomas turned to him. 'Do not jest. Brother, I have served him for many years, and I will not see him kept gaoled like a common felon.'

Stephen gave a harsh laugh as he clapped a hand to his wound, which was stinging badly. 'You think that this is a common gaol?'

'Enough! We must storm the hall,' the friar said. He had a sword in his hand already, and the desperate look in his eye reminded Stephen of the days when they used to poach venison from the game park.

They had been born at Dunchurch, a small manor fifteen or twenty miles from here. It had been a good life. John, their father, as was a stolid, hard-working yeoman, and his reputation ensured that his sons were favoured.

First Stephen was taken into the household of a baron and taught how to fight and ride; then Thomas demonstrated his quick intelligence, and was soon learning his letters and advancing himself. Now he was a papal chaplain. It still struck Stephen as odd to think that his little brother could have risen so far, so swiftly. Of their two other brothers, John was often in trouble, guilty even of rape and murder, and had been declared an outlaw. Only Oliver was likely to die in comfort in his own bed.

Stephen seriously doubted that the same would be true for him and Thomas.

'Ballocks to this,' he grated. 'We have to get out of here, Tom.'

'I will not leave without . . .'

'. . . seeing us both dead. Not I, little brother. Nay, you remain here if you want, but I am riding away while I can. The others are not here. It is only you, me, and some peasants over there who dare not run over the ward to reach us. What is the point of our dying here? Eh? We must escape while we may.'

Thomas shook his head grimly. His fist clenched about the sword hilt, and he rose on the balls of his feet, a hand steadying him on the storeroom's wall, and then he glanced back at his brother, his lower lip held between his teeth. 'Are you coming?'

Stephen shook his head.

'Don't blame you. I'd be mad to try it!' Thomas said with black humour as he, turned and squeezed past Stephen to get to the farther side of the little building.

It was tight here, a shrinking channel between the curtain wall and the hut, and at the end only one man could stand and peer out, shoulders sideways.

The clink and rattle of arrows hitting stone was slowing a little as Thomas poked his head out. He withdrew to the safety of the corridor. 'It's not too bad. Twenty yards to the gate, and the gate is still open.'

'Our horses?'

'I am a friar. I don't hurry on horseback,' Thomas said loftily. 'But I can run like a greyhound if I feel an arrow behind me,' he added.

Stephen took a deep breath. He stared ahead at the gateway, so temptingly open, so temptingly close.

'Oh, ballocks, brother. Let's dodge a clothyard.'[1]

In the White Hall he had heard the shouting, roared orders, the tolling of the bell and doors slamming shut, their bolts rammed home, and in his chamber, Sir Edward of Caernarfon leaped to his feet, staring about him wildly.

1 yard-long arrows

His guards had been removed when he renounced his crown, months ago. He was no longer considered a threat to those who ruled his kingdom, he had thought. But now he realised his foolishness: it meant there was no one to protect him!

So: this was how his life would end, with an assassin's attack. Just as Piers Gaveston had been waylaid by Sir Edward's enemies, so he would in his turn fall to a murderer's blade, here, inside one of the strongest castles in the land.

It was what he had expected, yesterday afternoon. When he heard the door open, and turned to see the stranger standing there, he had thought that his hour had come. But no assassin would have bent his knee. And, as Edward had stood there, frozen, awaiting a blow, the messenger had produced that astonishing letter from the Bardi.

Edward had read the parchment with incredulity. It had not occurred to him that he had loyal subjects so committed to helping him even now, in these desperate straits. It was heartening to learn that, although he had been dragged down, others were still honourable supporters of his cause.

The parchment he had given back to Dolwyn, for fear that it could be discovered, but its contents had filled him with renewed hope. With luck, he could be *freed*!

There was more shouting, a shrill scream, and he swore aloud, 'I'll not die here like a coward!'

He drew his sword, the blade's point unwavering, and allowed himself a small smile of satisfaction: they could take his crown, his throne, his realm, but they would not make him cower like a dog.

There was a bellow outside his door, and he stepped away as the latch was opened. Three men rushed in, and he lifted his sword, ready to fall upon them, until he realised that the three had no interest in him. Two pulled the door shut behind them and shoved the bolts over to lock it, while the third darted from one window to another, peering out into the court and cursing volubly.

'What is happening?' Edward demanded. 'Is it assassins? Murderers?'

'Sorry, Your Highness,' the man at the window responded. He was still staring down at the inner ward. 'There's an attack on the castle.'

'To kill me?' Edward said.

'What?'

And at the sight of his surprise, Edward felt his breath catch at the sudden realisation: the men attacking intended to *rescue* him! The man with the Bardi letter was not alone!

More shouting. There was a steady metallic clattering, then a rattle and hiss, and Edward glanced at the open windows. Arrows flew through the air, and he narrowed his eyes. Some of the men must have got into the castle, then, but having gained that inner space, they would find every door closed and barred, against them. They would be trapped.

A roared command, to 'Fall back! To the gates!' and Edward knew that the attempt to save him was doomed. Stumbling slightly, he made his way over to a seat at the window, from where he could see out.

There were four bodies lying in the court. Two were moving; one appeared to be trying to crawl to the gate, but then a guard hurried from a doorway with an axe, and hacked at his head until he was still.

Edward shuddered. To have gone from the conviction that he was in immediate danger, to the belief that someone was attempting his rescue, had left him drained. He did not acknowledge the men as they unbolted the door and left, allowing a page to enter. As the lad wandered about lighting candles, seeing to the fire and setting out the table for a small supper, Edward sat staring out.

But now he was not full of resentment.

He had rediscovered hope.

Dolwyn stood frozen to the spot as the last of the riders hurtled off into the distance. He was transfixed with horror, since from a simple situation in which he had anticipated being able to arrange the release of Sir Edward, he now felt as though he had been propelled into a nightmare.

Who in God's name were those fools? Had they no brains? No one without at least two hundred men could hope to storm a castle like Kenilworth. No, make that two thousand. And these congeons[1] had tried it with ten, perhaps twelve.

He wanted to roar his rage at the moon and vent some of the frustration he felt, as he realised that there was no possibility now that he could free Sir Edward of Caernarfon. The King would be secured tighter than a tick, and even with all his cleverness, Dolwyn would not be able to get close to him.

'Aw, *shite*,' he said with feeling.

Second Tuesday before the Feast of the Annunciation[2]

Caerphilly

Senchet Garcie stood beyond the drawbridge at Caerphilly and drew in a deep breath. 'It smells better out here, don't you agree?'

'Nah, it's not that much different,' Harry le Cur said grimly. 'Inside there it smelled of shit and piss, and out here it's the same.'

1 half-wit, imbecile
2 17 March 1327

Senchet looked from his friend to the men all around. 'So long as nobody tests his sword on me, I will persist in being happy.'

'Aye, well,' Harry said quietly. He too eyed the men about the castle. After a long siege, surrender was a dangerous time. 'Hold! Here's our welcoming party.'

It was impossible to be sad today, Senchet thought: they were out of the castle. There was a certain amount of tension in the air, in case the promises of safety had been lies, but he doubted it. They were being released with honour, and for that he was grateful. He would make a donation to a church . . . when he had some money.

The capitulation had taken an age to negotiate. All were to be freed without surrendering their weapons and had been promised full pardons. Even Hugh III, the son of Hugh le Despenser, was assured of his freedom.

Hugh III was bearing up well. His father and grandfather had both died hanged, drawn and quartered, and at only eighteen or nineteen years, Hugh III had shown courage that men double his age lacked.

The castle's guards had held out, honourably defending the King's last castle, as they had been commanded. Initially they had clung to the hope that relief would come, until news came of the execution of Sir Hugh le Despenser and the King's abdication. After that, they held on in order to secure the best terms. And so they had.

Senchet scratched behind his ear where a flea had bitten. 'No, the air out here definitely tastes better, my friend. Here, my soul feels free again.'

'There's a wind, true,' Harry grunted, but as he spoke his attention was drawn to the rattle and thump of wagons making their way towards them. 'What are they for?' he asked suspiciously.

Senchet gave a chuckle. 'The first thing any attacker would think of, naturally. They're here to take any loot.'

Harry gave a relieved sigh. 'To grab the King's gold, then.'

'And Sir Hugh le Despenser's, eh?'

'You can be assured of that, Senchet.'

'All those barrels. Five hundred pounds in each of 'em.'

'Aye,' Harry said. They had both seen the rows of barrels in the undercroft. It was a sight to gladden a man's heart.

'Except the last one. Despenser's contained a thousand pounds,' Senchet recalled with a sigh. 'Ah! It is sad to be a poor man, my friend. To think of that vast wealth in there. So desirable, so beautiful – and so far from us!' He held his fingers to his mouth, kissing them with a look of such mournful longing that Harry laughed despite himself.

'Senchet, such riches aren't for the likes of you and me. We have to seek out a new lord and plead for his largesse.'

'You have any thoughts about this new lord?'

'There are some who may welcome us,' Harry said. He took in the grey landscape about them. 'They're all a long way from here, though.'

'If we had but a small part of the money from the barrels, travel would be easier,' Senchet noted.

'And if we had wings, we could fly.'

'So we must walk.'

'Yes. And hope to find a new master,' Harry said.

He was not optimistic.

CHAPTER THIRTEEN

Near Kenilworth

Frere Thomas Dunheved shivered at the sound of thundering hooves approaching. He knew with a certainty that, were he to be captured, his life would not be worth a penny. They would kill him – once they had garnered all the information he held.

On hearing the horses, he had flung himself down into a thicket of brambles and holly, the only cover that lay about here. His black gown was all besmottered with mud, his hands, and no doubt his face, were smeared with it too, and he had a thorn in his thumb.

He could have sworn aloud at the disaster. All that planning and effort, gone to waste. God had not aided them, and Frere Thomas was once more on the run from the enemies of the true King.

How different things had been, once! The House of the Black Friars in London seemed a lifetime ago, a thousand leagues away. Was it truly only six months since his urgent flight with the King from London? It was difficult to believe.

But there were more pressing concerns. Where was Stephen? His older brother had pelted through the gate with him, the two of them thrilling with the sheer lunatic excitement while bolts and arrows fell all about them. Two others from their gang made it. The others . . . well, all perished in the storm of cloth-yard arrows and crossbow quarrels in that deadly ward.

Once outside, their predicament had grown clear. There were too many men in the castle, too much open land in front of it, and too much damned water in the moat, apart from anything else. They had been lucky that Stephen's horse was near to hand, another running wildly, crazed at the smell of blood, the shouting of fighting men. It was the action of a moment to snatch at the reins, leap into the saddle and, bending low over the horse's neck, ride away as fast as possible.

Stephen had been in front, just, when they pelted over the bridge and causeway, past a goggling priest, and thence to the road. They were delayed by a terrified carter, who stood by his horse, tugging at the rein. Thomas and Stephen had flown past him like hawks past a pigeon, but soon afterwards, they had heard the pursuit.

There was nothing to be done out here in the open lands other than whip, spur, and pray. Stephen was drawing away, but Thomas's brute was suddenly flagging. Stephen turned and would have stopped, but Thomas waved him on. No point in them both being caught. 'Ride on!'

He had reached some woods, and there he slipped from his saddle and slapped the horse's rump. Only then did he see the arrow protruding from the horse's back, just behind the saddle. It sent a chill down his spine to think how close that had come to ending his life. Only a couple of feet higher, only a tiny additional angle from the archer's perspective, and it would all have been over.

Then the horses were closer, and fear took hold. Thomas had run off, like a hare before the hounds, darting in and out among the thin tree boughs, hoping to deter any bowmen, but to be truthful, he doubted that they even noticed him. They certainly seemed to think they had better targets. He had heard one man scream in pain, but there was no telling who. Perhaps it was Stephen. He did not know.

He disliked admitting it, but there was no denying that if it *were* Stephen, it was more important that he, Frere Thomas, had survived. He was the strategist who had God's approval.

Frere Thomas lifted his head, brought back to the present. He was sure he had heard another horse from the east. Could that be them again? His nerves were tight as bowstrings as he strained his ears to listen, but there was nothing, no one to be seen. It must be his imagination, or maybe a rider ambling along at the extreme edge of his hearing, and passing now into a wood or gulley where the sound of his hooves could not be heard.

He blew the air from his lungs, rolled over and closed his eyes a moment. Yes, all that was yesterday. Last night he had dozed fitfully with his back against an old oak after walking miles over muddy fields. The peasants here would have good reason to curse the Dominican for the coming year, he thought with a weary grin. His feet would have disturbed their crops.

Today he had risen with the sun, wondering where on earth he was. Although raised not far from Kenilworth, this land was unfamiliar, and he peered about him warily before setting off again, making for the nearest church, which stood on a small hill a mile or two to the south. The priest there was entirely unwelcoming. A hidebound old fool, who believed that friars were only in his parish to steal his tithes, he made it clear that if he heard the friar preaching, he would come and chastise Thomas with a stick.

115

Personally, Thomas did not think this very likely, since the man looked so frail, but he did not want to raise attention to himself. He managed to persuade the priest to give him bread in exchange for his departure, and a brook was adequate for his thirst.

In the brook he caught sight of his reflection, and it exasperated him. He was used to a good life, to courteous discussions with the King and with the Pope, not to this indignity. Dear Heaven, what would the Pope say if he saw Thomas in this condition? Probably nothing, Frere Thomas admitted to himself, since the Pope would not have been told of a scruffy churl asking to meet him. Guards would have prevented him from entering the presence.

Now he rolled over and studied his injured thumb.

Recently he had been one of the most important men in the country. When there was a need for a cool head and diplomatic manner, King Edward II would send for Frere Thomas. Whether it concerned messages for the Pope, negotiations to assess the possibility of a marriage annulment – anything – it was to Frere Thomas that the King would turn. Sir Hugh le Despenser had been the King's best friend, yet he had the guile and subtlety of a hog cleaver, in Christ's name. He could hack, but when it was a silent assassin's stab that was needed, Despenser failed.

Well, the fool had paid for his manifold crimes. Hauled to a gallows fifty feet from the ground until almost dead, then dropped to a table where he had his genitals cut off and thrown into a fire before he was ritually disembowelled, the entrails also thrown into the flames, and his beating heart hacked from his breast. If it was still beating. Frere Thomas had his doubts about that. He believed that a man tended to expire a short time after his belly was opened.

He had no liking for Sir Hugh le Despenser, but he could sympathise with the man for his fate. It was difficult to think of any creature who deserved such a barbaric death.

Putting the ball of his thumb to his mouth, Frere Thomas bit into the broken-off stub of blackthorn that had stabbed him. It was a tough little imp, but he managed to tug it loose and spit it away, studying the marble of blood that formed, growing to a nugget of almost a half-inch diameter before running quickly down his wrist.

Frere Thomas sighed. As the fresh drops of rain began to clatter among the holly leaves, he closed his eyes, then cast a long suffering look upwards.

'Thank you, Lord,' he said, but then rose and made his way to the road. Here in this part of Warwickshire the land was flat, and in places very wet, and there was no jauntiness in his spirit as he stared off into the south, and began to trudge.

He wouldn't look back. That way lay defeat and misery. That way lay Kenilworth, where the man to whom he still owed his allegiance was held.

John wept as he pulled the hood over Paul's face, then stood stiffly, the wound in his flank hurting as he moved.

His friend was already cold. He had died soon after they left the roads and entered among the trees, falling from his horse before John could catch him, and gagging as the blood from that awful wound seeped into his throat and lungs. He clung to life with the desperation of a badger in a trap, grasping John's arms as though he could hold on to life the same way.

John closed his eyes again as tears moved down his cheeks. There was no shame in mourning the passing of an old friend, and there was no friend so close, so dear to his heart, as Paul.

117

That fight had been so sharp and swift, it took him a moment to comprehend that Paul was injured. Through the part-opened gates, he had seen the men falling, and realised his friend must be badly wounded in the same instant as he saw that face in the court: Sir Jevan de Bromfield.

It was enough. He slashed at his assailant, grabbed Paul's bridle, and fled.

He would never forget that ride. They had pelted along through the bushes, and Paul had seemed all right at first. Until they stopped.

It was astonishing he made it so far. The blade had cut deep, not through the vein or artery at the side – that would have killed him in moments – but opening his gullet. When he attempted to speak, no sound came. A bloom of crimson spread from his neck down the front of his chemise, and his eyes were desperate, like those of a dog gripped by a bear.

Later, when John could still his sobbing for his friend of so many years, he swore that he would take the body to a place where Paul could be buried decently, with a priest to look over his soul.

Those who had survived would have to meet to discuss what to do, now that they had failed so magnificently in rescuing the King.

Kenilworth

Sir Edward of Caernarfon stared into the yard below. There was little to be seen now of the carnage that had reigned last night. Only black stains on the ground, where flies squatted. As a dog wandered past, the stain rose, leaving behind the rust-coloured mark of dried blood, but then the flies returned, gorging themselves on a man's death.

The light had faded quickly behind the castle walls last night, but he had seen the bodies. Men dragged the dead to the wall, where they were left side-by-side. While he watched, two dogs trotted over, one to urinate, the other to lick and nudge, and he had wondered whether the latter was trying to waken its master, or whether it was testing the quality of the meat.

Sitting in a shaft of sunlight by the window with a goblet of wine, he was aware of a deep thrilling in his soul. He would soon be free. His subjects were coming to their senses. They *knew* they must honour their King: they had seen the error of their ways. Before long, Sir Roger Mortimer would be in chains in the Tower, and then he would die.

Isabella, his wife, who had committed adultery, would never know power again. It was incomprehensible how she could have rebelled against him – her husband, her lord, her King. Did she hate him?

She was a child when they married in the Year of Our Lord 1308, and he had been as kind to her as a brother to his sister. Happy days. But four years later his closest friend, Piers Gaveston, was murdered by a rabble of embittered barons jealous of their friendship. They slew Piers, and Edward was distraught. It was sweet Isabella who helped him then. He found in his Queen a woman of startling intelligence and compassion. In his hour of need, he discovered that this beautiful, talented, sympathetic woman understood his realm, his people, and him.

Strange to think that now, fifteen years later, she was flaunting her affair with his most deplored traitor.

She would be banished while he demanded a Papal Order annulling their marriage. She had made a cuckold of him, and betrayed his realm, and he could never forget or forgive. Just as he would not forget those who had joined in her invasion. All would pay.

Such were the satisfying reflections that engaged him as he sat in the window. When there came a knock at the door and his guard walked in, he could even smile thinly.

'Sir Edward, I'm glad to see you well,' Gilbert le Sadler said.

'I am very safe. You guard me well,' Edward said sarcastically. He raised his empty goblet, and his steward hurried to fill it for him. This man, Harold, was a good fellow. Not so attentive as his old steward, who had been with Edward for almost twelve years until he was cut down on the day Edward had been captured. One of so many who had died in his defence. Another pointless death.

Gilbert paid his words no heed. His brown eyes were strained as he studied his charge. 'Sire, this was no group of silly men who hoped to make you free of this place. They were thoughtful fellows who knew what they were about. This time they failed, but next . . .'

'So you are concerned that I could be released?' Edward said, venom dripping from each word. 'No doubt that is why you look so fearful. I would say you were *frit*, if I were to judge. Or is it fear for your own skin? You should be afraid, gaoler. You hold your King against his will.'

'Some while ago I received a message from Sir Roger Mortimer—'

'Do not speak that name in my presence!' Edward hissed. 'I will *not* hear it.'

'However, I must tell you the import of his message.'

Edward averted his face as Gilbert haltingly continued. 'I was warned, you see, that if at any time I felt you weren't safe, I should remove you,' Gilbert said. He chewed at his inner cheek. 'After the attack last evening, I think that time has come.'

'What do you mean?'

'Sir Roger suggested Berkeley Castle. It's safer. It's a pleasant place—'

Edward rasped, 'It is a charmless hovel with views of bog and marsh. It has little to redeem it, most particularly as it is the seat of the Berkeley family.'

'They're honourable men.'

'By their own lights. They are also allies of Mortimer. Lord de Berkeley is his son-in-law, and he is my sworn enemy.'

'Sir Roger commands me to escort you there. I am sorry, these are my orders.'

'What would the world be if a serf did not carry out his orders? Tell me: if you were ordered to kill me, would you obey that, too?'

'My . . . Please, I—'

'Would you feel happier to thrust a knife into my bowels here? Now?' Edward said, holding his hand to his belly. 'If your esteemed Sir Roger, the traitor, were to command it, would you do his bidding?'

The steward stepped forward as though to protect him, but Edward waved him back.

'He is honourable,' Gilbert said miserably. 'Murder would be—'

'You think Mortimer has not considered such a contingency? He has thought of transporting me from Kenilworth, in which there are few who bear me ill-will, and instead install me in the castle of his friend and ally. I like this not, master. I consider this a most ungenerous suggestion. If I could guess, I would say that Berkeley is likely where I shall die.'

He spoke the truth. In his mind's eye the castle of the Berkeleys was draped in a perpetual twilight, a foul black outline against the sky like a tomb. His tomb.

A thought struck him. 'How did he know of the attack? Is he here?'

'No. He is a day's ride away, in Wales. But a strange thing happened two days ago. A man masquerading as a messenger came to the castle. He escaped before I could catch him, but I deemed it necessary to let Sir Roger know.'

Edward could have cursed. So Dolwyn had been seen! He tried to sound off-hand, but only succeeded in peevishness. 'So, a man tried to harm me, and you'll send me to the man who wishes me dead?'

'You'll be better guarded there than here.'

'By the son-in-law of Sir Roger Mortimer himself. Yes, I will be well guarded. To the death.'

'I shall ride to Berkeley with you, if it would please you.'

'So, my gaoler and those whom he selects shall take me to my death. How reassuring!'

'My lord,' Gilbert coughed, 'if it would help, is there some-one I could have join us to protect you on the way? A man or two whom you would trust?'

Edward of Caernarfon passed a hand over his eyes. 'Someone from our kingdom to protect me? Whom should I ask, I wonder.'

He went silent. There *were* two men who had proved their valour to him, out on that pasturage in Wales just before his capture: he saw his steward fall, his body cloven by a sword, he saw the men pounding towards him on their great destriers, and he saw the two who strove to get between him and his enemies. Two knights, one with the black beard that followed the line of his chin, the other with the serious eyes that watched so carefully.

He gave the guard their names: Sir Baldwin de Furnshill and Sir Ralph of Evesham. 'If you can win these two men for my party, I shall agree to go wheresoever you wish to take me,' he said.

CHAPTER FOURTEEN

Wednesday before the Feast of the Annunciation[1]

Bubenall

Father Luke peered out from the little barn in which he had passed his second night up north of Kenilworth. It was a clear, cool dawn, and the grass was bejewelled with dew. Luke would normally have felt his heart lighten at the sight, but not any longer.

The battle two days ago had shocked him to his core. In the past he had imagined what a battle might look like, but never had he thought to witness one. It was hideous.

Luke had stood gaping, only dimly aware of his own danger, as other men were shot down. It was only when an arrow fell with a loud *thwock* into the ground near him, the clothyard quivering, that he too fled.

He was over the causeway when he heard the rumble of pursuing horses and knew that his ordeal was not yet over. In

1 18 March 1327

terror, he hurled himself into a muddy ditch, pulling his cowl over his head and praying with a desperation he had not known since he was a child. His urgent entreaties appeared to work. The posse of men-at-arms galloped past him, the men screaming their war cries.

As the terrible hoofbeats died away, Luke sat up cautiously, dripping, and watched with horror as the riders caught up with the small group of fleeing attackers. He saw weapons slashing, and then there came a great paean of fierce joy as they trampled the bodies with their hooves, making sure of all their victims. But they had not forgotten the two on horseback, and soon the party was off again.

He didn't know whether they had caught up with the purveyor or not. In fact, Luke did not care. He knew that Stephen Dunheved had been associated with the attack, thereby placing Luke's life, and Ham's, in danger. He could not forgive that. Crawling along the ditch, shivering as the mud plastered his body and robes, he eventually rose and made his way across the fields safe from view.

At least this morning was dry. Luke left his barn in daylight, walking slowly along the road with the sun on his left shoulder as he went. He was fearfully hungry, but the effort of searching for a cottage where he could beg for a mess of pottage or crust of bread was too draining. He would remain on this road and hope to find somewhere as he walked.

He sighed deeply at the thought of getting back to Willersey. He had no idea where Ham was, and to have to explain what had happened to Agatha would be taxing in the extreme.

Poor Ham, he thought. That tired-out old beast of his would never be able to escape the men who hunted him and the purveyor. Ham must have been caught, and likely cut down. The Kenilworth posse would not have wanted to listen to explanations. Perhaps they paused to kill Ham and let the purveyor and the other man free? Those two could have escaped, the Dominican Frere Thomas and the purveyor Stephen Dunheved. What in God's name were they doing in the castle? Why were they fighting the garrison?

And then the other thought returned to his mind. He stopped in the roadway, his mouth falling open with his dismay.

He had lost the King's gold.

Kenilworth

Sir Edward of Caernarfon was deeply religious. Here, at the altar in the castle's chapel, the chaplain mumbling his way through the service, he could almost forget the last year. Kneeling before God, he could sense a little of the peace that he had once felt at his chapel at Westminster.

He closed his eyes as a fragment of bread was placed in his mouth, and he sipped the wine with that tingle that he knew of old. It was still the same. Every time he took communion, it was there, sometimes stronger, sometimes weaker, but the sensation was there, a tickle in his spine that reached up to his scalp. The idea that this was the body and blood of another man like him, innocent of any crime, was strangely thrilling whenever he participated in the Mass.

Opening his eyes, he looked up at the crucifix. It seemed that Jesus was looking into his eyes, and Sir Edward of Caernarfon felt tears spring up at the thought that Christ was here right now, with him. No matter what the guards here said or did to him, he would show the fortitude expected of a King.

He thanked his chaplain with a nod as he rose, but in his chamber he sat staring into the distance as though he could see his own future, bleak and short. A black mood settled on him.

The door opened, and a laundrymaid entered with a heavy basket of clean clothing, but he scarcely noticed her.

He was fooling himself, thinking he could be protected. Mortimer wanted him dead so he couldn't retake his throne. And escorts from Berkeley would consist of men who were devoted to Lord Berkeley and his father-in-law, Sir Roger Mortimer. Even with two knights to defend him, it would be easy for Mortimer to order Sir Edward's death. A knife in the dark, a sudden knock on the head – almost anything could happen on such a journey.

He shivered. The assault on the castle which had promised so much now struck him as the precursor to his murder. Mortimer would say that the assault was proof of an attempt on his life, not his rescue. Perhaps it was: Mortimer could have arranged it, either to see to his death, or to give an excuse to have him pulled from Kenilworth to Berkeley. He might be despatched with ease on the way.

Yes. Mortimer would like to ensure that Edward was slain *en route*, because it would be embarrassing to have him killed while under the supervision of his son-in-law.

The laundress had set a pile of clean chemises and braies on the table now, and she looked at him. Something in her demeanour made him take notice. She was staring down at the pile in a way that was somehow meaningful. He had no idea what she might . . . Then he saw the scrap of parchment.

Taking a few coins from his purse, he dropped them into her hand even as his right hand took the slip.

CHAPTER FIFTEEN

Berkeley Castle

There was a rash of messengers, and in the midst of the men hurrying to and fro, Benedetto Bardi found it hard to make himself understood. He and the six men he had brought with him as bodyguards were forced to remain outside, a frustrating insult to the head of the House of Bardi.

'You want my Lord Berkeley, you'll have to wait here,' the guard at the door grated uncompromisingly. 'We've got better things to do than deal with merchants.'

Benedetto swallowed his anger. It was he who maintained the Queen Mother and King Edward III. Still, the guard wasn't to know that.

Matteo was on his way to meet Sir Roger Mortimer, he knew. It made him wonder what Sir Roger's motive was. Sir Roger had his own spies, and it was possible that he would try to use Matteo's sources. He would not want a second network in the country that could find better information than his own.

The bank depended upon its sources for its profit. They could not compromise that. Matteo must resist any such demands.

He looked about him. Berkeley was a strange little castle. It stood on the edge of a marshland, but anyone gazing at it would think it was unprotected. The land was all green, and from a distance it looked as if stood in the midst of a pasture.

Thomas, Lord Berkeley was master here. Benedetto had met him a few times. He was a strong, thirty-four-year-old man, healthy and intelligent. For five years, since the Barons' war, he had been held in gaol, not permitted to see his wife. His father had died in Wallingford Gaol, and all his lands and properties had been despoiled by Despenser. It was a miracle he was not bitter and resentful, but he appeared resigned to the fact that he had lost those years and was keen to renew his life and forget his intolerable imprisonment.

'Ha! Signor Bardi.'

'My lord.'

'Why are you waiting out here?'

Benedetto glanced at the guard expressionlessly. The fellow did not meet his eyes, but waited tensely for the word that could cause him to be flogged, if his lord was displeased.

'I wanted to remain here,' he said, and saw the guard's relief. 'The air is so clear, away from London.'

'Yes. I prefer this land to any other,' Berkeley said, stalking onwards, up the short flight of stairs to the hall. He strode across the floor to the dais, where he took his seat on the great carved chair, before courteously waving Benedetto to the seat on his right. 'Please.'

Benedetto dismissed his henchmen, took his seat with a thankful smile, and accepted the mazer of strong red wine. It was not so much to his taste as the Tuscan and Umbrian wines he enjoyed so much when he was in Florence, but it was not entirely bad.

'Your health, my lord,' he said, lifting the mazer in a toast.

Lord Berkeley reciprocated and then, speaking quietly, said, 'You have messages?'

'Yes, my lord. I saw your father-in-law only yesterday,' Benedetto said, pulling the notes from his scrip. 'He sends you his fondest regards and hopes you are well.'

Lord Thomas opened the wax seals, reading the notes quickly, his brows rising in surprise. Then, 'Steward! Bring another jug of wine. I have cause to celebrate.'

'What is that, my lord?' Benedetto enquired.

'I am to be Keeper of the King's Peace for Gloucestershire, along with Sir William de Wauton. We are to maintain the peace throughout the county.'

'There is another message, I think?'

'This is curious,' Lord Thomas said as he read. 'There has been an attempt to release Sir Edward of Caernarfon from his retirement. 'Sir Roger says he has received a warning from Kenilworth. He asks me to go there with as many men as I can muster, and bring Sir Edward here. Well, that will be no trouble,' Lord Thomas said, frowningly. 'But it will take time to organise. I have other responsibilities before I can depart . . .'

His steward brought more messages, and Lord Berkeley leafed through them. 'Ah! This is from Kenilworth,' he said, ripping the seal open. 'Sir Edward of Caernarfon demands that Sir Baldwin de Furnshill and Sir Ralph of Evesham should accompany us. Why we should need two more when I have my own guards . . . Well, at least it gives me more time to prepare.'

'You will not leave at once?'

'No, Master Bardi. I wait for Sir Baldwin. When he is here, I shall leave for Kenilworth,' the man said. 'No need to hurry unduly.'

'No, naturally,' Benedetto smiled. 'No hurry at all.'

Stoneleigh

The chill had not affected Dolwyn so much overnight. He too had slept rough, because he had little money left. After spending a day kicking his heels trying to think of any means of getting to Edward of Caernarfon in safety, he had still no better idea than the one that had occurred to him before – the laundress. It was not the safest idea, but the only one that seemed even remotely possible.

He had lain in wait out near the entrance to the town that lay north of the castle until he saw the laundress leaving the main gate. It was unthinkable that she could have lived within the castle. It would be too much of a temptation to the men of the garrison. Bad for discipline. She would be allowed in for her duties, but would be expelled before curfew.

'Maid, may I help you with that basket?' he asked as he joined her.

She shot him a doubtful look. 'Why?'

He had to smile. She was not quite such an ugly old crone as he had thought from a distance. Perhaps five-and-thirty years old, she still had a fresh complexion, and although she was painfully thin, there was a vivacity about her that was not unappealing. But her eyes were shrewd and held a feminine cunning, he thought. He must be cautious.

'May a man not offer help to a maid? Especially when she's—'

'If you want a whore, look elsewhere.'

'No, maid, really, I—'

'Master,' she sneered, 'don't "maid" me. If you followed me from the castle, you'll know I work there. I get all sorts of men offering me their "support". I have no need of help of that sort.'

'I wanted to offer you money for something else.'

She turned eyes on him in which the doubt was driven out by pure suspicion.

'Mistress, all I ask is that you listen to me. Let me buy you a pot of wine and explain.'

And she had listened, and agreed. He wrote the note on a strip of parchment and gave it to her, explaining that the attempt to free Edward had made matters more difficult, that he would return, and that Edward must remain patient.

The castle had been in uproar. He had heard chatter on the streets that there were fewer than thirty men in the attack. Fools! And now the garrison was running around like a cat with a flaming torch tied to its tail: eyeing anyone from the town with suspicion, sending men into the town to search for any survivors, scurrying about the countryside to find two men on horseback – one a Dominican, in Christ's name!

All they had achieved was to force Dolwyn to leave the town and seek anonymity on the road. He couldn't remain here in the locality and risk having to answer unwelcome questions. It was too likely that he would be uncovered as the man who had been in the castle the day before the attack. Instead he found a grassy spot in the bend of the river, and spent his morning dozing, soaking up what sun there was.

Later he walked to meet the woman again, at a quiet stable which had an ale-house next door, and there the laundress told him the news: they were to take the King to Berkeley Castle, to instal him in a cell there from which it would be more difficult to release him.

It was enough to make a man curse. What had been a moderately easy task, to rescue Edward from Kenilworth, had now become impossible. Where *was* Berkeley anyway? The laundress had said it was somewhere to the south and west, and that the King would be taken there before long.

So here he was, walking along a grotty little lane in the middle of the day without any idea where he was going, except that he was heading south and west.

The main question in his mind was: if he made his way there, what could he achieve? He was one man. It would make more sense to try to spring Edward of Caernarfon from the party escorting him to the castle, than to dream up a plan to help him escape from Berkeley. That would be suicidal.

In the distance he saw a cart, and called out: 'Hoi! You there!'

The carter gave him an unfriendly look. Dolwyn said politely, 'Friend, would you have space to help a weary traveller rest his feet for a mile or so?'

'Can't do that,' the carter said. He was a man of about Dolwyn's age, with brown hair kept long. His eyes were dark, and they kept moving fretfully over the road, the fields, and Dolwyn himself.

'Only a short ride, master,' Dolwyn wheedled. 'I've walked a long way.'

'Where from?'

'The castle at Kenilworth. It's a lovely place, isn't it?'

'Why do you say that?'

'I thought you must have come from that way, master, that's all,' Dolwyn said mildly. He smiled, and after a moment or two, the carter tried to return it, but his look was so fearful that it turned his face into a ghastly mask.

'I have passed by the town, yes,' he said.

Dolwyn nodded. 'I am sure you have. It's a long way from there, though. You must have rested for a day or two.'

'Eh?'

'There's straw on top of the cart. I guess you had it hidden in a barn somewhere to have thrown all that hay over it.'

'Why'd I do that?'

'Anyone who's been hiding would know the signs,' Dolwyn said shortly.

The carter glared at him for a moment, and then Dolwyn drew his knife, and spoke quietly and calmly. 'I know what you were doing, carter: you were supporting those boys at the castle, weren't you? Your life's worth nothing, because if the new King heard that you tried to free his father so he could take back his throne, I think he would have your ballocks for soup. And if he didn't, Sir Roger Mortimer would. So how about we forget all the shite and agree that you'll give me a ride. That's all I ask. *A ride.*'

Ham stared at him, terrified, then nodded.

And that was the beginning of Ham's nightmare.

Thursday before the Feast of the Annunciation[1]

Willersey

Father Luke's legs ached abominably as he limped into the village again after his long march. The way had not been too hard, but it had been quite hilly, as was normal in these parts.

In the beginning, his only thought had been for the danger in which he had placed himself. The memory of those men-at-arms riding towards him at such a terrifying pace was enough even now to turn his bowels to water, and the worst of it was, he had no real idea what on earth the fight was about. Oh, certainly, when a force of men was gathered together and there was plenty of ale or wine, it was common enough that there would be bickering, and with an armed garrison, that would often mean a fight, but even though he was not experienced in

1 19 March 1327

the ways of warriors, the priest was fairly sure that they did not spontaneously erupt into open battle. There had to be a reason why they had started to draw their weapons, and he was sure that the purveyor Stephen Dunheved must have had something to do with it.

It was enough to persuade him that he never wanted to return to that castle. No: not to *any* castle.

He still had no idea what had happened to Ham or his money; all he knew was that the whole purpose of his journey had been to deliver the chest of gold, and he had failed quite spectacularly.

It put him in a foul temper, until he reflected that Ham could well have been caught by the posse that rushed past from the castle. That made his anger leave him in an instant. The idea that Ham was dead was awful. Luke would be happier to think that he had stolen the money and that the coins were going towards his family's upkeep. At least Jen would have a dowry, if that was the case. He prayed that it might be so, and that Ham was even now in his house with the money.

Later he could find out.

For now, he reminded himself, he was a servant of God, and after the last days he should remember his duties. So rather than marching straight home and resting his sore feet, he first went to his church. Opening the door, he peered in, a little anxious in case a thief might have stolen the chalice or . . . But no, it looked the same as usual. When he opened his chest, all was there, safe and well. Thieves, drawlatches and outlaws had become commonplace in recent years, and they were daring enough to rip the very crucifixes from the walls if they could see a profit in it. Nothing was sacred to such men.

The floor was a disgrace, though. Someone had been in here with muddy boots, and Father Luke tutted to himself. Before anything else, he must sweep. He fetched a besom and began to clean his little church, sweeping the dirt away from the red and cream floor tiles of which he was so proud, until there was a fine mist of particles hanging about the whole place. The sun illuminated these dancing motes and created bright columns of light in the church that gave it a still more magnificent aspect. Leaning on his broom, Luke felt his tiredness leach away, and a calmness settle upon him.

He returned his broom to its corner, and walked the length of the nave to kneel before the altar, hands clasped together.

'Lord, forgive me for my anger and black choler, and I praise You for this peace. It is surely true that a man must seek comfort in the little things, in prayer, work, and—'

Just then, the door was thrown wide, and Father Luke snapped his eyes open, turning to see the woman striding towards him.

'Where is he?' Agatha demanded. 'Where's that good-for-nothing churl of a husband of mine? I suppose you left him in some ale-house where he could watch the wenches with his tongue hanging out? We've work to do here, and the fool is hiding somewhere!'

'Agatha, I was going to ask you the same question!'

'Me? How would I know where the useless prickle was? He was away with you, Father.'

'But I haven't seen him in days. I thought he was already here,' the priest protested.

'Oh, yes, of course you did. That's why you sidled into town like a cur expecting a boot up its backside, is it? I wasn't born yesterday, Father. I know you men. You promised you wouldn't tell me, eh? You can say this, though: when will he be back? I need to know that, at least.'

'Mistress Carter, I do *not* know,' Luke told her. 'We reached the castle three days ago, but as we got there, a fight broke out, and many men were killed. I was sure that your husband escaped, and . . .'

Father Luke slowed and stopped. In his mind's eye he saw again that furious posse hurtling along the road, falling upon the group of fleeing men and cutting them to pieces, before carrying on after the purveyor and the Dominican. If they had come across a lonely peasant with a cartload of money, Ham wouldn't have stood a chance. The men-at-arms would have slain him before checking his cart. If they did check and saw the weapons . . .

No, surely not! They were riding after the other two, the blackfriar and the other. He had seen the arrows flying after them, and shortly afterwards the posse poured out of the gate-house. They must have passed by the carter on their way after the two – if, indeed, they even noticed him.

'Yes, he must have escaped them,' Father Luke said reassuringly. 'I am sure that he is fine, mistress – you will simply have to be patient. He will return.'

'Aye, as soon as he's used up all his pennies, I suppose,' she declared. She tugged at her belt, hitching up her breasts as she did so. 'Well, I hope you're right, because if that niddicock isn't back soon, I don't know that I'll be responsible for my actions!'

CHAPTER SIXTEEN

Balsall

The cart rattled along comfortably enough, while the carter strode beside it, and Dolwyn jolted and rolled on the thin plank that served as a seat. This cart was a goodly size. It gave Dolwyn a feeling that it could be useful somehow in releasing the King. Not that he had any idea how that might be achieved.

'Where are you from?' he asked conversationally.

The man was uncommunicative, as so many peasants were. Dolwyn had wandered into a small town on his way up here to Kenilworth where the grubby urchins in the street eyed him with unconcealed alarm. They were incapable of speaking with him, because he was foreign. He came from more than ten miles away. It was the sort of insular attitude which had always upset Dolwyn when he was at home.

He was about to press the man, when a grudging comment came: 'Willersey. Small vill down southwest.'

'What were you doing up there?'

'Purveyor, he said he was. Came and told me to bring my cart. Said the castle wanted lampreys brought, and perry, and that I'd be well paid. Huh – never saw one penny. Then he set a load of swords and maces on my cart and there was that fight, and now I'm a hunted man, I think.'

'You are,' Dolwyn said with quiet conviction. 'But so are a lot after that attack. What is your name, anyway?'

'They call me Ham.'

'So then, Ham Carter of Willersey, what will you do now?'

'Go home, I suppose.'

'That would be sensible. But when you get there, what then? If they can trace you – and the King and Mortimer have very good spies – will you have brought danger to your wife, children, friends?'

Ham plodded on, but his head sank in dejection. 'What should I do?'

'My friend, I am sure that you will be safe enough. I merely asked. Now, for me, I will strike out westwards, away from the castle, and then follow the River Severn for a while. That will take me away from any search, I think.'

'How can you be sure of that, sir?'

'Good Ham, you can call me by my name: I am Dolwyn of Guildford. I am sure enough because only a strong force would dare to attack the Earl of Lancaster's castle at Kenilworth. Not only is it a mighty castle, it is owned by the second most powerful man in the realm.'

Ham's face grew longer. 'Master Dolwyn, what can I do? I am only a simple yeoman, when all is said and done, and I don't want any part of this sort of nonsense.'

Dolwyn smiled. He felt for his dagger. 'Look, friend, let's take our rest, eh?'

Nodding, Ham led the cart off the road onto a patch of

common land, and began to unhitch the pony as Dolwyn climbed down.

He wouldn't feel a thing, Dolwyn told himself as Ham turned away to pull a pot from the cart for boiling water. He would make it quick, he thought, his hand on the knife . . . But then he changed his mind. Not yet – not today. For now, travelling with a second man was perfect, in case anyone was looking for him. On his own he would stick out like a priest in a brothel. Here, on a cart with a man who was almost local, he would be less noticeable.

And this fool was too scared of him to be dangerous.

Friday before the Feast of the Annunciation[1]

Willersey

Agatha felt the soreness in her tired eyes as she tried to concentrate. There was so much to be done: animals to feed, protecting the emerging crops from birds and mice in their strips of land in the communal fields . . . She needed her man back. Where was he?

It was shameful to think that Ham would be running about the place free and happy with the money in his purse from the job with the cart, and not sharing anything with her or Jen. They needed the money. God's teeth, it was enough to make her weep!

The priest knew something, she was *sure* of it. She should watch him.

She held to her word through Mass that morning, her eyes fixed on Father Luke. He was calm and strong at first, but then,

1 20 March 1327

progressively, she became aware of his eyes moving towards her. He looked like a naughty boy consumed with guilt. Perhaps he had argued or fought with Ham, killed him and left the body ... But that was a laughable idea. This pasty priest was no match for her husband. Ham, for all his faults, was a hale and hearty man.

It was difficult to hold her tongue through the service. Instead, she aimed an accusing stare at Father Luke.

He definitely knew more than he was saying.

Abergavenny

Alured had ensured that Matteo Bardi was safely deposited at the castle's gates before seeing to the horses and finding a secure billet for himself and the other guards.

It had been a hard ride, but their reception was unfriendly. As soon as they entered the town, he felt the curious stares of the men and women. In fact, Alured got the impression that this town wasn't part of England at all. The people spoke in some weird tongue. They weren't like the folks of Kent or the men from the far north. These fellows actually spoke a whole different language, and it was disconcerting.

He felt out of place here. He was a London man. Those little alleys and streets were to him the essence of freedom. Without them, he felt lost.

His mood had not been improved by the way Matteo's nervousness had increased, the closer they came to Wales. Alured had not wanted to come here in the first place, but it was not his choice. What did he want with a four- or five-hundred-mile journey?

Alured could at least appreciate Matteo's alarm, having heard his suspicions about his brother Benedetto's murderous plan to wrest power from others at the bank. Alured himself doubted that Matteo's fears were justified, since Benedetto didn't seem like a killer to him. Still, it explained his trepidation. That and the fact that he was here to see Sir Roger Mortimer. No one would meet that man without a sense of grave danger. Sir Roger had not achieved the most powerful position by affability.

Yes. If Matteo was correct, Alured would have to be careful in the presence of Benedetto Bardi, but for his money, the more dangerous man was the one in the castle, Sir Roger Mortimer, not Benedetto.

Hunilege

Ham smiled at the man's jokes, but there was something about him that Ham didn't like. Dolwyn's smile, which appeared as easy and unforced as a taxman's while demanding more money, it was enough to make any man suspicious, he reckoned. What's more, as they travelled along, Ham noticed that his companion's eyes were all over the countryside.

Dolwyn caught him staring and gave him one of those long looks of his.

'What?' Dolwyn said.

'Nothin',' Ham protested feebly, feeling doubly foolish for blushing like a maid. 'It's just, you remind me of an old soldier I knew once. He always had his eyes on the hills about us when we were travellin'.'

'A man with sense, then. For I tell you now, when I look around here, all I see is danger. It's full of trees to hide a bowman, and old holes in which a thief could lie, and the hills themselves could hide a hundred outlaws.'

'So you were a soldier?'

Dolwyn looked at him. 'I have served the King. In peace and in war.'

'But now you're without a master?'

'Seems like it,' Dolwyn said. He saw no reason to mention the Bardi. 'There are many of us in the same position.'

Ham nodded to himself. It was no surprise to him. 'Are you married?' he asked next.

He half-expected the man to laugh at him. The idea of a warrior for the King having a wife and children was ludicrous, somehow, but to his faint surprise, the man gave him a slow, considering stare. 'Why?'

'Just wondered. I have a daughter. Lovely girl – little Jen. She makes my life whole. I'd die for her.'

Dolwyn turned to look at the road ahead. 'I did have a daughter once,' he admitted. 'But she died.'

'Well, I am sorry to hear that. A child is a comfort.'

'Yes. I . . . I envy you.'

They did not speak again. Ham walked alongside the cart, guessing how many days from the vill he had travelled, but occasionally throwing a look at Dolwyn, increasingly convinced that if he remained with this man for too long, he would pay dearly – possibly even with his life.

Dolwyn himself was back in the past: seeing his cottage lighted by the flames, the smoke billowing above the thatch, and hearing from inside the screams of Julia and Rose until at last they were stilled, and he was allowed to drop, weeping, to his knees.

Saturday before the Feast of the Annunciation[1]

Road south of Beausale

It had happened when they had stopped last night. Ham, the fool, had been setting about the horse as though to unlimber

1 21 March 1327

him from the cart, and Dolwyn had carefully clambered down, stiff and uncomfortable from the day's journeying. He was still thinking of Julia and Rose, and his flight after the terrible fire . . . when Ham struck him hard on the back of the head with a branch.

He'd slumped to his knees instantly, and heard a muttered apology, before Ham clubbed him again – and suddenly he was lying in the grass, uncaring about Ham, his horse or his creaking eyesore of a cart, which was currently rattling and clunking into the distance.

He had eventually managed to climb to his feet, but weakness forced him to sit with his back to a tree and doze through the night. Collecting firewood was impossible; the thought of cooking made him want to vomit. And he had no food anyway. The carter had taken the lot.

However this morning, although his poor head felt like a dented kettle, he was still alive.

There was the sound of water, and he made his way to a brook that ran past the road, lying on his belly and sucking up his fill. The coolness ran down his throat with the promise of life renewing; the chill as it struck his belly was like the first wash of ale on a summer's evening, and he was soon able to sit up and take more of an interest in his surroundings.

The land here was gentle, rolling farmland and pasture, with woods sprinkled here and there. He had no means of telling in which direction the carter had gone, but he recalled the man saying he came from a place called Willersey – and that, if Dolwyn was right, was down near Broadway. He could easily find his way there. There were tracks when he looked: and the cart was big enough that it would stand out.

143

Damn that bastard! He would find his way to Ham Carter's town, and he'd teach the swyving scrote a lesson he'd not forget in a hurry! No one knocked Dolwyn of Guildford down and got away with it.

CHAPTER SEVENTEEN

Willersey

Father Luke went about the work in his church, scarcely conscious of his actions and incapable of concentrating for more than a couple of moments at a time.

Last night, in his dreams, he saw the posse riding at him, swords raised, and he felt one slash at him, shearing right through his arm and sending it flying away; then a lance pierced his breast, lifting him up, high over the head of his killer, and he rose, staring down the great hole torn in him – and that was when he woke.

The mare planted these thoughts in his heart, and Father Luke knew that, no matter what he did today – whether he worked in the fields until exhausted, or knelt and prayed for hours on end, or slumped in Widow Lizzy's buttery and drank a gallon of her best ale – it would make no difference. Tonight he would still have that same dream and wake in a muck sweat.

Agatha had come to Mass this morning, and as he stood before the congregation, he could see her staring at him with those malevolent little eyes of hers. She had a suspicious nature and now she had a focus for all her bile in the man who had, she was sure, some idea where her good-for-nothing husband disappeared to.

No. He was being unfair. She was just a lonely woman, wondering where her husband had gone – and why shouldn't she? It must be worrying for her.

Last night she had appeared at Vespers like a cog entering a harbour, her heavily-built frame slowly moving across the nave until she was standing close to the altar. From there she focused her gaze upon him, as if she could suck the truth from him by staring.

She had been hard to ignore, but still less so was Jen. The little girl stood at her mother's side, and Luke felt certain that she was about to burst into tears at any moment. It made him feel as guilty as if he had actually killed her father. Because now, with still no sign of Ham, Father Luke was losing hope. Something must have happened to him. It shouldn't have taken him this long to return.

Poor man! Poor woman! Poor daughter! All of them suffering because of the purveyor, Stephen Dunheved. No matter what the man's reasons were, there was no excuse for coming here and taking Ham away and getting him involved in a fight in which many men died. It was unforgivable.

He went through the service, murmuring the Latin words that were so much a part of his life. Other priests, he knew, were happy to pretend. They had learned enough to become priests, but after that enjoyed lives of moderate peace without straining themselves to become more effectual at the cure of souls. That was not Luke's way. He intended to make sure that all who lived within his parish would be well served.

146

Afterwards, the peasants filed out as Father Luke finished the last of the communion wine and wiped the cup with a cloth saved for the purpose. However, as he placed his vestments in the chest behind the altar, he knew that two remained.

'Agatha,' he sighed.

'I want to know where he is, Father. You must have some idea.'

'But I don't. I am very sorry. Perhaps if we pray for him, God will bring him home again.'

'Why wouldn't he have come straight-away, like you?'

'I told you of the fight. Perhaps he had to run in the wrong direction.'

'Or you think these men caught him? But what if they did? He was only a poor carter passing by.'

'Men suspect peasants with money,' he said without thinking.

'What money?' she bridled. 'You know how much he had in his purse? We manage on very little.'

'True,' he agreed hastily. 'But posses can be unreasonable, especially after fighting.'

'You know more than you're saying.'

He felt his shoulders sag. 'I wish I could tell you more.'

'So there *is* more to tell?'

'No! I mean I wish I knew more so I *could* tell you.'

From that moment, whenever he saw Agatha and Jen, the suspicion grew in his mind. It was not his secret to divulge if Ham had decided to run away. But it was a cruel thing to do, if that was what Ham had chosen, to disappear taking the King's money with him.

Agatha would never forgive her husband, Father Luke knew. God save the poor fellow if she ever caught up with him!

Monday before the Feast of the Annunciation[1]

Furnshill, Devon

It had been a long, weary ride from Exeter, and Sir Baldwin de Furnshill felt every one of his four-and-fifty years as he rode up the incline towards his home.

As Keeper of the King's Peace he must often attend courts, but today he had witnessed two hangings, and it had left him sad.

One, a fellow called John from Wefford, had stabbed a King's verderer when he had been caught poaching, and for that there was no excuse. He was hanged. But Baldwin knew John and also knew that he was desperate to feed a growing family who would now suffer without him.

The second man, Piers Rookford, Baldwin suspected was innocent. Piers was accused of stealing plate and candles from the church at Coldridge, but the sole evidence was given by a watchman who stated that he had seen Piers leaving the church after dark. Since Piers was known for fighting, the jury had decided that the watchman was correct. Piers Rookford was hanged too.

At last he could see his home. There was the broad swathe of pasture before the house, the trees at either side and behind, and the smoke lazily drifting about it. The scene was, to him, one of unutterable beauty. Heaven, for him, would feel like this: a homecoming, knowing that his wife and children were waiting for him. The cares of his duties, his fears for the realm – all could be left here in the roadway.

He rode faster, eager to reach his hearth. The last few yards

1 23 March 1327

he covered at a gentle canter, the smile broadening on his face as he rode up the lane to his doorway, dropping from his beast and bellowing for his grooms.

It was then, as the door opened and the stranger appeared, that he felt the first premonition of disaster.

Abergavenny Castle

Matteo Bardi had been forced to wait – a pointless strategem to make a man realise his relative unimportance. As a tactic it failed, for Matteo was entirely confident of his own position. However, when he was called into the great hall, that confidence evaporated just a little.

Mortimer was seated on a large wooden chair on the dais, and studied Matteo with cool disdain which served only to increase the man's nervousness.

The chamber was decorated with gorgeous hallings that portrayed glorious hunts and acts of remarkable chivalry. A man rescuing a maid from a dragon, raches and alaunts holding a pure white hart at bay, knights jousting – it was a heady vision. A fire sent sparks high into the air, and there must have been ten pounds of candles flickering and smoking from the sconces and candle-holders set about the floor and on the table.

Sir Roger inclined his head graciously as Matteo entered, and then, once the Florentine got over his stammering, proceeded to speak with great charm and wit, but Matteo knew that he was meant to feel overwhelmed. After all, Sir Roger was the man to whom all must look if they wished to see how the King would order his realm. Sir Roger held all power. What was curious was that such an esteemed individual should have asked Matteo here. It didn't make sense.

'You asked to see me?' Matteo enquired when they had at

last exhausted all the polite chitchat which was demanded of them.

'What do you think of your brother, Benedetto?'

'He is a very capable, sensible man,' Matteo said.

'I've heard you are the more powerful of the men in your bank.'

'Sir Roger, I fear I am only a clerk. I listen to those who know what is happening, and then I pass on such information as I think will merit—'

'Your brother is an intelligent fellow,' Sir Roger continued as though Matteo had not spoken, 'but he is less keen on change. I know your brother Manuele was reluctant to aid me and the Queen when we had all the trouble last year. Benedetto, I believe, is formed from the same mould. Those with little imagination can only see what is right in front of their noses. Those with intelligence can see one grain of sand and conceive a desert. You are like that, I think.'

'I am honoured that you consider me so much more important than I truly am,' Matteo said, bowing.

'We both know your value. I wish to use you, because I appreciate it too.' Sir Roger took up his goblet and sipped the strong wine. 'You are wasted where you are.'

'I do not know how I could assist you.'

'You have your spies. It is your circle of friends that I need. Without you, it will not function. So I am prepared to offer you a bargain. Use your people to aid me and you will be rewarded. Your House will benefit from the money which the King will farm from his people.'

'I see,' Matteo said. He had to struggle to keep his voice calm. This was a glorious opportunity! To be spymaster to Sir Roger would give him and the House of Bardi more power than any other bank in the realm. It would put them on a higher footing than the Peruzzi or those Venetian *banditti* . . . and then he realised that Sir Roger was still speaking, and he had to concentrate hard to try to catch up with his words.

'Yes, you see there has been an attempt to free Sir Edward of Caernarfon from Kenilworth. Astonishing, but these rebels thought they could do it.'

'The K . . .' Matteo cleared his throat. 'Sir Edward is safe and well? He is not harmed?'

'Ah, so you think as I do that this foul attack was to harm the King's father? There are some who are not quick enough to see the danger which surrounds Sir Edward. But you and I, we appreciate it, I think.'

A short while after that, Sir Roger gave Matteo his instructions: he was to ride to Kenilworth and deliver a letter to Lord Berkeley. He would have left Berkeley Castle, so Matteo should meet him at Kenilworth.

'What is it?' Matteo asked.

'An indenture to pass control of the King's father from the Earl of Lancaster to the Lord Berkeley. He will now take over duties of protection and control.'

Furnshill

Sir Baldwin drew his sword in an instant. 'Who are you?'

There was a low chuckle, and as he looked, the stranger was yanked away, and in his place appeared Sir Peregrine of Barnstaple. 'Sir Baldwin, I don't think you need trouble yourself about running me through. I am not your enemy.'

Baldwin thrust the sword home into the scabbard again. 'Where is my wife?' he demanded.

'She is here, perfectly safe,' Sir Peregrine said, standing aside.

In a moment, Jeanne walked from the doorway and stood decorously before him. 'My lord, I am sorry I was not here to greet you,' she said.

Baldwin felt his heart swell. Jeanne had red-gold hair, and the perfect pale skin to match it. Her eyes were the rich blue of cornflowers, but her nose was tip-tilted, and her upper lip was more full than the lower, giving her a stubborn appearance. He adored her. She was, to him, the picture of beauty, and never more so than at times like this, when she gave that slow smile he knew so well.

'My lady, I have missed you,' he said.

'It has been only three nights,' she pointed out.

'To me, that feels a lifetime,' he said.

He took her arm and walked with her into his hall. In the last year or two he had spent too much time away from home. In the King's service, he had been sent to France as a guard to the Queen, he had returned with Bishop Walter in order to protect the King's son, he had been sent to Thorney Island to serve as a Member of Parliament, and he had been called away to fight for the King.

'So, Sir Peregrine, how can we serve you?' he asked.

Sir Peregrine of Barnstaple was one of those rare men, a knight banneret with integrity. He had been an acquaintance of Baldwin's for several years, and in all that time Baldwin had not learned to fully trust him. He was too devoted to the removal of the King's advisers and replacing them with men better, as he felt, suited to the task.

Now that the King was gone and his son Edward III crowned in his turn, Sir Peregrine had seen all he had desired come to pass. He was a happy man. Especially since he had now married.

'Your good lady has been kind enough to entertain us,' Sir Peregrine said, bowing to Jeanne.

Jeanne beamed. She had always been more keen on Sir Peregrine than Baldwin was.

'I am sure that will surprise neither you nor me,' Baldwin smiled. 'How is your own good lady?'

He spoke kindly. Sir Peregrine had almost married more than once, but he had been exceedingly unfortunate, and each woman had died. Now, he had been fortunate enough to meet with a widow, Isabella Crok, who was as fond of him as he was of her. They had married late the previous year.

'My lady Isabella is contented, I hope. She has taken a cruel dislike of a soldier's decorations, and seeks ever to improve my poor hall with her tapestries and hallings, but I remain convinced that it is easier to maintain a happy home by acquiescing in such matters than by debating.'

Jeanne's grin broadened. 'You would do well to remember such wise words, husband.'

'I have no need, my wife. You will be sure to remind me regularly,' Baldwin said drily.

He called for wine, and his servant Edgar was soon in the hall, carrying jugs. Baldwin cast a look up at him, and Edgar met it serenely, which was enough for Baldwin. His servant's judgement was usually faultless, as was that of his great mastiff, Wolf, who was lying by the fireside, head nodding gently. There was no apparent need for concern here. Not that he would expect danger from Sir Peregrine.

'There was a terrible shock last week,' Sir Peregrine said. He lifted his mazer and drank half his wine in a draught. 'Have you heard?'

Baldwin shrugged. 'I have been in court. All I know is that a butcher had a half-lamb stolen, a pastry cook was kicked by his mule, and a drunken shepherd fell in the well at the Cock at

Crediton and drowned. My interests have been, as you might say, rather parochial of late.'

He was utterly unprepared for the banneret's next words.

'A force stormed the castle at Kenilworth, Sir Baldwin,' Sir Peregrine said sombrely. 'They tried to free Sir Edward.'

CHAPTER EIGHTEEN

Willersey

That afternoon, Agatha sat by her hearth and made oat cakes. And for some reason, she kept weeping.

Ham was gone – she knew that. Her husband of fifteen years had left her, and the whole focus of her life was unbalanced. Here at her home, she felt completely out of place. It should have Ham in it.

'Why are you crying, Mother?' Jen asked as Agatha rose to sweep the floor.

'Quiet! Can't you see I'm trying to get some work done?'

Jen turned away, hurt, and Agatha felt a fleeting guilt, but then her thoughts were back on her husband.

She knew that her neighbours thought she had no affection for Ham, just because she shouted at him when he infuriated her. True, she complained about his laziness, his drunkenness when he returned from the ale-house reeking of cider, his snoring, his sudden deafness when she needed him to listen, or his inability to remember anything she told him for more than a

155

moment or two – and yet she needed him. He was infuriating, but he was hers. And without him, life lost its savour.

The church bell tolled, and she set her broom in the corner of the room where it always stood, next to the family's rolled palliasses – the large one which she and Ham had always shared, and the smaller one that she had made for Jen when the girl was old enough. It had taken an age to save up enough material for their daughter's bedding, but Agatha had been determined that they would not always share their bed with their children, like so many others. Better that there was a little peace for parents. They always set the beds there, near the corner of the room. It was like so much of their life: ordered and tidy.

Agnes had set upon marrying Ham from the first time she had met him, and this had been his house, with his parents. When Ham and she were wed, making their vows out in the pasture late at night after the midsummer feasts with five of their friends around to hear them, they had been only fifteen, both of them. It was frightening to leave her parents and come here, to be inspected by her father-in-law. But he was a kindly old man, and it was a black day when he died, Ham's mother too a short time later.

Later, when her friend Alice married and left, she began to feel the first stabs of envy. Alice's husband was an apprentice, but soon he took over the business, and the couple lived in luxury. Mild vexation grew to disgruntlement that her own husband could not provide so well.

Still, they had the house, and the land about here was abundant. Fruit grew thickly on the trees. The cider here was the best in the land, she swore, and no man need go hungry. They did not suffer hardship.

She saw that over the fireplace, hooked in the hole in the wood where the plaster had fallen away, was the old goosefeather which Ham had bought her for dusting and cleaning. It was a silly thing, just a length of feather, nothing more, and yet the sight of it was enough to make the tears flood her face. The feather held so many memories for her – of times when she and Ham had been happy, when Jen had been a little child. So many happy things to recall, and all now in the past. Ham had left her – had gone away to find a new life. She could almost wish she had been less shrewish.

'Mother?'

Agatha opened her eyes and looked at her daughter. The girl was anxious, wishing to console, but sad too, to think that her father was gone – because Jen was no fool. Agatha held her arms open and embraced her daughter, and soon she was sobbing like a maid. The emptiness in the cottage, the anxiety about her husband, all conspired to bring her to an emotional collapse.

It was not that she feared he was dead. Rather that he was alive and well, and enjoying another woman.

'I miss him so much!' she wailed, and the sound of her despair scared her.

'Mother, what did Father Luke mean? He said there was money. Papa had no money, did he?'

'No, of course not.' Agatha wiped her eyes. 'Must have meant the purveyor.'

Jen blew her nose. 'Why did Father Luke have to go with them?'

'I don't know,' Agatha said. But now there was a vague memory . . . She cast her mind back to that fateful day. Father Luke had approached her to ask where her husband was, hadn't he, and a little later she had heard that the priest was joining Ham and the purveyor. Ham had said he must go to the church to fetch something before he and the purveyor left. The words he muttered made her think it was a heavy item belonging to the priest.

Heavy. Coin was heavy. Gold was heavy. Could it be that the priest had something valuable to carry? What could a priest have that was worth anything, she scoffed. But there was a niggling suspicion at the back of her mind. Was that why Father Luke was so determined to tell her nothing about Ham? Poor Ham! What had happened to him?

'Ma?' Jen said.

'Don't worry,' Agatha said. 'I think there's something the Father forgot to tell us.'

Furnshill

Baldwin stared in astonishment. 'At Kenilworth? They must have been mad!'

'It was a bold attack, from all I have heard. No subtlety, just a simple assault. They almost reached Sir Edward, but then they were repulsed and several killed.'

'And?'

'And all the Keepers of the King's Peace are expected to be alert for any signs of such malefactors in their areas, and should arrest all those who appear to have plotted or who may plot the escape of Sir Edward of Caernarfon, lately King of England.'

Baldwin nodded, but did not react. Sir Peregrine knew that Baldwin had been an enthusiastic supporter of the King. No matter. So had many others.

'I shall be vigilant,' he said.

'Sir Baldwin, I am sorry, but I do not think you understand my mission. I was sent here by the guard at Kenilworth to ask you to join him.'

'What? At Kenilworth, you mean?'

'Yes. Sir Edward is to be taken away from that castle and installed in another. He is distressed. He believes his life is in grave danger, and he has asked that two men whom he can trust should go with him.'

'Not I?'

'I fear so.'

Baldwin was about to sneer at his words, when he saw the sympathy in Sir Peregrine's eyes. It was enough to stifle his response. 'Aye, well.'

'Not you alone, though. I believe you know Sir Ralph of Evesham?'

'I do. He was with me when the King was captured. He and I were among the last knights in his service.' Baldwin nodded his gratitude.

Sir Peregrine said nothing more, but both men knew that a fence had been leaped and both felt better for it.

It was obvious that Jeanne did not understand the undercurrent, but Baldwin could not explain. Not now.

King Edward II had been Baldwin's King for these twenty years past. Oh, Baldwin knew that his monarch had been foolish occasionally, but Baldwin was an intensely loyal man, who felt the solitude of his royal master's position keenly. Fractious barons, the Scots, and an inclination to unsuitable pursuits had all conspired to bring him low in the nation's esteem. Even merchants and peasants felt ashamed of a King who liked to join fishermen, who enjoyed swimming and acting, rather than more regal past times. In the eyes of his peers, he was foolish.

However, during all the long years since Baldwin and Sir Peregrine had first met, Baldwin had known that Sir Peregrine desired the removal of King Edward's adviser, Sir Hugh le Despenser. The latter was detested all over the realm, and yet

Baldwin would not join with any plots to bring about such an outcome. He remained true to his oath.

That Baldwin had served his King was a source of pride, because he believed in the importance of oaths and he had given his word to his King freely; yet the realisation, when he was captured, that he could be executed along with any who sought to defend the King had forced him to look back on his life and reconsider some of the decisions he had made.

If he had died, his wife and children could have become destitute. It was not a thought which had troubled him before, because a man in full strength rarely considers his own destruction, but now, more and more, he was aware of this concern. He imagined his wife being evicted, probably raped and beaten before being thrown out on the road with only the sobbing of their children to accompany her.

He felt as though, in seeking to serve his King, he had betrayed his own family. He could not do that again.

Willersey

The way that he tried to scurry from the church as soon as his service was over was enough to convince her.

'Father,' Agatha called. 'Father!'

He was already at the door, and seemed on the verge of bolting – but then she was at his side and he deflated like a punctured bladder.

'I want to know the truth,' she said grimly. 'What has happened to him?'

'Mistress, I don't know,' he protested weakly.

'I don't believe you!' She thrust her face forward. 'You wanted Ham to take something heavy, and so valuable that you didn't dare leave it to him alone. You had to go with him, didn't you? That's what you were saying when you spoke yesterday.

The money you mentioned, that Ham could have taken – did you put it on his cart?'

Luke stared past her towards the cross. He did not know whether to tell her all, or even a part of what had happened. Surely to divulge her husband's flight would be more cruel than allowing her to think that she was widowed? She could forget her man, continue with her life – perhaps find another husband.

And that brought him up short. What if she did find another and came to him, her priest, to ask that he marry her again? He could not do so, not while he remained convinced that her husband was no more dead than he was himself. No! He must tell her the truth, and that right soon.

'Mistress,' Father Luke confessed quietly, averting his eyes, 'I think that he stole my money and has fled.'

Furnshill

It was late that night when Jeanne heard her husband climb the stairs to their solar.

'You are weary, Baldwin.'

She saw him grin at her as he reached over to set the candle on a spike by the doorway. 'I admit it freely, my love. I am tired.'

'Was it Sir Peregrine?'

'The man exhausts me. His presence is a trial in its own right.'

'He is a different man since his marriage.'

Baldwin looked at her. 'No. He is the same man with a thin veneer of suavity.' He sat and began to tug off his boots. 'His marriage to Isabella has given him new interests, it is true, but his own desires were always concentrated on removing the Despenser from the heart of government. To achieve that, he knew that he must see the King replaced. Now that King

Edward II has given up his throne and passed it on to his son, Sir Peregrine considers his function in the world achieved, and he is content. But he knows that my own loyalty will remain with the King anointed in the sight of God, and none other. For no other King will exist for me until Edward II is dead.'

'But what does that mean?' Jeanne asked. She felt a flicker of fear awaken in her breast. 'You will not go against the new King, will you?'

Baldwin sat back and she saw his dark eyes study her for a long while. 'No,' he said at last, and her heart begin to calm. 'No, I could not involve myself in the kingdom's politics. Not willingly. I think that I have done my part in the last five years. I am keen now to remain as I am: a lowly rural knight. I have no affectations, no ambitions. I wish to enjoy what life is left to me with my family. That is all.'

He turned away and pulled his tunic over his head, tugged off his chemise and bundled all his clothes into a ball, setting them on top of the chest. He climbed into bed naked, and Jeanne snuggled closer. 'Ach, you're freezing!'

He chuckled, pulling her towards him, and kissed the top of her head. 'We shall be safe enough down here,' he said comfortingly.

Jeanne smiled to herself as he kissed her again, and lifted her head so he could kiss her mouth. She felt the familiar thrilling through her body as they began to make love, but later, when she opened her eyes again, close to sleep, she saw that her husband was staring up at the ceiling intently, like a man considering an unpleasant task.

Last year, at the time when he had been called away to protect the Duke of Aquitaine on his journey to Paris, knowing he was to desert her, he had worn a remarkably similar look on his face.

He looked at her now, and murmured, 'I think I am glad I collected my sword.'

His words were spoke lightly enough, but the look in his eyes was enough to chill her blood.

CHAPTER NINETEEN

Vigil of the Feast of the Annunciation[1]

Willersey

It was no good, she couldn't sleep. Agatha surrendered herself to the fact that she would remain awake throughout the night, and rolled from her palliasse to her feet, then shuffled in the dark towards the table. She sat on the stool and leaned her elbows on the table, chin resting on her fists.

That *prickle*!

It was the only thought that kept running through her mind. She wanted to scream and lash out at anyone who came near. But in truth, deep down, all she felt was despair at the thought that the man with whom she had expected to spend the rest of her life had deserted her.

Her man must have told Father Luke, since the latter was so certain. Perhaps Ham had confessed in church, or when he

1 24 March 1327

got drunk. Ham may have found some accommodating bitch who tempted him. Perhaps that was it – not money, just a drag-gletail, and he was off after her like a dog. All men were the same. Even Ham.

'Why now?' she groaned.

She could have made something of her life if he'd died years ago. When she was in her twenties, there were men who'd shown an interest in her and she could have made a good match. Instead, here she was – a raddled old wench, her face lined, her body sagging and worn. No man would want her now. She took her hands from her face and studied them: the calluses and warts, the horny skin. Once she had been pretty enough, and if she had been saved from this life of endless effort, maybe she would still be comely.

In time, she hoped she would accept the idea that he had left her. It was terrible to think she might not. A life full of bitter-ness was no life at all.

She looked over at Jen sleeping on her palliasse, her mouth dropped open, faint snores ensuing, and felt another surge of sadness, tinged with determination.

They would survive, even if Ham had left them. *They would survive.*

Ross-on-Wye

Matteo de Bardi rode stiffly still, the pain in his back a reminder of his vulnerability. It did not matter whether a fellow was a lord or a king – if the mob decided to remove him, it would do so. A word in the right ear and a crowd would stab him to death without a moment's hesitation.

The thought brought another twinge of pain.

Death had not left his mind in the last days. At Abergavenny Castle, danger had felt so close; on leaving, he felt as if he had

165

sloughed off a heavy cloak – and with the cloak went all his fears and troubles. Outside the town's gates he felt like a man renewed.

'Are you well, master?' Alured asked at his side.

'Yes,' Matteo smiled.

Matteo Bardi knew he was little known outside the bank, and yet it was he who wielded much of the real control. It was the information he gathered which led to the new directions being taken by the bank. Especially since the others rarely realised that they had been manipulated.

In recent years he had never once been in error. His informants were competent, from an Earl all the way down to a lay brother in a small priory. All knew their duties, and all were proficient if not prolific. It was the most arduous task, Matteo knew, to sift through the distraction of base rocks to search out the twinkling motes of pure gold. Other banks, even Florentine ones, were put to great effort to decide which information was accurate, which was guesswork, which was spurious or intended to cause confusion.

Matteo was happy that all that work had been done already. He paid well, and his sources knew that even if they had no information, he would still pay them. And because he did pay monthly in gold, his men continued to give him important tidbits when they had them. They trusted him.

And they were right to do so. He would support and protect them. Until they became dangerous, in which case he would instantly remove them.

It must have been something of this reputation which had helped recommend him to Sir Roger Mortimer. And now the latter had asked him to deliver the indenture to move Sir Edward of Caernarfon from Kenilworth. Matteo had considered it an honour, and had been happy to wait for a day while the parchment was drawn up by Mortimer's clerks.

However now, sitting astride his horse, he was assailed by doubts.

Matteo knew that Earl Henry of Lancaster and Sir Roger were vying for power. Earl Henry had better contacts in Parliament and could count on winning debates there, but Sir Roger was the Queen's lover. If Sir Roger wanted to take the old King from Kenilworth and place him in Berkeley Castle under the control of his son-in-law Lord Thomas de Berkeley, that must give Sir Roger the edge. While Earl Henry had him at Kenilworth, he could threaten to return Edward to his throne and oust Sir Roger. Without Sir Edward, his position was greatly weakened.

At least *he* would be safe enough, Matteo told himself. He was a mere messenger, one who was impartial in this matter.

Thank the Good Lord that Dolwyn had not been discovered, nor the Bardi letter found, he thought.

West Sandford

There were times when he hated that lazy prickle. Gurt hoddypeak[1].

Hugh scowled at the boy and aimed a kick at his backside. 'You know 'tis not what I meant, you boinard[2],' he snarled.

'How'm I to know what you mean? You never explain anything to me!'

Rob was a whining, idle, ferret-like boy whom Hugh's master Simon Puttock had somehow collected when he was living as Keeper of the Port of Dartmouth some while ago. The post had been intended as a reward to Master Simon, because he had served his lord, the Abbot of Tavistock, well – but the good abbot had had no notion of how devastating his kindness

1 simpleton
2 fool

167

had been. Removed from his beloved moors, Simon had been like a fish out of water. His wife was reluctant to move to Dartmouth, because their daughter Edith was the sort of girl who'd fall for the first fellow to come along, and the idea of her being exposed to a bunch of rough sailors was not to be borne. So the family had separated, Simon going to the coast while his family remained in Lydford.

This little wretch had been his servant there in Dartmouth. And he still couldn't wake up in time to make the morning's fire.

'More logs, I said,' Hugh hissed.

'Oh, "more logs, more tinder, more wine, more everything, Rob. Just do as I say, and don't argue"!' the lad said bitterly, mimicking Hugh's voice. 'You just don't know what I—'

He broke off as Hugh hurled a short stick at him. 'I said, *more logs*. I want a fire for the master when he returns.'

'You need a slave, that's what you need,' Rob grumbled.

'Shut your noise, boy, and fetch the logs,' Hugh rasped, and watched from black brows as the lad sulkily dragged his feet out through the doorway.

Hugh made a small pile of twigs in readiness, then held a hand over the ashes of the night's fire in the hearth. There was some heat in one corner, and when he blew gently on it, he saw a faint glimmer, but when he set a twig in it there was not enough heat to make it smoke.

Instead he took a little charred cloth and set it on his lap, preparing flint and steel, and then striking down sharply with the flint. The spark was so tiny, it might have been a mote of dust. He struck again, then four more times rapidly, until he saw the gleam of red on the black material.

Quickly picking it up, he blew to make it glow strongly and surrounded it with some wisps of old man's beard and some fine twigs and birch bark. Soon smoke was rising, and he carefully set it down over the hottest part of the ashes, placing the handful of twigs overtop, and blowing soft but steady into it. There was a flicker of flame and he nodded, satisfied.

Hugh had been born not far from Drewsteignton, on a farm that was noted for its sheep. There, as a boy, he had grown wild with the animals. He had cared for few people, only his sheep and his dog, and it was not until Simon Puttock took him on that he discovered the pleasure of companionship. He had never regretted joining with Master Simon, although he wished that his own marriage has lasted longer. His wife and child had died in a fire, and many had been the times he had wished that he had died with them.

His own son would never have grown so bone idle as this, that much he knew.

There was a muttered curse, and the fellow appeared in the doorway, arms filled.

He wasn't *so* bad, really, Hugh reminded himself. The lad had grown up in the port, son of a woman who gave herself in exchange for ale or wine. He had never known his father. The man was just one in a succession of sailors who had been entertained by his mother. It would have been a miracle for him to turn out any better. Most lads like him were dead before they were thirteen, and if not, they became sailors themselves. Fishermen or warriors for the King, it made little difference. Being employed by Simon had probably saved young Rob's life.

'Get the fire going, lad,' Hugh said, having blown the little sparks into life, and rising from his knees, grunting to himself, he lumbered from the room.

This was his sanctuary, the small buttery at the farther side of the screens passage, in which the household's ale and wine was stored. It was only a small chamber, but for Hugh, who had grown up without walls while he lived on the moors, it was as good as any man's grand hall. He sat on a stool and drew a quart of ale into a leather jug, drinking deeply.

He was still there when he heard the rattle of hooves outside.

Near Mickleton

Dolwyn woke in the early light, head aching, bones sore and rubbed, and cursed the sun. Another hour of sleep would not have hurt him.

All the way here, he had hurried, desperate to catch up with Ham. He was used to it. In his time he'd been forced to hurry to battles, as well as away from them afterwards. He had bolted from homes when he learned that a posse sought him, he had joined posses in search of felons when told to, he had ridden at speed with the King's messages from York to London and back. Once he had run from a woman's husband, leaving his hosen, belt and knife behind somewhere on the bitch's floor in the dark.

And in all those years he had never flagged, whether he was quarry or hunter.

He knew Willersey. Some years ago he had been to Gloucester, then was sent to Warwick, and on the way he passed through Broadway and Willersey. They had struck him then as ideal places for a man like himself. He could have taken the vills with very few men, and the rich land all about there would have fed and watered a goodly-sized force. Perhaps it was close to time for him to think again about such things. If he didn't manage to free Edward of Caernarfon, he would have to think about another opportunity; perhaps he could raise a force in order to free him.

First, though, he wanted food, followed by revenge – the chance to silence a man who had seen him too close to the castle where Edward was being held. He also wanted that horse and cart.

He just wished his head didn't hurt so much where that bastard had hit him.

Once up, his blanket rolled, he returned to the lane where the wide-set wheel-tracks stood out so strongly.

'Right, you son of a pox-ridden whore!' he muttered, and set off again, his bruised skull pounding with every step.

West Sandford

At the door, Hugh heard a familiar voice bellowing. It was almost enough to make him spill his ale. He walked to the hall, where the boy Rob was kneeling and blowing furiously in an attempt to keep the fire going, then along the screens passage to the open front door.

'Sir Richard,' he said.

'That's right, Sir Richard de Welles. Good God, man, you look like you swallowed a turd! Where's your groom, eh? Someone needs to come and take me horse and see to it. Simon indoors, is he? I've a throat as parched as a wild dog's in the Holy Land, and the idea of an ale is very welcome. If there's a little cheese and bread, that would be good too. Or some cold meat. Anything, really. What, lost your tongue, man?'

'Sir Richard, my master's not here.'

Sir Richard de Welles stood with his legs spaced as though preparing to fight, his hands on his belt – a tall man, at least six feet and an inch in height, somewhat heavy in the paunch, and with bright, genial eyes set in an almost perfectly round face. His brow was broad and tall, and his beard was so thick and long it looked much like a gorget. He had a mass of wrinkles on his amiable features, most of which had been carved into his flesh by laughing.

Hugh knew the knight moderately well. Sir Richard had first met Hugh's master Simon in Dartmouth some three years ago, when his skills as a coroner had helped Simon and Baldwin discover a murderer. Loud, apparently impervious to all types of drink, no matter what the quantity, with a head like an ox and a memory for foul jokes of all forms, he was an example of the sort of rough and crude, but honest and kindly, knight whom Hugh could respect.

Now Hugh frowned, his head low on his shoulders. 'There's some cold meat and ale. And bread.'

'Excellent! Capital! You know, this reminds me of a manor I used to know a long way from here. Up towards Wiltshire,' the knight said, staring out over the view. A happy smile spread across his features as he stood surveying the little plot of pasture, the field beyond, the small coppice and shaw, and the hill that rose steeply in the distance, thick with old trees. 'A pleasant little farm, that was. And they brewed some fine ales there. Hah! I hope yours is as good, eh? Where's the hall, then?'

Hugh called for a groom, cursorily throwing the horse's reins over a tree's limb, before hurrying inside.

The house was a simple one: the cross passage was screened from the hall, and two doors on the right led to the buttery and pantry, while beyond was the little dairy. Margaret had persuaded Simon to modernise, and now there was a chimney rising from the hall itself, a recent innovation that did little, to Hugh's mind, to alleviate the thick smoke that always filled the room.

In fact, he could see Rob still blowing ineffectually at the fire, trying to force a glimmer from it, while Sir Richard strode inside. The knight was peering down at him with a frown on his face, watching intently.

'GOOD GOD, BOY!' he bellowed at last. 'DO YOU HAVE NO IDEA?' He pushed Rob aside, then went down on all fours, blowing steadily. In only a short time there was a strong crackling noise and Sir Richard sat back on his haunches, studying the burgeoning flames with satisfaction. 'That's how you get a fire going, boy! Now, off with you. I need bread, cheese, ale, some scraps of salad if you can find them, and if you have a meat coffin, so much the better. A little pasty always works a wonder on an empty stomach. Oh, and if the ale's thin, a pint of wine too. I need to keep me strength up. Stop!'

Rob, who had been sulkily making his way to the door, paused and turned to look at the knight.

Sir Richard's eyes narrowed and he subjected Rob to a short study. 'You are the boy from Dartmouth, eh? The one the good Keeper of Dartmouth found?'

Rob gave a surly nod.

'Ah. I had cause to chastise you there, I remember. You didn't get up in the morning, did you? Don't make me have to do so again, lad. Go on, be off! And look sharp, too!'

Sir Richard shook his head as the fellow darted into the buttery. 'Master, that churl deserves the whip more than a number of the felons I see before me in my courts. He needs a firm hand, eh?'

Hugh said nothing. The boy needed discipline, it was true, but Hugh didn't need help or advice from the knight. He had taught enough dogs to know how to raise animals.

The food arrived shortly, and Sir Richard looked at the wooden platter with an approving eye as he seated himself. Picking up the quart jug of ale that Rob placed at his hand and sniffing it with every sign of pleasure, he raised it to his mouth, closed his eyes, and sank a pint in three immense gulps. In a few more moments, the second pint was gone and the knight gave a belch of happiness as he passed the empty container back to Rob. 'Refill it, boy.'

He then pulled a knife from his belt and began to cut his meats, shoving each piece into his mouth with gusto. Only when the bread was gone, and his trencher clear of all meats and leaves, did he lean back and take up the third quart of ale, a beatific smile spreading over his face.

'There now, that feels much better,' he said. 'Where's your master, Hugh? Did you say he was away? What about his wife, eh?'

'They're at Exeter. Seeing their daughter and grandson,' Hugh said.

'That so, eh? Right. I've urgent messages for him. You'd best tell me how to reach him there.' Sir Richard glanced out through the open window. The sky to the south was darkening, with pink and red and orange clouds standing still as the sun sank to the west, out of sight. 'Can't go tonight, though. We'll have to go in the morning.'

'I can't leave here,' Hugh objected. 'My master told me to stay and look after the place.'

'He'll want you with him, when he hears my news,' the knight said with certainty.

CHAPTER TWENTY

Mickleton

Alured and the three men guarding Master Matteo di Bardi were conscious of the trees and bushes on either side as they rode up towards the village, and their eyes moved from one possible hiding-place to another.

For a London man, this landscape was alarming. Alured would rather be walking alone and unarmed in a narrow alley in London, than here. Any tree trunk could conceal a bowman, while all the greenery about the ground would be ideal for a determined band of outlaws ready to make an ambush. Alured had heard of many bands which roamed about the kingdom preying on poor travellers, and he had no intention of becoming one of their victims.

It was as they were approaching the village, dusk darkening the countryside around them, and as the men about him were beginning to relax, that they saw the man walking along in front of them.

He looked as though he had spent many days on the road already, and from his scuffed and muddied boots to his worn hat, he was a picture of exhaustion. Alured paid him little heed, but when he heard Matteo give a sharp intake of breath, he hurriedly turned in his saddle. 'Master?'

'Dolwyn?' Matteo was staring at the fellow with a gaping mouth. 'I thought you must be dead! What have you been doing?'

'You want me to tell you?'

Matteo threw a look at Alured. 'No, no, you are right. Master Alured, please take these other men with you to the vill. Find a tavern to rest in. I shall follow on shortly.'

'I'll stay,' Alured said. 'You could be in danger.'

'There is none here. You know my man . . . He is my confidential adviser.'

Alured looked from Matteo to the tatty man glaring at him. 'I remember Dolwyn. I have told you before these other men that I don't think I should leave you,' he stated. 'If you insist, I will go, but I don't like it. Will he guard you to the town? This is dangerous country.'

'Just be gone,' Matteo said wearily. 'I shall join you at the tavern as soon as I may.'

'Very good, Master Matteo.' Alured called to the others, and clucked his horse, urging it onwards. They were soon in the little village, and there Alured busied himself with arranging accommodation and food, but all the while, his attention kept returning to the roadway.

The tavern-keeper lighted candles and told him, 'I'm supposed to keep the door closed and locked at night.'

'You will be paid. This door remains open until my master is back.' Alured held the man's gaze for a long moment, until the landlord looked away and nodded.

Alured sat up and waited for Matteo to return, sitting on a stool outside the tavern's door, staring back the way they had come, wondering what on earth Matteo was doing with the man.

Willersey

It was late when Ham steered the cart into the side of the roadway at the top of the enormous hill that spread out east of Broadway, and he sat there for a long while, staring down into the plain. In the gathering gloom, he could make out little twinkles of light where candles had been lighted, and there was a series of columns of smoke rising in the still air. It looked so peaceful.

Down there was his home.

He had thought often enough that it was a prison. It was a place he'd been tied to by land, by custom and by duty. So many times he had thought about breaking free, running away and finding a new life. But it was a dream, that was all. There were bonds that kept him here, especially his love for his daughter.

On occasion he had thought of the death of his wife, with a kind of longing. He could never kill her himself, but the idea of her death was attractive. Agatha was like a leaden weight about his soul, preventing him doing any of the things he wanted. Lonely, without the comfort of a woman's love, Ham existed in a world of unremitting toil.

To his friends he was an object of amusement. They looked on him with affectionate sympathy, knowing he was a slave to his wife's will. Ham was no dullard – it was just that his opportunities had been too fleeting, his disasters too numerous and overwhelming. At every point, when he had thought that he could make a good profit either the money didn't materialise, or it was soon lost in taxes or some other expense.

Just like this time.

Agatha couldn't help being disappointed by him. She herself was strong-willed, and if she had been born a man, her indomitable spirit would have won her an empire. As it was, she was a woman whose husband could not provide her with the life she craved.

He climbed down from his cart and hitched up the front of his tunic to piss at a tree – like a dog, he thought.

At first, when they had been newly wedded, he had wallowed in the happiness of his life with her. They could not help but be merry and cheerful in each other's company. But gradually they slipped into this grim, passionless existence. It was after Alice went off to Warwick. The bitch was always dropping sarcastic little comments about Ham when she deigned to return to her old home, wearing jewellery to impress and incite avarice. She resented him because before Ham married Agatha, she was Agatha's closest friend. And now Agatha resented him because she felt he had let her down: he should have made more of himself, like Alice's husband.

Ach, it wasn't only her. He too was jealous. Other couples had big families, while he and Agatha must needs survive with Jen. Their daughter was an angel, but there was no denying that Agatha and he could have done with a boy, to keep crows from the crops, to dig the vegetable garden, to take a hand mending the fence about the pigs. But they would have no more children. She appeared barren, or felt she was, and rejected him whenever he tried to . . . She didn't want him near her. That was an end to it.

It was not the life he would have picked.

Anyway, returning home wasn't safe. That vill, so placid in the evening's murk, could be teeming with men searching for him.

Oh well, even if he was captured the next day, it would be good to see Jen. And even Agatha, he admitted. Wearily, he walked back to the cart and took hold of the reins. He'd have to lead the old brute down the hill. It was steep here, and he must go cautiously.

All those miles north and east, only to turn about and return, and all for no payment. He was exhausted, mind and body. The way had been hazardous, never more so than when he had met Dolwyn.

He mused on the lethal nature of the fellow all the way down the hill. Dolwyn was the sort of man who would draw a knife and argue later. Ham was glad he had put so many miles between them. But a nagging doubt did remain, even as he led his old horse along the main roadway towards Willersey. He wished he had taken the final step and actually killed the man. He suddenly recalled what he had said to Dolwyn. He had mentioned his home, hadn't he? And his own name, of course. There were many here who would be able to point him out to a stranger. A chill ran through him.

That was daft, he chided himself. Dolwyn would not want to walk all the way here to find him. Ham had nothing to make such a journey worthwhile. He was only a poor villein, when all was said and done.

It was almost full dark now. He had planned on getting to his home, and bracing himself to listen to a torrent of Agatha's complaints, but now he stopped in the road, and stared ahead, to where his wife would be readying herself for her bed.

The vill was serene. Houses lay dotted about, encircled with wraiths of smoke. It was a clear evening, and the ponds reflected the setting sun and the salmon-coloured sky. A dog barked, and he was sure that he recognised his own brute's voice. It would be typical of the old fellow to recognise the sound of his cart's wheels even from such a distance, Ham thought with a grin to himself.

Darkness enveloped the world like a blanket as he listened to the lowing of cows, the occasional call of an owl, the lone bark of his dog.

This was his home, and it was strange to him. He was filled with trepidation and sadness, and he dared not go down into the vill. Perhaps he should stay out here tonight, and face his wife tomorrow.

All would seem better in daylight, he told himself. He looked about him, then led the horse to the side of the road. Here there was a narrow clearing, where he unharnessed the horse, set the cart down, then hobbled the horse with leather straps before wrapping himself in a blanket and sitting with his back to a tree. He drew his hat over his eyes, and his hood over his face, and settled to sleep.

It was already dark when Dolwyn approached the vill. He stepped quietly, because a man who has once strayed onto the wrong side of the law knows all about the dangers of being found at night. After curfew, any man would be at pains to explain why he was wandering about near people's homes. There was no criminal so loathed as a robber of houses after dark.

He heard some horses, and stepped into the shadows behind a large beech tree. The moon was not full, but there were no clouds, and the area looked to him as bright as daylight. No people. He heard a creaking, as of leather, and turned to eye the space between the trees, but there was nothing he could see, even in this light. Carefully, he took one step, then another, and gradually made his way forward, anxious at every point that he might stumble or break a twig and alert someone nearby.

Men walking about at night were always liable to be slain, for only outlaws wandered the country in darkness. And Dolwyn did not want to be stabbed as he sought Ham.

He would find out what this creaking was, but then settle and have a sleep.

The crackle of twigs made Ham half-open his eyes for a moment, but the evening was chill, and although he was usually a light sleeper, tonight, after so many long journeys, he was too weary to get up and investigate. Besides, as he told himself, the sound was probably just the horse moving. He often raised one hoof, then set it down again, crunching the twigs beneath the shoe.

Another crackle. Then another.

The brute must be unsettled to keep shifting so. As he listened, caught in the twilight world between wakefulness and dreaming, it occurred to Ham that the noise was regular; it could be someone moving stealthily through the darkness, attempting to approach without alerting a dozing carter.

That last crunch was close, he thought. He opened his eyes and sat up, blearily staring about him, and saw the . . .

'Hey!' he called as he took in the scene: someone was at his cart. And then . . . he felt the blow on his head, 'What are you doing?' he demanded angrily, and would have climbed to his feet, were it not for the strange ponderousness of his legs. He rolled slightly, and felt the second blow strike, and this time he was stunned, falling back.

'No!' he said quietly, looking up. 'Please, I—'

All he could see was that hideous axe, dripping with blood, and suddenly he realised that he was about to die. This was no dream, no mare sent to terrify, but the solid, terrible truth. His death was here.

He tried to open his mouth to plead, but there was no strength in his muscles or his voice. He tried to crawl away, but only succeeded in exposing his pate once more, and the axe slammed into the top of his skull, hammering his face into the twigs and dirt of the ground. He felt the teeth of his upper jaw snap on a pebble, the agony at the back of his jawbone as both hinges dislocated with the force of the blow, then the ripping horror of his skull's bones as they opened out, exposing his brain to the cool night air – but that was all.

His soul was a shiver on the breeze as it left his body and drifted away.

CHAPTER TWENTY-ONE

Wednesday, Feast of the Annunciation[1]

Exeter

The baby was crying again.

Every time Simon heard that sound, it pulled at his heart. It was so like the cry of his firstborn son, little Peterkin.

The baby boy had been a delight to Simon and his wife when he was born. Small but sturdy, he had been utterly different from their daughter Edith. She was tall, slim and fair, whereas both Simon and his wife Margaret felt sure that Peterkin would be short and dark.

Their dreams ended in disaster when Peterkin was struck down with a fever, and gradually over three days his crying became weaker and weaker as he succumbed. The little fellow's death had profoundly affected Simon and Margaret, but it was Simon who felt the guilt, because by the end of the third day, he

1 25 March 1327

was desperate for the sound to end. It tore at his nerves to hear it, and when the noise ceased he felt a kind of horrible relief.

When their second son was born, it seemed only natural to name him Peter as well. But Simon always quailed at the sound of a child's crying since it brought Peterkin's death home to him once again.

This time, though, the crying was the natural demand of a child for his mother and milk. Incredible to think that this was his own grandchild.

Simon passed the little bundle to his daughter, and watched with pride as she untied the laces at the front of her chemise, releasing a breast for the baby.

'He's a good pair of lungs,' Simon observed.

'Henry is a strong little boy, aren't you?' Edith cooed. 'Father! Get that look off your face.'

'What look?' he protested.

'The one that makes you look like a lapdog staring at his mistress.'

'Well, I'm happy,' he objected. 'How do you expect me to look?'

'Are you going to stay at home now? Mother was very distressed about your absences last year.'

'I know, but there was nothing I could do.' Simon sighed. 'Now that the kingdom is calm again, there is no more need for me to worry. I am just a farmer, whatever the great lords may think.'

'You're more than that, Father,' Edith protested. 'You were the Abbot of Tavistock's man for years.'

'But the good Abbot has been taken from us.' Simon shrugged. 'I know little about what happens at Tavistock now, and care less. I will not risk my family again by thrusting myself into politics. Not that I meant to before,' he added.

There was a loud knock at the door, and Edith called to her maid, Jane, to go and answer it. Before long the maid was back, but before she could open her mouth, Simon grinned. 'Bring him in.'

'How did . . .?'

The bellow of greeting as Sir Richard de Welles entered was enough to make the child stop suckling and start to cry. Edith looked up in consternation. Her mother walked in shortly afterwards and said, 'Sir Richard, it is good to see you, but surely you wouldn't mean to distress my daughter as she feeds her child?'

'Hah! Madame Puttock, as God is my witness, I wouldn't wish to upset her *or* you!' the coroner said in a loud whisper. 'My apologies, ladies both, but I was too overjoyed to see Master Puttock once more. And Madame, you look extraordinarily well just now.'

'It is kind of you to say so, Sir Knight,' replied Margaret Puttock.

Simon was about to speak, when he saw the shuffling figure in the doorway. 'Hugh? What are you doing here? You should be at home.'

'*I* brought him,' Sir Richard beamed. 'Master Puttock, I have to ask for your help.'

'Help? How can a farmer help a knight, sir?'

'I need a posse. Men have tried to release the last King from the castle where he's held. Damn their souls, the fools would threaten the realm's stability if they let him go.'

'No,' Simon said immediately.

'Simon, this is not a request from an elderly knight. It is a *demand* from the King. King Edward wishes to ensure that his father is safe.'

'He is held in a castle, in Christ's name. How might *I* help protect him? There are many others who would do a better job.'

'As I said, men have tried to break into Kenilworth Castle to free the King's father.'

'Sweet Jesus,' Simon murmured as the knight's words sank in. 'Who could want to do that?'

Sir Richard grunted and sat on a stool. 'I don't know – someone out to earn themselves a good purse of gold and a future secure from debt? Whatever the reason, I have been told to get up there with help. You and I, Simon, are to assist in transporting the old King to a new home.'

Willersey

It was early in the morning that Agatha saw the sudden burst of activity over near the church.

She had been out seeing to the chickens, throwing a little corn to the stupid creatures as they pecked at the grit and rubbish about the yard. They were the most foolish animals. Even more dim than sheep, Agatha reckoned, and she had little enough respect for their intellect. Throw corn down, and they would likely peck at the stone next to the food, rather than the grains themselves.

Jen tried to help her, but Agatha could see that her heart wasn't in it. The poor chit was anxious about her father. It made Agatha look more kindly upon the girl. But then she saw her making a pile of their precious grain and asked. 'What are you doing?'

'I was only thinking they could come and gather all they want,' Jen said. Her eyes were huge in her thin little face. 'I thought it would be easier.'

'I am spreading their food here already,' Agatha spat. 'And you go wasting good grain like that? Well, if you want to take over, do so, maid. You obviously know better.'

'No, Mother, wait! I'm sorry, I was only trying to help.'

'Well, you didn't,' her mother snapped. She walked to the precious corn sack and carefully let her apron down to release the golden grains back inside it. 'If you can't think, you're no help at all.'

Jen was silent, and Agatha saw the glistening trickles at either cheek. There was no satisfaction at seeing the hurt she had caused, but neither was there any guilt. You couldn't go wasting grain.

It was then, as she strode back towards the house, that she became aware of some drama going on, up at the church. Jen heard it too, and Agatha saw her staring at the great building. Together they watched the short, stocky man talking to the priest. The man, who wore a leather jerkin over a faded green tunic, was pointing back up the road. The priest put his hands to his face as though in horror, and then there was a general movement by a small crowd in that direction, following the ashen-faced priest and the fellow who had fetched him.

'Where are they going?' Jen asked, and instinctively reached for her mother's hand. Surprisingly, this once Agatha did not give her a stern reprimand, but squeezed her hand gently. Then, the two slowly trailed after the others.

Jen knew that this was evil tidings. It was there in the way that the priest walked, as though bludgeoned with bad news. She felt sorry for him.

They were at the woods now, and Jen recognised this as a place where her father used to bring her to collect wood in the autumn. They would coppice the trees, taking the spare twigs as bundled faggots for the fire, while the long boughs would be used for renewing buildings, for tool handles, or for carving into bowls or spoons. This was one of her father's favourite places, she knew. Here, he could find some peace from her mother's endless nagging.

There were three men standing at the edge of a little clearing. Jen knew them from the vill. They, and the other men and women, were looking at her with sorrowful eyes. Jen could scarcely breathe. She was paralysed with dread.

. . . And then time moved on and she saw the blood, the axe – still embedded – and then she was on her knees and there was a roaring sound in her ears as she reached out to her father to try to console him . . . and then the noise reached a peak and was stilled, as the girl toppled forwards and knew no more.

Tavern two miles west of Broadway

John of Shulton strode into the ale-house with every bone in his body telling him that it was likely to be a trap. Even the scab of his wound was burning as though in warning.

He had hated deserting Paul's body. Paul and he had been together from the days when they had joined Despenser's household. At least he had managed to find a priest. The man took his money and swore that Paul would receive a full Christian burial. It was enough for John.

The ale-house had one long chamber. A fire smouldered in the hearth in the middle of the room, and over to the far right was a little alcove in which a man stood and served cider from a barrel. About the fire was a big group of men huddled together. He saw a flash of metal, and felt his hackles rise, then a hood was cast back and relief swamped him as he recognised Stephen Dunheved, beside him Frere Thomas.

He nodded to the other men as he approached: William, son of William Aylmer, John Boteler, Sir Edmund Gascelin, and more – all men who had sworn to free the King.

'Where is Paul?' Frere Thomas asked.

'Dead. I did all I . . . I did all I could,' John said. He saw that gaping wound, the blood . . . and then he saw Sir Jevan's face again. It sent a ripple of hatred through his body.

'I am truly sorry,' Thomas said softly. 'I shall pray for him. It was a terrible slaughter in that castle.'

'It was a disaster,' Stephen corrected. 'We were so close, but the failure was mine. All mine!'

'Brother, we've been through this before,' Thomas said.

'And I'll go over it all many times again, I expect. It *was* my fault: I was late. If only I had reached the castle sooner, the weapons would have been there and ready.'

John dragged up a stool and seated himself. 'Perhaps. And perhaps not. We'll never know.'

Stephen nodded, staring at the ground. 'What can we do?'

Thomas leaned forward and slapped his face with his open hand, hissing, 'Bestir yourself! This is not some game in which we can afford ourselves the luxury of defeat. We have a duty to complete our work!'

Stephen looked at his brother, then at the others, and the despair in his eyes was, to John, almost as shocking as Paul's death. It was unlike Stephen Dunheved to admit to failure.

'Stephen,' he said firmly. 'If you cannot help, it would be better that you leave now.'

'You think I am a broken man?'

'Sweet Mother of God!' John cried, and leaned so close he could feel Stephen's breath on his face. 'We need resolution and determination, man! It's not your courage I doubt, it's your conviction. Do you have faith in yourself'

'You doubt me?' Stephen growled. 'When it was I who planned Kenilworth, I who determined how to free Sir Edward?'

'He needs us to be strong, Stephen. Not flinching at shadows.'

'I will not flinch.'

'Good.' Thomas leaned back. 'Are we satisfied? My brother and I will perform our part.'

John was content with Stephen's resolve, but now he glanced about him. 'We need more men. Look at us – we are hardly enough to rob a child of a toy.'

'We are dedicated,' Sir Edmund said loftily.

'Yes, but that doesn't mean we can survive against a hundred men at once. Kenilworth will not be easy to break into a second time – not without surprise on our side,' John pointed out.

'This is true.' Thomas was downcast, his voice quieter.

John set his jaw. 'Come, fellows. Perhaps we should all take our leave and agree to meet again when we are likely to have more—'

He was cut off by Sir Edmund, who stared into the fire and prodded the logs with his dagger as he said, 'According to rumour about Gloucester, Lord Thomas of Berkeley is gathering a force to fetch the King.'

'You think he'll have the King taken from Kenilworth?' Thomas said.

'I've heard Sir Roger Mortimer is in Wales, close to Berkeley. If you were he, would you want King Edward held at Kenilworth by your rival or held under the control of your own son-in-law?'

'How quickly could we gather our forces?' Stephen Dunheved asked his brother.

'They are scattered, but we could bring fifty or more together,' Thomas said, frowning. 'It would not be enough.'

'No,' Sir Edmund said. 'If we make an assault on Lord Thomas's party, the King would be in danger.'

'You think they'd kill him?' Stephen said. He gave a short laugh. 'Do you think they'd dare?'

Sir Edmund looked at him coolly. 'If I held a hostage, and was attacked, *I* would kill the hostage. Certainly, Lord Thomas would kill the King and any companions with him as a matter of necessity. So if we don't have enough men to ensure success, we should hold back until we do.'

'Until they're in Berkeley, you mean?' Stephen spat. 'Another castle? No, I say we attack while they are on the road.'

'What does your brother say?'

Frere Thomas said, 'I agree with Stephen. If there is the possibility of a successful ambush, we should exploit it. If we can, I would avoid assaulting another castle. At Kenilworth we had men inside to help us, and still things went awry. It was a miracle more of us did not die.'

Sir Edmund snorted, leaning back in his seat.

'You wish to add to your comments?' Frere Thomas said.

'I know Berkeley. The land all about there is a bog. You may be able to find a route across it, but if you do, you will not be able to run in knee-deep mud.'

'So, we take the road,' Stephen said.

'Which is the direction upon which all their artillery and bows will be concentrated. You'd not get within a matter of yards.'

'What would you suggest then, Sir Edmund?' Frere Thomas asked quietly.

'Strategems,' the knight said, leaning forward again. He set his elbows on his knees and looked at each of the men in turn. 'Berkeley is being renovated. When Despenser despoiled it, he did a good job. They're having to rebuild walls and towers. They have need of workmen.'

Frere Thomas stared at him. 'You are sure?'

'At Kenilworth we had a few inside on one day. All depended on the success of that one day. At Berkeley, labourers and

191

masons will be welcomed inside. Position your men, and then mount your assault. If we've enough men inside to raise hell, this time they won't be able to stop us.'

'We will need more comrades,' Stephen said.

Sir Edmund nodded. 'Earl Donald of Mar. He's devoted to Sir Edward of Caernarfon. With forces like his, Berkeley will fall.'

Frere Thomas looked around him. He felt a warm glow of appreciation for this rough knight. Like all experienced warriors, Sir Edmund was shrewd. The men nodded their assent, and Frere Thomas urged them to bend their heads while he spoke a short prayer for success.

'We ask this not for ourselves, Good Lord, but for the safety of Your son, Your anointed King, Edward of Caernarfon,' he finished, and began the *Pater Noster*.

John found his attention wavering. He looked about at the other men, and knew that none of them felt the same dread as him. Sir Edmund had called the King by his demeaned title, merely 'Sir Edward of Caernarfon', and it seemed like a bad omen. There was a coldness in his belly – the certainty that soon he would be with Paul.

The blackfriar finished: '*Amen*. Godspeed you all. Be careful, be cautious – and be suspicious of all men whom you do not know. And never forget, this is the work of God, and He demands our best efforts to ensure success.'

John nodded, and rose with the others. They began to filter from the chamber, and he was about to follow them when he felt Frere Thomas's hand on his arm.

'A moment, my son.'

Thomas waited until the room was emptied before sitting at John's side. He spoke quietly.

'This will be a difficult time for us. The King deserves our loyalty, but it will be troublesome to save him when there are so many ranged against us. It is truly in God's hands, not ours, as to whether we succeed or not.'

'I will do all I may,' John said. He looked down at the floor, missing Paul. It was Paul in whom he had always placed most trust, and to think that he was dead, that he could never again utter those barbed remarks, never give John that twisted smile – and never issue that shriek of terrifying blood-lust as he rushed headlong into battle . . . It left John feeling empty. The organ on which he depended for love and loyalty appeared to have shrivelled and died within his breast.

'You mourn Paul. I liked him, but it was always clear that he was your companion.'

'He was my constant friend,' John sighed.

'But he is dead. Are you committed to our task?'

'I will do all I may,' John repeated.

'Then there is something which you alone can do.'

'Me, Frere? I will ask all my followers to join us, of course, but I do not see what more—'

'We need a man on the inside of the party escorting our King. A man who can join with them.'

John frowned. 'How?'

'You must ride to Berkeley and offer your services. They will ask whence you came, and you can tell them all the truth, that you came from near Dunhead, that you are an experienced man-at-arms, and that you need a new lord since your old master has died.'

'Why would they take me?'

'Because there is no taint of dishonour or felony about you. You are the perfect man to join them. Ride with them, my friend, and bring the King back with you. With luck you shall return by way of Gloucester, and that means you may stop at

Llantony-next-Gloucester for a night. The Lord Berkeley is fond of the priory, so you should find that easy.'

'There is one problem,' John said. 'At the castle gate I saw Sir Jevan de Bromfield.'

'You know him?'

'He is a Lancaster man. Paul and I fought with him before. He may remember me.'

Frere Thomas reassured him. 'The Lord de Berkeley is taking our King from the men of Lancaster. They won't want one of Lancaster's men on the journey. Keep from him while at Kenilworth, and you will be safe.'

John nodded. Fatalism overwhelmed him. The Dominican might be right. If not, well, John would try to escape if he could.

'There is a man at the priory . . .' Thomas continued, and began to speak quietly of the man that John must meet.

CHAPTER TWENTY-TWO

Broadway

Dolwyn of Guildford led the horse through and past Broadway at the earliest moment. Up before dawn, he had made sure that the beast was harnessed and ready before he had eaten anything, and then he set off with a hunk of bread ready to satisfy his hunger as he walked.

The roads here were quite level and easy. There was a steady rise coming, he could see, but for all that he was content that his route was moderately fast. Much better than other parts of the country where the roads were constantly climbing or falling. With a horse and cart, leading the brute down a steep gradient was as bad as trying to make the animal climb. Carts were ungainly vehicles at the best of times. With a slow, old or recalcitrant horse in the shafts, they became a torment.

He had found the beast hobbled a short way from the cart, and it took him little time to have it in the shafts and ready. It would be foolish in the extreme to hang around, and he was on the road again in short order, hurrying on past Willersey and heading on down the road. He could see the church, the steeple rising from a mist, and he made a broad sweep around it, to avoid any early risers. He kept a wary eye on the road ahead, but a more careful watch on the road behind: that, he knew, was the direction any danger would come from.

He heard the first riders from Willersey before noon. A group of three horses galloping down the next road, their hooves striking sparks from the stones. At the sound, he ducked down, eyes scanning the hedges and the lane up behind him in case it was a posse. He had deliberately chosen these little grassy tracks, rather than a busier road. Speed had been sacrificed for concealment.

The riders were away past him in a flash, and he rested for a while, staring after them. They had been quick. He had hoped to get further from the crime before a posse had formed. He would obviously have to be very careful.

Pebworth

They were up long before Matteo was ready. He yawned and stretched when he was on his mount, but was glad that he had made time to speak with Dolwyn.

'Master Bardi?'

Matteo turned to see Alured at his side, walking along at Matteo's speed. 'Yes?'

'You were with Dolwyn a long time, Master Bardi.'

'What of it?'

'I was worried about you.'

'You had no need to worry,' Matteo said, feeling happier than he had in a long time. Sir Edward of Caernarfon had been glad of the letter, Dolwyn had told him, and had burned it in his presence, so there was nothing to connect the Bardi to him. If he should ever become King again, he would know that the House of Bardi had supported him; while if he failed, the family were safe.

In fact, there was only one connection to the Bardi from Sir Edward, and that was Dolwyn himself.

But Matteo did not think that Dolwyn was a risk.

Willersey

The house was neat, he had to give Agatha that, Father Luke thought as he rapped on the door. It was a good cruck house, built when Ham's father had been young. The wattle and daub was old but it had stood up well, thanks to Ham's annual lime-washing of the walls.

'Agatha, how is Jen?' he asked as he ducked under the lintel and peered about him in the gloom. The little girl had been brought home from the scene of her father's murder, and put to bed in a fainting fit.

Agatha was seated by her daughter's palliasse, from where she could reach the fire and stir some thickened pottage, and she stared at him, her features pale. 'What do you want?'

'I came to see how you were,' he said earnestly.

There was no reciprocal warmth in her eyes, he saw, only a deep suspicion – as if she expected him to try to rape her or rob her. He was, after all, the man who had led her husband from the vill and to his death.

'Oh really?' she asked, her tone silky, but venomous.

'I wished to console you both. Please, I should like to help you, mistress. Perhaps we can pray together?'

'You think I'd ever touch your hand again, Priest?' she screeched. 'You lied to me about my poor Ham. You said he'd run away, and yet he came back to me! He came all the way back to me!' She started to sob, and the girl whimpered in her sleep.

'Mistress, calm yourself.'

'It was me, wasn't it?' she said with a low, quiet certainty. 'It was because everyone thinks me a cold, unfeeling cow who doesn't care for anyone. You believed it too, didn't you? You thought he would do anything to run away from me. That was it. You reckoned he'd found some whore and chose to stay with her than coming home to me. But he loved me. And I loved him. He was mine – and now he's dead.'

'The man who did this will be found.' Father Luke promised. He had taken a step back against her sudden outburst, and now he tried to introduce a calming note. 'Mistress, you are overwrought. You should rest, let someone help you and young Jen.'

'They tried. Three maids have been here,' Agatha said, placing a cool cloth over Jen's brow, 'but I won't have them. She is my little girl, and I will look after her. Just as I shall see to my husband's body. I will clean him and clothe him in his winding sheet as a widow should. No one else.'

'The coroner has been sent for. With luck he will be here in the morning,' Father Luke said.

'So? You mean someone may be found?'

'We will do all we can.'

She sighed, the emotion of the morning taking its toll. 'Just bring my cart. I'll have to see to the horse before the poor thing collapses. At least it's not cold up there.'

The look on Father Luke's face made her scowl. 'What now?'

'Mistress, whoever killed Ham must have taken the cart. I'm sorry.'

'No, that cannot be!' she declared, wringing her hands. 'It *must* be there.'

'Perhaps he lost it on his way here,' Luke suggested. 'He could have had it stolen on the road.'

'No! The axe – that was the one he kept on his cart.' Agatha shuddered. 'It must still be up there.'

'I am very sorry,' Luke said.

'Stop saying that! It is there, it must be.' Her breast heaved with dry sobs. 'Oh, God. What will become of us?'

The priest knew that the cart would have guaranteed an income for this widow and her daughter. With Despenser's money, he could have helped them both so much. Thinking of Jen, he glanced down at the girl on the palliasse, and to his shock he realised that she was wide awake and listening.

'I am scared,' Jen whispered. Her eyes were deep wells of despair and fear as she looked up at him.

He tried to imagine how terrible it must be, to lose a father at such a tender age, and by such violent means. 'There is no need to be,' he said gently. 'You will be safe here.'

Jen looked up and gripped his hand. 'I want my father back,' she wept.

And the priest knew that no words of his could comfort her.

CHAPTER TWENTY-THREE

Exeter

'You want me to go with you *where*?' Simon said. 'No. Absolutely not!'

The older man sat back and leaned against the wall. 'Come, Bailiff, it is not so far as your journey to France last year. You can easily travel that distance.'

'I am not going anywhere,' Simon asserted. 'It's ridiculous! I've only just got back to my home after all the troubles last year, and you want me to head off with you again now?'

'Not me alone. It's a small force, but there are a few other fellows to ride with us. I swear I shall return you here to your home as soon as the King's father is safely ensconced in his new home.'

'And where will that be?' Simon demanded bitterly. 'Halfway to Scotland? I don't want to ride all the way to Kenilworth only to take the King's father on a long journey north!'

'We won't be going north from there, I promise you,' Sir Richard said smoothly. 'Hah! Can you see *me* travelling all that way? Still, we have been asked to go and there's not much we can do about it.'

Hugh had walked in now, and stood in the corner of the room with a dour expression on his face, as was his wont. Simon threw him a look. 'And what about *you*? I thought I told you to stay and guard the house. Dear heaven, you haven't left that fool Rob alone, have you?'

'Old Penny has gone to stay there with him,' Hugh muttered.

'Penny, eh?' A local man, Penny was a farmer to his fingertips – so he would know all the tasks Rob should be doing. And he was a brawny fellow, too, more than capable of protecting the place.

'So, Simon, we shall have to leave in the morning.'

'I cannot leave my wife again.'

Margaret clucked her tongue. The thought of Simon riding away had filled her with distress when Sir Richard had first mentioned it, but now she took a deep breath. 'Husband, please do not worry about me. I am perfectly content to be in Devon again. If Edith does not object, nor her husband, I will stay here with them until your return. It would be good for me to spend time with our grandson, and I may be able to help Edith, too.'

'Would you, Mother? That would be wonderful,' Edith said.

Simon scowled, eyeing them both suspiciously. Margaret smiled at him; it was plain enough that she would be overjoyed to remain here longer. He threw a look at Sir Richard. 'I don't know . . .'

His wife had suffered badly last year. He had been separated from her then, and the result had been a near disastrous brain-fever. She had survived the Siege of the Tower of London, only to become enclosed in Bristol as the Queen's men encircled the city, and Simon's departure so soon afterwards had weakened her. It had taken all this time, four months, to get her back to her usual good health.

'I am perfectly well now,' she told him. 'Now I know that Edith and Henry are fine – well, that eases my mind. As it should yours, too. You go and help Sir Richard. You don't want to refuse to obey the new King, do you?'

'This is truly a request from the new King?'

'Yes.' Sir Richard lowered his voice. 'I think he suspects that his father could be in danger, were the party sent to guard him to be chosen by another. There are many who might seek to have Sir Edward permanently removed, if you see what I mean.'

'Yes, I do.' Simon stared at the floor, thinking it all through. Then he made his decision. 'Very well. I'd best join you. Hugh, you will come with me. Since you've developed a taste for travelling, even when you've been told to stay at the house, you can join us on the ride to Kenilworth.'

Hugh said nothing. His dark glower spoke for him.

Morrow of the Feast of the Annunciation[1]

Exeter

The next morning was one of those perfect March days in which the world appears a better, kinder place. Margaret woke in the chamber below her daughter's solar to the sound of her grandchild demanding milk, beside a gently snoring Simon, and smiled at his relaxed face.

It was good to see him so at ease. In the last year he had been kept away from their home, and the vile Sir Hugh le Despenser

1 26 March 1327

had given both Simon and Margaret great heartache. He had cost them their new home in Lydford, he had almost cost them their daughter, and all for the sake of his ambitions.

When she thought of how close Simon had come to breaking down in Bristol, she shuddered. To have seen her strong, reliable husband nearly in tears, was shocking. She remembered his face as he stammered, his drawn features, his sudden, apparent old age. At the time it had scared her.

No longer. From the unglazed window she could hear birds singing merrily. The sunlight was already bright, and when she got up and walked to the window, she could see the sky was perfectly clear.

Simon snored again as she pulled on a tunic. She went to kiss him, and smelled the sour odour of stale wine. He and Sir Richard had sealed their compact last night when Simon finally gave in and agreed to join the knight. It was always an error, she knew, for Simon to drink with Sir Richard. The man had a stomach that might have been constructed by an armourer.

The baby was giving that sobbing cry that always sounded to her as though he was demanding '*Mi-i-i-ilk*' over and over again. It had been a call she had adored with her own babes, because it meant she was needed. Those moments were all too fleeting.

Children grew so swiftly. It seemed only weeks since Edith was a gangly little girl of seven or eight, and yet here she was now, a woman of seventeen, with a husband and her own child. The time flew past, and before a woman knew it, her children were old enough to lead their own lives, and the task of the mother was done.

Margaret knew that at her age many other mothers would be dead already, many of them in childbirth. At almost thirty-six, she too could still be killed by another baby, but she considered the likelihood with equanimity. There was no point in becoming disturbed by death. All a woman could do was work for her family and place her faith in God.

Leaving the solar, she walked through to the parlour, and found a grim-faced Sir Richard poking the fire.

He looked up. 'Morning, mistress. That wench is no good at lighting a fire. When I was a lad, it was the first thing you were taught: how to make a fire so your lord could have a hot drink. Now, the youngsters seem to think that all they need do is lay a few twigs and show them a spark, and the fire will take hold, just like that. Hah!'

'How is your head?'

'Me head?' He looked up with such obvious bafflement that she had to laugh.

'My husband is snoring still, and I doubt not that when he wakes he will be like a bear at the baiting. How much did you drink?'

Sir Richard blinked and set his head to one side as he calculated. 'Oh, I don't know . . . Perhaps a pair of quarts of wine, but then the maid told us that supplies were low and begged us to try her ale. It was good, too,' he added reflectively. 'I could do with some of that now. Oh, and there was some cider. A little harsh, that was. I needed another ale to take away the taste.'

'You shared all that?'

'Shared?' he repeated, an expression of bemusement on his face. 'No: *each*, me dear.'

She eyed him with renewed respect. For a man to drink so much and be able to wake the following morning was, she felt, rather admirable.

'You needn't worry about your husband, Madame Puttock,' he said, and she was about to protest that she was not concerned, merely deciding to leave him to sleep off his hangover, when

Sir Richard nodded seriously and continued, 'I'll look after him.'

'I am most grateful,' she said quietly, trying to control the urge to giggle. If there was one man whom Simon would not wish to have looking after his interests, it was this one, she felt sure.

Simon, she knew, would feel like death on waking.

Near Broadway

John sat up with a jerk, staring wildly about. In his dreams, he had been enjoying a drinking session in an ale-house in London with Paul, a little before the sudden rise of the London mob, and waking here under the branches of an elm left him feeling completely disorientated.

The memory of that dream stayed with him. All had been on tenterhooks at the time. The knowledge that Queen Isabella was raising a host of men from Hainault was enough to make all the men of Sir Hugh le Despenser's household anxious. Many were the discussions about their future prospects.

In the ale-house, John had been sitting and drinking by the fire with Paul, and the men around them were singing and laughing, teasing the three wenches serving ale while trying to negotiate for their company. One woman was soon dallying in the farther corner of the inn with a guard, and Paul eyed her sadly.

'What is it?' John had asked. 'There are other women.'

'No, it's not that,' Paul had answered. 'I just feel that our best times are past.'

'You feel all you want,' John had responded. 'I've plenty of time left in me, mate!'

'Aye, me too,' Paul chuckled, and the two knocked their mazers together and drank. But later, John had seen Paul staring into the fire, and now, after reliving those moments in his dream, he wondered whether his old companion had been granted a vision of the future and his own painful death.

John stood, and draped his blanket over a low branch to dry off the dew while he tidied his camp and began to pack his goods. Thirsty, he wandered to the little stream and filled his skin, drinking enough to assuage his thirst, then topping it up. He opened his saddle-pack and took out a loaf, which he broke in two. Half went into the pack for his lunch, and he took a bite from the other, squatting by his fire of the night before while he took a stick and began to scrape at the ground.

He had found a rabbit in a snare late last night. Some poacher had set a loose twine loop in a rabbit track, and no doubt intended to return later to collect it. John had got there first. He had paunched and cleaned it, then wrapped it in some large leaves and set it in the earth before lighting his fire over it, a little to one side. Loosening it from the soil now, he unwrapped the leaves and pulled off a hindleg. It was a little tough and dry, but tasted good, and he enjoyed the rest of his meal. With another draught of water in his belly, and the remainder of his piece of bread, he felt fit for the day.

Saddling his horse, he rode north. This was the time of day he knew he would miss Paul the most. It was strange, perhaps, because neither was communicative at such an hour, but it was that very companionable silence that he missed now. They could be up and break camp, then ride all morning without speaking, and yet enjoy each other's friendship as much as another man might enjoy a two-hour conversation.

His thoughts were still on Paul as he jogged along the lane towards Broadway.

After the arrival of the Queen, all had changed. Before, they had led a life of relative peace, enjoying Despenser's largesse. They had food and drink, good clothes, the best arms and armour . . . But when the Queen's forces landed, life had become a sudden explosion of urgent travel. First they had ridden to Bristol, and formed part of the last guard that went with the King to Wales. There they had been set free of their oaths. It was better that way. They had missed the last desperate days: the flight to Caerphilly, thence to Neath and capture. The humiliation of Despenser's execution.

John had hoped that there would be peace. He knew that his master had ruled with a determined avarice that appalled many, and alienated the Queen from him. But now Sir Hugh was dead, it seemed the Queen herself was taking on his role. Before, there had been an uprising of men who had been impoverished by the King and Despenser; now there was a force of disinherited whose sole crime was that they had remained loyal to Despenser. It was the replacement of one injustice with another.

He wondered whether the land could be ruled more justly.

Behind him there was a metallic clatter. It sounded like a stone under a horseshoe, and he turned around to stare, all thoughts of dreams and his friend flown in an instant.

Three men were trotting towards him, and the man in the front was the one knight he did not want to meet: Sir Jevan de Bromfield.

John pulled his horse's head round, raked his spurs down the brute's flanks and thundered off through the trees as fast as his steed could carry him.

Furnshill

Baldwin woke to the feeling of cold steel under his left armpit.

It was one of the easiest ways to kill a man. A sword thrust in quickly would meet little resistance as it pierced the lungs, filling them with blood so the victim drowned; if fortunate, the blade might also strike the heart and stop it. A fast death, and a kind one.

Baldwin was wide awake in an instant. He was in a field near Paris, and the men standing about him were all men-at-arms for the French King. The sword blade was being pressed gently into his flesh, but for some reason it wouldn't penetrate . . . He reached through the fog of sleep to find he was not in France but in his own bed, in Furnshill – and the hideous wet weapon was Wolf's nose.

'Get off, you stupid brute!' he exclaimed, bringing his arm down to cover the soggy patch where the dog had nudged him. 'Go and bother Edgar or Wat – they should feed you.'

He kissed Jeanne's neck and rose from his bed. For all his disgust at being woken in such a manner, he was pleased to be up and about. The weather looked fine and dry as he pulled on a chemise and pair of hosen before taking up his new sword and walking down the stairs and out to the grassy area before his house.

While a Templar, he had learned the importance of weapon training and keeping fit. One of the keys to the Order's fighting brilliance was the training that all the knights and sergeants underwent. Rather than being a loose accumulation of men gathered together for a fight in which few had any interest other than serving their liege lords, the Order provided a force of men who were used to fighting together in a compact unit, each seeing to the defence of the others, riding in tight formation, wheeling on the command, galloping in unison, and using specific martial skills that had proven themselves over time. The Templars were unbeatable under most conditions because of this emphasis on preparation.

Drawing the sword, Baldwin stood with his legs apart. And then began the mock-battle which he underwent every day. It was a series of simple routines, designed to test every muscle in his upper body, reminding him of all the possible attacks, and how to block, parry or avoid each. It was as much a part of him as his beard, this daily ritual, and soon he could feel the blood coursing faster through his veins.

However, today there was a problem which affected his movements and a strange dullness in his right ear, put his balance off: it reminded him of when he had been swimming, and occasionally water would enter his ear and remain there until he tipped his head to the side, when he would find his hearing restored. But today, although he pressed his little finger into the hole and tried to scrape out whatever might be causing the blockage, nothing could move it.

He shook his head and determined to continue with his training. When he'd finished, he went back to the house, feeling disquieted.

'You look as though something is unsettling you, sir,' his servant of almost thirty years observed. Edgar was a tall man, suave and elegant, and when the mood took him, as lethal as a viper.

'It's my ear. I can barely hear,' Baldwin said pensively. 'I feel as if I have gone deaf overnight.'

'Perhaps you have, sir.'

'Why should I suddenly lose my hearing?' Baldwin scoffed. 'There is no reason for it.'

'How often did you fight in the lists? In how many battles did you get belaboured about the head with a sword or mace? The ringing of an axe on a helmet could deaden your hearing.'

'But no one has hit me in recent years,' Baldwin pointed out. 'No, it must just be something stuck in there.'

Edgar agreed to investigate for him, and spent some while with a candle held dangerously close to Baldwin's ear, peering into it, but when the knight heard the crackle of hair singeing, he quickly decided to halt that form of enquiry.

'When do you leave, Sir Baldwin?' Edgar asked.

'As soon as I may,' Baldwin replied. 'The old King will not wish to have matters delayed any longer than necessary, in case they choose to move him without us there.'

'Would they dare? If he has expressed a desire to have you with him . . .'

'They do not treat him with any respect,' Baldwin said shortly. 'And there is an urgency now because of the attack on the castle. Mortimer will be terrified that the next attack might succeed.'

'It is a terrible place, Kenilworth Castle,' Edgar mused. 'I'm astonished that a raid managed to storm it.'

'I doubt they reached far inside the place,' Baldwin said. 'From what I have heard, the party broke into the main gate, but did not succeed in getting further. No, that is not what concerns me. It is the idea of taking the King from Kenilworth to Berkeley. On that long road, it would be a great deal easier for a group of men to break through a circle of guards and get to him.'

'And then what?'

'That is what I wonder. Were they there to rescue him, as so many reckon? Or were they there to kill him. Mortimer might well like to remove this constitutional embarrassment. When else has there been a King and that King's father, both alive? The usual route to kingship is for the son to inherit his realm, but this poor father was forced to surrender his crown.'

'What of it?'

'Simply this, Edgar,' Baldwin said with feeling. 'I do not know the law, but I daresay that it will prove to be a very fine point, as to whether a King who was forced to relinquish his crown can do so. If God installed him and saw him anointed with oil in the manner that He has decreed, which man has the right or authority to gainsay God?'

'And so?'

'Sir Roger Mortimer is not a man who likes to have loose threads lying about ready to be picked at,' Baldwin said. 'The old King is one such thread, and an impediment to the new King.'

'So you will go?'

'I must. I still hold my vow to the King to be in force. I made that oath before God, and I will not be forsworn.'

Edgar nodded. 'In that case, I will come too.'

'No, old friend,' Baldwin smiled. 'I must have you here to protect Jeanne and the family while I am gone. And in any case, you have your own family to consider.'

'Sir Baldwin, for one thing my family is safe enough. I remained here against my better judgement when you rode off last year, and a poor show it was. If I had been with you, you would not have been struck down and almost killed.'

'I doubt whether—'

'I shall not make the same error again.'

'What of my wife, Edgar? I need you here to see to her safety.'

'I think that is unnecessary.'

'*I* will decide what is needful in my own house,' Baldwin stated.

His wife's voice cut across his words as she walked towards him. 'No, Baldwin. This time it is my choice. And I will not be gainsaid.'

CHAPTER TWENTY-FOUR

Exeter

Margaret Puttock's prediction was all too accurate, sadly.

Simon came awake very slowly. His eyes were gummy and sore, and when he finally opened them it felt as though sawdust was trapped beneath the lids.

'Bloody knight,' he muttered to himself as he sat on the edge of the bed and paused, legs on the floor. After dealing with Sir Richard de Welles over some years, Simon could quickly evaluate the level of his poisoning. This was not so bad as that time in Exeter when he had immediately been forced to spew on waking . . . He winced at the taste of bile in his throat, and got up and walked to the window. On the floor beside it he had placed a little jug of ale the night before. It was soured now, but at least it took away the flavour from his mouth as he gargled and spat out of the window, and then swallowed a good mouthful.

He had first met Sir Richard in Dartmouth, where the man appeared to know everything about the town, pointing out where the best brothels and ale-houses had stood in his youth. The knight had always appeared to be in the most deplorably robust health – completely immune to the after-effects of excess wine or ale. But for all that Simon would often regret the day they had met, Sir Richard was a truly kind, compassionate man who had, early on in life, married a woman whom he adored, and then been forced to see her die. Perhaps that was why he had such an iron constitution, Simon thought: he had learned to drink heavily on his own after his wife died.

'How are you, Bailiff?' Sir Richard asked now, marching into his chamber.

'Please,' Simon said with a pained look. He put his hand to where it felt as though his brain might explode, and was glad to see his Meg stand and fetch him a goblet of wine.

At breakfast, Sir Richard picked up a chicken thigh and slurped at the meat, sucking the bones dry and licking at his fingers as he went. He smiled at Simon, who essayed a weakly grin in return, before pulling apart a large slice of bread and shoving it into his mouth, easing its passage down his throat with a gulp of red wine. 'Not bad, this,' he said. 'So, Simon, if you can have a bit of something to break your fast, we'd best be off.'

'What?'

'To Kenilworth. We have to get a move on, eh?'

Simon winced and burped carefully. 'There's no hurry, is there?' he said queasily. 'How about tomorrow?'

'Hah! So your head is hurting then – eh, Bailiff? No, seriously, old friend, we should be on our way as soon as we can. Our path is a long one, so it's best we get started now.'

'But I'm not ready!'

'You'll soon be ready when you get some fresh air in your

lungs, man. That and some food is all you need.' The knight smiled with a demon's amiability.

'Yes,' Simon whispered. He didn't nod. His head hurt too much.

Near Broadway

John stopped his horse as soon as he was convinced he had lost his pursuers. The woods here were dangerous to ride in at speed. After spotting Sir Jevan de Bromfield, he had pelted through the trees at full gallop, bent so low over his mount's neck that the saddle crupper had stuck in his belly. Behind him he knew that the other three were not gaining, but neither were they slackening. It was only when he saw ahead a low bank of holly bushes, that he hoped he might be able to lose one or two of them, and he had jerked the reins right at the last minute. In a moment he was flung almost from the saddle as the great beast hurtled off in a new direction, and he risked a quick glance behind him. He saw that one rider had been thrown by the suddenness of his manoeuvre, and gave a grin of savage delight to hear the scream of pain as the man fell into the thorny leaves.

Then he was facing forward again. Just then, his beast put a foot into a ditch. It could have snapped his leg like a dry twig, but somehow the magnificent animal recovered and set off along the road. Still, when John looked back, he saw that the first man was much closer, and it was Sir Jevan himself.

Sir Jevan de Bromfield: it was a name to make a man shiver. He was the dedicated servant of the last Earl of Lancaster, before King Edward II had him executed, and he hated all the followers of Despenser as much as his master had.

Sir Jevan had seen John at Kenilworth. And he would kill him if he caught him. It was as simple, and as deadly, as that.

Charlton Abbots

Dolwyn felt as though he was almost safe. There had been no sign of any pursuit since that first posse, and he wondered whether his pursuers had given up. After all, in these difficult and fearful times, there were many who deserved punishment more than him to seek.

He pulled the reins and the brute finally began to move again. The animal appeared to have made up his mind that he disliked Dolwyn and wished nothing so much as to leave the road and crop the grass. When Dolwyn pulled, the horse had taken to setting his ears flat back on his head and whinnying angrily. It took three firm cuffs about the head to make the animal obey him, and then only because he kept a firm hold of the reins.

It was a short while after this, still about the middle of the morning, when he heard a horse trotting towards him. Dolwyn was on a grassy track that was only just wide enough for the cart, and as soon as he heard the hooves approaching, he knew he would soon be in trouble.

'You! Have you seen three men-at-arms here today?'

The man was younger than Dolwyn, and he was dressed in a pale green-coloured tunic with a red cloak at his shoulders. He was sitting astride a huge grey, who pranced and prodded at the ground as the man watched Dolwyn suspiciously. His side had been injured, Dolwyn could see. The material of his tunic was rent, and there was a stain about it, as though he had bled there profusely a little while ago.

'Why?' Dolwyn asked. He let his head drop, and spoke sullenly like a villein who resented being questioned.

'Answer me, churl!'

'No.'

The knight nodded, but absently. Now he was looking at the cart closely. 'Where are you going?'

'Goin' 'ome,' Dolwyn said. 'Back to Gloucester.'

'Where did you find this cart, fellow?'

Dolwyn scowled. 'Why?' he said again. 'I've 'ad this for years.'

'Years, eh? That is curious: this cart is like a friend's whom . . . I saw this only recently, at Kenilworth. Where did you get it?'

'I said I've 'ad it years,' Dolwyn repeatedly sullenly.

'I heard you,' the man said, drawing his sword. 'But I don't believe you. It is what all felons would say.' He was staring at the bed of the cart. 'What do you carry?'

'Usual rubbish.'

'Show me!'

Dolwyn looked up at him. The rider may have been injured, and did appear to be favouring his right side, but he was yet on a fleet horse, and Dolwyn could not hope to outrun that. Commonsense said he should be as gracious as the situation allowed. Accordingly he imitated a peasant with a grievance, but stood back and allowed the man to investigate the cart.

Still on his horse, the fellow poked about with his sword's point, lifting the blankets and tapping the two perry barrels. 'What else do you have in there?'

'Perry.'

'I didn't mean the barrels, man. What else is there here?'

'That is it, sir. I'm only a wanderin' tranter,' Dolwyn whined.

'Really?' The fellow stared hard at the cart and horse as though he knew them, and he was about to speak again, his eyes on the small chest that lay between the barrels, when he sighed and muttered like a man distracted, 'I have too many troubles to worry myself about this. Move aside, you fool, and let me pass!'

Dolwyn did as he was instructed, and soon he was watching the man trot off up the roadway. But when he reached the bend in the lane, the man stopped, whirled his mount about and came hurtling back up the roadway towards Dolwyn. It was only by a miracle that Dolwyn wasn't struck by the flailing hooves as the beast thundered past.

Then there was a bellow, and he turned to see three men with the badge of the Earl of Lancaster on their breasts, pounding down the roadway towards him. He rammed his back up against the cart, but the last man was almost thrown as his horse balked at the narrow gap. Snarling with rage, the man-at-arms raked his spurs along his mount's flanks, screaming abuse in his frustration, and then he slashed down at Dolwyn with his sword.

Dolwyn felt the blow like a punch. He flinched and his horse, unnerved by the man's fury, jerked onwards. The cart began to judder on sluggishly, and Dolwyn fell beneath it, rolling between the wheels, too surprised even to feel anger yet. The cart moved over him, and when he peered up, he saw that the rider was off.

'I will remember you, master,' he said through gritted teeth. In an instant it felt as if his entire flank was on fire, and he put a hand to his side, and met shredded cloth and blood. Lots of blood. He set his jaw and forced himself to his knees, then up to his feet, staring after the man riding off so swiftly.

A tall man, wearing the Earl of Lancaster's badge, smooth-shaven, with dark brown hair and green eyes set in a square face. 'Yes, I will remember you – and I'll cut your ballocks off for what you've done to me!' he swore, writhing as the pain burned at him.

Bishop's Cleeve

Senchet was already tired out. The weather had been wet and filthy for several days, but yesterday, as though to add insult to their injury, it was suddenly bright sunshine, and while the warmth was welcome after the last days of chill, the sudden dryness made their clothing chafe their throats and armpits. Senchet's rough hosen rubbed his inner thighs raw, and it was all he could do to forget the pain as he stumbled onwards.

His friend was in no better shape. Harry trudged, head hanging. He sorely missed his horse, especially now his old boots had given up the ghost. The left sole flapped pathetically with every step, and his foot was a mass of blisters. In the wet he had been more comfortable because wet mud was slick, but now dirt and stones cut and scratched his bare sole.

'Harry, we must find somewhere to rest. And get food.'

'And how do we buy food? We have no money, Senchet.'

They were in a long lane, with wheel tracks at either side forming a morass of mud with a narrow channel of grass struggling to grow in the middle. Hedges on either side with thick brambles deterred passage.

'Harry, let us just take a rest.'

With a bad grace his companion agreed, and after another slow, painful hundred yards or so they managed to find a tree that had fallen, and both could at last sit and stretch their legs.

Senchet glanced back the way they had come, then up ahead, and was struck by the gloomy conviction that they had travelled scarcely two miles since their last halt. So far, they had slept out three nights in the last four, and the result, with the cold and the rain, was that Senchet himself felt certain that he was to win little but a fever from this long tramp.

'My friend, I am thinking maybe we should have stayed back there in the town.'

'They wouldn't have let us,' Harry grunted. 'You think they'd want two men from the King's host to be hanging about the town? Any of the garrison which remained would suffer the risk of a short rope and a long drop.'

'Perhaps better that than *this*, eh?' Senchet said with an emphatic gesture at the roadway. He rubbed his brow. 'There must be a lord somewhere who needs men like us.'

'Perhaps.'

'You sound unconvinced.'

'I am. Now the war is over, the lords will send their men home. What need have they of great forces? Men cost money,' he added gloomily. 'Even the lords who distrust their neighbours will seek to disband their feudal hosts. It's spring. They want their men back in the fields, not standing in armour looking shiny.'

'We are,' Senchet observed, 'not the most desirable of men, are we? Perhaps I should return to my homeland. There may be more work there.'

Harry nodded. He wanted to rest his head, but knew he would fall asleep instantly. They must keep on going, but it was hard, very hard. He was too old for all this. Too many fights had taken their toll and his back was giving him grief – a common complaint after the years of soldiering. There were injuries, too, on his ribs and thighs, but nothing compared with the throbbing misery that was his poor leg. He dared not remove his boot for the thought of what he might find.

'Why bother,' he muttered to himself.

'It all comes down to money. I wish it grew on the trees that we might reach up and pluck what we needed.'

'Only the rich would take it.' Harry looked at his friend pityingly. 'You dream about money, but me, I'll dream about a solid meal, a warm chamber and a dry palliasse.'

'With money, you could buy them all.'

Harry shook his head. A bite of food, that was all he needed, but both finished their meagre rations two days ago. 'What I wouldn't give for a loaf of bread,' he said sadly.

'What's that?' Senchet said, alert.

From the road ahead there came a rumbling of hooves. Mingled with the squeak of leather was the clatter and rattle of metal, as of pots and pans.

The two men exchanged a look.

'*Shit!*' Harry forced himself to his feet. 'I can't run like this, Sen. You get away while you can, and leave me to them.'

'I will not leave you to the mercy of some vagabond of the roadway,' Senchet said firmly. 'Hah! You think I should give up my companionship with you so that we can both be cut down on our own? No, I prefer to make a stand together.'

Harry hissed with pain, teeth gritted, but set his hand to his sword's hilt and tested the blade. 'Come on then. Let's see what these bastards are like in a fight,' he said, and grinned weakly.

CHAPTER TWENTY-FIVE

North of Exeter

They had left by the east gate of the city on the Sidwell Road, riding out into the broad, flat expanse of farmland, and immediately turning north on the Longbrook Street, past the rows of cheap hovels scattered about, the roadside dotted with trees and little strips of fields in which the peasants were bending and working. Some stopped and watched as they rode by. Simon knew that as they passed out of the environs of Exeter, and began to ride along roads where they were strangers, there would be danger not only from outlaws but from suspicious locals as well. Many a traveller had been attacked by crowds wielding stones because his face made someone fearful. There were many primitive little vills on the way from here to Bristol.

The weather was at least clement, but although the sun shone, it meant that before long Simon was feeling the sweat soaking into the collar of his tunic. His hat was intolerably warm, and he was forced to remove it after a while, holding it in his left hand, occasionally lifting it to shield his eyes from the blazing sun as he peered ahead at the road.

It was the duty of the Keepers of the King's Peace to see to it that the verges of roadways were kept clear of all brambles, trees and shrubs, so that there should be less risk of ambushes. These roads had recently been surveyed, but it did not help Simon. He felt foul, from the soles of his sweating feet to the stickiness under his armpits. His mouth was disgusting and dry, his tongue felt woollen and revolting.

By contrast, Sir Richard was enjoying his ride. 'Magnificent weather, eh?' he trumpeted. 'What more could a man ask for in this beautiful kingdom of ours than an open road, sunshine, and the promise of a pleasant journey.'

'A bed,' Simon said, and belched acid.

Behind him, Hugh said grumpily, 'And a pot of ale.'

'Come now, Simon, Hugh. The sun has been up for an age. Only a child would wish to sleep through a day such as this. Or a poxy monk sitting in his scriptorium. No, Simon,' he said, warming to his theme, 'this is the way to live. Not hiding away in a warm room, but out in the open air.'

On any other morning, Simon would have agreed – but this day he was not inclined to support the knight. 'How far is it?' he mumbled.

'To Kenilworth? Oh, less than seventy leagues. Up to Bristol, thence to Gloucester, Evesham, and on up to the castle.'

'Seventy leagues?' Hugh asked. He had never enjoyed riding, although some years ago he had grown accustomed enough to the distances that he must cover with his master. But in recent weeks he had not travelled so widely, and it was plain from his expression that he would have been happy not to have to renew his acquaintance with this saddle.

'Two hundred and ten miles,' Sir Richard said. He lolled back against the cantle and sighed happily. 'And if it's all as pleasant as this, we shall have a wonderful time. Tell me, Simon, did I ever tell you the joke about the man who borrowed a horse? Eh? He—'

'Yes, I think you did tell me.'

'Ah, well, then, Hugh, you will like this: the man spoke to the stableowner and paid for a beast, and the stableman said, "You are a very clever man to pick that fellow. It's the best in my stable. You must be like Ben Bakere".

' "Who?" asked the man.

' "Ben Bakere. If he went to a stable, he always picked the best mount. He had an infallible eye, that man."

' "Oh," said the man.

' "Yes, and if he went to the wine merchants, he always got the best wine. A perfect nose."

' "Oh," said the man.

' "If he negotiated to buy hay, he always got the best deal. If he needed harnesses, he could find the best quality at the finest price. He was clever, was Ben Bakere. The cleverest man who ever lived in jolly old England. The wisest, shrewdest, kindest and pleasantest."

' "You said 'was' – has he moved away?"

' "No, he died."

' "I'm sorry. It's hard to lose a friend," the man said.'

Sir Richard chuckled richly, glancing at Simon to ensure he appreciated the full perfection of the tale.

' "Friend? he's no friend to me."

' "But from what you said, I thought he was a close friend?"

' "No. I never met him. But I married his damned widow." Ha! You understand, eh? Talking about his wife's first husband, you see?' And the good knight laughed without affectation, delighted with the simplicity of the joke.

223

Simon smiled thinly. Seventy leagues of this . . . His headache grew suddenly much worse.

Bishop's Cleeve

The noise grew, and Senchet was aware of the hair on the back of his neck standing up on end. There was still no sign of the source. He glanced at Harry, and the two men edged closer together.

'Senchet,' Harry said quietly. 'I've not said it before, but I've been glad of your company.'

'Friend Harry, I have been grateful for your companionship also.' Senchet pulled his sword out with a slow slithering of metal. 'I do not like this phantasm, though. How does a man fight with a wraith? It is not to be borne.'

'It's no wraith,' Harry said suddenly, and pointed.

There, before them, a cart with one tired nag pulling it, crossed the road.

Senchet felt relief flood his body. 'For a moment . . .'

'Never mind that, let's ask him if there's somewhere near,' Harry said urgently.

It was astonishing what hunger could do to a man's feet. Senchet lurched into a trot and stumbled off along the roadway after the cart, hallooing and waving his arms wildly.

The cart was large, and in the back were sacks and blankets. The carter himself was a shortish man, hooded, who lolled and nodded as the wheels bounced and rattled over the ruts and holes. Ranged along the outer side of the cart were pots and pans, which clattered so much it was a miracle that the driver could doze, Senchet thought to himself.

'Hi! Hey there, fellow! Wake yourself, and listen to me! Wait!'

Although the man didn't react, the horse heard him, and drew to a halt so that Senchet could hurry to catch up.

Senchet was surprised to see that the horse itself was close to collapse. It had been forced to carry on long after it should have rested.

'Sir,' he panted. 'Do you know how far to the nearest village? My friend can hardly walk, and we are both famished.'

The man on the board gazed at him listlessly, then shook his head as though trying to waken himself. 'Village?'

'Where are we?'

'I . . . don't know . . .' the man said, and closed his eyes again.

'Listen, we need to find our way to a place for some food. Do you—' Senchet suddenly saw that the man's flank was soaked with blood. 'You are injured?'

'Jumped on – men from Earl of Lancaster few miles back. Got lost. Don't know where I am,' the man mumbled. His eyes closed again and he slowly toppled over. Senchet caught his body, grunting with the effort.

There was one good thing. The man might be in a bad way, but Senchet had a strong conviction that there was food in his wagon.

Friday following the Feast of the Annunciation[1]

Willersey

All had been . . . satisfactory, Agatha supposed.

The coroner had arrived yesterday afternoon – a pasty-faced young knight who coughed and sneezed all over everyone, sneered and shouted at the jury, and swore at his clerk, an inoffensive little man at least double the man's age. The conclusion

1 27 March 1327

of murder was hardly surprising, since the axe was still in Ham's head.

She felt her heart constrict at the sight of her husband's naked body, lying there as all the vill's men and women stared at him, the coroner measuring each wound, wincing at the insects buzzing about and then deciding on the fines to be imposed, noting the names of the 'First Finder', the nearest householders, the members of the jury and all the others who could be forced to pay for the breaking of the King's Peace. He made a perfunctory enquiry about who could have been responsible, but there was little he could glean. No one had known Ham was back in Willersey, after all.

Everyone knew Ham had left the vill with the purveyor almost two weeks ago. The only motive that could be inferred was based on the fact that his cart and horse were missing, but no one in the jury mentioned that in case there would be a further fine imposed for the theft. Nor did anyone there trust this cunning-looking knight with the streaming nose. He was not of a mind to be accommodating or kindly.

Walking back to the vill yesterday, with her husband's body pushed in a handcart by two farmers, all Agatha could think of was the injustice. Ham had been so late coming back, yet there was no money. If only there had been a little to help her and Jen. Just the coins promised by the purveyor would have helped, let alone those the priest had mentioned. She had no choice now: she would have to depend on the charity of the Church. While there were alms, she and Jen should not starve. And given time, a man would be found for her. She could not expect to depend upon the others in the vill for the remainder of her days. When a local man lost his wife, Agatha would be prevailed upon to make an arrangement with him, and marry. Any widow who refused would find herself without friends.

Men needed women, and to fight against the natural way of things was a certain way to make enemies.

Yesterday they had undressed Ham, she and Jen, and washed away the worst of the blood about his face. His jaw was broken, and when she saw his teeth had snapped off, it made her stomach lurch. The axe-wounds were less horrific; they were merely broad cuts in his flesh, but the sight of what had happened to his face was appalling. It was a relief to be able to wrap him in muslin and cover his sad eyes.

Jen was pale, slightly greenish, as she helped her mother. She worked methodically, concentrating on the wounds she was cleaning. It made Agatha's belly knot to see her so distraught.

Agatha sat up all night with his body, Jen beside her. Ham wasn't there: this corpse wasn't him. The man she had known was gone, his soul flown, and there was nothing of him left behind, only a husk. After the cleaning and washing, even his odours were gone. She could scarcely believe this was him. All her life was in turmoil, and she knew only utter emptiness.

But even as she sat beside him, she railed inwardly. It was so unfair! Where were Ham's horse and cart? The man who stole them had stolen Jen's future. He was the focus for her bile and rage.

If she met him, she would *kill* him.

Close to Warwick

The carter's wound was at least clean. Senchet and Harry were trained in dealing with injuries of many types.

'It must have been a sword wound,' Harry guessed. A bad cut, but not septic. Last night he had washed it and placed some linen over it, but this morning, when he saw it in daylight, the man's flank was bloody again. Harry frowned. The carter was losing too much blood.

'We must place him in his cart and take him to the nearest vill,' Senchet said.

Harry shivered. His belly was better after he and Senchet had eaten some of this man's food yesterday, but he was still suffering from the after-effects of their enforced starvation. 'We can't leave him here,' he agreed.

'He needs hot food, or I'm a Saxon,' Senchet said.

Harry was already gathering more sticks and pieces of wood for a fire. The two men worked together quickly, collecting enough to make a small pile, and Senchet struck sparks from his flint until his tinder caught. Before long the two men were setting a pot over the flames to heat some water. In the man's pack they had found some dried sticks of meat, and they placed these in the pot with some herbs and leaves they found about the area.

Harry broke bread into a bowl, and then they spooned the gravy over it. The watery pottage thickened well, and both had a little before they tried to feed some to the injured man. He moved his head as they attempted to pour a little of it into his mouth, but then he started to swallow, and soon his eyes flickered and opened.

Senchet held up the spoon so he could see it. 'You need this, my friend. Can you open your mouth?'

The man nodded, and soon he was eating hungrily. Only when the last of the gravy had been wiped away did he settle back again, eyes closed.

'Are you well?' Harry asked, and received a nod in return. 'Are you from near here? Is there somewhere we can take you?'

'My name is Dolwyn,' he said weakly. 'I don't know this area at all.'

CHAPTER TWENTY-SIX

Passion Sunday[1]

Berkeley Castle

It was miserable that day. Benedetto had joined Lord Berkeley in the small, cramped chapel for Mass, and the chill had eaten into his bones. How he longed for the warm climate of Florence!

The service must have left the chaplain feeling as cold as the congregation, because he hurried through the last parts and completed it in what seemed like indecent haste.

Benedetto left the chapel, trailing out behind the lord and members of the garrison, and was momentarily blinded by the brightness. The sun was concealed behind a series of clouds that ranged over the sky, but for all that her glow was apparent, especially after the comparative gloom of the chapel.

Benedetto sighed as he crossed the yard. Last night he had dreamed that Manuele was alive again – and the realisation as

1 29 March 1327

he awoke that his brother was still dead had coloured the rest of his day with a black melancholy. If truth be known, Manuele had been his favourite brother. Matteo was always a little reserved, as though he was still spying even when with his own family, whereas Manuele had been a pleasant, cheery fellow.

It was noon when he saw a man ride under the gateway. A strong, tall knight, with a beard and piercing eyes, behind him a man on a good palfrey. Both men looked experienced fighters, and Benedetto was impressed by the manner in which the second dropped from his mount and looked carefully about him, before steadying his master's beast. With them was a large, long-haired mastiff with tricolour markings. A handsome brute, Benedetto told himself, rather like the farm dogs of the Swiss rebels. He could have been tempted by the fellow.

The knight pulled off his gloves as grooms rushed over to see to the horses, and asked for Lord de Berkeley.

'Sir Knight,' Benedetto said, 'he is hunting. May I serve you? My name is Benedetto di Bardi.'

'Signor Bardi, I am Sir Baldwin de Furnshill.'

'I am honoured,' Benedetto said, with a small bow.

The knight gave a perfunctory bow in return, but his dark eyes ranged over Benedetto, enough to make the Florentine flush, as though he had reason to be ashamed.

'You are one of the famous banking family?' Sir Baldwin asked.

Benedetto was not surprised that his fame should have reached all the way here, but he was confused by this knight's cool response to his name. 'Yes, we are bankers,' he said.

'I am very honoured to meet you too,' the knight said, his voice stiff. 'I know you were the banker to Sir Edward, the King's father. And I suppose you support the new King now?'

'Yes, we have assisted the new government,' Benedetto agreed. 'No modern government can survive without money.'

'And when there are many foreign mercenaries to pay, I suppose the money is even more necessary,' Baldwin said drily.

'How the money is used is up to the King, of course,' Benedetto said smoothly.

'Of course,' Baldwin said. 'I apologise if you feel I insulted you. It was not my intention. However, to lend money at high rates does not seem to me to be Christian.'

'How else would the government operate? And after the last year, anything that can ease the flow of money is to be applauded.'

'And the profit you make on such loans?'

'Is high, because the risks themselves are high. It could be that we lend, perhaps, tens of thousands of pounds – and then there is a change in government and we lose every penny.'

Baldwin smiled thinly. 'And that would be dreadful.'

'For the House of Bardi, my friend, yes.'

Willersey

In the church, Agatha stood staring at the cross while Father Luke led the funeral service. The words flowed over and around her, but even when the priest spoke in English, she barely comprehended. She held her feather in her hand, the goose quill that Ham had given her, as if it was some sort of token, but it gave her no consolation.

Jen was beside her, but the two did not touch; their grief separated them. Agatha was tormented by the feeling that she had failed Jen. Occasionally she felt the girl's eyes upon her, but did not turn to meet them.

She knew she was the topic of gossip in the vill, but she didn't care. There was nothing anyone could say to her that would make her feel worse. Her guilt, her shame, her inner revulsion, all combined to convince her of her utter inadequacy.

And then there was a flicker in her breast. A sudden thought that gave her a tingle of excitement. *Someone had taken her husband's cart and horse*. There must be some means by which she could announce the theft and see them returned. Perhaps a word with the local officers, or . . .

The priest was finished, and now they were going to carry Ham to his grave. She followed the wrapped body out into the sunshine, and found herself at the edge of his grave, staring down into it. It looked very narrow. The men carefully slid Ham into the hole, the sexton taking his feet. But his hips stuck. The men above were forced to heave him upwards again, and then move him further down the grave's pit, the sexton tugging at him with many a muttered imprecation. No one cared for Agatha's feelings as the body was shifted this way and that. In the end, it was firmly pressed down, and one shoulder was set higher than the other. Jen wept quietly.

A couple of women were watching her and Jen, and partly in order to escape their gaze, Agatha put her arms around Jen and hugged her tightly so she wouldn't see. She threw the feather in as the sexton clambered out of the grave and took up his shovel.

'Father?' she said to the priest.

'Yes, daughter? A sombre occasion. How are you?' Father Luke smiled at her, and at Jen, and Agatha took a deep breath.

'Father, I need to find my cart,' she said in a choked voice. 'Will you help me?'

Kenilworth

Matteo reached the inner ward and sat on his horse, peering about him. Kenilworth was busy, and entering had been difficult. The portcullis was down when he and his men clattered over the drawbridge.

'I am sorry, master,' Gilbert said when he finally allowed them inside. 'We have had an attack. We can't be too careful.'

'Of course,' Matteo said, looking about him. The place showed no sign of violence, he thought. He clambered from the saddle, and stood on the ground with his hands on his back, rubbing the tightened muscles.

'Where is the Earl of Lancaster?' he asked.

'He is travelling down from York,' Gilbert informed him. 'He will be here in a few days.'

'Then we shall wait for him,' Matteo said with a smile.

Berkeley

John watched as the knight spoke to the merchant with the rich clothing, his henchman nearby, and felt the relief wash through his blood.

'Sir Baldwin, do you remember me?' he called, and crossed the yard to the knight's side. 'I am right glad to see you again. It is some months since we last met.'

'But of course. It is John, is it not?'

'Yes. I was with you in the last days of my master, Sir Hugh le Despenser.'

'You are now a servant of Lord Thomas?'

'My Lord Berkeley has been good enough to allow me to join his household.'

'You proved your loyalty to your lord. I hear Lord Berkeley is to travel to Kenilworth?'

At this point, Benedetto bowed and excused himself.

'Yes,' John said, when the banker was gone. 'Lord Berkeley will leave as soon as he may. I think he was waiting only for you to arrive.'

'Our presence was commanded by Sir Edward of Caernarfon himself,' Baldwin said.

'I confess I still find it difficult to call my King by that name, as though he was merely a knight,' John said, glancing around cautiously.

'I think that after the last months he would be glad indeed to become an ordinary knight. But be careful who hears you speaking like that. There are those who would be glad to accuse you of disloyalty to your new King,' said Baldwin.

'Aye. Well, I cannot throw off my allegiances as easily as some,' John said.

'We ride soon?' Baldwin asked, by way of changing the subject.

'My Lord Berkeley has gathered together all the men he can for this escort,' John said. 'There has been an attempt upon Sir Edward already.'

'So I heard,' Baldwin said. 'It is a curious thing that someone should have tried to attack a castle to free him. Surely they would know that the castle would be all but impregnable. How did they do it?'

John hesitated a moment, and then answered. 'I heard that they had men already inside the castle, and although those men were searched for weapons, they had a cartload on the way. If the weapons had been there, the attack might have succeeded. It was a bold plan.'

'Was it to free Sir Edward – or harm him, though,' Baldwin said thoughtfully.

'What a question!' John laughed. 'Who would want to have him harmed?'

Baldwin looked about him at the men thronging the court, preparing horses and harnesses for the journey. 'I cannot imagine. But think of this: bankers need excellent communications. They control numbers of spies and messengers all over the countries in which they operate so that they can see what is happening – before the King himself in many cases.'

'So?'

'The Bardi is here for a reason, my friend. I do not know what that reason may be, but let us imagine the fellow has contact with Sir Roger Mortimer. Sir Roger holds on to power with his fingernails because of Queen Isabella, but if someone were to release Sir Edward of Caernarfon, Sir Roger's authority would collapse. He would be exposed as a felon who stole the throne, stole the Queen, and imposed his will over the King's heir. So if you ask me who could have a desire to kill the man you and I still consider our King, I would answer: Sir Roger. He would find it difficult to explain Sir Edward's death to the Queen and her son; but better that than to have to try to explain himself to the King, were Sir Edward back on his legitimate throne.'

John listened, his heart shrivelling in his breast. The idea that there could be more civil war, more unnecessary deaths, was utterly repugnant to him. In his mind's eye, he saw Paul's dead face again. It made him want to weep.

Edgar walked up and was introduced. He gripped John's hand, and John could not help but wince.

'You have some pain?'

'I have reached that age in life, where sometimes I twist or move foolishly, and as a result receive quite a painful injury,' John lied, putting his misery to one side. 'I pulled a muscle a few days ago. I fear I grow old.'

'Then there can be little hope for me,' Baldwin chuckled.

John smiled politely. 'Sir, you will be joining the good Lord Berkeley on his way to Kenilworth?'

'Yes,' Baldwin said. 'We go to accompany the King back here.'

'May I ride with you? The journey will be strange, with so many who are not devoted to Sir Edward.'

Baldwin smiled. 'I should be pleased to have your company.'

CHAPTER TWENTY-SEVEN

Tuesday after the Feast of the Annunciation[1]

Near Warwick

It had been a long journey, and as Simon and Sir Richard rode along the main road towards Warwick, they were too tired to talk.

Over the last day or two they had spent much of the time chatting quietly, sometimes even the normally taciturn Hugh joining in with a comment or two, but now, all fell quiet.

For Simon, the peace was a relief. He did not dislike the knight – on the contrary, he was fond of the man – but Sir Richard's taste in humour ran to quantity rather than quality, and so much delight from such a kindly, generous, but above all exceedingly *loud* companion, was very wearing. He had memories of travelling with Baldwin – long hot rides in the sun and torrential rain – yet, never was he so worn down as now, with Sir Richard.

1 31 March 1327

Hugh, he could see, was more resilient. The servant always complained about his poor riding skills, but for a man who was raised on a little farm in Dartmoor, who had spent his early days on the moors with the sheep, that was no surprise. Few peasants would ever be able to afford to ride a horse, whether their own or a borrowed one, because by and large, horses were for the wealthy. Men like Hugh were lucky to see anything more than an ox to work the farm, and perhaps a donkey for journeying. Not that the folks about Drewsteignton were likely to be a able to use donkey. The paths and tracks there were so poor that even packhorses found the going troublesome.

It was as they reached a little crossroads that they met the men.

Near Tidintune

Senchet and Harry were glad to have found the cottage.

The woman who lived there, Helen, had been very helpful, especially since there could have been few widows who would have welcomed three men to feed, but she told them that they were her guests, and if they needed food, she could provide them with some for one night.

Dolwyn had been weak when they arrived, but the following morning, while Senchet was hitching the horse to the shafts and settling the reins along his back and up to the cart, he heard Harry bellow. He sprang from the cart's bed and ran to the cottage. Inside, Helen stood wringing her hands beside Dolwyn's prostrate body.

'Help me, Sen,' Harry called, and Senchet hurried to his side.

'He tried to get up, and collapsed after two paces,' Helen said. 'He looked all right when he stood, a little rocky, perhaps, but now look at him. He is not well, gentles. Not at all well.'

238

'Helen, I think we will need to impose upon your hospitality a little longer than we had hoped,' Senchet said, his hand at Dolwyn's forehead. 'Ah, the poor fellow is burning up. Feel his brow – here, see? His body is afire.'

Harry wrinkled his face. 'Ach! He has a fever.'

'That is bad,' Senchet said. He glanced down at Dolwyn's flank, where the knife had penetrated. 'We should look at the wound.'

Harry nodded, and reached out for the man's tunic.

'No,' Helen said. 'Leave me with him. I shall nurse him to health, God willing. You two must make yourselves useful. Fetch wood for the fire and fill my pot with water. You will have to make a pottage. There are plenty of leaves in my garden. Go and seek out what you may. And one of you, can you find some meat?'

Senchet nodded and hurried out to the vegetable garden. It was difficult to know what to fetch for the best. He knew the physician's favourites for an invalid: hot plants or cold, dry or wet, to suit the different humours. But he had no idea whether this man was choleric or phlegmatic, sanguine or melancholic. Without that most basic information, it was impossible to decide what would be the best remedy for his illness. Probably best just to fill the poor man's belly, he decided, and took some handfuls of the leaves from the meagre vegetable garden.

When he returned, Harry had already filled the pot from the well outside, and was lighting the fire. Soon the room was filled with the clean odour of scorched bark as Harry blew on his tinder.

Senchet left him to it, wandering outside and looking for some means of capturing a bird or rabbit. There were nets in a small pile in an outside house, and he looked through them with a frown. Perhaps suitable for catching rabbits if he had a ferret, but nothing else. What he really needed was a bow to shoot a pigeon from a tree.

He knew that there was some food still in the back of the cart. Rather than waste time now, he returned to it, hunting through the items on the bed while he searched for the bag with the food in it. When he had last seen it, it was just beneath the plank on which Dolwyn had sat, but when the horse was taken from the cart last night and the shafts rested on the ground, all the items in the cart had slid forward. Now he must pull the bags out of the way.

It was the first time he had looked at all the stuff in the bed of the cart. He pulled one large blanket bound about something, and frowned as he felt the weight of it. As he dragged it free, he heard the rattle of steel inside. Opening it, he realised that the sack was full of weapons, and he whistled to see the swords, axes, maces and other devices designed to kill.

Near Warwick

The sight of the three men approaching was alarming, especially when they spread out like those who are used to fighting.

Sir Jevan stiffened his back as he watched them approach. 'Wait,' he said to his two men-at-arms.

'Sirs, are you bound for Kenilworth?' he asked as Simon and Sir Richard de Welles were close enough.

Sir Richard answered. 'Yes. Perhaps we go there for the same reasons, hey?'

Sir Jevan inclined his head, keeping his eyes on them. 'I am with the garrison there.'

'Aye? What are you doin' here, then?'

'There was an attack on the castle, and we have been scouring the lands for the men responsible.'

'Thought you had been riding for a while. There's a lot of mud on your tunic. You must have ridden out after the attempt to free Sir Edward—.'

Sir Jevan smiled. 'You are observant, my friend.'

The older knight's eyes wrinkled in delight. 'Even an old fool like me can see when I bother to open my eyes, my friend. I am Sir Richard de Welles. Coroner to the King.'

In a few moments the men had introduced themselves. Sir Jevan rode alongside Sir Richard as if equals alone should ride at the front of the party. He gave Simon a hard stare when he joined them. It was enough to make Simon begin to fall back, until Sir Richard said, 'Hoi, where are you going, Bailiff? You think you're too good to join me and Sir Jevan, eh?'

'I thought you would want to have some privacy,' Simon said coolly.

'Well, ye thought wrong. Now, Sir Jevan, we've heard that some idiots tried to grab the Ki . . . Edward of Caernarfon, that is, from Kenilworth. Are they the men you were seeking?'

'Yes. They killed the porter, Squire Bernard, and four of the garrison before they made off, but luckily we caught and slew several of them before they could escape.'

'Must have been mad, the lot of them,' Sir Richard said comfortably. 'Moon-struck. The idea that a handful of men could burst into Kenilworth and do as they please was sheer foolishness!'

'So we are all to join together to guard him on his way to another castle,' Sir Jevan said.

'Aye,' Sir Richard agreed. 'To Berkeley. Shouldn't take long. Now, how many were there in the gang? Do ye know who any of them were?'

'There were some who were recognised: two brothers, a man called Stephen Dunheved, and his brother, a Franciscan, Frere Thomas.'

'You know these two, Bailiff?' Sir Richard asked Simon. 'You know half the felons and outlaws in the kingdom.'

'No, I don't think I've heard of Stephen,' Simon admitted. 'But the friar's name is familiar.'

'This Stephen is a renowned felon. He killed a man some years ago, and was forced to flee the realm. He abjured and travelled to France, I believe. No doubt he returned recently.'

'If he is trying to release Edward, I greatly doubt he would have come over with the Queen's men,' Simon said. 'She would not have given her protection to a man who was known as a loyal servant to her husband.'

'I would doubt he told her so,' Sir Richard chuckled. 'No, a fellow like this Dunhead would have been careful to keep that matter secret, I daresay.'

'Dunheved,' Simon corrected him.

'All the same to me,' Sir Richard said blandly. 'When his head's off, it won't matter much.'

'Good,' Sir Jevan said tersely. 'He should die for the murder of my companions at Kenilworth. It was a foul attack.'

'What of this Franciscan?' Sir Richard said, throwing a look at Simon. 'You say you know of him?'

Simon racked his brain. 'I seem to remember hearing about him when I was at court with Baldwin. Wasn't it Frere Thomas who was sent to Avignon to meet with the Pope? Our King used him as a messenger.'

'It was said that he was sent by Despenser,' Sir Jevan said, 'and told to arrange a divorce between Edward and Queen Isabella. Our Pope refused to consider such a plea, so the fellow was forced to return empty-handed.'

Simon nodded. 'Any others you know of who were involved in the plot?'

'No, not by name, but there are some I would recognise by sight,' Sir Jevan said with cold certainty. 'And when I see them, I will kill them. One I hunted for miles to the south, and almost caught him, but he escaped because my men and I were thwarted by a peasant with a cart. I should have executed the churl there and then for his stupidity! Blocking the roadway, he allowed the man to escape. I hope to find him again soon, though. I am sure his face was familiar to me,' he added thoughtfully.

'He'll be far away by now,' Simon said. He shot a look at Sir Richard and caught a shrewd flickering in his eyes. It was enough to reassure Simon that Sir Richard did not like this stranger knight either. There was something about him that Simon instinctively mistrusted.

'No. He was heading up here,' Sir Jevan said. 'I think that there is another plot being schemed to release Sir Edward. We needs must be vigilant. Very vigilant.'

Kenilworth

Baldwin and the rest of his party arrived at the castle in the middle of the afternoon, and it was a great relief to meet with Sir Ralph of Evesham once more.

'My friend,' Baldwin said, offering his hand, but then the two embraced and Sir Ralph beat Sir Baldwin's back for a moment.

They had endured privations in the last year while both served the King in his last days of freedom. Those had been difficult times, with many of their companions being killed, while they were hunted all the way from Bristol to Caerphilly and beyond. Baldwin had a feeling that they were closer as a result than many men would understand. The bonds between these two warriors after their period of mutual danger were deep; their joint suffering had forged shackles neither could remove.

Sir Ralph had enjoyed the last months, from the look of him. 'You are heavier than when I last saw you,' Baldwin said.

'I don't think your waist is as fine as once it was, either,' Sir Ralph rejoined.

He was a man of a little more than middling height, with strong shoulders and arms, and a square, pugnacious jaw. Yet his grey eyes were calm, and because he blinked more rarely than other men, he gave the appearance of great concentration.

'How is the King?' Baldwin asked.

'Sir Edward is well enough, for a man who suffers so gravely the loss of all,' Sir Ralph said, his face growing sombre, adding, 'Please, be careful how you address him in this castle of enemies. Come, he will be pleased to see you.'

As they walked to the King's chamber, Baldwin and he spoke of the other men they had known. Sir Ralph's squire was recovered from a sword-blow that had scarred his arm, and two others with whom they had marched and fought, were joined with Sir Ralph, replacing two men whom he had lost.

Baldwin listened with half an ear, but as they reached the door to the chamber, and he saw the two guards outside, he gritted his teeth. These men should have been inside the chamber, guarding Sir Edward from attack, and instead they were here to guard him as gaolers.

'Your swords,' one of them said.

'What is your name?' Baldwin asked.

'I am Sergeant Gilbert.'

'Then, Sergeant, you will know better than most that a knight will not relinquish his sword for no reason. What reason do you give?'

'I would not have Sir Edward of Caernarfon in danger, sir,' Gilbert said stoutly.

'Nor would I, which is why I will carry this sword with me in his defence,' Baldwin said.

244

'I have orders.'

'And I have a fixed determination. Sir Edward has asked to see me. Open the door.'

Gilbert looked at him as though about to argue, but then he shot a glance at the other man at the door. That fellow shrugged, and Gilbert reluctantly stood aside.

Baldwin knocked. 'My lord?'

CHAPTER TWENTY-EIGHT

Kenilworth

Edward of Caernarfon stood when the knock came. He had already heard voices outside, and although they had not been raised in anger, he was aware of tension.

'You may enter,' he said now. He felt that tingling in his breast again, as though he was readying himself for a sudden attack once more. The flesh of his scalp was moving, and he could feel his heart pounding in his breast.

And then his fear left him and he almost fell to the floor, so great was his relief. At first he could not speak, his throat closed with the emotion that seemed almost to suffocate him. And then, as the two men knelt, their eyes on him, he held out his hands. 'My friends.'

'My liege,' Baldwin replied. 'I am here as you ordered.'

'And I am heartily glad of it,' the King said. 'I had feared that I would die before you arrived, but now, to see you both with me once more, I begin to feel sure that I will survive.'

'We have heard of the attack on the castle.'

'I am glad of it, Sir Baldwin. But you do not, perhaps, comprehend the full enormity of the attack.'

'You believe that they may have been intending to kill you,' Baldwin said. 'It was my fear also. That is why I am here.'

'I am sincerely glad of it, too,' the King said. Then he glanced at the door, and beckoned the other two over to the window at the farther wall. He looked from Baldwin to Sir Ralph, and then placed a finger at his lips in token of silence. 'There is more,' he whispered. 'A man came to see me before the attack on the castle, and he managed to pass me a note. He said that the Bardi were prepared to advance me money to help rescue me, and that they would give me all the aid I require.'

Baldwin exchanged a startled look with Sir Ralph. 'Are you sure of this?'

'You doubt me?'

'I would be suspicious of any such message. At Berkeley on my way here, my liege, I saw the head of the House of Bardi, but he is entangled with the new regime. He provides the money that the Queen needs to pay her mercenaries.'

Edward of Caernarfon smiled. 'And would they not do so, in order to inveigle their way into the affections of those in power, so that when the moment came, they would be ready? I think you will find that the Bardi are ready to reinstate me.'

Wednesday before Palm Sunday[1]

Kenilworth

It was the sight of the massive castle that made Simon realise the enormity of the Dunheveds' task.

1 1 April 1327

MICHAEL JECKS

'Christ's ballocks, they tried to storm *that*?' he breathed at the sight.

Sir Richard de Welles looked up with a measuring gaze. 'Hey? Oh, yes, that's the castle. A good fortress – solid footings on rock, I expect, with a lake for a moat. Not much chance of the fools getting inside without a stratagem of some kind. No doubt they were so confident they thought they could walk to the doors and open them.'

Sir Jevan shook his head. 'They thought themselves too clever to be captured, my friends. They sent a man in the day before, and learned from him where the King was held, and then the next day they infiltrated many of their companions into the castle, pretending that they were bringing food and drink. Some of them had been delivering goods to the castle for many weeks. It shows how good their planning had been, eh?'

'They had some foresight,' Sir Richard nodded. 'But without the ability to run to a set plan, all that was a waste of time and effort. They were fools. Better by far to jump upon us when we leave.' He placed his hand on the crupper and cantle, and turned in his saddle, peering around at the men behind, then gazing off at the road along which they had ridden. 'Yes. On that road. But not here, so near the castle. No, if I were them, I'd have the ambush planned for somewhere nearer the destination. Perhaps along the last five miles. Just at the stage when the plodding escort with the King will be both bored and tired, and ready for a break. That would be my plan.'

'You have no need to worry about your plan,' Sir Jevan said with calm confidence. 'The rebels will not dare to try again so soon. They will need to gather their strength.'

'Really?' Sir Richard said with a smile. 'Hah, that's a relief. I'd thought that a mob like them, with fifteen men to spare in

248

a frontal assault, may have one or two others about the place. This Stephen Dunhead – was he a local man?'

'I think his lands were not far,' Sir Jevan said tightly.

'Oh. And the others with him – were there any knights?'

'Some who looked like knights,' Sir Jevan agreed. He glanced curiously at Sir Richard. 'What of it?'

'And all these fifteen men who were inside the castle, they weren't known to the garrison as locals? Or else they'd have been taken, wouldn't they?'

'Of course.'

'So, we have a man who's a local boy, who has lots of friends, we can guess. Yet he also has enough friends who're not known hereabouts, to be able to raise a little force that can come and attack without fear of recognition.'

'Why do you assume he has lots of friends about here?' Sir Jevan scoffed.

Sir Richard smiled broadly. 'Because I have fought many times in me life, my friend. And if there's one thing I've learned, it's that it's better by far to assume that your enemy is much cleverer and more populous than you and your own men. Ye know why? Because that way there are no unpleasant surprises.'

'There will be none on our ride,' Sir Jevan said with cold certainty. 'Not with the force assembling here. And if they were to wish to surprise us, they would find it difficult. We leave tomorrow, as early as we may.'

Willersey

Agatha knew now that no one could help her.

She had gone to see Master William, the reeve, and he had quickly put her straight. No, the cart had not been there. It couldn't have been, because if the horse and cart had been stolen when Ham was killed, the coroner would come back and fine the vill deodand for the stolen goods. But no one had seen a horse or cart, therefore no one could state that they had been stolen. Perhaps they were lost miles away, and Ham had walked home. It was possible. Mention of the cart now would only lead to embarrassment and expense, he told Agatha. And, he hinted, the vill which was expected to support a widow and child would not be so willing to do so, were that widow to expose the whole vill to more costs.

The law was terrifying. It was there for men, not women. Women did not exist in law except as chattels of husbands or fathers, and even though it was obvious to the meanest intellect that Agatha had been deprived of her family's goods, she had no right to bring a case against anyone. She was only a woman.

But she was not going to surrender immediately on the word of the reeve. The cart and horse were hers. Jen and she needed food, and the horse and cart together were worth a lot of money.

A clerk in Holy Orders could help a widow. He had a duty to each member of his flock. A priest was educated, he would understand the courts and help her to win the justice she needed. From all she had heard, Father Luke had an interest in finding the cart, too.

She had seen the tyre marks of a cart when she went and looked. The tracks were some distance from Ham's body, but distinctive. Even days after his death, they were plain on the ground. She knew that he had done as he usually did: hobbled the horse, set the cart in a quiet, hidden place among trees, and then gone to sleep a short way away.

Someone had found the cart, or discovered the horse hobbling about, and took them, together with all the valuables on the back of the cart. Well, Agatha wanted them all back.

She heard the priest knocking on her door and calling. It took her no time at all to kiss Jen, make her promise to listen to the other adults in the vill, and to see the neighbours if she had any difficulties, then collect her food and drink, wrapped in a large square of muslin, and join the priest at the door.

'You are sure you wish to do this, mistress?' he asked hopefully. He would prefer to avoid another walk.

'Of course I am,' she snapped. 'I have to look after us now that Ham's dead, don't I?'

Father Luke nodded sadly. The journey to Worcester was a long one, and he had already endured enough travelling to last him many years. Even the prospect of a pilgrimage to Canterbury, which he had until recently viewed with enthusiasm, was not to be borne. No, if he could, he would remain here in Willersey for the remainder of his days.

'Come on!' she called. 'If we don't leave now we'll never get anywhere.'

He glanced about him at the little vill as she set off, stumping heavily up the roadway. Jen stood in the doorway, her hands on the doorpost, staring wide-eyed after her mother, like a child who feared she would soon be orphaned.

All her confidence was gone now, Father Luke saw. The little girl who only a few weeks ago had continually surprised him with her maturity and intellect, was lost. With her father gone, she had realised that the world was infinitely more dangerous than she could ever have foreseen.

He set his jaw, took his staff, and moved off after Agatha, filled with a grim resolution. He would find that damned cart, and the chest – and he would keep it. The man who had been King had no use for the money, for it would not change his life one whit, but here, in this vill, it could work a wonder. It could even save that little girl from living in fear.

Somehow, he would find that money.

Kenilworth

Matteo walked down to the yard as Lord Berkeley's men gathered there. The lord was giving orders to his men, and Matteo bowed as he presented the indenture.

'My lord, this is for you. It is the authorisation for you to take Sir Edward of Caernarfon to your own castle.'

Lord Thomas took the parchment and opened it. 'Good. Where is the Earl?'

'He is away,' Gilbert said reluctantly. He had been standing over at the entrance to the hall, but now he stepped forward. 'May I help you, my lord?'

'This is an indenture for the release of Sir Edward into my hands. I am to take him to Berkeley,' Lord Thomas said pleasantly. 'It is signed by the King.'

'My lord, I have no . . . Please, can you wait until my lord the Earl returns? He should only be a little while longer, and I am sure—'

'I have urgent business,' Lord Thomas said tersely. 'Prepare Sir Edward for his departure.'

'My lord, I—'

'*At once.*'

'My lord, I do not think you should attempt to remove Sir Edward until Earl Henry has viewed the indenture,' Sir Jevan said.

'You are?'

'My name is Sir Jevan de Bromfield.'

'You are a household knight of the Earl of Lancaster? I am glad to meet you, Sir Jevan. However, I have been ordered in the name of the King to remove Sir Edward for his own protection. It seems that the defences here were insufficient. Perhaps that was intentional – I don't know. However, my task is bring Sir Edward to safety and that, Sir Jevan, I shall do. If you wish to thwart me and my men, I think you will find it difficult.'

Thursday before Palm Sunday[1]

Kenilworth Castle

'Morning, Master Puttock. How are ye this morning, eh? It's a fine morning for a sore head, I daresay. Good God, breathe that air. Makes you glad to be alive, hey?'

Simon heard Sir Richard approach from the far side of the outer ward where the good knight had been glancing over his rounsey, and now he nudged Simon with a beaming smile. 'Bad head, eh? I know what it's like. You need a quick cup of strong ale to settle your stomach, man, that's all.'

The thought was almost enough to make Simon spew again. He had already had to stick his head out of the window when he woke, and after trying to eat a little breakfast, he had resorted to running for the midden, where he had brought it all up again. It was outrageous to suggest that he should take more ale when his head was entirely due to the knight's carousing the night before!

'No,' he said weakly.

'Well, if you don't want a solid cure for your head, man, you only have yourself to blame, eh?'

Simon gave him a sour look and walked over to the horses. His own beast was looking well enough after almost a day of rest, and he was glad to see that a patch where the saddle had rubbed on its withers appeared to have healed, after the groom had spread some goose fat over the area.

---

1 2 April 1327

'There he is,' the groom said with a nod of his head towards the inner ward's gates.

Simon turned to see Sir Edward of Caernarfon walking past.

'He looks sad,' Simon said quietly.

'He is, I expect,' said Sir Jevan, who had been patting his own horse a short way away. He joined Simon. 'Hard to imagine how he must feel, eh? His children won't see him, his wife hates him, and his subjects have forgotten him. What a disaster it must seem, to see all his works set aside.'

Simon shrugged. Perhaps the King was experiencing a little of the horror that had been visited upon the people of his realm. In his opinion, the King did not deserve any more sympathy than Despenser.

And yet Simon still found himself feeling sorry for the man.

There was a goodly number of men around the King as he trotted to the outer ward. Beside him was a squire, whom Simon recognised from the King's household in Westminster, although he could not remember the fellow's name. At the other side was the King's Gaoler, a Sergeant called Gilbert. Then came more servants and a contingent of guards. None of them terribly prepossessing, he thought.

Mostly they were scruffy-looking fellows with long knives, leather jerkins and toughened leather caps on their heads. Welsh, from the look of them, he thought. Mortimer had many Welsh friends, and was trusted by the Welsh, as was Sir Edward of Caernarfon himself. It made for confusion among the peoples of the Principality when Mortimer decided to rebel.

'Ho! Looks like we should mount,' Sir Richard said. He left Simon and swung himself onto his beast, settling instantly like a man born in a saddle. Simon took a little longer, and when he was seated, he saw Hugh scowling ferociously while two grooms tried to curb their amusement, holding his pony still for him while he attempted to get his foot in the stirrup.

Watching Hugh, Simon did not pay attention to the others, and he was surprised to find that a man had ridden up close. He looked across – and felt a little of his sore head dissipate at the gladsome sight.

'Baldwin! What in God's great name are *you* doing here?'

'Old friend, I was about to ask you the same question,' Baldwin said, gripping Simon's arm.

There was a shout at the gate, a slow rumble as the great baulks of timber swung open on their huge hinges, and then amid a loud trumpet blast, Gilbert gave the order for the unruly mob to ride off. Soon all fifty men were moving, Gilbert in the lead, while the old King was surrounded by the majority of the men-at-arms behind him.

CHAPTER TWENTY-NINE

Kenilworth

John climbed into the saddle with a sigh of thankfulness. He had no desire to be on horseback again so soon, but anything was better than remaining here in the castle. He constantly felt the need to keep his head down. It was a relief that he had been billeted outside the castle itself, along with many of the Berkeley men. There was not room for all inside.

It was impossible not to be worried. No matter where he looked, he saw men against whom only a few days before, he had fought. That fellow there, to the left of the main gates, he was one of those who had stood in John and Paul's way as they tried to rush the gates; that fellow by the windlass, he was one of those John had seen in the yard. All about him were men who would be sure to recognise him at any moment. His nerves were in tatters.

A shiver ran through his frame at the thought that this was the place where Paul had died. It was here that John himself had killed the guard at the gate. More blood, he thought, more unnecessary death.

Already the horns were blaring their strident call, and the first of the men were beginning to walk on their horses towards the gates, led by their two commanders, Lord Thomas de Berkeley, and his brother-in-law, Sir John Maltravers, who both made a show of hardly acknowledging the presence of their charge. Lord Thomas gave Sir Edward of Caernarfon a curt nod, John saw, but nothing more. It was deeply insulting, and he seethed with indignation on Sir Edward's behalf. Not long ago, those two men were in gaol because of their disrespect and treachery to their King. And now they felt they could treat that same man with the contempt usually reserved for a villein from their estates. For his part, he felt only sympathy and sadness. Like him, Sir Edward had lost all his closest friends and companions.

He clapped spurs to his beast's flanks and clicked his tongue, and soon he was moving off with all the others, and as he went, his worry about being discovered was blown away with the wind. Once the cavalcade was outside the gates, and away from that dread garrison of men loyal to Earl Henry of Lancaster, it would be time for him to follow with the rearguard. At that thought he felt renewed, and could look about him with his head held high once more.

And then he saw that among the last men to leave the castle was Sir Jevan de Bromfield on his horse, and John felt his heart sink to his feet as he ducked his head down and pulled his hood over his brow.

Kenilworth Castle

'So where have you been hiding?' Baldwin said.

'Hardly hiding,' Simon grunted. They were thundering over the causeway now, and the low, grumbling sound was making his head pound still harder. 'Sir Richard met me at Edith's house.'

'Oh, he is here, is he?'

'Hence my head.'

Baldwin smiled. A man who was abstemious himself, he rarely suffered from hangovers, but he could at least sympathise with a man in as much pain as Simon. 'Hopefully it will improve as we ride. That is the pleasure of riding in good, clear weather.'

'Apart from the dust,' Simon pointed out grimly.

Already, as the lead horses left the wooden causeway and trotted over the dried earth of the roadway at the other side, a fine mist was forming in the air.

Baldwin nodded and pulled at his neckerchief. He would tie it over his face, now the dust had become worse.

'When did you get here?' Simon asked.

'Three days ago,' Baldwin said with a grin. 'Apparently Sir Edward asked to have friends whom he could trust to join him on the road.'

'Why you as well?' Simon wondered. 'Aren't there enough here already?'

'We're here to help guard him from *you*, Simon, and the rest of the men here,' Baldwin said.

Simon winced. 'I don't think I want to hear any more.'

'We will be well enough,' Baldwin said. 'Sir Ralph is riding with the King, and we agreed that I would have a look over the rest of the men in the escort. I would be glad if you would too, and let me know if you see or hear anything suspicious, old friend. It is good to know that you are here, and Sir Richard. If ever there was a man less likely to be a danger to the King, it would be him.'

'I have heard nothing,' Simon said. He cast a look about them, idly studying the men nearest. 'The only fellow I have encountered here is a man called Sir Jevan. Do you know him?'

'By reputation. He is one of the new breed of knight,' Baldwin said dismissively. 'One of those who lives by the sword and seeks only enrichment, the same as those who flocked to Despenser's side – not that Sir Jevan was one of them. I believe he hated Despenser with a passion. Still, he is a man who thinks that the strongest deserve praise by virtue of their power.'

'I was not impressed,' Simon admitted.

'Good,' Baldwin chuckled. Then a cloud of dust rose and enveloped them and he coughed. 'Dear heaven, this ride will be as pleasant as riding across the Holy Land.'

'A little less hot, I hope,' Simon muttered.

'So do I,' Baldwin said.

'So, why does Sir Edward of Caernarfon think he needs protection?'

'Because he thinks you, or someone else here who has no reason to remember him with fondness, will attempt to assassinate him.'

'You jest.'

'Oh, no, Simon,' Baldwin said, and Simon saw the truth in his eyes. 'I do not make jest at all. He believes it. And so do I.'

South of Kenilworth

John rode as far to the back of the mounted men-at-arms as he could, keeping his hood over his head and a strip of cloth over his mouth. Many others were covering their faces against the rising clouds of dust that clung to the inside of a man's mouth and nostrils like flour in a mill. It was a horrible sensation, true enough, but it was not so revolting to John as the sight of Sir Jevan.

He gritted his teeth. It would be impossible to feel safe while that bastard was with the escort. If Sir Jevan so much as caught a glimpse of his face, John was done for. It was a miracle that he had not already been recognised. Fortunately he had changed his clothing when he arrived at the castle, giving his tunic and hosen to the laundress who had joined the party, which was perhaps why he had escaped Sir Jevan's attention so far. That, and the strategic use of his hood, had probably saved him.

He would have to try to keep out of Sir Jevan's way. With so many men sprawling over so large an area, it was easy enough to remain undetected. Here at the rear, John was nearly a quarter of a mile or so behind the knight.

The only other option was to escape entirely and leave the party. Or kill Sir Jevan.

Kenilworth

Simon stared at him, and then gave a guffaw of laughter. 'Me? What, you reckon Hugh and I could try something?'

'Not alone, Simon,' Baldwin explained. 'But think about it from Sir Edward's point of view. He was captured, saw his closest companion hacked to pieces, and was brought there, to Kenilworth,' he jerked his thumb at the great castle, 'and there, while protected by a mass of men, a tiny group managed to penetrate the defences. They forced their way into the outer ward and would have got further, were it not for a little bad luck. They were discovered as the curfew was imposed, and killed.'

'All?'

'All those who remained in the castle. A posse was sent to capture the others outside the castle walls, but it was curfew and growing dark, and although a few were found and slain, they suspect the ringleaders escaped. Or weren't there,' he added as an afterthought.

Simon grinned. 'You're being evasive, or merely impenetrable?'

Baldwin chuckled. 'No, merely I find conversation so much more elevating when I hold it with myself! Sir Edward thought that this transfer to Berkeley was a pretext. Away from Kenilworth, it would be easier to have him killed.'

'Ah!' Simon breathed. 'You mean Mortimer.'

'He did,' Baldwin said, shooting him a glance.

'But you don't?'

'Of course not! Why would Sir Roger kill Sir Edward? Killing the King must inevitably come back to haunt him, because it would be impossible to keep such a scheme secret. So the fact of the assassination would become public knowledge, and then King Edward III, Sir Edward's son, and his mother, Isabella, must both turn upon Sir Roger. They could not support him if they learned that he had ordered the death of Sir Edward.'

'But removing him . . .'

'Serves no useful purpose.'

'It would prevent another freeing him and installing him once more on the throne.'

Baldwin shook his head. 'Who would support Sir Edward? Some few, perhaps, but when it came to a battle, would his men stay at his side against his son, the King? The risks of killing Sir Edward are greater than those of holding him in comfort. The rage that Queen Isabella would show, were she to learn that her husband had been murdered – that would scare me!'

'But she and Mortimer are lovers.'

'I know that is the rumour. But once she loved her husband. Still, that is not important. What is important is that she is a most pragmatic lady. If it were to become thought that she had colluded in his death, she would herself be guilty of gross treason. And she would also think of the danger to her own son. If a king could so easily be done to death, her son would run that same gauntlet through his life, should a powerful baron rise against him. No, she is a French princess. She would not dream of insulting her peers and her blood in such a manner.'

'So who . . .?'

'There is nothing to say anyone will try to assassinate Sir Edward.'

Simon closed his eyes. 'My head hurts, but were it a little less painful, Baldwin, I would knock you from your horse, knight or no knight.'

'It is not confusing. Mortimer may well have pretended to attack Kenilworth to show that Edward was not secure there. Kenilworth is held by my lord the Earl of Lancaster, is it not? To slander the Earl by showing that his guards and precautions are not sufficient, then to have Edward taken to another castle, which is run for Mortimer and which would keep the King under his closer control, would be perfect for Sir Roger. It upsets Lancaster at the same time, for which he would be grateful.'

'Unless the guard at Berkeley Castle show themselves to be less reliable than Sir Roger thought,' Simon guessed.

'Which is not likely, since the Lord Berkeley is Sir Roger Mortimer's son-in-law,' Baldwin finished.

'That all makes sense,' Simon agreed. 'So why is the King worried?'

'Because all this is *my* reasoning, not the King's. He thinks that there will be an ambush, and someone will attack us on the way to Berkeley.'

'To kill him.'

'Yes.'

CHAPTER THIRTY

Worcester

It felt stifling.

Agatha had been to Worcester several times in her life, to markets and twice to see the executions, but today was different as she continued with Father Luke on towards her goal, the huge cathedral that stood in the middle of the city.

'Let us enter and pray before we go to see him,' Father Luke said as they reached the massive west door. He looked up, she saw, as though in profound piety, like a saint about to enter his named church, but it didn't impress her. When they had entered the city, she had seen the way that he had eyed each tavern and low ale-house. He was no better than any other man, and was as keen on a drink as her own Ham had been.

Ham had loved coming to the market. There was always a good profit to be made, he reckoned. Not that Agatha saw it. He'd come, sell his produce, make money, and then spend it in a tavern and doze on the cart on the way home. She said he was a purse, accepting coins from one man and passing them on to another within the day.

He had been so enthusiastic when he was young, had Ham. He had plans then, for making money. It didn't matter that he wasn't a free man, he would say. Others had managed to build good flocks; buy houses and rent them – take a field or two and charge for pasturage. And he was right. Even the Bishop here at Worcester would be pleased with a serf who made money, for the Bishop took a tenth of everything the serf earned, as well as the best of his animals when he died. The system worked for everyone.

But then his enthusiasm waned. He was too comfortable, that was the trouble. He liked an easy life. That was why Agatha found the idea of Ham stealing the priest's money so believable. He would have taken that opportunity if it fell into his lap.

In the thirty-odd miles to walk here, away from the vill and Jen, away from the daily drudge of milking, cleaning the sty, seeing to the chickens, preparing food and drink, listening all the while to Jen's chattering, Agatha had had time to reflect, and not all her thoughts were comfortable.

For instance, she had always bemoaned her fate, thinking that her husband had cost her a better life. Alice shone as an example of how her life could be improved. Yet now she wondered whether Ham had ever felt the same. Maybe he thought that *he* could have done better without her. There were women who inspired their menfolk, she knew. They would flatter and cajole, promise favours later in their beds, and in other ways persuade.

Not all succeeded, for there were three women in the vill who were thought either to be shrews who deserved a thrashing, or foolish chits who should be regularly beaten. In Agatha's mind, all were equally stupid. A woman who didn't expect her husband to treat her with respect was a fool. If Ham had ever tried to beat her, she would have made him regret it. Without a doubt some of Ham's friends looked down on him because he couldn't cow her. So be it. If a man tried to thrash her, she'd soon give him reason to regret his temerity!

Father Luke was at the door now, and she came to with a start. For a moment there, she had been back in the past with her memories. Now she recalled that there was a sterner purpose to her visit here. She nodded and walked in after him, and stood in the vast, echoing nave.

It was busy. Three merchants stood at the side, arguing loudly about a sale, while a peasant with two grey raches stood, head lowered, brows beetling as he stared truculently towards the altar. A woman knelt on the stone floor, weeping and pulling her hair while two boys and a young girl stood at her side looking baffled and anxious. A couple at the back of the church were holding hands, he pretending to be entirely unaware of the woman at his side, while she gazed adoringly up into his face. Two old men sat on the floor, backs to the wall, playing a game of knucklebones, one chuckling throatily and holding out his hand for a penny.

A priest was trying to catch two boys who darted in and out among the congregation, but he was too fat and slow to make any headway. The boys ran laughing loudly, while the incense soared up to the roof and priests mumbled their incomprehensible words. It was enough to make a body give up on the Church, she told herself.

They prayed, and then waited until Father Luke could speak to a cleric. Soon Luke was beckoned, and he followed the cleric out.

Agatha did not mind. Women would not be welcome in the Bishop's Palace, she knew, and she was content to leave Father Luke to conduct the interview. He was too simple to think of bilking her and trying to get out of the arrangement. For it was in his interests to find that money now, too. He was an old fool, to be sure, but he seemed to think he had the vill's future to think of. He would work hard to bring the money back to Willersey.

'Well?' she demanded as he strode back to her where she waited outside, some while later.

Looking up, he registered how far the sun had moved across the sky. 'Past noon already,' he muttered.

'Well?' she repeated. 'What did he say?'

'He said, if I thought he had time enough on his hands to call on the posse and organise a search for one cart and one horse, no matter what was on the cart, I was a fool and didn't deserve my living at Willersey. He let me understand that if I didn't find enough to occupy me there, he would find someone else who would be happy to take my place, and further, there were posts in much colder, less pleasant places, where recalcitrant priests could be sent. Then he told me that if no one had reported the theft of the horse and cart when Ham was found, perhaps neither was there in the first place. And if it was true that a horse and cart were stolen, then the vill had been trying to evade their fair taxes.'

'Did you tell him about the money?'

He looked at her. 'You see this church?' he asked rhetorically. 'It costs a lot to run. If he heard of any money, that would be the last the vill would see of it.'

'Oh.' She sighed. At least that meant that only she and Father Luke knew of it. The secret was safe. 'So we must return, then?' she wondered. And then what – just leave the cart to whoever had stolen it?

'I will not,' Father Luke said. 'The good Bishop has no time for such matters, but your husband is dead. The man who committed that murder and stole your cart and horse deserves punishment.'

'What now, then?'

Father Luke stared at the altar as though seeking inspiration. Slowly, he said, 'We could go to our lord and beg his aid.'

'To Berkeley?'

'Yes. My Lord Berkeley owns our manor. It would be reasonable for him to send men to hunt down this thief and murderer.'

She looked at him, and then slowly nodded. 'If you are sure.'

'I am.' His face showed a stern determination. Agatha could not see that within his soul, he seethed at the way the Bishop had spoken to him.

'Why do you seek this cart, Father?' the Bishop had demanded satirically. 'What is so fascinating about it?'

'It is a matter of distress to Ham's widow,' Father Luke said.

'Ah, see – and is this widow buxom? Has she a good broad hip to take hold of?' the Bishop laughed.

'My Lord Bishop, she is only recently widowed, and besides, my vows would not permit me to consider her in that light!'

'So you say, so you say,' the Bishop said easily. He had a mazer full of wine, and now he drained it, studying Luke over the brim. 'But you listen to me, good Father Luke. I will not have my priests attempting to take advantage of the women in their care, you understand? If I hear you've been trying to get under her skirts, you will find yourself in my gaol faster than a drawlatch on Christmas Day.'

Agatha caught a little of his black mood. 'What did he say to you?'

'Nothing that matters,' he lied. He had seen the clerk and asked that a priest be sent to Willersey for some days while he was away. He hoped only for a matter of a week or so, but it was impossible to say. 'What *does* matter is that we should make our way down to Berkeley now. It should only take us two or three days. And there, with fortune, we may be granted a little justice.'

Friday before Palm Sunday[1]

Near Tidintune

Harry le Cur heard the man roll over. There was a quiet moment, in which Dolwyn opened his eyes and glanced about him, and then he tried to sit up, and groaned loudly.

'You should rest yourself,' Harry said. He walked over to stand at Dolwyn's side. 'You've been very ill.'

'It feels like I've been squashed against a wall by an ox,' Dolwyn said gruffly. 'My whole body aches.'

'Aye, well, you should be glad you have any feeling. You ought to be dead,' Harry said.

'What happened?'

'You were stabbed in the side, remember? We came across you in the road, but you collapsed. We're lucky that the woman here was prepared to help and nurse you. She saved your life.'

'I am grateful,' he said. His eyes were still dulled with the fever that had ravaged his body for the last days. 'Is she here?'

'She sleeps,' Harry said, pointing to the palliasse on the floor a few yards away. Helen was exhausted and deeply asleep, snoring very faintly and whistling. 'She's nursed you for three days. Without her, you would have died.'

Dolwyn nodded and sank back on his bedding. He shivered slightly, and pulled a blanket up over his body. 'You said three days?'

'Yes.'

1 3 April 1327

'That cannot be.'

Harry looked down at him. 'You can take my word on it.'

'But I must get away!'

'To deliver your weapons?'

Dolwyn went quiet, watching like a rabbit who fears the snare. 'Weapons?'

'We found everything. Why would a carter have need of so many weapons?'

'I don't think . . .'

'It interests us. But I suppose it's none of our business.' Harry looked at him doubtfully. 'We found a casket there, too. Filled with riches beyond my dreams – and my dreams are vivid.'

'It isn't mine,' Dolwyn stated blankly. Riches? A treasure? Who had put that there?

'I was sure of that already,' Harry said drily.

'I was taking provisions to Kenilworth with a purveyor, but there was a fight when we arrived, and he ran off. I had to hurry to ride away myself, too, and all the load remained. It must have been his, I suppose,' Dolwyn said, still confused, thinking, *What was that carter doing with a box of money?*

Palm Sunday[1]

Llantony Priory

Their journey had been a lengthy one, but they were making good time, Edgar thought as he jogged along behind Sir Baldwin.

They were approaching the abbey of Llantony-next-Gloucester, which was where they intended staying for the

1 5 April 1327

night after two days of steady riding. Edgar was wary whenever he was riding about country he did not know – and today he had a firm conviction that they were entering a place of danger. It was not the location that was threatening: it was the fact that all those in the party guarding Sir Edward felt so secure. The guards were confident that no one would try to attack them while inside an abbey, and that meant they were unconscious of the potential dangers. Because of this, Edgar experienced a nervous tension that he had not known since the days when he and Sir Baldwin had been in flight in France after the arrest of their companions in the Templar Order.

Llantony-next-Gloucester was a small abbey that nestled to the south of the great city of Gloucester, a daughter-house of the priory in Wales, and one in which Edgar felt sure they must be moderately safe, but it was this last stage before reaching it that made him anxious. The houses began to crowd in upon them, and instead of the broad swathe of open verge, where he felt secure from all but a crossbow bolt, now they were riding in among buildings that overlooked the road. Assassins in those jettied rooms would find it easy to brain any number of the men in Sir Edward's guard.

Not that Edgar himself was fretting. His tension came from an appreciation of dangers, not a terror of them – unlike Sir Edward himself. All had seen how the man who had once been their King was bowed down with troubles.

Edgar had seen a man like that before, and for the last day or two he had tried to bring the man's face or name to mind, but there was nothing to spark a connection, until he saw Edward glance around at a sudden crash. The noise was caused by a horse slipping on a wet cobblestone, but in Edward's eyes Edgar saw a sudden terror mingled with a kind of hope, as though this could at last be the end. That was what Edgar saw in his eyes: a longing for it to be over.

Baldwin was nearby. 'What is it, Edgar? Something wrong?'

'No, I was just reminded of the servant who stole the bread at Acre.'

Baldwin winced at the memory.

It had been a dreadful siege. Although the Christians held on, all knew that they would not be able to keep the Mameluke forces at bay for ever.

And then the lad – what was his name? Balian or something similar, a lad of some seventeen years like Edgar and Baldwin themselves – had given in. He tried to steal a crust of mouldy bread, and when he was seen, he drew his knife in a frenzy of hunger, and slew the owner.

Yes. Sir Edward wore the same look as Balian had as he was dragged away to execution: a look of mingled terror and relief. Terror to be slain, but relief to know that at last the long wait was over.

But Sir Edward's torment was *not* over.

CHAPTER THIRTY-ONE

Near Tidintune

Senchet Garcie had spent many years of his life travelling. Originally from Gascony, from the English territories that had been recently stolen by deceit from the English crown, he had spent most of his life on the road, so when he found a comfortable billet, he tried to remain there for as long as possible, making the most of regular meals and drinks. A warrior's life suited him, there was no doubting that, but times of peace were also welcome. And the break here had done him and Harry good.

'Well?' Harry said, finding Senchet sitting on a log in the yard.

'We should be getting on our way.'

'Aye,' Harry said. He sniffed, hawked and spat. 'And?'

Senchet smiled at him with the easiness of a man fully rested. 'And when we're on our way, we can ask him more about this money. Where it came from, and where it was going *to*.'

Harry gave a slow nod. 'He's ready to travel?'

'He'll live. For a while longer.'

'Good.'

Senchet and Harry exchanged a look, and then both rose and went to the horse and began to prepare for the journey.

Llantony-next-Gloucester

Riding into the abbey grounds, John looked about him with nervousness tinged with relief. Here he felt safe, for he was protected by the Abbot.

It was the purest good fortune that he had not been spotted yet. He had pulled his hood low over his head and intentionally kept far from Sir Jevan, but his best protection was that no one would believe that one of the attackers of the castle could be so foolish as to join the men guarding Sir Edward.

Llantony-next-Gloucester was a simple Augustinian abbey. Ahead was the church and cloisters, while to his left were the stables and farm area. He could see the fishpond over to the right, two lay brothers standing with their robes rolled up and bound about their knees, holding a net.

He left his horse in the hands of a groom, and took his saddle-bags, throwing them over his shoulder with his blanket and cloak, before walking off to the open pasture outside the cloisters. There were already forty or more men-at-arms and servants milling about, preparing tents and lighting their cook fires. John dumped his belongings before wandering off to find a drink.

His legs were stiff and his backside felt as though it had been pummelled by a stave of wood. It seemed to be one enormous bruise. More concerning to him was his flank, which was still sore and painful, and he put his hand to it as he walked, wincing.

'My friend, are you in pain?'

273

The man who asked was a tall, thin monk, who eyed him slightly askance.

'Are you Brother Anselm?'

'No, my name is Michael. And you are with the King's men.'

'I am for the King,' John said, and felt the relief flood his body at hearing the passwords confirmed.

Brother Michael glanced at him. 'Your side, it is giving you pain?'

John nodded.

'Come with me. Let us see if we can give you some comfort.' The monk led the way along the side of the cloisters to a small room.

'I am glad to meet you,' John said.

Michael held a finger to his lips and walked about the chamber, looking under the tables and peering through the shutters on the window. He beckoned John to the back of the chamber, and spoke in a hushed voice.

'There are many places here where a man could listen. You must speak very quietly.'

'Do you know when the attack will come?' John whispered.

'It has taken time to gather the men, especially since Kenilworth, as they are spread all over the shires. But they *are* gathering.'

'That is good,' John said.

'You sound unconvinced?'

John pulled a grimace. 'The men at Berkeley will be waiting. They have already foiled one attack at Kenilworth. They'll expect us to try again.'

'There will be news soon that will distract them,' Michael said knowingly.

'Will there be many with us?'

'As many as the Dunheveds can gather,' the monk said. 'It is not an easy task, for since Mortimer captured the King, many went into hiding.'

John nodded. He knew most of his own companions had themselves disappeared. There were too many among Sir Roger Mortimer's forces who had grievances against those from the old regime. He tried to put aside a vision of men scaling ladders, arrows, war-hammers cracking skulls. Men dying, heaped at the foot of the walls . . .

'That is good,' he said, trying to smile. 'The sooner we can release him, the better for all.'

There came a tap at the door, and Brother Michael put a finger to his lips again, and then walked to the door. He opened it, and a slim, dark, sallow-faced man slipped in quickly.

John gazed from one to the other, and then he grabbed for his sword. The monk shook his head, but the other man stood with his arms held high, palms towards John.

'I'm no enemy. I'm with you!' he said.

The sun had been dreadfully hot today, and Matteo was relieved to ride within the cool shadow of the priory's gatehouse. On their journey here the heat had been overwhelming, but he didn't care. Even the thick dust that rose and clogged his throat was a cause for a prayer of thanks.

Since delivering the note to Lord Berkeley, he had felt an increasing sense of joy. He was aware of the weather and the little delights that greeted him every day – the sight of flowers, of tall trees, of rolling green hills.

He had heard that others who had come close to death often described it as a meaningful, almost religious event. They spoke of falling into a pit, and then being pulled back. One man said he had felt that he was being drawn upwards to the sun, to a land that flowed with milk and honey, in which angels flew and sang, and where a multitude waited to greet him. And then he was made to understand that he was not to come here yet, and returned to earth and life with a reluctance that now coloured all his remaining days. He could not wait to go back to that heavenly land, he said.

It had not been so for Matteo. He had limped homewards from the brink without any memory of a glorious light or singing. All he had was a terrible headache that made him sick, and a ferocious pain in his back. The fever had nearly carried him off. And then, he had been so riven by doubts and fears that his miraculous survival had not struck him.

It must be this ride. Perhaps it was the sheer act of journeying that had helped clear his mind. If so, he could see the merit in pilgrimage. Because in truth, he felt as though he was entirely renewed.

Alured was still at his side. He was the only man whom Matteo entirely trusted. After all, Alured had saved his life. Benedetto must have tried to bribe him, but Alured had not accepted.

'Alured . . .' he began.

'Master Bardi?'

Matteo dropped from his horse and passed the reins to a groom. 'When I lay dying, I was very fortunate because you found me.'

Alured caught his serious tone and looked at him. 'I know.'

'There is always someone who benefits from a murder. Only one man could have benefited from my death: my brother Benedetto.'

'As you said before.'

'If he could, he would have finished me off.'

'No, master. I didn't tell you before, because I thought it would worry you, but when you were unwell, he visited you.

He could have killed you then, while you were fevered and weak. I left him with you at least twice. It would have taken no effort for him to finish you.'

'Did he offer you money?' Matteo damanded. How could Alured have left him alone with Benedetto?

'For your keep, master. That was all.'

'He said, "Take this. You will be doing me a service. *Look after* my brother for me",' he sneered.

'Nothing like that,' Alured protested, and frowned. 'Really He was being kind and offering to pay us for your food and cleaning. He was generous.'

'My brother is a clever, clever man,' Matteo said. 'I don't think he ever makes a simple request. He may still be at Berkeley, Alured. When we reach it, I want you to swear to me that you will watch over me all the more carefully.'

'Very well. I swear it,' Alured said, but he did not believe there was any need. Benedetto struck him as a pleasant soul.

John was not of a mind to be convinced by a statement. 'Who are you?'

'I am William atte Hull,' the man said. 'Nephew to Michael here.'

'He is telling the truth,' Brother Michael said urgently. 'You have to trust him, as you trusted me.'

John felt his resolution waver. His flank was hurting abominably, and he was confused and lost without Paul. If Paul were here, he would be able to understand better what he should do for the best. Now, on his own, he was unsure about everything.

'I was sorry to hear of your companion's death,' William said. 'I heard about the attack. It must have been terrible to see so many good men die.'

'Paul was indeed a good man. He and I rode together for many years,' John said. He looked from one to the other, and made a decision. If these two were enemies of his, he was already lost. They need only shout and half the escort would come in here to take him. Sighing, he thrust his sword back in the sheath. 'He was the sort of man in whom you could place your trust. Not perfect, because he had his faults like all of us, but he was yet a kindly man. Honourable and courteous.'

'I know. I met him a few times,' the monk said, 'when he was here with the King.'

'He and I used to travel with our lord, Despenser, and the King quite regularly. They knew that they could count upon us. But he died after the adventure at Kenilworth.'

'What actually happened there, John?' William asked.

'We were sorely beaten,' he said shortly. As if in sympathy, his wound flared again, and he had to put a hand to his side with the pain.

'I forgot your injury!' Brother Michael castigated himself. 'You are in pain. Come over here and let me see to it. I have some skill with curing ailments.'

John disliked the idea of taking his mail off, but the notion that this kindly-looking old monk might be seeking to hurt him was on the face of it ludicrous.

He began to tell them about the attack, while William helped him to remove his tunic and mail, setting them on a nearby bench until John was down to his braies. He had spoken to no one of that awful day since the meeting in the tavern, and to be able to unburden himself felt good.

'We'd stopped earlier to pass the weapons to Stephen, as was agreed, but by the time he got to us, the rest would have been in the castle some hours, all of them waiting for us and the cart. God knows what he was thinking of, but he

278

stopped at an ale-house, and that delayed us all. So when we reached the castle, the gatekeeper was already bellowing to have the gate locked. Stephen rode on ahead to try to delay that, because without the cart of weapons, we could achieve nothing. Paul and I went to assist, and suddenly all hell was let loose. A man in the gateway was preventing us from getting in, and there were arrows everywhere . . .' He broke off, remembering. 'I was stabbed in the flank here by a man with a lance or something. The same fellow managed to strike Paul in the throat.' He swallowed. 'There was nothing I could do.'

'I understand,' the monk said, peering. 'You have been lucky, indeed, my friend. The blade stabbed into your ribs – and painful though it is, that injury prevented the point from thrusting into your vitals. If your lungs or liver had been penetrated, you would not be here now.'

'He paid for his attack,' John said bleakly. 'I saw to that.'

'Good.' The monk had a wad of cloth in his hand; he smeared some honey onto it, then added some paste from a jar. 'You have a melancholic appearance. This should help soothe the injury.'

John winced as the thick pad was placed on his wound, and then Brother Michael began to wind a length of muslin about his chest and shoulder to hold it in place. He tied it up and stood back to survey his work. 'That should hold for you,' he said. 'You must avoid any excessive strains with that arm.'

'Is that intended to be a joke?' John demanded, swinging his sword arm to see how painful it was.

Michael gave him a nervous smile. 'No. I am sorry.'

John gave him thanks, and then began to dress once more. William helped, and then stood back as John bound his sword-belt about his waist.

'You will be able to ride tomorrow when they leave?' William enquired.

'Yes, I will. What of you?'

'I shall join you, I think. I have heard that there is a need for builders at the castle at Berkeley. I can carry a hod well enough.'

John nodded, then glanced at Brother Michael.

'I, my son, will remain here,' the elderly monk said. 'It would be difficult for me to leave my priory without a lot of tedious explanation.'

'And the less there is of that, the better,' William said briskly. 'This whole business is too important to leave to you and a few others, Master John.'

CHAPTER THIRTY-TWO

Llatony Priory

Edgar was walking back from the stables, in search of Sir Baldwin, when he saw John stalk out from the small chamber. He knew that the man had been injured, after all – his stiffness and occasional winces had been noted, and John had explained that he had pulled a muscle – but he felt that John had a curiously shifty look about him now, and he moved off in a hurry as though eager to be away from the door.

Shortly afterwards, a friar appeared in the doorway too, glancing furtively about the court as he stepped aside to let another man out. Then he locked the door behind him, giving Edgar a challenging stare as he did so, as if daring him to comment.

Edgar was not the sort to be easily intimidated, so he simply smiled back and was about to walk onto the field in which the tents were being erected when on a whim he dawdled, and made his way slowly in the same direction as John.

'Ride all this way, and then they expect us to set up camp for 'em too,' Hugh grumbled. He was shuffling his way along the outer perimeter of the cloister, and had caught up with Edgar.

'That man,' Edgar said, pointing with a jerk of his chin at John. 'Do you know anything about him?'

'He came to Kenilworth with you, didn't he?'

'Yes, but I begin to wonder about him. He does not look like an ordinary man-at-arms.'

'He's just a guard who's been with us from the castle,' Hugh grunted.

'He's no knight,' Edgar said. 'He's been injured though, hasn't he?'

'He said he'd pulled his muscle. What of it?'

'Nothing, I daresay,' Edgar said, and bestowed a beatific smile upon the glowering Hugh. 'But it was curious to me that he arrived here with us and instantly appeared to know where he was, where to go, and what to do here. He knew a friar, and has already been treated for a wound, when the larger portion of our group are still erecting the tents.'

Hugh frowned. 'He went to the infirmarer, did he? So what?'

'Probably nothing,' Edgar said easily. 'But we are transporting a highly important man, friend Hugh. I would not wish for something unpleasant to happen.'

'Nor me,' Hugh said with certainty. 'I'm going to sleep like a newborn pup when I get to my bedroll. Nothing'll wake me.'

'I am glad to hear it. For myself, I think I shall sleep more lightly tonight,' Edgar said. He watched as John glanced about him, and then walked off towards the stables once more.

Hugh might not find anything suspect about the man, but Edgar did – and Edgar was too experienced a warrior to ignore his instincts.

Monday after Palm Sunday[1]

Llantony Priory

John was in the saddle as early as possible the next morning, keen to avoid Sir Jevan. The man scared him.

He had not passed a comfortable night. The lump of sticky material placed next to his skin felt odd, but he had to admit that this morning, the pain was somewhat abated. He had much more freedom of movement with his left arm than before, too. It was almost as easy as it had been before that bastard had shoved his lance at him . . .

'Ready to ride, master?'

John stared at Edgar, who had spoken. John had no reason to be concerned about his master: Sir Baldwin, to him, was just an elderly, scruffy-looking knight from some obscure manor far to the south-west – a spent force. Edgar, however, had the look of a competent warrior. There were many folks to keep an eye on, from carters and sumptermen, to the two women who tagged along with the baggage, but this knight's servant kept his attention fixed a little too firmly on John for his comfort.

'Aye, I am ready. What of your knight?'

'He is always ready for any little journey,' Edgar said with a cool gaze.

'Well, you can tell him that today's journey will be a short and easy one,' John said. 'There are only some five leagues or so to Berkeley, so we can hope to be there by noon.'

'Noon? Perhaps so,' Edgar said.

John nodded and patted at his horse's neck, ignoring the impudent churl. He was glad to hear the fellow ride away a short while later. As though he could be intimidated by some

1 6 April 1327

knight's servant! He only hoped that Edgar's unwelcome attentions would not become obvious to others. Especially Sir Jevan.

He eyed the others in the party again. When they had set out he had been so terrified of being seen by Sir Jevan that he took little notice of the others. Now, however, he paid more heed to them as they came closer to Berkeley and the possibility of an attack increased.

Most of them were not of the highest calibre. There were all kinds of dullards among them, lads who should be back at home prodding oxen, as well as some aged warriors with more white than grey in their hair. But there were the odd few to watch out for. That servant of Sir Baldwin's, and also Master Simon, who was clearly a close companion of the knight. He looked a dangerous man, and while his servant might ride like a sack of turnips, he had a belligerent look about him. The other knight, Sir Richard, was too fat and slow to pose any kind of a threat.

Of course, there were others: Gilbert had four or five men about him and the King who looked competent with their weapons, and there were another thirty or so amongst the rest who could be challenging, too, but overall John was content. The garrison of Berkeley, if these men were representative, could be overwhelmed by a strategem.

A shout, and the rattle of steel, and the King appeared walking slowly from the abbot's house. He stood bleakly surveying his guards, his long fair hair moving in the wind, his shoulders still strong, a powerful man, but yet a man broken. He no longer stood erect like a knight, but bent, like an old man. When he moved to go to his horse, he shuffled at first, as if the weight of his worries was all but unsupportable.

It was not difficult to see why, John thought.

As he walked to the horses, another man pushed rudely past him. Without even glancing at the man who had been his King, Lord Thomas de Berkeley strode to his horse, pulling on soft pigskin riding gloves. He reached his mount and sprang up into the saddle in a moment, gazing about him expressionlessly. The only time he smiled was when he saw his friend Sir John Maltravers. That knight strolled indolently along the court to his horse and climbed up easily. Both men were enormously resilient, John thought, bearing in mind how long each had been in gaol or exile in recent years.

The former King Edward II – he who had ensured Lord Thomas's arrest and Sir John's flight – must surely feel all the horror of the last years lying heavy on his conscience. He had done so much damage to the kingdom, to his God-given inheritance – and now all that harm was being repaid, with interest. The kingdom itself had finally rejected him. All could see how the Queen's departure for France, her ensnaring of her own son to join her, and now her taking of the kingdom, had affected him. And then, of course, he had seen his friend Sir Hugh le Despenser literally cut to pieces. His best friend and most loyal adviser, and yet he could do nothing to save him.

Yes, he thought, Sir Edward must bear a hideous weight of guilt.

Baldwin watched Sir Edward stumble across the court to his horse, and with the help of a page climb up into his saddle.

'He looks like a man on the way to his noose,' Simon observed.

'The thought of what must be going through his mind does not bear considering,' Baldwin agreed.

'Ha! There are some who wouldn't mind seeing his pain eased,' Sir Richard stated. He was quiet for a moment, then continued: 'The thing is, no man knows what goes on in another fellow's mind. He's taken many poor decisions, based on poor advice given him by poor advisers. Is that a reason to blame him? He only saw a limited number of men each day, after all. If they were churls and incompetent, it was not his fault, but the fault of his advisers.'

'He allowed free rein to Despenser,' Simon said. 'I can never forgive him that.'

'Despenser has paid for his crimes,' Baldwin said.

'Yes. And is no longer here, which is a blessed relief,' Simon said, looking up at the sky. 'Should be good weather.'

Sir Richard tilted his head back and gazed up at the small wispy clouds floating by. 'Aye, you're right.'

There was a blare of horns, the herald shouted a command, and the men began to file off towards the gate.

At the last gate, Baldwin saw a friar with thin, ascetic features. He noticed that Edgar was watching the man.

'That friar,' Edgar muttered, 'was with the fellow John yesterday. I conceived a dislike for their companionship.'

'For all you know, the two may be brothers,' Baldwin said. 'This John is an honourable man, I deem.'

'Perhaps,' Edgar said. 'In which case it will hurt no one if I keep my eye on him.'

'Your man has a good brain in his head,' Sir Richard remarked to Baldwin.

'I know. But like a good guard dog, sometimes he is inclined to bite first, and ask questions afterwards,' Baldwin said, smiling at Wolf, who stood sniffing at a wall nearby.

Sir Richard chuckled at that, and although Edgar kept his eyes on John and the friar, who had started to walk alongside the guards, he saw nothing that led him to suspect that there was any foul play planned.

Until they met with the cart, there was nothing out of the ordinary on their ride that morning.

Near Berkeley Castle

Senchet was walking alongside the cart when he spotted the first of them. Harry was dozing on the board, and Dolwyn was lying back on the bed of the cart, his eyes closed in pain.

'Harry,' Senchet called desperately, 'wake up!' but it was already too late. The leading horsemen had seen them, and now three men-at-arms approached, calling to them to halt the cart.

Senchet bowed politely as the riders approached. 'Mes Sieurs, how can we help you?'

The leading man was a squire, and he appeared young and calm, but the man behind him was a more dangerous fellow, a large, strong-looking, green-eyed knight. Senchet saw his eyes moving to Harry and back to Senchet, noting the weapons both carried, and then moving aside from the squire so that if Senchet tried to attack, he would have complete freedom of movement. No fool this one, Senchet thought.

'Where are you from? Where are you going?' the squire demanded.

'We are travelling from Wales, m'Sieur, to the north, in the hope of finding a new lord.'

'Who was your lord?'

'My apologies, but why do you wish to know?'

'Answer him, *now*!' the second man hissed. His horse had arrived at Senchet's side, and Senchet found himself staring along two and a half feet of gleaming steel.

'If you insist,' he shrugged. 'We were loyal members of the old King's household.'

'Really?' the man said. He kept his sword at Senchet's throat.

'Sir Jevan, please, lower your weapon. There is no need to threaten them,' the squire said.

'Perhaps, Squire, but we would be foolish to take any chances. This fellow should drop his weapons, and his companion too. Squire, please send your man-at-arms to my Lord de Berkeley and warn him that we have a cart blocking our path. Suggest that he comes here to speak with the man.'

'Very well,' the squire said. He was a young man of perhaps five-and-twenty, who surveyed the countryside with a world-weary air. 'But I do hope you can be swift. I was looking forward to a good lunch at Berkeley, and I am sure that Sir Edward would appreciate it too.'

'We shall see,' Sir Jevan said. He glanced at the man in the back of the cart. 'Who are you? Are you injured?'

'I was set upon by footpads, and I have a wound in my flank. These kind gentlemen have saved my life, taking it upon themselves to bring me to safety.' Dolwyn had spoken with his eyes closed, but now he opened them and suddenly took in Sir Jevan's face. His face paled as he recognised him.

Sir Jevan saw his expression change, and his attention quickened. He peered at Dolwyn's face closely, his eyes narrowed. 'You were the churl who slowed me when I chased the felon!' His glance fell upon the cart, and he saw the shape of weapons concealed by a blanket.

'Climb down from the cart very slowly,' he advised them. Harry and Dolwyn moved obediently. Senchet tried to slip sideways, but Sir Jevan spun his horse about. 'Move further, man, and you will lose your head. *Comprenez?* You are to come with us.'

Senchet smiled, but there was no humour in his face. 'What now?'

'Drop your sword-belt and any knives about you.'

There was the sound of approaching hooves. An order came from behind him, and Sir Jevan turned to see the chief guard of Edward of Caernafon.

'*Dieu ou diable?*' Senchet muttered. 'Sieur Gilbert?'

'You haven't hanged yet then, friend Senchet?'

CHAPTER THIRTY-THREE

Near Berkeley Castle

It was the bad fortune of the age, John reflected. He was unlucky enough to have been born in a period when no man could live an honourable life, free of fear. Everything conspired always to swyve the best plans possible.

He fretted on his horse, staring ahead at the huddle of men, and it was all he could do not to shout and demand that they get moving again. He had to keep his head down below the back of the man in front so that Sir Jevan would not see him, but even so, he flinched every time Sir Jevan glanced in his direction.

'Why have we stopped?' a man asked him, and it was all he could do not to punch him for his stupidity.

He spoke with frigid precision. 'There is a cart in the road. Perhaps it is the cart of a local farmer, eh? But what if this wagon is the property of a man who has a desire to kill Sir Edward of Caernarfon? There are many about who have cause to hate him, are there not?'

'Oh.'

John could see Sir Baldwin talking to the three who stood by the cart, but from here it was impossible to discover what they were saying. Lord Thomas de Berkeley gave a command to Sir John Maltravers, he saw, and Sir John rode forward at a fast trot, four of his own guards riding with him – which left only a handful of men-at-arms guarding Sir Edward of Caernarfon.

Almost without thinking, he kicked his horse into motion and rode towards Sir Edward. Gilbert was ahead of him. The man was turning in his saddle: he looked as though he was going to say something, but then, as he came closer, John saw that there were only a couple of men between him and Edward.

There was a rushing in his ears. It would be the work of a moment to trot forward, right alongside the prisoner, draw a knife and cut his throat. And then – no more fighting, no more strife. No more deaths like Paul's.

'In God's name,' he prayed to himself, and would have spurred his beast, but then he felt a hand at his knee, stilling him.

'Not now, my friend.' It was William. 'You could not grab the King and ride three-score paces with him before someone would bring you down. Look about you, at all the men here. There are plans already to rescue him. Do not risk yourself.'

'I wanted to—'

'I understand,' William hissed. 'I do, truly. But there will be better moments, believe me. For now it is better by far that we wait. Trust me, John. If not, all is lost! He *will* be rescued.'

John nodded, but as he drew the reins, about to return to the rear guard, he cast a final look at Sir Edward.

He had not meant to rescue him. *He had meant to kill him.*

Berkeley Castle

'Hah! This is more like it, Sir Baldwin, eh? A good castle with beef to eat and strong ale to drink – I swear I shall rest well tonight, no matter that the French King's host should come knocking on the door!'

Baldwin smiled thinly. It was ever the same when a large household arrived at a stop-over, whether it was a large inn or a castle: first there would be the dawdling about while the senior people were escorted to their rooms and made comfortable, their beasts taken aside to the better stabling and cared for, their baggage all taken up to their chambers ready for them, while maids and servants darted hither and thither with trenchers and platters and mugs and drinking horns. By the time all their needs were catered for, the last poor devils were allowed in to take up any spare room for their horses, and then finally try to locate any space where they themselves might collapse and sleep.

'Perhaps, Sir Richard,' he nodded. 'However, it may be troublesome to find space for so many people tonight, including ourselves, do you not think?'

'Don't see why, sir! No, we shall soon be accommodated, I'm sure. First, *food*.'

At that moment, a young maid went scurrying past. She had thick, curly black hair under her coif, and her grey eyes were panicky.

Sir Richard put on a kindly smile. 'Maid! MAID!'

She almost fell to the ground before his bellow. 'Sir—'

'My dear, you are busy, I appreciate that, but I have need of ale, food and a spot for me bed. Now, where can I find all these?'

'Sir, I am sorry, I have been ordered to take these to . . .'

Sir Richard was already gazing down at the tray she bore with every sign of satisfaction. 'That looks perfect.'

'It is for the guard with Sir Edward.'

'Good. We *are* the guard.'

'But, Sir Knight, you can't just take it,' she pleaded.

'Is there more where this came from?' he asked.

'Yes, but—'

'You tell them that Sir Richard de Welles forced you to give it up – that he was most brutal and demanding, and you feared for your life. Because you would, wouldn't you, if I was to threaten you?'

She looked at his kindly eyes set in that round face with the thick beard. A smile broke out on her face. 'No.'

'You don't think me terrifying?'

'Not really. So, sir, I will take these to the men who ordered them.' She slipped around him, and then paused. 'But if you were to wait over there, by the stable, I may not be able to get round you again,' she said with a little smile, before disappearing on her errand.

Baldwin scowled. 'How do you manage that?' he wondered. 'You're old enough to be her grandfather, and yet you have her simpering like a maid with her swain.'

'Don't know what you mean,' Sir Richard said innocently. 'Only asked her for some help, that's all.'

'Yes,' Baldwin said, and glanced at Simon, who burst out laughing. The two followed after the knight as he made his way to the place she had pointed out.

Matteo eyed the castle with interest. Its age was evident. Ancient-looking stone was scarred with white where pigeons had roosted. Mortar between stones had been pecked away by generations of sparrows. There were three or four holes in the wall of the keep itself which he could see, and he decided to avoid standing beneath the castle's walls or the towers. To be struck by one of those lumps of red-gold stone would be to die instantly. He needed no second brush with death.

Whole sections of wall had been demolished. A pile of rubble lay at the base of one tower, and this made him frown in concern. The castle was not so strong as it appeared from without.

Matteo did not care for heights. While labourers climbed up and down ladders with their hods full of mortar, some apprentices scampered about like monkeys on the narrowest of walkways, defying death at every leap and sending Matteo's heart into his mouth.

The men-at-arms shouted and swore as their horses were taken by grooms and led away, and there was a rush of bodies towards the buildings as they ran to lay claim to beds, palliasses or even sections of filthy floor. Only then did Matteo see the cart again, with the three men found on the way here. It was clear that the three were viewed with suspicion, because they were kept apart from all the others, and a man with a long polearm stood watching them with his weapon at the ready.

Matteo saw Dolwyn's eyes move towards him, and quickly averted his gaze.

'Brother mine, I am pleased to see you,' Benedetto called. He was standing at the door to the hall, but hurried to meet Matteo, offering a helpful hand from his horse.

It was irritating, this patronising solicitude which Benedetto displayed towards his younger brother, but that was not why Matteo almost rejected his aid. It was the thought that this hand might have held the knife that stabbed him. Or paid the assassin who wielded it.

He took Benedetto's hand.

Throughout his life, Manuele or Benedetto had always been at Matteo's side, and while he often resented their casual treatment of him, he knew they needed him. Without Matteo and his network of informers, the House of Bardi would have lost a vast sum in recent years.

Alured slipped from his horse as Matteo and Benedetto began to stroll together. He followed them.

'Are you well, brother? You look tired,' Benedetto said.

'It has been a weary journey. I had to see Sir Roger Mortimer.' Matteo explained about his journey to Wales, and the delivery of the indenture to Kenilworth.

'Tell me, do you recognise any of those men there?' Benedetto asked, staring at the three by the cart.

Matteo felt his heart lurch. He looked at Harry, Senchet and Dolwyn, and saw Dolwyn's eyes glitter. The two beside him saw Matteo and Benedetto at the same moment, and Harry looked as though he was about step forward to speak with him, when the polearm dropped before him. Harry gave the guard a look of poisonous contempt.

'They are the two who came to see us in our house in London,' Matteo said quickly. 'On the day Manuele was murdered.'

'Perhaps they are here to finish us off?'

'Why?' Matteo scoffed. 'Because Manuele held back? I do not think so. They were angry with him, but it was the mob which caught him and pulled him from his horse.'

'True, I suppose. But I will ask Lord Thomas who they say they are,' Benedetto said. 'Even if they did not kill Manuele, if they were the men who attacked you, they should be made to pay.'

Matteo said nothing. Benedetto was right that the three men were dangerous, but he had no idea just what shocking information Dolwyn could give him.

Or did he? Matteo wondered again whether Dolwyn had been responsible for his wound. Benedetto could afford an expensive assassin. Dolwyn was bearded and filthy, so it was understandable Benedetto might not have recognised him, but if Dolwyn was *his* hireling, he would pretend not to know him. The possibilities made his head ache.

'Lord Berkeley will know what to do with them,' Matteo said at last.

'If you are sure,' his brother said. 'So,' he continued as they walked towards the castle's hall, 'you came from Kenilworth with Sir Edward of Caernarfon. How is he?'

'Sad,' Matteo said.

'A good thing we supported the Queen then, eh? Have you news from Sir Roger Mortimer?'

'None that he intends you to have,' Matteo said with a thin smile. 'He seeks to strengthen his grip on the country, but dare not alienate any. Especially now, with war brewing in the north.'

'Does he want war?'

'It has been forced on him. The Bruce demands that King Edward III renounce his claim to Scotland, that the first act of his government should be to relinquish his Scottish territories. Preparations for war are under way, and Bruce is ravaging the north. King Edward and Sir Roger must march before too long.'

There was more news to be relayed, and Benedetto listened carefully as Matteo spoke. He asked a few questions, then sought the advice which only Matteo could give. Soon they were finished for the present, and Matteo could find a chamber in which to rest.

He lay back and closed his eyes. It was a blessed relief to lie on a good bed, but as soon as his back touched the mattress, his wound hurt. It was inflamed after all the journeying, and he grunted, 'Bencdetto, it was you, wasn't it?' as he rolled over.

Benedetto had wanted to position the bank wholeheartedly behind the Queen and her son. He hadn't wanted Matteo to stir up confusion by supporting the old King.

There was no man alive so ruthless, Matteo thought before he fell asleep, as a man of money seeking to protect his wealth.

In the court, Alured had listened with astonishment to the brothers talking. If *he* had suspected a man of knifing him, especially his brother, he would never have been able to walk with the bastard. It would have turned his stomach.

Meanwhile, it was interesting to know that those two scruffy scrotes with Dolwyn were in London when the murders happened and Matteo got wounded. He surreptitiously glanced at their boots, but whatever they may have looked like five or six months ago, they were now so scratched and covered in mud that they could have been a hundred years old.

He should stop this. There was no point in trying to find a murderer from so long ago. Also, it was ridiculous to believe the evidence of a witness who was drunk at the time, and could well be dead by now. There was nothing to say that the 'knight' he saw with the red Cordova boots was actually the killer, and not merely a man who had run along the alley to escape the crowds, and when he found the bodies, fled.

But Alured couldn't stop. The thought of those two youngsters slain for no purpose, stuck in his mind like a fishbone in a man's throat, and no matter how he struggled he could not shift it.

CHAPTER THIRTY-FOUR

Berkeley Castle

When they had finally managed to sort themselves out, the chambers at the castle were already gone. The King had a large room to himself, along with Gilbert and some few guards, as well as a friar, but the rest of the men must make shift to accommodate themselves as best they could. The men of the castle garrison made it plain that their additional protection was unnecessary here in the King's room, and Baldwin and Sir Ralph were removed from the main chamber in a polite, but implacable manner.

The pair had gone with Simon and their servants to the main castle building, but it was quickly apparent that they would not succeed in winning a space in the great hall itself. There would be no sleep for the poor devils who crowded about that room. Simon hoped that Baldwin and Sir Richard would exercise their rights as knights and demand a spot near the fire, but instead, to his consternation, they walked back out through the screen and along the passage to the main courtyard. There Sir Richard stood, his thumbs in his sword-belt, waiting, with a smile set on his face, eyeing the servants and porters milling about the inner ward.

'What's he up to?' Simon demanded.

Baldwin shrugged. 'There are some men, Simon, who go through life hoping that they will be granted that which they deserve, and there are others who *know* that they will receive, no matter what. Sir Richard is one such. He believes he will receive better treatment, and few would dare to deny him what he expects.'

Simon thought this sounded bizarre. From hard-learned experience, he knew full well that the best place always was as close to the fire as possible. It was lunacy to be out here, he thought, and pulled his cloak about him.

Hugh was grimly studying the walls about the inner ward. 'So, shall we get the horses saddled and find an inn, or go back inside?'

'Ah!' Sir Richard said, and nodded towards the kitchen. The same young maid was standing outside. She noticed Sir Richard, and wiped her hands clean on her apron, before rolling her eyes and walking towards them.

'You hungry still?' she asked.

'My dear young woman, the food was good, the ale excellent, and the company still better,' Sir Richard said heartily. 'But there is one last problem with which we must contend. We find that the whole of the guard party for the old King must contest a few meagre feet of cold stone floor.'

'There is a stable with a hayloft,' she said.

'Ah. Is there?' enquired the knight, smiling.

'You want me to show you to it?'

'Would a man with my trained physique be able to climb the ladder?'

She eyed him with a chuckle. 'Oh, follow me, then. There's a small chamber at the side.'

The wench had brought them all here, to a small shed set into the wall. It had a hearth at the wall itself, and a hole above to let the smoke out. Someone had used it for storage, and the floor was littered with pieces of wood and twigs. For the men, it was fine. Edgar began to clear the space nearest the fire, while Hugh set himself to fetching all their belongings, and soon they had their packs and blankets arranged neatly, with a fire roaring, and its cheery light illuminating the room.

'That is better,' Baldwin said. He looked about the chamber. 'Where is Sir Richard?'

Edgar cleared his throat. 'I think the maid felt he needed more comfort, Sir Baldwin.'

Baldwin gave him a look of baffled horror. 'She took him?'

'What I do not understand,' Simon said, 'is how he gets away with it. A man half his age, and more handsome, more polite and courteous, would not have half the luck of Sir Richard. Still, for my part, I don't care. For once I can sleep without the noise of his snoring to disturb me, and that is a wonderful prospect.'

From outside, in the hall, there came a loud cheer, then singing and some shouting. A celebration, it seemed, was underway.

A short while later, Sir Ralph entered their room, gazing about him with the look of a man who was grateful for any comforts which the world could offer.

'Sir Ralph, you are very welcome,' Baldwin said. Aside to Simon, he added, 'I trust you do not mind that I invited another to share our good fortune? This is Sir Ralph of Evesham, Simon. Sir Ralph, my old friend Simon Puttock.'

'Of course,' Simon said, offering his hand. 'You were with Baldwin when Sir Edward of Caernarfon was captured.'

'That is so,' Sir Ralph said a little stiffly.

'My apologies,' Simon said hurriedly. 'It was not my intention to upset you with unfortunate memories.'

'No, you do not upset me, but you will understand that those days were not my happiest,' Sir Ralph said.

'Of course. Please, be seated,' Simon said, and plied him with wine.

'You must be very competent looters to have gathered together so vast a store of provisions already,' Sir Ralph said, eyeing their food.

'One of our party is,' Baldwin laughed. 'Do you know Sir Richard de Welles?'

'Ah, so he is with you? That would explain much,' Sir Ralph chuckled.

Simon refilled Sir Ralph's mazer with wine. The man had already drained the first in a single gulp. 'I am most grateful,' Sir Ralph said, and gave a dry cough. 'My throat feels as if it's been scoured with rough stone. The dust on that journey was unbelievable.'

Simon nodded. His eyes felt the same. 'And soon we shall have to endure the long ride homewards, eh, Baldwin?'

Baldwin looked at Sir Ralph. 'What do you think, Sir Ralph?'

The knight shrugged and pulled a face. 'I think we shall not be here for very much longer. If all I have heard is right, soon we shall be ordered to muster for the march north with all our men and equipment.'

Baldwin nodded. 'This unhappy realm.'

Simon felt his pleasure at finding such a good billet fade away. 'You think they'll want us to join them?' he said to Baldwin.

'This is to be a long, hard war against the Scottish,' Baldwin guessed. 'The new King will wish to impose his will on the Bruce. Bruce is a cunning old devil, but there are tales that he is dying. He wishes to leave a firm inheritance for his family, I estimate. That is why he has begun to ravage the north again. It is a ploy of his, to destabilise the young King's realm so that Bruce can rule in peace in Scotland. But King Edward III is not made of the same fibres as his father. You remember how his grandfather, Edward I, was named the "Hammer of the Scots"? I have heard it said before that often one strong man will beget a feeble son, but that sometimes in the third generation the early strength and determination will reappear, and often with renewed vigour. Perhaps it will be so with our new King. He appears a determined and competent young man, from all I have seen.'

'He'll want the strongest army he can gather,' Sir Ralph said, adding quietly, 'if only to ensure that Sir Roger Mortimer is held in check.'

Baldwin gave a dry smile. 'I personally would not wish to trust him without an army at my back.'

'Well, at least we can return home first,' Simon said. 'I don't want to be up here any longer than necessary.'

'Quite so,' Baldwin agreed.

'Yes,' Sir Ralph said. 'As soon as we are confident that Sir Edward of Caernarfon is safe here, then we may leave.'

Simon saw Sir Ralph and his friend exchange a look at that, and his heart sank. No matter what they said to his face, it could be some little while before they would be able to leave.

Senchet and Harry watched the cart being taken away to the stables. Senchet wanted to keep close to all that lovely money in the chest, but even as he watched, two men lifted it down. There was a low stone building near the entrance of the castle, and the men hauled the chest over to it between them. There a man with keys, presumably the keeper, opened the door. The two carried the box inside, and a moment later they were out and the door was again locked.

Senchet felt utter despair at the thought of that lost fortune.

Matteo could smell the smoke, he could hear the screams and shouts, see his brother's horse rearing, Manuele flailing about him with his riding crop, while the mob attempted to pull him down, some with knives and hatchets, a butcher with his two-handed cleaver. Matteo tried to run towards him, but the throng was too thick, and his legs moved as if through treacle . . . and then he felt the grip of men's hands on his arms, tugging him away, back from the mob and their bonfire, backwards to safety.

And then he heard the shouts, the sudden pattering of feet, the bellow from old Andrew, his bodyguard, followed by the thud of stones landing all about him. And he felt the stone that clubbed him on the back of the head, slamming him to the ground, seeing the cobblestones rise up to meet his face – and his men running to save their own skins, leaving him to die in the dust.

He felt the single, quick stab in his back, and he screamed . . .

. . . and woke, sweating, the wound inflamed once more. He rolled over on to his belly, knowing it was only a dream, that the mares would bring the same visions to him night after night, that he would never be free of this horror.

It was a long time before he dared close his eyes again.

303

Tuesday after Palm Sunday[1]

Berkeley Castle

John had slept moderately well, and woke hoping that his growing beard would protect him from recognition.

The castle was stirring as he rose from his blanket near the wall in the main hall. He walked outside with his blankets and set the bundle on his saddle where he had left it, before studying the yard without enthusiasm. The land around was boggy. It would be astonishingly difficult for any party to storm the place. Still more so to achieve that and reach Edward.

'You are worried, my friend?' William atte Hull was at his side already, and he smiled to see John's startled expression. 'Don't panic. It is a skill, walking quietly, which poachers round my home learn when they are young.'

John whispered earnestly, 'The Dunheveds will not be able to take this place. It is too well protected.'

'You mean men?'

'Men, yes. There are too many here. If there were only a small garrison perhaps it could be attempted, but with *this* force? No. No one could get in here.'

'Perhaps not usually,' William atte Hull said. 'But with men inside the castle to ensure that the gate opened, and then helping us from within, then it would be different.'

'Not with so many guards,' John said bleakly. He looked about him at the men up on the walls, more men down in the yard, and even as he watched, a party of men rode in through the gates. 'And even without them, the land about here is too marshy for a force to reach the place. They would have to come along the road, and that would make them too obvious.'

1 7 April 1327

'There may be another way,' his companion said. 'And we shall discover it.'

'If you say so. But I am doubtful, friend.'

'There is always hope.'

There was a loud shout from the gate, and John turned to stare as a pair of shabby peasants approached from the mists.

'Who are they?' John asked.

William atte Hull looked up without interest. 'Beggars, perhaps? Either that or a priest and woman petitioning the Lord de Berkeley for some slight, real or imagined.'

John nodded. He felt as though he was in great danger all the time that he remained here in the castle. 'Sir Jevan saw me, you know, at the gate at Kenilworth.'

'If he sees you here, tell me,' William said. His gaze moved back to the two bedraggled figures at the gate. 'We may have to do something about him.'

CHAPTER THIRTY-FIVE

Berkeley Castle

Agatha felt the weight of the place as she stepped under the gatehouse. This castle was built, it seemed to her, of men's dreams and ambitions. And they were crushing.

'We are here to speak to the Lord de Berkeley,' Father Luke said to the porter at the gate.

The man looked the Father up and down, and kept his hand on his sword. Giving a whistle over his shoulder, he kept half an eye on the priest and Agatha, while peering out towards the roadway beyond them. Soon a small group of men-at-arms was gathered about them, and the porter could devote his entire attention to them. 'Where you from?'

'Willersey. It is—'

'I know where it is. Why're you here?'

'I said, to speak with—'

'Yeah. You said.' The man scratched at his armpit, gazing at Agatha. 'What's she want?'

'To speak with—'

'My Lord de Berkeley, yeah. Why?'

Agatha felt her indomitable spirit returning in the face of this petty official. 'I'll tell the lord himself, not his meanest servant,' she snapped.

'Meanest, eh?' the porter said, taking in her black garb. 'A widow are you, then? All in your weeds. So you're here to demand help from his lordship, I suppose? Perhaps some money to compensate you? You just go home to your donkey, mistress and—'

'HOI! PORTER!' Simon, Baldwin and Sir Richard de Welles had overheard this conversation from where they sat on a bench near the armourers' rooms.

'Yes, sir?'

'Let them in. I would speak with them.'

'Sir, they are . . .'

Sir Richard de Welles was unused to being denied his whims. Hearing the porter attempt to refuse him, he smiled and nodded.

The porter felt a vague unease, but continued nonetheless. 'Sir, I have been ordered to prevent any suspicious characters from entering.'

'Aye. Very sensible.'

'Anybody who is not known must be refused admission. Because of the prisoner.'

'Oh. Right.'

'So I cannot let these in.'

'Suspicious characters, eh?'

The porter looked at the large knight's face and felt a sinking in his belly. 'Sir, I . . .'

'The priest, eh? You think he's dangerous? He carries a poisoned crucifix, I suppose?'

'No, but—'

'The widow? You think she carries a siege engine upon her person?'

The porter wisely chose to remain silent.

'Let them enter,' Sir Richard boomed. 'If there's any danger it'll be to me, and I think I'll be safe enough, but if they overpower me, you have my permission to take any action you see fit.'

The man subsided reluctantly, muttering to himself about guests taking over the place, and curtly waved away his guards as he marched back to the gatehouse, Then Sir Richard beckoned Agatha and Luke to join them.

'Now, mistress,' Sir Richard said, looking at Agatha. 'What're you here for, eh?'

'My husband is dead. The man who killed him stole our cart and horse, and I want them back,' she glowered.

'Aye, I'm sure ye do,' Sir Richard said heartily. 'What of it?'

'I thought that the Lord de Berkeley would help me. I am one of his serfs,' she said.

'And you, priest?'

'I am Father Luke of St Peter's, Willersey, where this good woman comes from.'

'Oh.' Sir Richard looked at Agatha again. 'So, why do you think that the Lord de Berkeley will have time to help you?'

'It was all we had, that old horse and cart. The horse wasn't even a good one, but at least he was reliable. He drew goods all the way to Kenilworth, and then—'

'Kenilworth?' interrupted Sir Richard. 'When?'

Agatha shot a look at Luke, and in her heart there was horror at her betrayal. She hadn't meant to speak of that, and certainly not to bring Father Luke into her story so swiftly.

Father Luke smiled gently. 'Do not worry, Agatha, I am sure that this good knight will understand.'

Sir Ralph and Baldwin were leaning forward now.

Baldwin spoke softly. 'Madam, are you saying that you were there at the attack?'

'No, it was me,' said Luke. He shook his head. 'So many dead men, and all for nothing.'

'What were you doing there?' Simon demanded.

'There was money on that cart.' Father Luke went on to explain about the chest of gold which had been left in his care.

'And you think this gold was on the cart when it was stolen?' Baldwin frowned.

'I don't know where else it could have gone,' Father Luke said.

'Wherever it went, it probably went there a long time ago,' Simon said. He leaned back in his chair. He had spent so many years dealing with the law and enforcing it on Dartmoor, that he had a solid understanding of the mind of a felon. 'Whoever took your cart, mistress, has almost certainly sold it. If he had the brains to look in the chest, that money will be gone too. A man like that will not have gone far, though. If you look within a ten-mile radius of where you found your husband, I'd lay a wager that the thief will be there. Probably in a city with a bevy of whores about him, and reeking of cider or strong ale. He'll have spent it rashly, not thinking that tomorrow he'll hang for murder, because men like that never think.'

Baldwin was frowning. 'Mistress Agatha, this cart – of what type was it? And the beast that pulled it, what manner of horse was this? You say old, but what colour, what markings?'

Agatha shrugged. 'The cart was a good, sturdy one, with a plank to sit on. Two wheels, one either side. It was plain, but wider than most. As to the horse, well, he was a good height, with a broad chest, and a white flash on his breast like a fist. He had brown on his flanks and back and head, but there was a

309

white ankle on his left foreleg, and above the right rear leg he had a star on his rump.'

Simon had not been close to the cart when it was captured the previous day, but he realised that something was going on, and he looked at his friends with interest. 'What? What is it?'

Berkeley Castle Hall

This morning Matteo had woken tired and unrested amid the hubbub of the celebrations in the hall at the return of Lord Berkeley, as people demonstrated their joy at the fact that the lord's most despised enemy, the man who had seen him incarcerated for years – Sir Edward of Caernarfon – was now his prisoner.

Even when he did manage to fall asleep, Matteo kept seeing the same vision: Benedetto, chasing after him with that wicked knife in his fist and a look of cold hatred in his eyes.

Three times Matteo fell into a heavy slumber, and each time he was woken by that horrible mare. The last occasion, he had woken himself with a scream. After he had reassured Alured that he was perfectly safe, he had lain awake, staring into the shadows of his room.

Rising long after dawn, Matteo dressed slowly, and went to the hall to eat. Inside it was filled with benches and long tables. There were no spaces that he could see, and he was about to ask a steward where he might sit, when the lord lifted the tapestry behind the dais and walked in.

All those in the hall stood, their benches scraping and screeching on the tiled floor. Until the lord had walked to his seat and taken it, all his guests of lower degree must remain on their feet. It was a matter of protocol and good manners.

Lord Berkeley was a happy man, and although last night he had celebrated in grand style, this morning he was still in a cheerful mood, from what Matteo could see. His laughter rang out over all the other noises of the hall, and Matteo was irritated to see how the man smiled and clapped his men on the back. His own head was sore from lack of sleep.

At last the lord stood in front of his seat, staring at the assembled men before sitting. This was the signal for a general scraping of benches and stools, until at last all the assembled men were seated. Benedetto, as the head of the House of Bardi, was granted the unusual privilege of a seat at the lord's table, next to Sir John Maltravers, but Matteo was not given the same honour. He looked about him for a space at any of the messes, but there was none. Angry at being ignored, he strode from the room.

A kitchen maid took pity on him and offered him a crust or two of good white bread, along with a jug of strong ale, and he sat on a stool by the gate nursing his bitterness until he had finished his food. It soothed him, and soon he was engaged in conversation with the porter.

It was a useful chat. The porter was garrulous on the subject of the new prisoner.

There were several advantages to Lord Berkeley in taking on the role of Sir Edward's gaoler, Matteo learned. First among them was the fact that he now had funds to support an increased garrison. Matteo heard Sir John Maltravers mention the fee on the ride here: five pounds each day, just to look after the King's father. And it would not cost him that much, Matteo knew.

The chamber in which the sorry man had been installed was narrow and dank. It had a window that looked out over a little courtyard, and a smelly garderobe in the corner. It was a most deplorable lodging for a former King. From what Matteo heard, he felt it insulted not only Sir Edward, but the realm. Yet it provided the porter with great amusement.

Matteo chewed and listened carefully.

The money would be enormously useful for Lord Thomas because it was not merely for the upkeep of Sir Edward; it was to make sure that he remained in captivity without the opportunity of escape. Thus it would help with the cost of his rebuilding works, too.

Leaving the man, Matteo went to stand in the gateway, staring out over the landscape. Today the weather was almost warm enough for a Florentine, he thought. But too humid.

He could not leave the thought of Benedetto. How much longer could he maintain this pretence of civility to his would-be murderer without losing his mind?

He must force a conclusion somehow.

Sir Jevan eyed the men about him in the hall as he finished his meal. It had been a surprise to come across that churl who had held him up that day when he was pursuing the felon. Good to see that his sword had marked the man, but odd to find him so close to Berkeley. And then the fleeting glimpse of that other face: the man he had been chasing.

He had been so close to bellowing that the fellow there was one who had been with the attackers of Kenilworth – and yet as soon as he thought of it, the face vanished, and no matter how Sir Jevan sought him, he could not find him anywhere.

Oh well. He knew his eyesight was not of the best, so perhaps he had been mistaken. He would keep a close eye on all the fellows about the castle, just in case.

Matteo looked over towards the forebuilding, in which he knew Sir Edward of Caernarfon was being held. Irked by the thought of the horrible confinement of that once great King, Matteo set off in the opposite direction, around the main keep.

Matteo had good reason to wish to speak with the captive, but knowing *how* to was the problem.

There was a sudden shout behind him, and a young man hobbled towards him. 'A message,' he called.

Matteo recognised the lad. He was one of Benedetto's messengers who had been left with the Queen and Sir Roger Mortimer. He nodded, and took the proffered note. He checked the seal: it had been signed by the Queen herself, he saw. He broke the wax and glanced down the roll, and then whistled.

'Go and find yourself some food and drink,' he said to the messenger. 'You will need to rest, after riding all that way.'

The fellow gave him a grateful look, and followed his directions to the buttery, exhausted after his punishing ride.

'So,' Matteo said to himself. 'The Queen thinks her son would have a war, does she?' A war was good. There were endless opportunities for a bank to earn money during a conflict. As soon as he could, he would have to bring this to Benedetto's attention, he thought – but then gave a frown. Benedetto was not the man that Manuele had been when it came to decision-making. He was always weighing one argument against another, considering this compared with that . . . never making up his mind.

Matteo was about to walk back to the hall, when he saw the knight Sir Baldwin de Furnshill and the other, Sir Richard de Welles, heading towards the stables. With them were a woman in black and a priest. There was something about the way they moved that intrigued him – and he decided to sneak along behind them, to find out what they were up to.

The cart was standing a short way from the rest of the wagons, carts and paraphernalia of transport in the large chamber close by the little stable.

313

As Baldwin knew, usually horses and equipment would be stored away from the castle. Lord Berkeley's warhorses were kept at his great stables at Wotton-Under-Edge, and they would be sent for as required. Today the stables were still over-full from the arrival of so many men yesterday, but the old nag from the cart stood out even so.

Baldwin could see it from some distance away. The white fist was quite plain, and the star he remembered from the day before. It was exactly as the woman had described it.

Agatha glanced over all the beasts, but it was obvious when she spotted her own. A smile spread over her face, and she looked at the priest for confirmation. 'That's him.'

Father Luke nodded. 'It certainly is. I remember that fellow from all those miles to Kenilworth. That star is imprinted upon my mind. Where are the goods from the cart?'

Baldwin looked at Sir Richard. 'They are convincing, are they not?'

'Aye, like enough. So, good Agatha, what was on the cart?'

'I don't know – it was whatever the purveyor wanted to take. Some perry, I think, and lampreys.'

'And a small chest,' Father Luke said. 'About this size,' he added, gesturing with his hands.

'That was where your money was held?' Simon asked.

'Yes.'

'We shall need to speak with the fellows who brought this cart here,' Baldwin said, 'and the castle's steward will know where the items from the back of the cart have gone.'

'Where is the castle prison, do you think?' Sir Richard said.

Simon had seen a man leaning negligently against a wall at the farther side of the courtyard. Gesturing at him, he said, 'I would think if he isn't the gaoler, he will know who is.'

CHAPTER THIRTY-SIX

Berkeley Castle

When Sir Jevan de Bromfield caught sight of Benedetto Bardi, he gave the short bow due to a man of wealth, even if he were a mere merchant.

'Sir Jevan,' Benedetto said, bowing lower.

The knight smiled at his politeness. It was natural that a banker should be somewhat obsequious when faced with a man of noble birth. 'You have enjoyed your meal?'

'His lordship was most courteous.'

Sir Jevan thought, Yes, he would be. He knows you could lend him enough money to rebuild his entire castle. 'You are popular.'

'I am fortunate to be able to help people in need,' Benedetto said.

Sir Jevan detected smugness; it was enough to turn his stomach. 'The Queen must be very grateful,' he said.

'She appreciates the good I can do for her,' Benedetto said smoothly. 'I was glad to help her and the King.'

Sir Jevan commented, 'Your brother – he suffers from mares, I hear. He was very loud last night.'

Benedetto nodded; he had to step to one side as a man barged past on his way to the smiths' forges. 'Yes, Matteo was attacked by the mob in London. It was a terrible affair – I thought he would die.'

'Death is never pleasant.' Sir Jevan recalled for a moment the young woman's face, the shock on her swain's as his sword thrust into flesh. Those two deaths had been so long ago, he had all but forgotten them. But now there was something that brought them back to him. Benedetto – of course, he told himself. He had gone to meet Benedetto just after killing them both.

'He is a different man since the attack,' Benedetto said.

'Near-death is bound to affect a man,' Sir Jevan said, tiring of the conversation and the banker. He looked about him. 'Is that him?' He pointed to Matteo.

'Yes,' Benedetto said. 'My poor brother. I sometimes fear he will not live long.'

'Really?' Sir Jevan said distractedly, observing the group with Sir Baldwin, the priest and the woman heading towards the gaol.

He wanted to speak with that carter too.

Berkeley Castle Gaol

Dolwyn squatted at the wall. He had spent a miserable night incarcerated here, but it was no worse than the nights at Newgate, and he could contemplate his future with some equanimity.

He had seen the two Bardi brothers. That was interesting. He had taken money from one in order to kill another: if that story was not to be betrayed, the man in question should hurry and secure his release. Dolwyn was not going to the gallows without ensuring that those who had hired him suffered the same fate.

And he still had a parchment in his purse. That was something that plenty of men would be interested to see. Yes, he felt that he had some protection.

The other two prisoners showed little interest in him. They were more concerned with their own situation, and clearly they had reason to be alarmed. In recent months, they had been enemies of Lord Berkeley and Sir Roger Mortimer, the King's Regent, and could expect little in the way of sympathy from their captor.

There was no water to drink, other than a bucket of foul-smelling liquid that could have been dredged from the moat itself. It stank of mud and rancid weed. One other bucket was provided in the room, for which he was grateful. He had heard that many gaolers did not bother with such niceties. He only hoped that the two had not been mixed up.

It was just as he was beginning to think seriously about how long he could survive without some food, that the door's lock moved. There was the sound of keys turning, and they all stood up. It was better to face whatever might happen while on their feet.

The door was pushed wide, and outside there was a series of faces staring in.

'Father, do you recognise any of these?' a man asked.

Father Luke peered inside, studying Harry, then Senchet, and then his eyes fell on Dolwyn, and he shook his head.

'No, I know none of these.'

'But I do,' Sir Jevan said. 'I would like to speak with this man now.'

He had seen them over there, Benedetto and that tall knight, pointing at him. Benedetto looked like a farmer, pointing to which sheep he wanted slaughtered, Matteo thought. Not that he would use a man like Sir Jevan as an assassin. Not when there were cheaper men to be bought, like Dolwyn.

As Sir Jevan left Benedetto and hurried after Baldwin, Matteo walked across the court, Benedetto had scarcely been able to meet his eye. Matteo had that feeling in his back again, as though the blade had never left it.

He had never felt so lonely and threatened.

Baldwin was glad of the aid of Sir Jevan. With his help Baldwin was able to summons two men-at-arms, who stood nearby with their weapons ready as the three men were brought up the long, narrow stairs from their cell and out into the sun. There Baldwin called on them to give him their names.

Only one night, and the sight of them was already enough to inspire sympathy, Baldwin thought to himself. The foreigner, Senchet, was trying to smile, but his eyes betrayed his anxiety. Harry was more grim-faced, and spent much of his time peering at Edgar, who stood a short way to his side, wearing his usual easy smile. It was an expression designed to goad others to fury when they saw it, but Harry was clearly not angry, only anxious and wary.

It was the last man who attracted Baldwin's attention. He stood with his head lowered, rather like a bull preparing to charge. He did not look concerned at his incarceration. Indeed, he might have been a long-serving prisoner from the way that he glared at Baldwin and the others. He had the gaolbird's contempt for his guards. His only admission of weakness was the hand he held at his injured side.

'He was the man who delayed me when I was chasing a felon,' Sir Jevan said.

'You were in charge of the cart?' Baldwin asked. 'Sir Jevan here remembers you.'

'Aye – and I remember *him* well. He did this to me.'

'You were preventing me from chasing a criminal,' Sir Jevan said between gritted teeth.

'I was walking along a road when you and your companions rode past me. You were the one who couldn't pass – the others did well enough – and because you were enraged at your poor riding, you stabbed me.'

'You deliberately moved your cart into my path!'

'I was hiding *beside* my cart so as not to be struck by a fool's hooves.'

'You are lying!' Sir Jevan spat, and lifted his arm as though to hit him.

Baldwin shot a look at Edgar, who smilingly stepped forward and shook his head.

'Out of my way,' hissed Sir Jevan, but Baldwin spoke quietly.

'Sir Jevan, I am Keeper of the King's Peace and I will not have a prisoner maltreated in my care.'

'And I will not have him lie about me!' Sir Jevan roared. He had never been exposed to a peasant's humour before, and now he could see a sneer of delight twisting Dolwyn's features. 'I'll wipe that smile from his ugly face!'

'No, Sir Jevan, you will not,' Baldwin said firmly. He turned to Dolwyn. 'Why did you have weapons in your cart?'

'They were in the cart when I found it.'

Agatha spat, 'When you killed my husband, you mean. Coxbones! You deny you killed my poor Ham?'

'What? What do you mean, "killed Ham"?'

Baldwin was watching him carefully. The man's surprise was unfeigned. If Baldwin had to guess, he spoke the truth. 'You deny it?'

'Of course I do. I didn't kill this Ham. I didn't even see him.'

'You liar!' Agatha shouted. She managed to spring forward and clump him on the head before Edgar, distracted by Jevan, could stop her. Father Luke and Simon together pulled her away. She shook them from her, muttering angrily.

'What do you say?' Baldwin demanded.

'I didn't kill him. I was going to capture him if I could, because he knocked me on the head and left me by the road. But I didn't lay a finger on him.'

'Why capture him?' Baldwin asked. 'To rob him of his money?'

'No,' Dolwyn said. 'To give him a headache like the one he gave me.'

'So you took an axe and killed him?' Agatha said. 'God's cods! You make me sick. You killed my poor man to steal the little we had.'

Dolwyn looked at her. 'As God is my judge, no. I'll put my hand on His Gospels and swear, if you want. May He strike me down here and now if I lie. I did not kill him. I got to Willersey late, and settled myself to sleep in the woods. Next morning, I woke to the sound of a horse whinnying, took it and the cart, and went on my way. I saw no one about the place.'

'So you admit you stole the cart?' Father Luke said.

'I took a cart that was without a master, and a horse. They could have been stolen otherwise. Then, for God's sake, some fools rode past me and all but killed me. This *honourable* knight struck at me because he was in a rage at being slowed. Not because of me, but because his own horse was shy.'

'You say I was not capable of riding, eh?' Sir Jevan would have leaped forward, but for Baldwin and Edgar blocking his path. Sir Jevan put his hand to his sword, but so did Edgar.

Baldwin shook his head. 'There is no need for swordplay, Sir Jevan.'

'Your man,' Sir Jevan said tersely, 'is in my way.'

'You will not attack the castle's prisoners,' Baldwin repeated, before eyeing Dolwyn again. 'What of the weapons?'

'They were there because of the purveyor,' Father Luke said sadly. 'I can explain all.'

Cirencester

The town was quiet as the two rode into it, and Stephen Dunheved cast about him warily, looking for any possible threats among the people there.

He felt very exposed.

'Brother, the more you stare about you, the more likely it is someone will think you suspicious,' Thomas said. He sat on a large black stallion which they had stolen from the stable of a supporter of Sir Roger Mortimer. At the same time they had liberated cattle and sheep worth almost forty pounds, which was enough to keep the men happy.

Stephen nodded, but it was hard to look out for men sent to arrest him from under his hat's brim. In the end he surrendered to fate, drawing his hat down.

They stopped at a tavern, and paid an urchin to hold their reins for them.

The young lad eyed them pensively. 'A penny.'

Thomas waved a hand in a vague benediction. 'For both.'

'No, for one.'

'Boy, if you argue I will say a ha'pence for the two.'

'Then I'll leave them.' He dropped the reins.

Stephen widened his eyes. 'Have you been boxed about the ears recently, lad? You soon will be.'

'A penny each.'

Thomas chuckled to himself. He pulled a silver penny from his pocket and held it out. 'When we return – *if* you have looked after our beasts well.'

'A' right, sir,' the boy agreed with a smile.

'That was too much,' Stephen said as they walked away. But there was little point in haggling. It would only spark interest in them that was bound to be unwelcome.

'Come,' Thomas said, leading the way.

The streets were broad, the houses appearing wealthy with their yellow stone, the occasional house of wood with wattle and daub and thatch that Stephen was used to. But it was the wealth of the people here that was so apparent. Stephen was amazed by the signs of affluence.

'It is like a tiny London,' he breathed. This was the wealth that came from sheep, he knew.

'The abbey is very rich,' Thomas agreed. He stood at the corner of the street and looked about him. 'I think this will do, brother. Do you not?'

Stephen stood and stared about at the town. A sleepy, rural town, he thought to himself. 'Perfect,' he said.

'Then we shall take a wet to clean the dust from our throats, beg God's good will upon our efforts, and retire to collect our band together,' Thomas told him with a smile. He glanced about him again. 'Yes. This will serve our needs very well.'

Berkeley Castle

Luke sighed as the men all turned to him.

'I was given the chest for safekeeping,' he began. 'It was while the King's reign was ending, and I had no understanding of how much money there was in there. All I knew was that a servant of Sir Hugh le Despenser had asked me to look after a chest. I did so. And when I heard of his death, I recalled the chest, and went to look at it. I opened it and found it full of purses of coin, containing hundreds of florins. It was obvious I couldn't keep them, and just as obvious that Sir Hugh had no more need of them. So I bethought myself that it would be best to have the money passed over to he who had the most right to it – and that, it seemed to me, was the King.'

'Sir Edward of Caernarfon, you mean?' Baldwin said.

'Yes. So when I heard that Ham, this good woman's husband, was to take his cart all the way to Kenilworth, it seemed a good idea to join him. He was with a purveyor, and I thought I should be safe in their company.'

'And?'

'And then Ham, the fool, stopped at the wayside, and two men threw weapons onto the cart, and we were sworn to silence. I heard one say that my cloth would protect them as they tried to enter the castle.'

His face registered his shock and dismay at having been duped. He told them all about the attack, the sudden explosion of violence, the dead men and those who fled the place in terror.

'In all truth I do not know how I survived.'

'But you made your way home?'

'Yes. In the end. I finally reached my home and thought that my trials were ended,' Luke sighed. 'But then, as soon as I saw Agatha, I knew that I was being selfish. I could not leave her knowing nothing of her husband's end. I had to make her aware of what had happened. And then we found poor Ham's body in the woods outside the vill. It was a terrible discovery.'

Luke held his hands out in a gesture of pleading. 'We did all we could for him – but nobody saw him die. He was killed with an axe. A horrible sight.'

'What sort of an axe?' Baldwin asked. 'A war axe, such as was in the cart?'

'No,' Luke said. 'Just a small hatchet, such as any man might have for breaking wood for the fire.'

'Did your husband have such an axe in his cart?' Baldwin asked.

'He always had one,' Agatha responded. She was shaking with emotion, Luke saw. He went to her and patted her back. 'He kept it beneath the plank in front, where he might catch hold in need. He didn't have a sword, it was all he possessed to defend himself if attacked.'

'Check to see whether there is such an axe in the cart,' Baldwin said to Edgar.

Edgar wandered over to the cart. He searched all around the plank and beneath it before going to the weapons and goods in the bed. He riffled through them before returning with a shake of his head. 'Nothing there.'

Baldwin eyed Dolwyn. 'I don't know why you chose to do it, but I believe the evidence suggests you were guilty of his murder. The weapon used to kill him was probably on the cart, and you were found with the cart.'

'I had nothing to do with it,' Dolwyn said strongly. 'And there are men here who can vouch for me. Matteo Bardi will speak for me – and his friend Alured, I think. They both know me well enough.'

Baldwin heard running feet and turned to see a young messenger boy. 'Sir Edward would see you, Sir Baldwin.'

'Very well.' Baldwin looked over at Dolwyn. 'I hope you will be fortunate in calling these friends to speak for your character. We shall discuss this matter later. Edgar, return these fellows to the gaol.'

CHAPTER THIRTY-SEVEN

King's Chamber, Berkeley Castle

The room was a mean little cell for a man who had been King, Baldwin felt.

There were windows to the right and in front of him, and a table stood at the far wall, but there were no glorious hangings, nor pictures painted on the plain limewash of the walls. As Baldwin stood in the doorway, Sir Edward gestured to his steward and two pages. They bowed and left in unison.

'I am glad you could come,' Sir Edward said.

Baldwin could see he was distraught. His face was lined with worry, his eyes looked dull and faded, and his flesh was pasty, like a man who has endured a long fever which has only recently broken. Even his once-luxuriant hair was paler, and lacking in lustre.

'You look upon me as you might a leper: with pity but also revulsion,' Sir Edward said.

'I am sorry, my lord, it was just . . . you are so despondent. You—'

Sir Edward sighed. 'I know, my friend. You are a loyal subject.'

It was a miracle that he could retain any of his calm demeanour. Baldwin was not sure that he could remain so collected, were their roles reversed. To be confined in a chamber like this must be torture to a man who had been used to riding each morning, and who was of a gregarious nature. The King had loved feasts and dancing, tournaments and joining in the country pursuits of the meanest villeins. His was a world of activity, not that of a ascetic. But here he was now, shut away from all that.

'You know, at night in Kenilworth I used to plead with God for the love of a close companion. And do you know what I now beg for? That I never know another man so well, that there is never another beloved fellow so close to my heart. Because I am cursed, Sir Baldwin. All my loyal servants die. They must pay the price for being my friends. I never want to lose a friend like that again.'

'Your Majesty, I am—'

'No!' Sir Edward stared at Baldwin. 'Do not call me that. You can see that I am merely a prisoner, Sir Baldwin. I cannot come and go at will. To pretend that I am King is to play to my vanity. And I would hear the truth. It is less unpalatable than lies. Call me as the others do: Sir Edward. It is at least honourable enough. They have not removed my chivalry,' he added with an icy calm.

'Very well, Sir Edward.'

'My dear Sir Baldwin, you are yet true to me, are you not?' Sir Edward had turned away and was toying with the fabric of a cushion.

'Yes, Sir Edward. I will ever be faithful to my oath and to you.'

'There are so few who are,' he said, staring through the window. 'Look! They will not even permit a view of freedom. At Kenilworth I could see the Great Court. Here, all I see is a tiny patch of stone and weeds. I suppose I am old. I should accept my gaol and enclosing walls like a caged bird.'

'If you are old, I am decrepit,' Baldwin smiled.

'Please, Sir Baldwin, do not treat me as a fool,' Sir Edward said with a trace of his old asperity. 'I have not lost my brains. Flattery was part of my life in the days when I was a King. Now I am a mere prisoner. A man of no note.'

He faced Baldwin, and the latter saw the authority in his eyes again.

'Sir Baldwin, this is the place where I will die. Mortimer detests me, and he knows that if I am released, I will ensure his destruction. I would not have him live a day in my kingdom, and never, *never* would I allow him to escape the realm again to raise a host against me. So there is no other conclusion: when he may, he must scc me dead.'

Baldwin said nothing. He was not persuaded because he saw the risks to Mortimer: he would lose the Queen's support, the support of his leading Earls and Barons, the support of King Edward III; all would revile him, were he to stoop to regicide.

'So, Sir Baldwin, if I am to live,' Sir Edward said, carefully modulating his tones, 'I must escape.'

'I see.'

'Do you?' Sir Edward stared at him. 'There are many here who would happily slit my throat. I am in danger all the time I remain here.'

'You have loyal men here to protect you,' Baldwin said.

'There are plans to rescue me,' Sir Edward said. 'If I can survive one month, I may yet vanquish Mortimer. And after that, I will be freed, with God's help.' He fixed Baldwin with a stern look. 'I will be out of here within two months. It is your duty, and that of Sir Ralph, to ensure that I am safe until then. I have heard from those who would see me return to the throne. And afterwards, those who have aided me will be richly rewarded.'

Baldwin smiled and nodded. But he felt a dreadful pang as he walked from that chamber.

It seemed plain to him that the man who had been King was losing his mind.

Sir Jevan was disgusted by the behaviour of those fools. They had no idea how to get the truth from peasants! It was better to beat them, or cut them a little, if you wanted their co-operation. The cretins were not capable of opening their vile mouths without incentives. Any knight knew that.

He strode to the buttery and demanded a pot of wine, which he drank off in a couple of gulps. Rage was still simmering in his breast at the thought of that blasted carter – the idiot who had delayed him so much when he was trying to capture that felon and outlaw . . .

That was when he recalled the curious incident yesterday on the way here. The man whose eyes had seemed so familiar. The man riding at the rear of the party who had looked so similar to the fellow he had hunted: John of Shulton. Perhaps it was his imagination – after all, even the most foolhardy outlaw would avoid joining a party like the guard from Kenilworth. It would take a man of incomparable stupidity to try such a thing.

Or a most cunning one, he reflected.

Wednesday before Easter[1]

Berkeley Castle

John was out in the yard a short while before the noontime meal; he whittled at a stick near the hall as he waited, hungry, his eyes watchful for any sign of Sir Jevan.

'An exciting time yesterday,' William atte Hull said, walking up to him, wiping his hands on his jerkin.

'The felon?'

'Yes. Always satisfying to see a criminal brought to justice,' William said. 'They will convene a court for him, no doubt. That will encourage good behaviour. There's nothing like seeing a wrongdoer dangle by the neck.'

All in the castle had heard of the interrogation of Dolwyn the day before, but it gave John little pleasure. He threw his stick aside and sheathed his knife. He didn't feel as though there was anything to celebrate about yet another man who was doomed to die.

'You disagree? The fellow deserves his end,' William continued, seeing John's expression. 'And in any case, he's only a common churl from a vill somewhere far away. Who will miss him?'

'His wife, his children, if he has any,' John said.

'He shouldn't have killed a man and tried to hide his crime then, should he?' William countered. He glanced about them. 'Listen – I have spoken to the masons here, and there is work for at least another five men. If we can get even one more of ours into the castle, it will help a great deal.'

'Right,' John said. He felt his spirits sinking as he looked about him at the strong keep, the massive curtain walls and defences. 'And you think this could work?'

1 8 April 1327

William ignored his pessimism. 'I can get a message to one of our men. Then it will be up to you to keep an ear out for any suggestion amongst the garrison that a man in among them could be suspected. You understand?'

'You really think one extra man in here will help?'

'One additional man will always be better than none,' William said with confidence. 'And soon, very soon, there will be news of Stephen and Brother Thomas. They are preparing for a new battle. Yes, soon, very soon we shall be ready.'

The castle was quiet that afternoon as Baldwin and Simon and their servants left the hall, replete after their lunch.

'Sir Ralph is with Sir Edward?' Simon asked.

'Yes. I agreed with him that he would look after the King—'

'*King?*'

Baldwin gave a shamefaced grin. 'If you prefer, then, Sir Edward of Caernarfon, in the mornings, while I would see him in the afternoons. There is no need for both of us to be with him all the time. And I doubt most strongly that Lord Berkeley would want more than one knight in with Sir Edward.'

'He would not trust you to keep the knight in his chamber, then,' Simon said lightly.

'No,' Baldwin said with a grin. 'I think that he does not trust any who has shown loyalty to Sir Edward. It can scarcely be wondered at. If Sir Edward were to be rescued, what would happen to the lord? As the gaoler of our former King, I think he could imagine with great ease what his end would be, were the good knight to recover his throne. So while he is responsible for Sir Edward, he will keep those who are loyal well away from him.'

'How long must you remain here, Baldwin?' Simon asked.

Baldwin smiled sadly. 'I do not know,' he admitted. 'Perhaps a month, perhaps two. It is not a very long sojourn, I trust. What about you?'

'Oh, I hope to leave before too long,' Simon said. 'I promised I would return home before the summer is well under way.'

Baldwin nodded, but then he gave a fleeting frown. 'What do you think of her, Simon?'

Following his gaze, Simon saw the figure of Agatha. 'Her? Just a peasant's widow.'

'And upset to learn that her horse and cart were gone. So upset she travelled all the way here to try to find them.'

'What of it?'

'The theft of the cart surprises me,' Baldwin said. 'Just think: a man comes across a fellow with a cart and decides to steal it. How would he do so?'

'Knock him on the head or stab him,' Simon said with certainty.

'Yes. He would not rummage through the man's cart to find an axe. If he did, he would immediately go to the parcel at the back that clearly held weapons, wouldn't he?'

'Perhaps it was dark, and he couldn't see the weapons?'

'But if it were dark, it is even more surprising. Let us assume that it was. Ham was asleep. The killer went to his cart and felt around for a weapon. He would first have found those wrapped in the blanket, would he not? If the hatchet was under the plank, it would be the last weapon he would come across. Also, Dolwyn had a sword at his belt. Why on earth hunt for a new weapon when he already wore one?'

'Because he didn't want to have his guilt demonstrated? You know as well as I do that a sword can be matched to the wound it makes.'

'Yes, but not with accuracy. No one could affirm it with certainty – and he would know that. An assailant in the dark will wish to attack first and make sure of his victim, rather than riffling through a cart in the hope of finding a weapon.'

'But this man Dolwyn knew that there were weapons there,' Simon said.

'True enough. But did he know that there was a hatchet as well?' Baldwin wondered.

'He had been with Ham for some time, so he probably discovered that Ham kept a small axe there, and when he found Ham, he took that as being the nearest weapon to hand. Unwrapping the others would knock one against the other and make a noise,' Simon said.

'Yes,' Baldwin said. 'You must be right.'

But he was not convinced.

Father Luke rose from his place before the little altar in the chapel, and crossed himself devoutly.

He hated being here in this great castle. The place felt like a prison. Luke was used to the countryside about Willersey and Broadway. If he had wanted to be secluded, he would have joined a monastery.

Outside, the bustle of the men at the walls made his head hurt. He eyed the men on the scaffolding, the masons hacking at rocks with their sharp hammers and chisels, men up higher with only a hammer, tapping here or there at a recalcitrant stone as they tried to make the wall secure. Chips and small flakes of rock pattered to the ground like hail.

He was not used to all this noise. He was out of place, and this was not where he should be. He should be in his little church back at Willersey.

'Father?' Agatha was approaching him with a look of resolve on her face.

'Yes, my daughter?'

'How long do you think it will be before I can get my horse and cart?'

'As long as it takes for my Lord Berkeley to decide that it truly was yours and that it should be returned,' he said testily. 'It is not in my hands.'

'I know, but I want to get home again to my little girl.'

He wanted to shout that he too had no desire to remain here. The trip had turned out to be worthwhile because of recovering the King's gold, but now that he was here, he was as sure as he could be that he would never be able to touch the coins. Lord Berkeley would never let a parish priest and a peasant woman take any of the money back.

'You are right,' he said. 'It would be good to return to her.'

'I can't leave without my horse and cart. It would make all my trouble pointless,' she said.

'And mine,' he agreed. He set his jaw. He would have hoped that Agatha would show a little more appreciation for the lengths to which he had gone. Then again, he had never told her that he was intending to find the money so that he could use some of it to make her life and that of Jen easier. Why should she be grateful?

He about to walk off when he heard his name called again. Turning, he found himself confronted by a man-at-arms.

'You!'

'Father, I have sinned and I need you to hear my confession.'

'I will *not*! After what you did?'

'Father Luke, I must make confession. You wouldn't deny me that, would you?' John said, and gave a twisted grin.

CHAPTER THIRTY-EIGHT

Maundy Thursday[1]

Berkeley Castle

Dolwyn was sitting apart from the other two. They had shunned him since learning he had been accused of murder. Perhaps, he thought sullenly, they expected him to spring upon them during the night and slay them with bare hands and teeth.

The morning was well advanced when the upper door opened and five men unlocked their cell, calling on all three to follow them.

Traipsing up the stairway, Dolwyn was surprised at how leaden his feet felt. He had done without food for longer than this before, when he had been on the run, but that did not compare to this feeling.

The sudden glare made him cover his eyes as it had two days before, but today there was no direct sunlight, only

1 9 April 1327

bright clouds that gleamed like balls of spun silver high overhead.

There were two more men out here, both with staffs at the ready, and he eyed them as he passed. Seven guards for three weak and hungry men, Dolwyn thought to himself. It was heavy-handed.

They were brought to the hall. There was no fire today. Instead, the blackened hearth in the middle of the broad flagstoned room had been cleared, and the three prisoners were placed before it. A shame it was not lit. The stone walls absorbed any heat the sun might provide; in here it was perpetual autumn.

At the far end of the hall, sitting on his great seat on his dais, was Lord Berkeley, looking solemn. Ranged about the walls were men from the castle's garrison, and Dolwyn saw the priest, Agatha, Baldwin and the others. He eyed them with a feeling of apprehension. This was not to be a quick and easy hearing with allies to protect him; this was a dangerous chamber.

'You have been accused of the murder of Ham Carter of Willersey. How do you plead?'

Dolwyn knew that this court was convened to see to it that he was executed. A simple means for a lord to ensure that peasants would obey his laws was to hang a malefactor every so often.

'I am innocent.'

'What of the other two? How do they plead?' Lord Berkeley called, staring at Harry and Senchet.

'Innocent,' they both responded quickly.

Dolwyn looked at them. 'I did not find these two until after I had taken the cart. I was riding along the road alone when Sir Jevan there,' he nodded in Sir Jevan's direction, 'saw me and stabbed me. They have nothing to do with the matter.'

'Is there anyone who can speak for these two?' Lord Berkeley asked.

Gilbert nodded. 'My lord, I know them both. They were loyal servants to Sir Edward when he was King. He would speak for them, if you wish, I am sure.'

There was some annoyance in the face of Lord Berkeley when he heard that, but after a muttered discussion it was decided by the lord and his steward that the two could be released.

'What do you have to say for yourself then, Master Dolwyn?' the steward asked with a sneer. He was a medium-height man in his forties, with a protuberant pot belly. Grey eyes watched closely as Dolwyn responded to his questions, narrowing slightly when the answers he received were not to his liking. It was plain that he had at one time been given some legal training from the way he posed his questions, glancing down at the clerk who scratched away with his reeds as he spoke, making sure of the facts. He enjoyed his task as prosecutor.

Naturally there was no defence pleader. An innocent man had no need of a specialist: innocence spoke for itself.

'So, your name is Dolwyn of Guildford. And you stole a horse and cart.'

'I stole nothing. I *found* a horse and cart. There was no one with them. It's not stealing to take something that's been left.'

'But it was only left because you had killed the owner. You took an axe and cut his head off.'

'That wasn't me,' Dolwyn said.

'Master Steward,' Luke said, 'the head was not cut off.'

'But an axe killed him?'

'Yes,' Luke agreed.

'Very well. This man took an axe and slew the owner, Ham, and left his body to rot while stealing his horse and cart.'

'I did not see him and did not murder him.'

'Then who did? Do you accuse the other two who were not

with you when you were discovered by Sir Jevan? Did they kill Ham so you could steal his cart?'

'I had nothing to do with his death and did not meet these two until after Sir Jevan stabbed me. I've been ill for days, and those two men saved my life.'

'So you say.'

'My master will speak for me,' Dolwyn said. He was looking about the hall already.

'Which master is that?'

'Matteo Bardi, brother of Benedetto Bardi.'

'Are they here? Call for them!' the steward demanded after a short glance at Lord Berkeley. The latter would not want the Bardis insulted – they were too important to his father-in-law and the Queen – but if this man truly was their servant, they might wish to protect him.

It was an anxious time for Dolwyn as he waited.

Soon the two brothers walked into the hall. Matteo looked concerned, and for his part, Benedetto was fretful. His eyes were on Dolwyn as he crossed the floor, and even when he had stopped, his attention was on Dolwyn and not the steward.

'Sirs, this man says he knows you. Do you know him?'

Matteo nodded. 'He was lately in my service. Before that he was in the service of the King.'

'Can you vouch for his character?'

'Of course. I would not have a servant who was not entirely reliable,' Matteo said.

Benedetto was peering, but finally nodded. 'This man is known to my house.'

'Where is your house?' the steward asked.

'London,' Matteo said.

'And yet the fellow was here. What was he doing so far from your home?'

'He had been sent to deliver messages,' Matteo said with some hauteur. 'I often send servants with messages, as does your lord.'

'You think that his theft of a cart was suitable for delivery of your little notes?'

'I think that if he found a cart and horse wandering, he would be right to bring them to the nearest town. It would be his duty.'

'So you are not aware of his having stolen anything else before?'

'No. Not of his *stealing*,' Matteo said.

There was a sudden hush. Matteo shot a quick look at his brother, then at Dolwyn, but would not meet the steward's piercing eye.

The steward was not fooled. 'What crimes has he committed?'

'I could not speak of them. Any crime he could have committed was long before I knew him,' Matteo said.

'I won't have this,' the steward declared. 'Do you know of any crimes of which he has been accused?'

Matteo looked despairingly at Dolwyn. No one spoke, until Dolwyn sighed heavily. 'It was murder, Steward. Murder. I was accused of it before I served Master Matteo.'

William had secured a place for John at a tavern in the town. It was the better option, he said, in case Sir Jevan saw him, and John felt sure he was right. If he were to remain in the castle all day long, the risk of being seen was high, and then his fate would be assured.

William had advised him to keep away from the castle. He would be called if he were needed, but if he were to go to the castle, Sir Jevan would have to be slain first so he could not identify John. Because if John were to be seen, and his part at Kenilworth remembered, the whole project could be thrown into disarray – and that, William made clear, he was not prepared to tolerate.

John was more than content to remain here in this tavern, away from Sir Jevan and the castle. The more he thought of it, the more terrible the idea grew of freeing Sir Edward from his captivity. As soon as he was released there would be more fighting. More battles. More blood spilled.

John had seen enough of war and death.

The room was silent after Dolwyn's quiet intervention. Then the steward turned to him, his voice dripping with sarcasm.

'Oh! The felon recalls now, does he? All of a sudden he remembers that he has killed before.'

'I didn't say that!' Dolwyn declared fiercely. 'I said I was accused. I wasn't guilty.'

'Were you found guilty in a court?'

'No.'

'But the coroner recorded that you were.'

'No, only that there were some arguments that day.'

'Tell us, Master Dolwyn of Guildford, were you serving the King's household at the time?'

Simon looked at the accused man and would have sworn that he rocked back on his heels at those words. He had not expected to hear that, Simon guessed. The man had assumed that his past was secret. How, Simon wondered, had the truth been betrayed?

'I was.' Dolwyn's voice sounded as though there was an obstruction in his throat.

'And who were you accused of killing?'

Simon could feel the tension in the room as though all the people in the room were waiting, but Dolwyn did not speak.

'I ask again,' the steward said in a tone of heavy patience.

The accused man blinked and struggled with his breath as though suffocating. Eventually he whispered 'My wife. My child. They died,' Dolwyn went on. 'But it wasn't murder. I wasn't hanged.'

'Because you ran? You abjured the realm?'

'No.' The voice was ragged.

'What happened to your wife and child?'

'They were in the house. I was out for the night at the tavern, and I'd had a lot to drink. When I got home, my wife was in a rage with me. I hit her.'

'You killed her.'

'No! I swear it! But she had been shouting at me, and all I did was punch her. And then I went out to cool my head, and when I came back the place was on fire. I tried to rescue her . . .'

'You killed her. She fell into the fire, and the house caught light.'

'I tried to get back inside to save her and my daughter, but the men in the vill stopped me. They held me back.' How did this steward know of all that? Dolwyn had told Matteo, but no one else.

'So this is the sort of man you are. A killer even of your own family. A danger to others. My lord, I have no more questions. Here is exactly the kind of fellow who would take advantage of a traveller, kill him, and rob him of all he possessed.'

'I did nothing! My family wasn't meant to die!'

'You expect us to believe that?' the steward spat.

'What of the jury?' Lord Berkeley asked.

The men who stood at the wall nearest Simon fell to talking amongst themselves, and then they nodded to the steward. He asked if they had reached a conclusion. There was a muttering, and then he asked them for their decision.

'He's guilty, master.'

The steward addressed Dolwyn. 'You've heard their conclusion. What do you have to say?'

'I didn't harm him. I wouldn't have, because I knew he had a wife and child at home. After he told me that, it would have been impossible for me to lay a finger on him. I'd not have hurt him any more than I'd have hurt them. Master Matteo, help me!' he pleaded, turning to Matteo.

Matteo nodded, and Simon saw him give a quick frown as if of reassurance. The gesture was so swift, Simon could almost have believed that he had imagined it, but then he saw Matteo's hand pat his purse, and understood. The Bardi would pay to save him.

Lord Berkeley leaned forward. 'Well, this is my court, and I believe that the jury is fair and just in their conclusions. So it is my belief that you are guilty. You murdered Ham, you stole his horse and cart, and you would have made off with your booty if the brave knight here had not prevented you. I find you guilty, and my decision is that you will be hanged until you are dead. Take him away.'

Simon looked at Dolwyn. He barely appeared to care. There was something about him that was ineffably sad. He opened his mouth as if to speak, but suddenly another voice intervened.

'WAIT!'

Simon winced at the bellow from his side.

Lord Berkeley and his steward peered round.

'Who said that?' the steward demanded.

'I did,' declared the smiling Sir Richard de Welles. 'You can't do that.'

Lord Berkeley raised his eyebrows. 'Really? You think a lord cannot decide his own judgements in his own court?'

'Oh, that's all right, me lord. No trouble at all,' Sir Richard said with a genial smile. He pushed three men from before him and stepped over to Dolwyn's side. 'But you cannot send him to hang.'

'And why not?'

'You know the law, me lord. It's illegal for you to execute any man without the approval of your local coroner. He has to be there to witness the execution and make sure all is in order.'

'Oh, and you claim that privilege?'

'No, I am not coroner here. You have to ask your local fellow to come. Who is he?'

Lord Berkeley looked at his steward, then at Sir John Maltravers. 'Well?'

Neither knew the name of the man responsible for the area.

'In that case, me lord, I am afraid you may not have this man's head,' said Sir Richard apologetically. 'I'm very sorry. Be a good thing, removing an arse like this, especially since he's a known killer. But against the law.'

'Is there any man here who would stand by him?' Sir John demanded. He was a big man, almost as tall as Sir Richard, although younger, and with a powerful, heavy body that was not fat, but accumulated muscle. He had only a couple of days' growth of beard, which gave him a belligerent appearance.

'I will,' said Sir Richard happily. 'Sorry, me lord, but we can't break the King's laws.'

'I too,' Baldwin said. 'As a Keeper of the King's Peace . . .'

'So am *I*!' Lord Berkeley stated angrily.

'I was about to say, my lord,' Baldwin finished smoothly, 'that as Keeper of the King's Peace yourself, you would hardly wish it known that you had deliberately flouted the King's laws in your own court. Bring the coroner here so that he may witness the execution. That is all. It need not be a lengthy process.'

'True,' the lord said, frowning at Baldwin and Sir Richard with a baleful eye. 'Very well. Put him back in the gaol. He can wait there until the coroner arrives.'

CHAPTER THIRTY-NINE

Good Friday[1]

Berkeley Castle's Hall

'I still think you are both mad,' Simon said as he took a mess of fish cooked in a white wine sauce. 'He was furious with you when you told him he was not allowed to execute his own felon.'

'When you get to my age,' Baldwin said, 'you realise that there really isn't much to fear about standing up for what you believe is right, Simon.'

'No,' Sir Richard said, belching behind his hand and reaching for the mess himself, decorously scooping out a large bowlful, setting it on the table before him and sighing happily. With a hunk of bread in his hand, he began to eat. Swallowing noisily, and sticking his tongue out to catch a stray drip from his moustache, he turned a beaming face to Simon. 'And he couldn't

1 10 April 1327

344

argue. Not with all his people there, as well as us and Sir Jevan. He knew that there were too many for him to cow us.'

'Why did you both do it?' Simon asked. 'He is a felon, isn't he? He did take the cart.'

'Mayhap he is, but if we allowed this lord to hang a man illegally, what sort of example would that leave, eh?' Sir Richard said reasonably.

Simon nodded. 'And?'

Baldwin grinned, dropped his bread onto his wooden trencher and said, 'There was an indecent haste about the way Lord Berkeley convened his court to investigate the murder of a complete unknown. The lord himself will never have heard of this "Ham", after all – so why the need for such speedy justice? Because the lord feels anger at a peasant's death? I doubt it. Because he loathes the sight of this man Dolwyn? Why should he? Or is it because Dolwyn is a threat to him? Again, that would be hard to believe. But perhaps the lord wanted to make a point. To cow someone else?'

'Dolwyn's master?' Simon guessed.

'Yes,' Baldwin agreed, and a faraway look came into his eyes. 'But there was a striking lack of support from Bardi, wasn't there? I cannot help but wonder whether there is something going on between the Bardi and Lord Berkeley.'

Simon had to agree with that. He too had noted that Matteo had appeared reluctant to support Dolwyn, his servant. 'You think the Florentine had reason to desert his servant?'

'I've never known a banker do anything unless it was in his interests,' Sir Richard said with certainty.

Baldwin smiled at his comment, but he looked round at the sight of Harry and Senchet being brought into the hall. 'Look. The Lord Berkeley decided they were innocent, after all.'

'Good,' said Simon. 'From all I've heard, they had nothing to do with the murder, no matter what the facts about Dolwyn.'

'There, I believe you are correct. About those Bardis, though,' Baldwin said. 'I should not trust such men. What sort of interest could such bankers have in the fate of a servant like Dolwyn?'

Sir Richard guffawed and poked Baldwin in the flank with a finger as thick as a sausage. 'Hah! You are too innocent, sir. If one of my servants was to open his mouth and babble to a clerk, I'd worry. And so would half the women in west Devon, I'd be bound! You may not be a fellow for the women or for the delights of the chase, but perhaps the fellow Bardi has a happy wife and a happier mistress, eh? A wise man tries to keep them apart, but it would only take a word or two from an old retainer to bring a little more fire into the home than a man might like, eh?'

Baldwin set his head on one side. 'A London man would scarcely be anxious about his wife's hearing something in Berkeley,' he argued reasonably. 'If there were cause for him to be alarmed, it would be his business, not his love affairs. Perhaps he has been less than scrupulous over his accounts. He was the old King's banker, and a man like him could be tempted to perhaps hold on to a little more of the King's gold than he ought, during a time of civil war. Suppose Bardi kept back monies that should have passed to the new King and his mother? That would be a cause for great embarrassment, were a reliable servant to announce such news to the son-in-law of the King's Regent.'

Sir Richard's mouth stopped moving as he absorbed that. 'D'ye think the foreign bretheling[1] would dare a trick like that? We'd have his ballocks if he did!'

1 git

'*If* he was discovered,' Baldwin said.

'It's possible,' Simon judged.

'It is one possibility, in any case,' Baldwin said. 'Perhaps we should ensure that the gaol is watched? It would be a great shame were the Bardi to insinuate a weapon into the gaol. Or poison. His servant may well be the only witness to another crime, and I would not have him slain because his master sees him as an embarrassment.'

'What will you do, then?' Simon asked. 'Go and question him?'

Baldwin sipped wine from the mazer before him, pulling a face at the flavour. 'Not today. I will pay the gaoler to stop men visiting the prisoner, and plan on seeing him tomorrow. If there is an attempt upon his life, we may catch the culprit. In any case, he will have spent four days in prison by then. Time for him to have realised how unpleasant his life could become, were he to remain there. Yes, tomorrow I shall speak with him.'

Matteo had seen the knights talking at their table, and felt a certain quivering in his belly at the sight. It would be better if Dolwyn was dead. The man was a danger to the bank, and to him personally. And Matteo had no idea how to deal with him.

He walked about the yard, musing over his servant, and thinking too about his brother. There was so much danger it was hard to isolate the greatest threat. But as he walked, he saw Benedetto, and he felt certain that this was the time to seek to resolve one issue, if he could.

Benedetto had taken power so quickly after Manuele's death, he reminded himself. Now he bent his steps towards his brother.

'Benedetto, I would have a moment,' he said.

'Of course,' his brother answered, waving away the two guards who were always behind him. 'This is a magnificent castle, is it not? Who could wish for a more comfortable and congenial home? And the lord keeps it in such splendid condition, especially with all the reworkings. They will enhance it, I have no doubt. I think . . .' He noticed at last the expression on his brother's face. 'Why, what is it, Matteo?'

He had grown more confident in his position, Matteo saw. From a young age, Matteo had lived in two worlds. One was that of the business, in which he knew he was a crucial part of the entire structure; but in the family, in which he was the youngest member, he had a constant battle to remind himself that he was now a grown man. But it wasn't him alone, he knew. His brother Benedetto was also aware of the disparity in their ages. Benedetto was the older and would for ever have the increased maturity that age conferred. In the family, Matteo would always submit to Benedetto's whims. A part of him was still the little boy who could be bullied.

It should not be so. Matteo was an adult now. Such foolishness hampered his clarity of thought.

'Benedetto. I am worried.'

'Yes? And by what?'

'You.'

Benedetto stopped and eyed him with surprise. 'What do you mean, little brother?'

For Matteo, that term was confirmation of the contempt in which he was held by his brother. He said sharply, 'I may be younger than you but without my efforts, our bank would be out of business. You would have joined Manuele in supporting the old King, and the House of Bardi would have collapsed, as did his reign. So don't call me "little brother", like some idiot child. I am the head intelligencer for the bank. Treat me as such.'

'Of course, Matteo,' his brother said with a touch of injured aloofness.

'What I mean is, I have had a lot of time to think since my injury.' Matteo said, 'and I must know. Did you send a man to kill me that day?'

'Me!' Benedetto cried. There was no mistaking his hurt.

'You disappeared so quickly. I was stabbed a moment or two after seeing our brother die. It was almost as though someone paid the mob to kill us both. That would have left you with total control of the business.'

'Matteo, listen to yourself,' Benedetto said pleadingly. 'I had to return to my house because I was due to meet a man. I was gone from the bank in great haste. I did not see Manuele's death because I was already halfway home. How can you think that I would do such a thing? I am your brother, Matteo, and that means as much to me as it does to you! I couldn't plot your death. I couldn't.'

'Whom did you have to see? Someone from the King's household?'

'No. It was Sir Jevan. He wished to confirm that the money needed by the Queen would be sent to her. It was as we had discussed in the meeting.'

'You had already decided?' Matteo said, eyes narrowing. 'You had plotted with her before we had the meeting?'

Benedetto grimaced. 'You know how things were that day. It was clear to all that the Queen was going to win, and that the King's power was on the wane. What would you have expected – that I should have waited for Manuele to agree before guaranteeing the security of the bank? The only thing I could do was

349

ensure that we were safe by speaking with the Queen's agents. I am not ashamed of it. I would do it again.'

'Sir Jevan?' Matteo muttered. '*He* was an agent of the Queen?'

'You are our best intelligencer, and didn't know?' Benedetto chuckled. 'Yes, Sir Jevan was there that day. I agreed that we should support the Queen above all others. It did lead to our being involved right from the first . . . You look worried, brother. What is it?' His face suddenly fell. 'You think that because you were discussing your letter to Sir Edward, I sent a man to kill you? Matteo, we are brothers. If a man may not trust his own blood, how can he trust any man? I could not hurt you any more than you could hurt me.'

Matteo nodded, and when Benedetto threw his arms about him, he did not even flinch.

Saturday before Easter Sunday[1]

Berkeley Gaol

Dolwyn squatted on the floor, waiting with a patience that was close to madness. He was alone in this dark, dingy chamber. There was one little sewer that ran along the length of it, a mere trench cut in the rock, which fed into a small pit at the farther end. From there the moisture sank somehow into the soil beneath the castle, he assumed. This cold, befouled prison was the most noisome and repugnant he had ever seen.

He had no idea what would happen to him. They had not dragged him out to die, since that knight's words. The coroner

1 11 April 1327

had postponed his death, thank God! Otherwise he would have been taken out and pulled up by the neck until he was strangled, as that block-headed ribald[1] of a lord had wanted.

The Bardis wouldn't want him to talk, so they had better be careful. Very careful.

The door creaked open at the top of the staircase, and he felt his breath catch in his throat. The footsteps coming down the stairs must be those of a pair of guards, and he instantly began to shake, as though these men were going to take him up to the fresh air and the light and slip a rope over his head in an instant.

And then he heard a voice . . .

'Come with me, my friend,' Baldwin said. 'You will not wish to be questioned down here. Let us go together and enjoy some food and drink.'

Within a few minutes, Dolwyn found himself seated on a bench, and before him was set fresh, warm bread, a block of cheese, a bowl of thin stew, and a pot of ale. He touched the food with a restraint that was torture. 'What do you want?'

'The truth. Perhaps to save your life?' Baldwin took his seat opposite Dolwyn. 'Eat.'

Dolwyn took a little bread and chewed it slowly, savouring the flavour, and then he picked up the pot of ale and drained it in one long draught. Sighing with pleasure, he put it down again and set about the cheese and bread with gusto.

'There is a reckoning, of course,' Baldwin said. 'It comes to men no matter what they think of the justice. But if you were truly innocent of the murder of Ham Carter, I would not see you punished for that crime.'

1 fool, worthless man

Dolwyn eyed him. It would be all too easy to admit to a past offence and be hanged for that, he guessed. He must be cautious. At least he could be honest about Ham.

'I quite liked the carter. He was a fellow as I was once. More than a little hen-pecked. He reminded me how I was before my wife's death.'

'How did that happen?'

A convulsive shiver ran through Dolwyn's frame. 'I killed her – and my daughter. But I had not meant to hurt either of them. I could never have harmed my little girl. She was all the sweetness in life to me.'

Baldwin could see that the man was affected, unless he was an excellent actor. 'Go on.'

'My woman was always over-willing to chastise me. That was why I used to go and drink, sometimes too much. That night I returned and we had a row, as usual. The vill heard and some of the men came to demand that we keep the peace and stop our wrangling, but she berated them in insulting terms. I could see that they were horrified to be addressed in such a way. So, after they left, I determined I would try to correct her behaviour. I took up a stick, and threatened her.'

As he spoke, he saw again the cramped room that was their home, little Emily terrified in her bed, the glow from the rush-lights throwing a fitful orange light over everything. Maggie stood with her hands on her hips, her face turned sharper, more like a ferret's. He had been standing beside his barrel of burned cider[1] with a cup in his hand. A stiffener before bed, he had thought. Something to strengthen his resolve before his wife started to lay into him with her tongue. And then she began.

1 distilled cider to make a strong spirit

She had taunted him, telling him he was less of a man because he couldn't hold his drink. 'You used to be someone I could admire, but look at you now,' she jeered. 'A pathetic dog is what you've become, with the sense and courage of a rabbit. Once our Emily looked up to you, but these days she would be happier with Saul Archer as her father. You're nothing but a drunken wastrel.'

'What about Saul?'

'I should have married him after he swyved me before you,' she said spitefully. 'He is worth ten of you.'

He could recall throwing aside the cup of spirit, and screaming at her to shut up, to just leave him alone, and then he lashed out with his stick and saw it catch her cheek, and he remembered throwing his stick aside and trying to catch her to hug her, but then she had drawn her knife, and the blade caught his forearm. The sting of it stirred his rage. He punched her, with all the malice and fury that seven years of marriage had given him, and saw her fly to the ground.

He left the house. Saul's was only a few hundred yards away, and he remembered staggering dangerously up towards it, the anger sparkling and fizzing in his blood like acid. But before he could get close to Saul's, he stumbled. It was only by a miracle that he managed to throw himself to one side before he tumbled into the narrow well at the roadside, and he lay there, on his back, panting, before throwing up. He had the presence of mind to turn away from the well, so he did not pollute the water, but even as he was vomiting, he felt the waves of self-disgust rising and washing through him.

She was right – he *was* weak. How could she or Emily respect him, when he was a miserable brethel without prospects or skills to create them? He stood up, determined to show her he could be worthy of her. It was true – she did deserve better than him. And if she had rolled in the hay with Saul, what of it? That was more than seven years ago, if it was before they had wed. He would not hold that against her.

353

That was when he had heard the screaming. Emily must have been screaming for a while before that, he assumed, because Peter and John were there with buckets, and others were, bellowing to the girl and her mother to escape.

Completely sober now, he ran for his door. The flames were already leaping up and the thatch had caught a spark. Smoke rose in black clouds, and then there was a hollow roaring noise, and a warm flame lazily rolled from the door, throwing aside the thin oiled screen at the window, and a strange thudding detonation came to his ears, and he knew instinctively that it was his burned cider.

The barrel-staves were found later near the fire in the middle of the hearth, and gradually he pieced together what must have happened. His wife had decided to destroy that spirit that had taken him so long to make, and rolled the barrel to the drain-hole at the rear of the cottage, opening the taps to let the drink run away. But some had reached the flames, and the liquid caught fire. The barrels themselves exploded like flour in a mill.

He had tried to make his way inside to save them. God knew, he had tried – but John and others held his arms and pulled him away as the flames licked about the doorframe and the window. If he had gone in, he would have died, there was no doubt.

Baldwin listened carefully. The man's sorrow was plain enough. 'So afterwards, you said you were pardoned?'

'I was accused, but it was agreed that I had not killed them. I was outside when my little girl screamed. And I tried to get in to save them. I wasn't actually pardoned. There were discussions about my having tried to harm them, and the coroner recorded them, and the facts of our shouting at each other, but the court agreed I was innocent. That was that.' He gave a long, shuddering sigh.

'I see.'

'Sir, I know how this must look,' Dolwyn said, 'but I had nothing to do with Ham's death. He was a sad little man, who inspired sympathy in me because he reminded me of how I once had been.'

'A pathetic churl. But one with a chest of gold and an array of weapons that might be sold,' Baldwin said.

'I knew nothing of gold. That was hidden from me. Like his axe.'

'So you say you did not know where his axe was?'

'I didn't know he had one. I did find the weapons, but not his axe.'

'You still state that you did not slay him?'

'Sir, I state that I did not even see him. Alive or dead, I did not see him that night. I found the horse and cart and bethought me that they gave me more chance of evading capture in the days following the attack on Kenilworth.'

'I see.'

'Sir, is it true that you are loyal to the memory of our last King? I had heard the gaoler say that you were called here by Sir Edward to help guard him.'

'It is true.'

'Then, sir, ask him about me,' Dolwyn said, his voice dropping. 'Ask about the man who went to see him at Kenilworth.'

Baldwin's mind whirled. He remembered the King speaking of someone giving him a message. It seemed madness to think that this could have been that man, but he had heard stranger things in his life. 'Do you have a token he would know?'

Dolwyn licked his lips, and brought out from within his shirt a small purse. He untied the thongs that bound it, and passed Baldwin the parchment within.

Baldwin read it with shock. 'The Bardis?'

'Sir, they think that note has been destroyed, but I have guarded it with my life. Now, perhaps, it can help to save me.'

CHAPTER FORTY

Monday after Easter[1]

Berkeley Castle

It had been impossible, in the midst of the Easter feasting, for Baldwin to find a private moment with Sir Edward of Caernarfon. During the early morning, Sir Edward had been permitted to attend chapel with all the household of the castle, and afterwards he had been allowed a place at the table in the hall with Lord Berkeley. Not that he was engaged in conversation, as Baldwin saw. He was kept there as a sop to his past position as King, rather than from a desire to honour him. Nor did he eat much; for the most part, he picked at his food, seldom raising his eyes from his plate.

Today, as early as he could, Baldwin walked to Sir Edward's chamber in the castle. In his purse he held the parchment which Dolwyn had passed to him, and so, as soon as they were alone,

1 13 April 1327

356

he handed it to the former King, saying, 'Do you recognise this, sire?'

Sir Edward paled. 'Where did you find it?'

'A man in the dungeon,' Baldwin said, and explained about Dolwyn languishing in the gaol.

'Dear heaven! You must have him released immediately, Sir Baldwin. That man should be attempting my freedom.'

'He is held guilty of murder. The Lord Berkeley will want him kept here until the coroner can come and witness his execution. If he had his way, Dolwyn would be dead already. It is only Sir Richard's strong sense of demarcation that has prevented its happening.'

'Can we not arrange for his pardon?'

Baldwin said nothing. Sir Edward was unable to provide pardons now.

He realised his impotence even as he looked at Baldwin for support. 'Good Sir Baldwin, if that man speaks out, he could save his life by threatening mine. My gaolers would be happy to free him, if he were to speak of an attempt to save me. You must have him freed, Sir Baldwin – please! There must be some way in which the fellow can be brought from his cell.'

'Any influence I have would compromise you,' Baldwin said heavily. 'If I demand his release, men will immediately question *why*.'

'Speak with the coroner, Sir Richard, and ask whether there is some pretext on which he can be allowed out. I beg you, Sir Baldwin. *Try to have him released.*'

Tuesday after Easter[1]

Berkeley Castle

The castle was hideous to her. Agatha was staying in the vill nearby, where she and Father Luke relied upon alms from the church to eat and live, but apart from that, she spent her time at the castle.

It was some relief to know that their horse was being well looked after. She went to check on him regularly, always suspicious that one day she would find him gone, but so far there had been no cause for concern.

Today Father Luke was already at the court when she arrived, and she nodded to him as she peered over into the stables.

They were less crowded now, as the majority of the beasts had been passed out to the various farms in the area, and her own was still standing and munching happily on his hay. At least they had not lost him, she told herself. That would have been a terrible price to pay.

She could kick Ham for getting them all into this mess.

'Agatha, I don't know how much longer I can stay here,' Father Luke was saying.

'You won't leave me?' she said, panicked at the thought of being left here all alone.

'Mistress, I have duties with the souls in Willersey.' The priest was looking drawn and haggard.

'Are you all right?'

'I did not sleep well last night,' he admitted. He shook his head apologetically. 'It could be weeks before they hold a court to listen to Dolwyn's case, and I have the vill at home in Willersey to serve. The man I asked to take my place while I was absent will be wondering what has happened to me.'

1 14 April 1327

'Why can't they do it sooner?' she fretted.

'There is so much else for them to think of,' Father Luke said. 'And I don't know that the Lord Berkeley wants to have it handled quickly. I expect he hopes to keep the money.' There was a bitter note in his voice. How foolish, to think he could rescue it for the vill. The money was tainted, but he could have put it to good use in Willersey, rather than leave it here.

'If you go, there will be no one to speak for it and to claim it,' Agatha pointed out.

'If he wants, he can keep us here waiting for a year,' the priest said bleakly. He looked about the court like a man seeing it for the first time. 'What a horrible place. Nothing is what it seems here. It is full of savagery – greed and violence. Agatha, you should come home with me – home to Jen. She will be missing her mother.'

'I cannot,' Agatha said. 'How will we live without that money?' She was about to plead with him that he should remain at least one more week when she was cut short by the sound of hooves.

A man cantered in through the gates. 'My Lord Berkeley – urgent message for Lord Berkeley,' he panted as he threw himself from his horse.

The shouts and rattling of hooves in the court drew Baldwin to his feet. Wolf lay by the door, and opened an eye.

On hearing the noise, Sir Edward looked over at the window, remarking peevishly, 'There is to be never any peace in this place. What is it now?'

Baldwin was in Sir Edward's chamber, carrying out his increasingly irksome protective duty. While Sir Edward sat quietly and read his books, occasionally staring out through his window, fingers tapping on the desk before him and sighing fretfully, Baldwin was forced to remain quiet and attentive. It was not a task to which he was suited.

'Please be seated, Sir Baldwin,' Sir Edward said irritably. 'You distract me. Can you not see that I am reading?'

'My apologies, my lord,' Baldwin said, striding to the doorway and peering out. Here, there were always two guards on duty, and beyond them, a small guardroom. There was movement in there, and he soon saw three men coming out, all gripping weapons. They ran along the corridor, and then out to the main court. But from this chamber there was no means by which Baldwin could see or hear what was happening.

Edgar was not permitted to join him in here during his enforced incarceration with the prisoner, because apparently Lord Berkeley did not trust Baldwin's servant any more than he trusted Baldwin himself. Instead, Baldwin had told Edgar to remain in the court and listen and watch for danger.

There was no need. Soon after the urgent hoofbeats came hurrying in, there came the tramp of booted feet, and bellowed orders. Baldwin stood back from the door and felt for his sword as Wolf stiffened. He knew where those feet were coming: here, to Sir Edward's room.

The sound had stirred Simon, who had been dozing in the court while Sir Richard de Welles waxed lyrical about the pleasures of such a fine castle.

All had enjoyed the fruits of the additional money supplied for Sir Edward's confinement, but few had done so well as Sir Richard. He had the roseate glow of a well-fed fellow, for his little maid was as infatuated with her rotund knight as any maiden with a noble squire.

'I don't know how he does it,' Hugh grumbled more than once, much to Simon's amusement.

It *was* ridiculous that such a heavy, hoary old man should have won the heart of such an attractive little wench, but that he had was not in doubt. Whenever she came into the yard, she would look for him, and when she saw him, her face would light up like a child's seeing her father. Perhaps that was it, Simon reflected. It was just that she saw something of her own father in Sir Richard. Not that any father would behave with his daughter in such a manner, he added to himself censoriously.

Hugh glanced over the court towards the gaol's door. 'I heard that the man thought to have killed the carter had killed his own wife, too.'

'Baldwin said his wife and child died in a fire,' Simon said quietly, eyes still shut. He knew how Hugh missed his family.

'I'm all right,' Hugh said grimly, 'but I'd kill him myself if it was true.'

Before Simon could speak, he was grateful, for once, for Sir Richard's intervention.

'HOI!' he called, nudging Simon. 'Look at this, eh?'

The messenger had dismounted by the time a bleary Simon had rubbed the last of the sleep from his eyes and could take in the world once more. 'What?'

'Messenger from the King. Wearin' the King's colours,' Sir Richard said, but there was no humour in his tones now. 'Think we could be in for a little local trouble. Christ's bones, you don't think the King's comin' here, do ye?'

'No, not while the Scots are fighting again,' Simon said, and with that thought both stared at each other, even as the shouting and horn-blowing began.

'Oh, God's blood,' Sir Richard complained. 'Just as you get comfortable, they decide to muster us all for a damned war in Scotland, eh?'

*　　*　　*

361

Rumours began to fly about the castle in moments. Agatha and Father Luke heard the news from one of the grooms, who was laughing as he ran past them to his duties.

'What is it, boy?' Father Luke demanded, catching hold of his jerkin.

'War, Father. God be praised! Young King Edward's going to lead us to war. We're to gather our belongings for the ride.'

'Dear Heaven,' Father Luke said with despair. 'Not again.' In his mind's eye he saw once more the bodies outside Kenilworth, and heard the screams and shouts of the dying. Now he saw that same vision, magnified.

He saw John's face too, as the man-at-arms made his confession to him in the chapel: he had confessed to killing the guard at Kenilworth, plotting to release Sir Edward, and meeting others of the same mind. John of Shulton was sunk deep in infamy. He had told Father Luke all of this – and all in the confidence of the confessional. That was why the priest was so desperate to be away from this dreadful place.

Agatha was smiling with a fiendish glee. 'You know what that means? They will *have* to deal with the man now before they leave the castle, won't they?'

Luke gazed about him. 'I will stay one more day. But no more,' he said. 'I swear, no more.'

'Simon! What is happening, my friend?' Baldwin said breathlessly as he reached the bailiff and Sir Richard. 'It is true that they are called to muster?'

Simon indicated the hurrying servants. 'They've been ordered to the lord's stables, to fetch his destriers, carts, wagons – *everything*. The garrison is to leave with him.'

'What of the prisoner?'

Sir Richard answered that. 'They will leave a skeleton guard here. The larger part of the men are to go with Lord Berkeley and ride to York.'

Baldwin winced. 'The Scots, then?'

'Yes. They must be there by Ascension Day, so they have a month and a week or so, but they have to stop at Bristol first, to collect all the armour and weaponry there, as well as commandeer wagons to transport it all northwards.'

'It will take them almost a month,' Baldwin said pensively. 'What of us, Simon?'

'Me?' Simon said. 'I am staying here. You too, surely. I know that Gilbert, Sir Ralph and others dedicated to guarding Sir Edward are to remain.'

'I don't know,' Baldwin said slowly. 'If it is a full muster, I may be expected to join them. I shall have to find out.'

It was very soon that he learned his fate. His name was specifically mentioned on the muster.

Sir Baldwin de Furnshill was to ride to war again.

Sir Ralph was sitting in the seat facing the door of Sir Edward's chamber, wondering what the commotion was all about. His oath had been given long ago, and he felt he had behaved honourably to the man who had been his King, but this service was irksome. He had travelled with the King all the way across to Bristol and beyond last year, and all he had to show for his duty was dead companions and the loss of his manor. After Sir Roger Mortimer saw King Edward III crowned, he had taken Sir Ralph's lands for his son.

It would be interesting to see how the new King would cope with such a bold, avaricious adviser, he considered.

He was happy to be here, to be fed and billeted in the castle, but he did not seek companionship. Least of all with Sir

Edward. His oath was still valid, but Sir Ralph would not strive to return the old King to the throne. He felt the country had seen enough of war.

'What is all the noise about?' Sir Edward demanded peevishly from the window.

'Sir, would you like me to send a page down to find out?'

'No. Someone will deign to tell me eventually. I wouldn't have them think they had me anxious. Better to remain composed.'

'As you wish.'

'You are a good man, Sir Ralph,' Sir Edward said. He dropped moodily on to his chair. 'I am glad of your company.'

'Thank you, sire.'

'Do you think . . . do you think my wife would let them kill me?'

Sir Ralph felt as though the room was moving beneath his feet. 'Your *wife*?'

'Does she truly hate me so much? I never wanted to hurt her.'

'I am sure she wouldn't,' Sir Ralph said, and was relieved when there was a loud knock at the door.

A guard from the castle entered. 'Sir Edward, Lord Berkeley wishes you to know that he is to march. The King will bring war to Scotland.'

'When do we leave?' Sir Edward demanded. He stood, eyeing the door keenly.

'No, sir, you and Sir Ralph will remain here. Lord Berkeley will leave with his host, leaving a decent garrison to protect you here.'

Sir Edward said eagerly, 'I think I shall be needed to fight too. My wife would not leave me—'

'I am sorry, my lord,' the guard interrupted. 'That's all I was told to say.'

As soon as the door closed, Sir Edward turned and walked to the window again – but not before Sir Ralph had seen the tears on his cheeks.

It should have been a sombre meal that evening, but as Simon walked into the hall he became aware of a holiday atmosphere.

This first service was full of ribald laughter and boasting about how those present would put paid to the ambitions of that mad felon Robert, who called himself the Bruce. He had been excommunicated and the whole of Scotland forced to suffer anathema because of his ridiculous claims that he should not be a vassal of the English King; however, no one paid him any attention. While he had succeeded in harming some English forces, he fought with a low cunning that was despised by men of chivalry.

The fighting men of Scotland preferred to hurry into England on their sturdy little ponies and commit various acts of violence upon the people of the north, harrying the peasants and farmers all the way down to York. They were a warlike, violent people, but obviously no match for the brave young English warriors, and with their new King to lead them, with the Regent at his side, the English must prevail.

That was the mood of the place, Simon saw. But it was not matched by Baldwin's.

'These young fellows have not fought against a desperate foe before,' he said. 'This war will not be so easy as they imagine. It would take three or four wars for them to become accustomed to the ways of the Scottish.'

'Hah! You will be fine, my friend, and so will they,' Sir Richard de Welles boomed from Baldwin's other side. 'These Scottish churls will be shocked to see how massive are the forces ranged against them this time.'

'They want their freedom,' Baldwin murmured. 'That is something many men would think worth fighting and dying for.'

'It all looks worthwhile fighting and dying for – until you're standin' in line with a wave of English clothyards[1] aimin' at your proud Scottish heart,' Sir Richard chuckled.

'Perhaps,' Baldwin said, but Simon could see that he was not convinced.

Although he racked his brain for something that might divert his friend, Simon could think of no suitable topic to lighten the mood. It was a relief when Matteo Bardi arrived at their side and asked to speak with Baldwin.

CHAPTER FORTY-ONE

Berkeley Castle

Simon and Sir Richard walked with Baldwin out of the court, through the open gate and out into the wide space before the castle.

'Well?' Baldwin asked the Florentine.

'I am worried that I will die soon, and I would prefer that others whom I trust were told of my suspicions and fears before I am killed.'

Sir Richard snorted rudely. 'Who'd be bothered to kill a banker?'

'Tell us,' Baldwin said.

Matteo glanced quickly at the castle before striding away towards the bridge over the moat.

'This murder of the carter – it was not the first killing,' he began. 'You have heard that I was attacked and left for dead during the rioting in London? Well, my brother Manuele, head of our bank and our family in England, was slain that day. It did not occur to me that it was a malicious attempt to slay me at the

same time. I considered it more likely that I was the unfortunate victim of the fury of the mob, and that I should forget it.'

'But?' Baldwin prompted.

'The day of the attack I had been to a meeting of my family,'
Matteo said. 'We discussed whether to throw our influence
behind the Queen or the King. I was unsure, while my brother
Benedetto wished to support the Queen, and Manuele wanted
to remain on the side of the King. It was that same day that
Manuele died and I was almost slain.'

'You think your brother Benedetto could have stabbed you in
London?' Baldwin said.

'Yes.'

'Hah!' Sir Richard exclaimed. 'That is a terrible suspicion
to harbour – but you haven't acted on it before, have you, eh?
Why now?'

'Because now I have learned that he had a meeting with
the Queen's agent that very same day,' Matteo said. 'With Sir
Jevan de Bromfield.'

Baldwin was puzzled. 'I do not see how that affects you.'

'If Benedetto was so determined to throw the weight of the
House of Bardi, behind the Queen, would he not also have been
forced to silence all those stood in his way? Like me. And he
would have wanted to remove the man dedicated to the old
King: Manuele.'

'Possibly so. But other explanations fit,' said Baldwin. The
tale Matteo told corresponded with the note Baldwin had given
Sir Edward, and yet . . . 'I was in London myself about that
time, and I saw the effect of the rifflers on the city. It is quite
likely that you and your brother *were* unfortunate, that it was
just the mob howling for blood.'

'Yes, it could have been – but who else had a reason to kill
me, Manuele, and also my servant Dolwyn?'

'What of him?' Baldwin asked.

'Just this: is it not curious that the man who carried a note from the House of Bardi to the King should be the same man to find this horse and cart? Perhaps someone heard he was passing that way, and decided to have him killed. By accident the wrong man was found and slain. Maybe the carter was asleep, and the assassins found him snoring, and slew him thinking he was the messenger they sought.'

Baldwin's face screwed up as he considered the implications of Matteo's words. 'You assume that someone was able to track the man that efficiently, and yet miss him and kill the wrong one? And it follows on from an assumption of the possible guilt of your brother, which is itself dubious at best.'

'These are only my suspicions, but if I die,' Matteo said, 'please do me the service of enquiring after me.'

'Very well,' Sir Richard said. 'Now, is there anything else you would like to tell us? Because if not, my friend, we should return to the celebrations.'

'Yes, of course,' Matteo said disconsolately. His head was low on his shoulders, a picture of abject gloom. 'I am sorry to have troubled you. But remember what I have said, sirs. I believe my life may be the next to be taken.'

Wednesday after Easter[1]

Berkeley

'Simon, I am sorry to leave you here,' Baldwin said.

'I am sad you are to ride off,' Simon replied. There was much he wanted to say, but the only words that came to mind were

---

1 15 April 1327

platitudes that had no place in their friendship. 'Do you want me to take a message back to Jeanne?'

'No. I hope I shall be able to speak to her myself,' Baldwin said with a smile, but he was tense as he listened to the shouted orders from the front of the column.

Sir Ralph was in the ward, and he strode to Baldwin's side.

'I hope you have good fortune, my friend.'

'And I you,' Baldwin said. 'Good luck with your charge, my friend. You must look after him as best you can. If you need aid, speak with my friend Simon. He is reliable, honest and trustworthy.'

'I shall. Godspeed.'

'Sir Baldwin? It is time,' Edgar said. He was seated on his great rounsey, who pranced and chewed his bit, eager to be off.

Baldwin nodded. 'Aye. We must away, Simon.'

'Godspeed you back, Baldwin,' Simon said.

His friend gave him a quick grin, and turned to his horse. He patted Wolf, and was about to mount, when he saw Sir Richard. Quickly, he crossed to the latter and had a brief word, then mounted, waved once, and was off with the rest of the cavalcade.

The whole rattling mass was deafening. Cooking pots and pans, dangling from carts, clashed and clanged; iron-shod wheels thundered and hammered against the cobbles, while the hooves of many horses together produced a cacophony of noise that was painful on the ears. Simon knew they would be lucky to manage twenty miles each day. More likely, they would only complete about fifteen, what with the ox-wagons lumbering along at the rear. The huge creatures needed so much time to rest each day, and the party must travel at the speed of the slowest.

Simon was about to re-enter the castle, when he saw Agatha hurtling from the gates, her face a tragic mask.

'My cart! They've taken my cart!'

It was a disaster. To think that only yesterday she had been upset at the thought that the priest might leave her here, and now her family's most valuable possession had been taken. It was hard to think of anything worse, other than that her house might collapse with her and Jen inside.

'What will become of us?' she wailed, and fell to her knees. 'I am ruined! No man to run the house, no cart! How can I provide for my little girl?' She began to sob with great racking gulps.

The man she knew of as the bailiff was walking towards her. 'Mistress?' he called, but she didn't pay him any attention.

'Mistress, come,' Simon said, and put his hand out to her.

'Get off me!' she snapped, and beat at his hand. 'You don't know what this is like. How could someone like you understand? I have nothing! How can I provide for my little girl, when everything is gone?'

'I have suffered too,' Simon said. 'I lost my house, my daughter . . . But all is well again.'

'I don't know what to do,' she wept.

Simon looked up at the men of the castle who were standing about, and caught Sir Richard de Welles's eye.

Behind the loud, obstreperous exterior, Sir Richard had a kindly soul. He stood over the woman with a stern expression, and trumpeted, 'Woman, how far is it to your home?'

'Many miles.'

'Your daughter is there waiting for you?'

'Yes.'

'Then you should return home to her. But before you go, I will give you a note which will confirm that your cart and horse have been taken by the lord's purveyors. It is clear that you will have to have a receipt to mark the confiscation. And when the lord's men return here, if you have any difficulty with them in terms of giving back your cart, you need only speak with the steward here.'

'They won't do as I need!'

'Madam, they will do anything you ask if it means they will not have to answer to me,' Sir Richard said with calm certainty.

'I thank you,' she said, wavering. It was only when she saw Father Luke that she hurried off to tell him too.

Simon eyed the knight with a grin. 'Can you do that, or were you raising her hopes?'

'It'll do her and her daughter no good to be separated. And as coroner, if I tell her that I'll try to recover her property, so be it. I will.'

'What was it Baldwin said to you when he was about to ride off?'

Sir Richard's smile faded. 'He told me the King – Sir Edward, that is – wants the man Dolwyn freed if possible. God Himself knows why.'

'You don't think he was innocent?'

'Simon, that fellow may not be guilty of this particular crime, but I'd lay odds that he is guilty of others. I doubt not he's a thieving, murderous scrote who deserves the rope and will get it before too many years are past. So no, I am *not* happy that Sir Baldwin wants him freed to please Sir Edward. If I could, I'd probably have him hanged as Lord Berkeley wanted in the first place.'

'*You've* changed your tune!'

'Eh?'

'It was only a few days ago that you decided to save his life.'

'I did no such thing, Simon. No, I simply stopped him from being hanged without the officer of the law being there to witness and ensure that all was done in accordance *with* the law.'

He sighed and looked at the near-empty courtyard. There were a few men loitering, three grooms having a morning wet after their efforts preparing the horses for their journey, and over towards the gate Simon saw the older Bardi with that stern-looking knight, Sir Jevan. Both were in heavy conversation, their eyes following the dust cloud that obscured Lord Berkeley's men.

'I just hope we don't regret this,' Sir Richard added in his quietest voice.

'What do you mean?' Simon saw Sir Jevan turn and meet his look with a cold indifference. The arrogance of the bastard, Simon thought to himself, and then he saw Sir Jevan's face change. A scowl of recognition seemed to pass over his features, and when Simon shot a glance behind him, he saw the man-at-arms, John. What had that fellow done to upset him? he wondered.

'Well? What do you think?' Sir Richard said.

Simon had not heard his comment. 'Eh?'

'If this fellow gives his oath, d'you think we can rely on his word?'

'Yes. For what good it'll do.'

'Does he understand making an oath on the Gospel?'

'Of course he does. Do you think him a fool?'

Sir Richard nodded. He turned to John. 'You! Go and fetch me the gaoler. I want a word with him.'

Dolwyn stumbled out into the sunshine with a baffled, anxious look about him. He was glad to be out of the gaol. Senchet and Harry joined him a moment or two later, brought from the chamber in the main keep where they had been held since their release from the gaol itself.

'DO YOU ALL UNDERSTAND ME?' Sir Richard roared. 'I am releasing you on your own oaths. You can help about the castle as best you may, you can walk about the court here, and if you want, you can wander outside a little. But every night you will return to us here and take your beds in the keep. You will be locked in, and released in the morning. It is possible that one or two of you,' he added, staring ferociously at Harry and Senchet, 'may try to escape the castle and run. If you do, you will be called to court and, I swear, you will be declared outlaw for your bad faith. If you run, I will personally hunt you down, and I will have your heads as outlaws. You understand me?'

All three nodded dumbly. Dolwyn felt his ears ringing from the man's bellowing voice, but he did not care. It was so good to be outside once more.

'You have been found guilty of murder, Master Dolwyn,' Sir Richard continued. 'It was a legal court, and the Lord of the Manor has declared your offence. That means you are living under sentence of death now. If the coroner agrees with the sentence, you will hang. But there's little need to keep you in the castle's dungeon since it would only hasten your end. So you have some freedom for a little. Use your time wisely. You two – I hold you responsible for him,' he barked at Hary and Senchet. 'If he escapes, you will be taken and held in the gaol. You understand me? You are his gaolers now. So look after him!'

There was no need of further words. The three gazed about them, Dolwyn in particular bewildered by the sudden turn of events. He watched the knight and Simon for a moment with his mouth open. Then: 'Where is everyone gone?'

'They've been called to fight the Scottish,' Simon explained. He felt less antipathy towards this fellow than Sir Richard did. To Simon's mind, his tale of finding the cart was believable enough. If he had wanted, he could surely have invented a better story than merely finding the cart and no carter.

Dolwyn nodded and looked around again, searching for the Bardis, but the only person he saw whom he recognised was that woman, the carter's wife, who glared at him balefully from near the gate. At her side was the priest, who watched him with more a look of sympathy in his eyes, rather than disgust or hatred. Dolwyn saw them both pick up packs, she with a stick to carry hers over her shoulder, while the priest had a length of cord bound through his to hook over his shoulder . . . and then the two turned away and walked out through the gates.

It was a relief. The poor woman had lost everything, but it was not Dolwyn's concern. He was glad to be alive, and free again. If she was to suffer, that was sad for her, but he had other matters to attend to.

If he was spared, of course. Since the lord was gone, he had no idea whether his life was to be taken soon or not.

'What are these men doing out of the prison?'

The voice made his eyes snap wide. Dolwyn looked over to the other side of the yard, where he saw the hated figure in a cream tunic once more. This fellow was called Sir Jevan, he now knew, and he looked at the man with trepidation.

Behind him he heard the booming voice of the coroner again. 'I released them on their own parole.'

'Their "parole"? You think that they understand the concept of honour? They should be returned to their cell at once.'

'I have taken their oaths. I will not send them back for no reason.'

'No reason? Three felons and outlaws, and you think they should be released?'

'They are not convicted.'

'They are *guilty*. Look at them!'

'I am a Coroner to the King, and I have some few little powers. One allows me to hold these men to their word.'

The other knight gazed at him with contempt, then spat into the dirt at his feet, turned and walked away.

Dolwyn watched him go. All he could feel at that moment was the flaring of the wound in his flank. That and his utter loathing of that bastard.

'Masters,' he said to Senchet and Harry. 'I feel I owe you much. I cannot pay you for my life, but I can buy you some ale. Would you join me?'

CHAPTER FORTY-TWO

Berkeley Castle

Sir Jevan sneered as he watched the coroner leave the court. A man who was prepared to release criminals did not deserve to be in the position of responsibility held by that tub of lard. Such a fat fool would be a useless comrade in a fight.

It was a relief to Sir Jevan that he himself had not been called upon to join the King's muster. He had no objection to fighting, of course, but he knew that his master would much prefer him to be here, to keep an eye on Sir Edward of Caernarfon. The latter was far too valuable to Earl Henry of Lancaster for him to be allowed to be killed.

Sir Jevan wiped his brow. It was hot, and he felt uncomfortable in his thick tunic. Still, better here than on a long march north. Those fellows would soon be in some discomfort, with the sun shining on them all day long. He knew – he had taken part in such journeys before. Dust clogged the throat, and sat on collars, sanding away at exposed flesh like a hone on steel, until a man could only jog along trying to keep his head still. Dreadful business.

He looked around the court and spotted a small company playing at dice at a low table. The bankers were both sitting on a bench, and two others were testing their luck with knuckle-bones. A maiden watched, serving them with ale as the bones were thrown. In the past, Sir Jevan had enjoyed such pursuits, but not now, of course. After the execution of his master, Earl Thomas of Lancaster, by the King, Sir Jevan had lost interest in gambling.

Thank God that the man who had been King Edward II was now merely Sir Edward of Caernarfon – a lowly knight, no matter his former status. It was satisfying at a deep level – and quite inadequate at all others.

Just then, he noticed Matteo Bardi observing him from beneath hooded eyes. It was enough to make him clench his jaw. The man had a discourteous manner. Turning away, Sir Jevan strode off. This was not the time for him to get angry with these people. There was still much to be done.

He was just mastering his annoyance when he saw the three men released from gaol sitting out near the hall. Rage arose in him once more.

Dolwyn of Guildford was lucky to be breathing, the prickle. It was not for Sir Jevan to impose a punishment here, but if this were his Earl's castle, he would soon ensure that the fool discovered that a churl's place was not in the way of a knight, no matter where it might be – on the road, in a castle, any damned where! The man seemed to think he was entitled to take his place with other free men. Dear God, if all peasants were to think like this, the kingdom would collapse.

It irritated him beyond measure, yet once again, the only thing he could do was walk away. The alternative was to run this churl through with his sword, and that would only bring embarrassment and might even cause a renewed rift between his master, Earl Henry, and Sir Roger Mortimer. That, he knew, was not to be desired.

He must not get into a fight here in the castle. But if he were to leave the place, and was followed, he would be justified in defending himself. And it would be his word against the peasant's . . .

The Town of Berkeley

John saw William approach, but kept his eyes on the road – watching for any men following. There was no one.

'There is a muster, I'm told,' he said. 'Has Sir Jevan gone?'

William shook his head. 'No, unfortunately. You must be careful and avoid him.'

'How *can* one man avoid another in such a small castle? He knows me, and if he sees me, he will try to kill me.'

'Then you will have to ride away,' William said dismissively. 'It is not my concern.'

'Well it should be, man! What if he does capture me and I am put to the *peine forte et dure*? No one can survive that for long. I would be forced to give something away – and I don't want to do that.'

William studied him for a moment. 'You may be right,' he said. He glanced over his shoulder at the door, and then, when he turned back, found himself staring down the blade of John's sword. 'What are you doing?' he hissed.

'You were going to draw steel, weren't you?' John whispered. 'A look over your shoulder to see there were no witnesses, and then you planned to take my head off.'

William scowled. 'You are a cretin, John. Just now I am your only true friend in the castle, and yet you threaten to kill me? I was looking to see that no one could overhear our conversation, nothing more.'

John slowly let his sword-point drop. 'I am sorry. I am so aware of the dangers here at all times, especially with Sir Jevan. I . . . I do not know what I was thinking.'

'Then start thinking again now! You need to escape here. That is clear enough. I suggest you pack, mount your horse and join Lord Berkeley's men. Ride with him and leave this to me. It is too dangerous for you here, and your capture would make the whole plan fail. We cannot afford that.'

'Very well.' John sighed, and began to make his way out towards the stables.

'Oh – and John?' William called.

'Yes?'

'If you ever draw steel on me again, you had best use it. Next time I will not be so tolerant.'

Berkeley Castle

As Dolwyn came out from the buttery with Senchet and Harry, all carrying jugs of ale, he saw Sir Jevan and his heart sank. There was no safety here, not with that bastard staying behind. It was curious, from here, to see how his hair lit up with the sun's kiss, as if he was a saint – supreme, sacred, safe. But then he passed beyond the gateway, and suddenly his hair was dark brown again.

Sir Jevan personified everything Dolwyn hated about so many knights. It was there in the impunity with which this knight had attacked him, as though he was irrelevant, like a fly in his way. A fly that could be squashed and destroyed.

On a whim, Dolwyn followed after Sir Jevan. He walked out through the gates, and stared out beyond. The knight was not there!

Dolwyn hurried forwards – and then there was a sudden jerk at his side as his arm was grabbed and he was pulled over

– and then he realised that there was a white-hot mark where a dagger's blade was set to his throat.

'Peasant, you want to harm me, don't you?' Sir Jevan hissed. 'Well, it will not happen. I am watching you all the time, and I am trained. Do you really think you can confuse me, or cause me to drop my guard for a single moment so that you can have your chance to kill me? It will not happen, I am warning you. You will die trying. And that is good. Because you know you deserve it, don't you?'

'Something wrong here, master?'

Dolwyn looked over his shoulder. There, a matter of a couple of feet away, was Alured. His sword was in its scabbard, but he stood on the balls of his feet in readiness.

'This is nothing to do with you,' Sir Jevan growled.

'I am an officer of the law in London, and it's my job always to prevent men fighting. Seems to me you're trying to threaten this man, and I won't have that.'

Sir Jevan was about to call for some of his men, but to start a fight within the castle's grounds, was sheer folly.

'Sir, you are holding a dagger to his throat,' Alured went on. 'I think you should take it away – *now*.'

Sir Jevan bit his lip, then withdrew the blade and marched off to the main gate once more, without giving either of them a backward glance.

'You all right?' Alured said, watching the knight.

'Yes.' Dolwyn swallowed, and wiped away the blood from his neck. 'I am grateful to you, master.'

'So you should be, Master Dolwyn. So you should be,' Alured said, but his attention was on the knight still, because from beneath the long tunic that Sir Jevan wore, he had caught a flash of dark-red boots: boots of Cordovan leather. And he wondered suddenly if those boots had tassels . . .

Thursday after Easter[1]

Berkeley Castle

Alured woke the next morning to the regular sound of snoring coming from a large, black-haired man with a beard and moustache that had not seen a barber's knife for at least a month. Alured blinked and found himself gazing into the man's open mouth. It was not a seductive sight.

The ale-house where he had spent the night was a scruffy peasant's house in which the only chamber was used for both drinking and sleeping. The accommodation was sparse, the palliasses thin and rank, but the food was plentiful and the ale excellent.

Rolling over, he put his arms behind his head, staring up at the rafters. There was a homely smell of woodsmoke and ale in here, the smells he remembered from his own home all those hundreds of miles away in London, and for a moment he thought about his wife and what she would be doing today – sweeping out the rooms, tending the fire, setting the pot on its trivet to boil some water, heating a stone to cook a little cake for her breakfast. It was a scene he had witnessed many times, and never before had he felt the full force of its importance to him.

Sir Jevan had reddish-brown boots. No surprise there. Many other men wore boots made of good Cordovan leather. Alured must have seen twenty or more such pairs of boots on the way here – and amongst the garrison he had seen others. So what made the sight of Sir Jevan's boots so uniquely surprising, he asked himself. And then he realised. It was not so much the boots on their own, but the boots combined with Sir Jevan's character.

1 16 April 1327

Most knights were intelligent enough, and although there were some who were prepared to flout the law and steal or rob, most of them were honourable enough by their own lights. However, Sir Jevan was not one whom Alured would trust. It was easy to believe that he could have been involved in the murder of those two youngsters. But *why*? That was the question that nagged at Alured.

He would see what he could learn.

Saturday after Easter[1]

Berkeley Castle

Simon had enjoyed his breakfast that morning. Sir Richard was already up and outside, so the good bailiff was able to relax and eat a leisurely meal, not attended, for once, by a violent hangover.

He was shovelling a large plate of eggs into his mouth when Alured appeared in the doorway. Simon did not know this man well. He was aware that he was some form of servant or guard to one of the Bardi, but that was the extent of his knowledge.

'Master Bailiff? May I speak with you?'

Alured stood looking down at Simon. He had a kind of steadiness in his eyes which Simon rather liked.

'What is it?'

Alured licked his lips, and then sat down at Simon's side. 'I think that I have discovered a murderer,' he murmured. 'I need your help.'

Simon's face hardened. 'That is a serious accusation.'

1 18 April 1327

'You think I don't realise that?' Alured grated. 'I am well aware of the penalty for a wrongful accusation.'

'Are you?' Simon asked. 'If you accuse a man of murder and it's shown he was innocent, you pay the price he would have paid. You would be hanged in his place. You do realise that?'

'It is worse that the man is a knight,' Alured mumbled.

'A *knight*?'

'Sir Jevan. He is a murderer, I am convinced of it.'

CHAPTER FORTY-THREE

Second Monday after Easter[1]

Berkeley Castle

Simon and Sir Richard walked together about the upper north wall. It was a place where they were guaranteed some peace, and could speak for the most part with the security of knowing that no one could overhear them.

It was not easy, Simon reflected, to find a place where no one else would hear Sir Richard's booming voice.

'Are ye sure?' the knight said in what he fondly assumed to be a quiet tone.

Simon nodded, looking down into the castle's court at the men milling about there. The place had settled into a new routine in the last few days since the departure of Lord Berkeley and his men. Now there were three men sitting out at the entrance to the main block where Sir Edward of

1 20 April 1327

Caernarfon was kept. Sir Ralph now shared the chamber with Sir Edward at all times. He was the constant companion, who shared in every meal, who watched over every visitor, and stood always between his former King and any possible danger.

If Alured was right, and Sir Jevan *was* a murderer, there were enough men here to capture him and make him safe. The garrison was reduced to a minimum, with perhaps thirty or so men, and the host of labourers was possibly larger than the garrison itself. There were only a few genuine men-at-arms, but they should be enough to help capture one man even if he were inclined to try to kill again.

'Ye know, not all murderers are maddened fools,' Sir Richard mused. 'Would it not be better to speak with this Sir Jevan and see what he has to say? The man seemed reasonable enough when we met him.'

'Perhaps. But I would be anxious that he might attack us and then flee.'

Sir Richard looked at him. '*Flee*? I don't think he'd get far if we had the gates locked first.'

'You think so?' Simon said. 'Those gates are so old, the lock so worn, I daresay he could pull them apart! But if you are sure, I would be happy to go and talk to him with you.'

'There he is,' Sir Richard said, pointing.

Down in the court Simon saw the knight speaking with the older Bardi brother, Benedetto. 'Let's go and tackle him, then.'

'Yes,' Sir Richard agreed, but his mind was elsewhere, Simon saw. The coroner was staring down past the two men towards a dark, shadowed doorway. 'Isn't that the other fellow?'

'Yes. It's Matteo Bardi,' Simon said. 'He's watching and listening to them, isn't he? And he did accuse his brother of trying to kill him. Do you think Benedetto and Sir Jevan could be in league?'

Willersey

Father Luke had never been so glad to return to his church. Travel, he thought, may broaden the mind, but for him, remaining here in his vill was infinitely better. The whole journey had been a disaster. He had learned that his bishop viewed him as a vile womaniser, just because he had tried to help a widowed parishioner in need. And then the wretched castle at Berkeley, with the lord and his men keen to steal what they could. A horse and cart were useful items – and the fact that the thief Dolwyn of Guildford had dropped them into the lord's lap made them only more attractive.

At least poor Agatha had her note from the kindly knight Richard de Welles, and he had promised to ensure that she did recover her property later. That was good. At least that knight was honourable, Luke thought to himself.

He was in his meagre garden, weeding and pulling the snails and slugs from his lettuces. It was good to bend and work like this, revelling in the sunshine and thanking God all the while for His bounty. At last, Father Luke felt that he was regaining a little of his composure.

Looking up, he saw Jen at the door to her house, a large pail of water from the well in her hand. She looked, if anything, more pale and fearful than ever, the poor child. She had been blooming before her father's death, but his dying had changed her for ever. Any child would miss her father if he was taken from her prematurely, but to see his murdered body, with the axe still in his head . . . that must have been traumatic.

He saw her glance in his direction – a pale, seven-year-old child, skinny from lack of food, with eyes as wide as a puppy's waiting for a thrashing, before she quietly slipped into her house.

Yes, it was terribly sad to see her in that state. He would pray for her. No young girl should suffer so much.

Berkeley Castle

Simon hailed the two as he and Sir Richard descended the stairs. 'Sir Jevan, Master Bardi. Could we speak with you a moment?'

Sir Richard smiled widely at the sight of the two men. Sir Jevan was a smaller man than him, but very wiry. He would be a tough opponent, Sir Richard felt sure, if they were to come to blows.

Sir Jevan snapped, 'Yes? What do you want?'

Simon pulled a face. 'It is a difficult question to pose. You see, I have been discussing with the good knight here a trouble-some matter.'

'My friend is reluctant to mention it,' Sir Richard said. 'Sir Jevan, it's said that you were in London at the time of the rioting last year. That right?'

'Yes.'

'And you went to have a meeting with this man, too,' he gestured to Benedetto, 'because you were arranging finance for the Queen, so we've heard. Nothin' wrong with that. But the same day, a couple of youngsters were killed behind your house, Master Benedetto. Did you hear of that?'

'Was it the same day?' Benedetto enquired. He had a well-meaning smile on his face that Sir Richard did not trust for a moment. 'I heard of their deaths, of course, but did not realise they had occurred on that very day. A terrible time. My brother was killed there, too.'

'Yes,' Sir Richard said without hesitation. Alured had told Simon it was the same day, and he was unlikely to have got it wrong. In one day, Alured had found rioters, seen the Bardi house invaded, found Matteo lying on the ground, and then discovered the two dead bodies. Sir Richard found such testimony convincing.

'I don't remember it distinctly,' Benedetto said.

'What of it?' Sir Jevan barked.

'There was a man seen with the two youngsters. He killed them. The witness said he wore good, Cordovan leather boots of a dark reddish-brown, with tassels to match,' Simon said. He looked down at the tunic of Sir Jevan.

'Half London wears good leather from Cordova,' the knight said without lifting the hem of his tunic.

'Perhaps so. However, half London was not in the area on that day,' Simon said.

'Do you accuse me?' Sir Jevan said, taking a small step nearer.

'I ask: was it you who killed these two young people?' Simon demanded.

'He was with me that day,' Benedetto interjected.

Sir Jevan eyed Simon. 'I do not recall the details of that day, but I do remember that there were many men running hither and thither. Any of them could have been a murderer, and yet you dare to suggest I had something to do with this crime? Your presumption is astonishing!'

'Do you deny it, then?' Sir Richard demanded bluntly.

'Show me the fool who dares accuse me,' Sir Jevan said. 'I will see him in court, and he will pay for his presumption!'

Sir Richard watched as he stormed away.

Simon looked at him. 'Well?'

'He did it,' Sir Richard said without hesitation. 'And so now I think we should be cautious, my friend. A man like him should be treated with care.'

Simon nodded. Then, 'I will warn Alured, too. He should beware of Sir Jevan's temper.'

Second Tuesday after Easter[1]

Berkeley Castle

The screams rose like those of a tormented banshee, and Dolwyn threw himself from his bench with the swift reactions of a man used to danger. He rolled to the corner of the wall, his fingers gripping his sword already, the blade a wicked grey blur in the air before him, his mouth slightly open as he listened intently.

'What in God's name was that?' Harry whispered from the farther corner of the chamber.

'My friend, I do not want to find out on my own,' Senchet muttered from between the two.

They had taken this room for their own after the lord had ridden off to meet King Edward III. It was a good-sized room in the castle's keep, with the added advantage that it was far enough from the guard rooms to leave them feeling safe from a possible stab in the dark, and the door had a lock that worked, and two bolts.

Dolwyn went to the door now, and tested the bolts. They opened smoothly. He had spread some butter thickly on them last week to make sure that he could slide them silently, and now that effort paid off. Without speaking, he pulled the door open and glanced out. 'No one there. Come on!' he whispered, and darted out.

He stepped quietly along the narrow passageway, listening. The screams came from farther up, and he moved cautiously,

1 21 April 1327

his feet finding the stone flags and testing each before he continued. The hairs on his neck rose, and he felt as though there was a band of steel wrapped about his breast, contracting with every step until to breathe was an agony.

Another ungodly shriek. Dolwyn felt sure that his lungs would burst with the strain – and then he saw a glimmer of grey in the corridor before him: a window, with the glorious bright moon illuminating the way. He pelted across the last of the stones and reached the window, feeling the cool night air flood his body, and then, as the next scream shivered through the very stones of the castle, he took courage and ran onwards, hearing Harry and Senchet close behind him.

He knew this place. It was a part of the tower where the outer walls had weakened and fallen. Below in the yard was the place where the labourers and masons slept, in tents and lean-to buildings. There were pieces of masonry all about, and he stumbled on rock chips as he went, searching for the source of those horrible screams.

When he saw the body, it was only the legs at first. They protruded, still kicking, from between two walls of rock, where the man had been deposited. Blood lay all around, and Dolwyn's feet slipped on it as the man struggled and thrashed about desperate to keep a hold of his life.

Road near Stoke-on-Trent

They had made good time in a week, John of Shulton thought as he stirred himself from his bed that morning and peered about him in the gloom of a foggy day.

He had caught up with the lord's men in only an hour or so of moderate riding, since the column was travelling slowly with so many carts and wagons in its train. Once there, he had made his way to Sir Baldwin, as being the most friendly face he knew. The knight nodded to him amicably enough, but Edgar's smile was a warm welcome to John, who felt so lonely still.

As he gradually eased himself upwards, he winced with the stiffness that came from sleeping in the open air.

'You slept soundly,' Edgar said. He was already squatting at the side of a small fire. Others in the camp had fires, too, but Edgar's was the only one which did not spit fitfully and smoke. Instead there were good flames licking upwards from the few sticks and chopped logs, and already he was about to set a pot on top to warm some water before making some soft bread.

'Don't I always?' John said with a smile.

'Not usually, no. It seems you are easier in your mind the further you are from Berkeley. Or the monk from near Gloucester.'

John felt a little silver of ice pass down his neck. 'Really?'

'Friend, I have no idea what you hurry from, but now you are joining us on a different adventure. We ride to war. There is no time for doubts and anxiety in battle. So whatever you flee, you are safe here.'

John tried to take comfort in Edgar's words, but all he could see in his mind's eye was Sir Jevan's face – and that was no comfort at all.

Berkeley Castle

The castle had soon been roused and almost at once men had grabbed Dolwyn, Harry and Senchet, and thrown them against the wall.

'We found him here,' Dolwyn protested. 'I was just First Finder – I didn't hurt him, nor anyone else, either. Let me go!'

But his words were in vain. As he and the other two were forced back, swords at their throats, more men arrived, gazing down in horror as the light entered the corridor with the rising sun.

'WHAT IS ALL THIS?' Sir Richard demanded as he barged his way through the press. 'Man killed, eh? Who is it? And who did for him? Where's the First Finder?'

It was a guard near Harry who responded, pointing to Dolwyn and describing how he was found, sword in hand, and blood all over his face.

'What d'you have to say to that, eh?' Sir Richard demanded, standing over Dolwyn.

'Simply that I am First Finder. I came because this poor devil's screams woke me, just as they did my friends here. And the man was almost dead when I got here. But my sword is clean. You look at it – no one's been stabbed with it.'

'Aye. Let's see it,' Sir Richard said.

A man indicated the sword. It lay near the body, in a pool of blood, where it had fallen when Dolwyn was forced to drop it.

'I was made to put it down,' he protested. 'I can't help that.'

Simon was crouching reluctantly near the body. 'There is an axe here, a small hatchet,' he said. 'This is what killed the man.'

'Who is it?' Sir Richard said. 'I haven't looked at him yet.' He turned to peer down at the body, and then shot a look at Simon. 'Is it who I think it is?'

'Yes, Sir Richard. It's Sir Jevan.'

CHAPTER FORTY-FOUR

Berkeley Castle

Simon spent much of the morning with the labourers and masons.

The hole in the wall of the chamber in which Sir Jevan had been found had been caused by a collapse in the outer wall of the tower itself, although that facing the inner ward was still sound. Like much of the rest of the fabric of the castle, this square tower set into the south-western corner of the wall had become sadly dilapidated during the period when the Despenser had overtaken the castle, because he wanted no strong fortresses at the edge of his own territories, and had deliberately weakened the buildings and walls.

'Did you not hear the cries in the night?' he asked a labourer.

He was sitting on a rock, while Hugh and two castle servants brought the workers to him. The responses were shifty at best. One man shook his head in frank denial, and pointed to his ears. Simon was given to understand that he was deaf. Another stated with conviction that the screams were those of the Devil carrying a soul to hell, but for the most part the men here denied hearing anything, or if they did hear, they didn't know where the screams came from.

That was understandable, Simon felt, looking up at the tower again. With the only window many feet above ground, and no other gap in the tower's wall facing this way, it would be hard for a man down here on the ground to know where the cries came from.

'What of you?' he asked the latest man to be delivered to him. 'Did you hear the cries last night?'

'Yes. But I didn't know who it was, nor where he was.'

'Where were you sleeping?'

'I was down here,' William said, pointing at the tent's canopy.

'With the other masons?'

'Some of them.'

Simon looked about him. 'Did you see or hear anything else after the screaming started?'

'We'd drunk well last night. It was Samuel's birthday, and we celebrated with a barrel of wine, so I don't think any of us was fast to waken,' William said. 'But when we did, we ran up to see what was happening. We all went together.'

Simon thanked him and sent him away. 'That is that, Hugh. They were all out here, but so drunk they scarcely knew what was going on. Whoever did it, how did he manage to escape when all the stairs and passages were full of men coming to investigate?'

Hugh shrugged. 'Maybe the fellow was right, and it was a devil.'

'And maybe the killer flew away, you mean?' Simon said, staring about him at the rocks fastened with ropes, ready to be hauled up. 'I don't think that there was a flying murderer, Hugh. A magical killer would have no need of an axe, would he? No, this was a normal, flesh and blood murderer. Same as any. But how he did it, that's a different matter.'

'*If* anyone cares about the knight dying,' Hugh shrugged.

'I care,' Simon said, but then he remembered Sir Jevan's face from yesterday, and Sir Richard's conviction that he was the murderer of at least two others.

'I care,' he repeated, with no conviction at all.

Second Wednesday after Easter[1]

Berkeley Castle

Simon strode along the court from the hall where he had broken his fast, and up to the corridor.

'Any sign of him?' Sir Richard asked.

'Not yet. I hope the man hasn't gone to war with the others,' Simon said.

'Not too much risk of that, I'd think. There are enough murders down this part of the world to bring in a respectable income for the King. He won't want to lose that.'

They had sent for the official coroner as soon as light permitted yesterday, but so far there was no sign of the man. Instead the castle was forced to try to run itself without allowing anybody in or out, as the law demanded. When a man was slain in a manor, the people living there were to be held until the coroner had come and held his inquest. Despite being a coroner himself, Sir Richard held no warrant for this county; he could not work here unless he had permission.

'Doubt if he'll make much sense o' this,' Sir Richard grumbled to himself as he eyed the corpse. 'A man killed in the

1 22 April 1327

middle of the night by an axe. Plenty of axes lying about here, and enough men willing to wield 'em, from what I've seen of Sir Jevan.'

'Do you think it was Dolwyn?'

Sir Richard cocked an eyebrow. 'Do *you* think it was him? No, of course not! Blasted fellow arrived at the wrong time, that was all. And the fact that the murderer used an axe just means he wasn't stupid. With all the rumours about the man Ham slaughtered on the way here, and people lookin' at Dolwyn all askance, it was natural they'd think it was him.'

'He was the man there when the guards arrived.'

'He was the man who slept nearest, so naturally he would have been first to wake and first to get to the body. More to the point is, what was Jevan doin' here anyway? What made him get out of bed in the night and walk over to that place?'

'Got lost on his way to the garderobe?' Simon wondered.

'And happened to meet a maddened axeman on the way? I doubt it, Simon.' Sir Richard sighed. 'Did you speak with Alured last night when you said you would?'

'Yes, but I incline to the view that he wouldn't have done this.'

'Why?'

'Because he seems devoted to the law and justice. He's a constable, not a maddened axeman.'

'Whoever killed Jevan,' Sir Richard said thoughtfully, 'was seeking to deliver justice. We must talk to Alured, Simon.'

When Simon and Sir Richard enquired, they learned that Alured was in the hall with his master, Matteo di Bardi.

'Signor Bardi,' Simon said as they walked to them. 'I am sorry, but we would like to speak to your man.'

'There is nothing you can say to him that you cannot tell me,' Matteo said.

He was sitting on a bench next to Alured like a pleader, Simon thought. All pale and thin, like the clerk he was. Simon had heard much about this man, how he would gather news and use it for the benefit of the bank. It reminded him of how Despenser had used informers all over the country. Simon disliked the idea of spying. Those who were supposed to be loyal should be so, to his mind. There was little point in giving an oath of loyalty if a man was going to renege immediately for Florentine money.

'Alured, you know what I want to speak about,' Simon said.

'Yes. Master Matteo may as well hear it too,' Alured said. 'He should be aware.'

'Tell us again, then, about Sir Jevan.'

Alured looked at Matteo as he answered, 'The day you were stabbed, master, a short way from you lay two more bodies. Just youngsters, they were. The girl had her head cut off, while the boy was stabbed. It happened while I was with you. I heard something and ran up the alley – and there they were, poor souls. I found a witness – a man who had seen the killer hurrying away.'

'You told me this. But he saw no face,' Matteo said.

'No. He was very drunk and lying at the side of the alley, but he *did* see reddish-brown Cordovan leather boots – like the ones Sir Jevan wore. And the style of death – the girl's head cut cleanly from her body – that was the act of a man-at-arms, not a peasant. The lad too was stabbed twice about the heart. I think he died in an instant, which also speaks of a killer experienced in war and killing. And Sir Jevan was that.'

'So?' Matteo said.

'A man could easily have stabbed you, then flown up the alley and stood there waiting to see if he was pursued. And if some youngsters came along unexpectedly, he might have killed them before making his way to his meeting.'

'His meeting – with my brother?' Matteo said, and his stomach lurched. 'So my brother did try to kill me. I had suspected it for so long, but to hear this . . .'

'Not your brother,' Alured said. 'Sir Jevan. He was on his way to see your brother, you told me, but he could have stabbed you and then the couple I found before he got there.'

'My brother . . .' Matteo said again, his face a mask of tragedy.

'There is no proof he's involved,' Sir Richard said with his low, rumbling voice. 'He may be completely innocent. Come, Master Bardi, I think before you contemplate an accusation you should be careful to consider the implications.'

'The "implications"?' Matteo echoed. 'The only "implications" I see are that I risk death whenever I see Benedetto!'

'Meanwhile, Alured,' Simon said, 'I would like to know where you were last night.'

'I slept on a bench outside my master's chamber,' Alured said. His expression told what he thought of the arrangement. 'I was there all night.'

'Was anyone with you?' Sir Richard asked.

'You think to accuse *me* of the murder?' Alured said. 'I deny it. I was on my bench and asleep from an early hour. I was tired – I still am!'

'I heard the screams and opened my door and he was there,' Matteo confirmed.

'So, will you arrest me too? You have three men in gaol. Why not make it a quartet?' Alured asked cynically. 'You can never have too many suspects, can you?'

'We ain't askin' all this for the fun of it,' Sir Richard boomed. 'It's our duty, and yours, to learn what we can about the murder of a knight.'

Alured looked at him, but he knew better than to pick a fight with Sir Richard.

'I think you one of the least likely killers in the castle,' Simon said. 'But we could hardly ignore the fact that you have been seeking the man for months. If not you, who else?'

'You know who *I* think it was,' Matteo said.

'Yes, your brother was involved with Sir Jevan, Master Matteo.'

'If he had paid the man to kill me, perhaps Benedetto wanted to see to it that Sir Jevan could not confess and put the blame on him,' Matteo said.

'Your brother could be a danger to you. Be aware, and act accordingly. Keep Alured with you at all times; do not go about without a friend whom you can trust.'

'Surely his brother will not attempt to kill?' Alured said. 'He had to enlist the aid of others to try to kill Matteo.'

His face suddenly froze as he realised what Simon was getting at.

'Yes,' Simon said gently as he watched Matteo. 'Be very cautious, because it is possible your brother killed Sir Jevan last night. Perhaps he has no need of agents to perform his killings now. He can do it for himself.'

Second Thursday after Easter[1]

Berkeley Castle

Benedetto Bardi was anxious and growing all the more so, the longer he was held in this castle. To think that only a few days ago he had felt that the place was pleasing! He had spoken to

1 23 April 1327

Matteo about the congenial atmosphere, the efforts which Lord Berkeley was expending to make it still more delightful . . . and now he could not look about him without thinking the place was no better than a midden.

There was a definite feeling of menace. Men on the walls stared down with suspicion, whilst the servants were surly and rude. If Lord Berkeley were here, Benedetto would have demanded of him that his staff remember their duty of courtesy to a guest, but without him, he dared say nothing. Not while the soul of Sir Jevan wandered the corridors. There was far too much death and sadness in this place, he thought.

He knew why they all looked at him askance: they knew that he was guilty. The letter which should never have been written had been found. That man Sir Baldwin had discovered it, and Lord Berkeley had seen it. Clearly that was the cause of all this suspicion.

Lord Berkeley had called for him soon after the arrival of the messenger from the King.

'Come in, sit down, my friend,' he had said as Benedetto entered his chamber.

It was a small room, this – dark, but warm.

'You like my private chambers? Cosy, which is how I prefer it. I don't like to suffer if I can avoid it,' Lord Berkeley said.

He sipped from a goblet, and held it out. The only other man in the room was his steward, who stepped forward in an instant to refill it. Oddly enough, he forgot to offer a drink to Benedetto, but the latter assumed it was merely the pressure of work that was distracting him.

Lord Berkeley peered at him over the rim. 'So, Master Bardi. You are an industrious fellow, I know. You have the difficult task of always being on the side of the men who will be in power – a balancing act that would torment the ability of a juggler. So difficult to maintain perfect harmony while trying to win the favours of Sir Roger Mortimer as well as Sir Edward of Caernarfon.'

Benedetto's smile was forced as he muttered, 'I don't know what you mean, my lord.'

'No? I suggest you search your memory. I know of the letter your family wrote to Sir Edward when he was King. You promised him your support. At the same time you swore to provide all needful to the Queen and Sir Roger. One letter to one side, another to the other. Did you not pause to reflect that the letters must become known? No matter who was to win, someone from the Queen's camp would be sure to find out about your letters to the King, and vice versa. And now they *are* discovered, and I have the interesting difficulty that I am not sure what to do with you. Perhaps I should just tell Sir Roger Mortimer and see what he would consider best.'

'No!' Benedetto blurted out. 'There is no need for that. Let me aid you, my lord, and we can—'

' "Aid me", you say? I think that would be a most improper course. You wish to include me in your schemes – entangle me in the web of lies you have constructed? I think not.'

'My lord, it was Manuele who wrote and signed those letters, not me. And I was already willing the Queen to overwhelm her husband. There must be something, a service I could provide . . .'

Lord Berkeley looked shocked. 'Do you mean you would offer a bribe to keep my silence?'

It was agreed in a few minutes. Lord Berkeley had very little money. So much had been despoiled when Despenser captured his castle, so many objects stolen, so much damage done to the walls, that the cost of returning the building to its former glory would be exorbitant. And Benedetto must agree to help with those costs. Lord Berkeley drove a hard bargain.

Benedetto knew from the looks which the others here in the castle threw at him that his deal was common knowledge. The steward must have spread the tale far and wide, the son of a whore! If he could, Benedetto would have him killed. Pay Dolwyn or some other fellow to slay him – or even perform the deed himself. The bastard had ruined Benedetto's position here.

But Dolwyn was in the gaol for killing Sir Jevan. At least it meant that he was secure.

Benedetto disliked having a dangerous man like him loose.

CHAPTER FORTY-FIVE

Near Macclesfield

Baldwin felt the cool air penetrating beneath his armour, and took a deep breath, clenching the muscles of his chest and shoulders against the chill.

They were making good time, even with the ox-carts holding them up. Where a horse could walk and take rests to eat and drink, an ox had to eat, then lie down to chew the cud, before being able to walk on. They were immensely powerful brutes, but Baldwin did wonder whether their ability to haul massive wagons was not offset by their slowness.

The party was making its way north around the wild lands, and soon would turn north and east towards York. That was where the King's Host was gathering. From what Baldwin had heard, it was clear the young King was determined to crush the Scottish. Their raids and depredations upon the innocent farmers and peasants of the north had appalled him, and he had set his heart on destroying them once and for all. He was calling upon all: Hainaulters,

Frenchmen, barons, knights and squires, to join him in this great endeavour. Many had already been summoned to meet the King at York for the Monday following Rogation Sunday[1] and it was thought that they would soon thereafter march on Scotland.

But to reach York would take time. All he could think of as he rode was his manor, his wife and his children. He was riding ever further from them with every passing hour. It felt as though he was being torn in two: his heart was with his family, while his head demanded that he carry on to York and to battle as a warrior. Baldwin had a duty to fight for the greater good.

They were in a broad plain when he saw a small contingent of men-at-arms veering off to the left. There were seven all told, and Baldwin frowned at the sight. There were all too many men who would 'ride out', foraging amongst peasants' houses for tidbits of food or drink. It was natural that a knight would expect those whom he protected to reward him for his efforts, but some took advantage of their position and would steal and harry without mercy. Baldwin had seen it in the Holy Land, in Italy, and in France, and recently he had witnessed it in England.

On a whim, he clucked his tongue and spurred his horse. Leading Edgar and John, he rode at a moderate canter towards the men. But he had misjudged them. They were not riding out; they had simply spotted a party of men trying to hide, and had encircled them with lances at the ready.

'What is this?' Baldwin demanded as he approached. There were eleven all told, and well-dressed in soft wools and linens. The leader was a little younger than Baldwin. He had dark

1 18 May 1327

hair and hazel eyes in a sunburned face that was square and as uncompromising as granite. As he eyed the men encircling him, his attention was more with the rest of the column than the men about him, Baldwin noticed.

'You!' he said to the man. 'What is your name?'

'David of Monteith. Who are you?'

'Sir Baldwin de Furnshill,' Baldwin said. 'You are many leagues from home, friend.'

'We travel south. To family in Wales.'

'Aye?' Baldwin eyed the men's clothing. They had all travelled in foul weather, from the look of the mud that had splattered about their boots and up their horses' legs. They were particularly well armed, too, but that was no surprise – travellers needed the means of protecting themselves. 'You have met with inclement weather.'

'What of it?'

'Not many would carry on in the worst of weathers. They would rest themselves and their horses in an inn. You must have great need to ride so far so fast. What is the cause?'

'We have no great urgency,' the man insisted. His companions murmured and their sturdy horses moved uneasily.

Edgar was at his side, and Baldwin knew that there was no need to trouble himself on that flank. Nobody would pass Edgar unless they killed him first, and that would require a more resolute man than most Baldwin had met.

'John, ride to my Lord Berkeley and tell him there are Scottish forces riding to spy on us,' Baldwin said calmly.

There was a moment's silence after his words. Baldwin was filled with a heightened awareness – of the men around him, but more, of the sound of bees among the flowers and grasses at his feet, the song of larks high overhead, the wind soughing through the branches of the furze.

And then Monteith dragged his sword free and bellowed his war-cry, spurring his beast at Baldwin.

Baldwin grabbed at his sword but it seemed to take a dreadful amount of time to clear it from the scabbard. Too slow: he must be run through by Monteith's sword, and then his new blade was out and flashing wickedly in the pale daylight. A gleam caught it, and it sparked in blue fire.

He was about to ride on to meet Monteith when Edgar flew past him, and Baldwin saw another man with a bow aiming it at him. He readied himself for the arrow, fully expecting to feel it in his breast at any moment, but before Edgar could reach the archer, Monteith was at his side, and had raised his sword. Baldwin lifted his own and parried, and as he was about to turn his steel to attack, Monteith coughed and groaned, and tumbled from his horse, the arrow planted in the back of his neck at the base of his skull.

Berkeley Castle

Simon and Sir Richard de Welles were pleased to hear the sound of horses approaching. The confinement in the castle was an intense irritation to all concerned. However, it was natural that the people of the household should remain together when a murder was discovered, so that the malefactor was prevented from running away. A killer abroad was a danger to all, because if a man would kill once, clearly he was likely to do so again. It was a basic premise of the law that a murderer should be punished by the loss of his life. Otherwise what was the point of laws? Such a man was a threat to the whole order of society. That was Simon's belief.

The law itself was, as he knew, more pragmatic. It required that the body remain where it was when it was discovered; this also applied to the people who had been near when the man was killed, so that their names could be registered. Then, when a Justice arrived on his tourn, the correct fines could be imposed on each of them.

'Sounds like him now,' Sir Richard said, standing up. The maid, who had been sitting on his lap, squeaked as he unceremoniously dumped her on the ground. 'Sorry, wench. Coroner's comin' and I need to have a word or two with him.'

Simon helped the girl to her feet before hurrying after Sir Richard.

He found the knight at the gateway, speaking with a slender, short man with grizzled hair and a thin, oval face. From his size and fine features, he looked more like a clerk than a coroner and knight, especially in comparison with the man behind him who travelled on a donkey. He was a clerk, from his tonsure and habit, but he had the build of a wrestler, and his black eyes were suspicious.

'Sir Ranulf, I am well indeed. And you?'

'My health has not been good of late,' the coroner said, and sprang lightly from his horse. 'I am plagued by afflictions that will, I have no doubt, carry me off before long. I must make the most of the time God has seen fit to give to me. It is not easy when you are prey to so many ailments.'

'It must be a torment,' Sir Richard said seriously.

'It is. Where is the body?'

'Come, take a little wine or ale first. You have had a long, wearisome journey, I make no doubt.'

'It has been wearisome, yes,' the coroner said. 'But a man must accept the trials imposed upon him.'

'So, food and drink first?' Sir Richard said hopefully.

'Sir Ranulf, if you refuse him, there could be another murder in this castle,' the clerk said.

'Master Rodney, kindly remember that I am the coroner, you are the clerk. I speak, you record. That is the basis of our collaboration. You recall?'

'Oh, yes. I recall. But, Sir Knight, if you want me to record for you, you will do very badly unless I have eaten first. My reeds will all break and smudge the pages, unless your amiable, obedient servant is fed.'

'In God's name, what a trial this fellow is. I swear,' Coroner Ranulf said. He eyed the clerk with a stern look. 'Come, man, have you no sense of duty?'

'My duties are to Him. And He would see me fed!'

'Ach! Then yes, Sir Richard, we will break bread with you. You can tell us about the man found dead while we eat, if you would be so kind.'

Near Macclesfield

John watched the body slump and tumble to the ground. When he was a lad and had helped the local warrener net and kill his rabbits, John had seen bodies fall like that. Not a twitch, not a sign of the passing spirit, just one moment alive, the next dead. The arrow must have penetrated his spine to kill him so swiftly, he thought, and he stared down in shock at the sight of David Monteith's body lying on the grass.

The rest of the Scottish knew as soon as their leader fell that their own position was hopeless. The archer sat in his saddle with his bow still in his hand, incapable of speech. Instead he stared at the body on the ground.

Baldwin rode over and took the bow from his unresisting fingers. 'You will come with us. Edgar and John, place the dead man on his horse. We shall take his body to Lord Berkeley. You, archer, what is your name?'

'I'm James, sir.'

Baldwin looked at the fellow. He was young, probably not yet twenty summers old. He had been aiming at Baldwin, John knew, and steeled himself for the knight's anger.

But he did not kill the boy. Instead, to John's amazement, Sir Baldwin put his hand on the archer's. 'You are to come with us. You have done enough in this war. Your arrow was directed by God.'

John was troubled as they rode back to the column. He knew that Monteith's men were due to join the Dunheveds at Berkeley. If Lord Berkeley spoke with James, he might learn of their plan to save Sir Edward of Caernarfon.

He listened as the men were questioned, and when James was released from Lord Berkeley's interrogation, badly beaten, he knew he must warn the Dunheveds.

A short while later, Lord Berkeley came and spoke to Sir Baldwin.

'Sir, you have an interest in protecting Sir Edward of Caernarfon, I think.'

'I feel it my duty,' Baldwin said levelly.

'I have a task that should be to your taste, then. I require you to ride back to Berkeley and warn the castellan that there are men gathering about the castle. These fellows would tell us nothing about their reasons for travelling, but I think that itself is an indication.'

'I don't understand, my lord.'

'Monteith was a vassal of Donald, the Earl of Mar. You know of him?'

'Yes.'

He would be known by all, John thought. A strong, fearless and resourceful Scottish knight, he was intensely loyal to King Edward II.

'He was at Bristol, I heard, before the city was captured by Queen Isabella,' Baldwin said.

'Yes, but he escaped. He rode to Scotland to demand aid for Sir Edward,' Lord Berkeley said, 'and if his men are riding down here, away from York, avoiding larger towns and cities, Mar is near too. I can see no other purpose in his journey but the rescue of Sir Edward.'

Baldwin's eyes narrowed. 'Excuse my bluntness, my lord. You know that I am devoted to Sir Edward of Caernarfon, yet you tell me to ride with messages to ensure that he will be kept confined?'

'Sir Baldwin, I do not wish it said I colluded in the murder of Sir Edward! Imagine, were a band of thieves, cut-throats and outlaws to raid my castle, what would happen to Sir Edward? He would try to escape, and entering the mêlée be cut down or shot full of arrows. My little castle may not be the largest in the land, but it is sufficient as a defensive fortress. I would not have him die there. I know your loyalty to Sir Edward, and you know your duty. Protect him. Ride to Berkeley, ensure they are aware that the castle is at risk, and you may save Sir Edward's life.'

Baldwin nodded, and glanced about him. 'Edgar, we return south,' he said wearily.

John had no wish to return to Berkeley, but he must. Someone had to warn the others that their plot was unravelling. He cleared his throat. 'Sir Baldwin, you may need a spare man if the castle is attacked. May I accompany you?'

'Perhaps,' Baldwin said, and now those dark, intense eyes were turned upon John. It felt as though the knight could see through to John's heart.

CHAPTER FORTY-SIX

Berkeley Castle

The little hallway in which Sir Jevan's body lay was beginning to stink. Simon, walking behind the two coroners, was struck by the odour long before they reached the corpse. Flies were everywhere.

'Damn these fiends,' Sir Richard said, waving his hand to keep them from his face, which bore a wholly untypical glower of disgust.

Simon had known Sir Richard for some years now, and had never seen him flinch at the sight of a corpse before, however ancient and noisome. But this was different. The stench in here was overpowering.

Sir Ranulf and his clerk walked with Sir Richard to stare down at the body.

'I think,' Sir Ranulf said, 'we should conduct this inquest as soon as we may.'

The clerk had thrust his face into the elbow of his sleeve. His voice was was muffled as he replied, 'Yes. And then have the poor fellow buried.'

The coroner nodded, still staring down at the ravaged figure, and then turned on his heel and was marching away. 'Right, Sir Richard, could you aid me in collecting together all the men in the castle and in the town for our jury. We shall require them to gather here in the morning. With luck we can expedite matters and have the body delivered to the priest by luncheon.'

'Of course.'

Sir Ranulf looked about him as they emerged into the daylight again. 'This is a good little fortress, isn't it? And I believe you have a prisoner here.'

'True. Sir Edward of Caernarfon is held in the back over there,' Sir Richard replied.

'I should like to see him,' Sir Ranulf said.

Sir Richard smiled. 'There would be no trouble with that, Sir Ranulf. But anyone visiting Sir Edward must remain tolerably polite.'

'But of course,' said Sir Ranulf. 'How else would one behave to our last King?'

Second Friday after Easter[1]

Berkeley Castle

The castle had returned to its accustomed quietness after the inquest, and the men of the jury had dispersed back to their fields and labours by early afternoon.

Simon and Sir Richard sat with the coroner and his clerk in the hall while the two ate.

Sir Ranulf was an astute man, Simon learned. This was

---

1 24 April 1327

another in the mould of Sir Richard, who appeared to have a genuine interest in discovering who was guilty of a crime.

'The man Dolwyn was not convincing,' Sir Ranulf said meditatively. 'And he is owed a hanging, I hear.'

'He had the manner of a man determined to remain in gaol,' Sir Richard commented, pulling the thigh from the chicken on the board before him and taking a gargantuan bite. 'I think he has a lot of secrets to keep.'

'But do you think he killed Sir Jevan?' Sir Ranulf asked.

'No. And I'm glad that the task of deciding his guilt or innocence is up to a Justice and not me,' Sir Richard told him.

Simon shook his head. Dolwyn had cut a mean figure. He had the pallor of a gaol-bird already, and his responses to all questions were insolent, as though he was already convinced he would hang for this murder. 'I think him innocent.'

Sir Richard glanced at him. 'Perhaps. Not our place to decide.'

The coroner for the county stared at his trencher with a frown. 'There would appear to be few friends of this Sir Jevan. Soon all the men here who could have committed the crime will be flown. Then justice will be difficult to pursue.'

'I am sure that Harry and Senchet had nothing to do with the murder,' Simon said.

'As am I,' concurred Sir Richard.

'Then, my friends, I recommend that you both bend your efforts to discover the true culprit,' Sir Ranulf said.

Simon looked at the food on his trencher. He had lost his appetite. The local courts would decide upon the guilt or innocence of Dolwyn, and the comfort of passing the responsibility to another was shattered. He knew he must seek the murderer.

Of the men who had cause to wish to see Sir Jevan dead, he felt sure that the Bardi brothers or Alured were the most likely suspects. He knew that they had motives: Benedetto to punish Sir Jevan for attempting to kill Matteo; Matteo in revenge for his injuries. Both would think Sir Jevan guilty, because Alured had shown them that the man was a murderer.

But whoever had killed him had used an axe and left it in the body, just as Ham had been murdered. And Dolwyn was accused of that murder too.

Sir Ranulf continued, 'I would aid you, but I have two more corpses to view.' He sighed, pushed his trencher from him and leaned away from the table. 'The last year has provided me with more corpses than I ever wished to see.'

'Aye,' his clerk said. 'And it will become worse.'

'How so?' Sir Richard said. 'The kingdom is at ease.'

Rodney looked at Sir Ranulf. 'Do you really believe the land is at peace? While Sir Edward of Caernarfon lives, there is a rallying point for those who would rebel against the new order. If we are not careful, he will be released and the wars will start again.'

'War!' Sir Ranulf said. 'I know little of war, but I do know murder when I see it. And there are plenty of men willing to free Sir Edward. They say that he is still the legitimate King.'

'We have to keep him safe,' Sir Richard said.

'From harm,' Sir Ranulf added.

Simon nodded too, but as he glanced at Sir Richard, he thought the knight sent a nod and slight wink in his direction. Sir Richard would help him find the murderer of Sir Jevan, he felt sure.

Cirencester

The news that they had been expecting came all too soon. Frere Thomas was already calmly sitting on a bench in the little tavern when his brother walked in.

Stephen was wearing a short tunic, a cowl and hood, like any number of peasants in the area, and the two brothers nodded to each other imperceptibly as their eyes met, but beyond that there was no sign that they had seen each other.

Thomas watched Stephen walk to the bar and lean on it, asking for ale, while all the time, Thomas's ears were straining outside. There was nothing to indicate that either had been followed in here, and all his anxiety fled as he realised that their plans had worked. They were safe.

He stood, made a smiling bow at the wench at the bar, giving her the sign of the cross, then walked out to the bench at the door outside. A few moments later a shadow fell over him, and he knew it was Stephen.

'Well?'

'As we thought, Tom, the King has demanded that all his men leave to join him up in the north. The lands about here are growing empty.'

'Good. Then we should begin to make their lives more exciting,' Thomas said.

Stephen said no more. The men in their gang knew what was expected. He walked away from Thomas, and the latter uttered a short prayer for success. He did not plead his case or that of Stephen, he merely asked that their patron, the man who had once been King, should be returned to his throne. As God must require.

And that thought itself was enough to make him content.

Berkeley Castle

Sir Ralph was surprised when the knock came, and a moment or two later Sir Richard and Sir Ranulf were in the chamber and introducing the coroner to the King.

'Your Highness,' Sir Ranulf said, bowing. 'I hope I find you comfortable?'

Sir Ralph smiled to see the expression on Sir Edward's face. It was that of a man who has been given a pot of iced water in a desert. 'As you can see, sir, it is not the accommodation I would have chosen,' he said deprecatingly, with a gesture around the room. 'But it suffices.'

'You have all you need?' Sir Ranulf asked.

'I have excellent company, my friend, but I lack books. That is my greatest sorrow.'

'I shall ensure that books are sent to you, sire.'

Sir Ralph frowned. It was unkind of the coroner to pretend to help. He thought he should interrupt, but was unsure how to.

'I would be grateful.'

Sir Ranulf glanced about the chamber with a critical eye. 'You must let me know if there is anything else you need, sire. And one other thing. Her Royal Highness, your wife, wishes me to tell you she thinks of you with fondness, and has asked me to arrange for some presents to be brought. Wine, some clothing, and choice meats. I shall arrange this with the custodian of the castle.'

Sir Richard appeared to stir himself. 'Hey? Do you have a letter from Her Highness, or anything to confirm all this?'

The coroner smiled. 'I was asked to visit to enquire about Sir Edward. It was simply fortuitous that you had a death here as well.'

Sir Ralph rose and peered at the letter with Sir Richard when Sir Edward had studied it.

'It is genuine,' Sir Edward said. 'Please tell my wife that I am glad, and grateful for her thoughts and gifts.'

Sir Ranulf spoke with Sir Edward for some little while, and Sir Ralph was glad to see his lord keenly enthusiastic all the while. Only when the guests had left the chamber, did Sir Edward's mask fall.

He fell into his seat and covered his eyes.

'Sir Edward?' Sir Ralph rose to his feet, perturbed.

'What does she wish to do? Torture me? Promising presents – books, clothes. Why, to remind me of all I have lost? Or does she tease me, showing me all the luxuries that her damned lover enjoys?'

Willersey

The day was overcast and heavy with the threat of rain as Father Luke walked from his church door to the little patch of garden, carrying his hoe.

'Hello, Jen,' he called with a smile.

She gave a startled jump like a young foal, and turned a face of tragic misery to him.

'Jen,' he said, shocked at the sight. 'Please, maid, come here and let me hold you.'

She slowly crossed the path to him, and he put his arms about her. 'Dear child, you are skin and bone,' he said. 'You must eat, or you will not flourish.'

'I can't,' she said quietly. 'I have no hunger.'

'Jen, your father wouldn't wish to think that his death would cause yours,' Luke said firmly. 'You need to eat and remember how good your father was, so that his memory, and your love for him, will live on.'

'*I miss him so much!*' she blurted out, sobbing.

He knelt before her, and she put her head on his shoulder, weeping with all the passion of a grown woman.

Father Luke cradled her skinny body and had to blink to keep his own tears at bay. This poor little girl.

He felt as though the despair of the world was resting on his shoulders.

Second Saturday after Easter[1]

Berkeley Castle

Simon and Sir Richard sat on a bench outside the gaol as Dolwyn, Harry and Senchet were brought to them.

The day was warm and humid, but of the three men, Dolwyn shivered like a man with the ague.

'Do you know why we've brought you here?' Sir Richard asked, his eyes resting on each of them in turn.

Harry spoke first. 'We know nothing, sir. We were asleep in our beds when the screams woke us, and we followed Master Dolwyn to find the cause, as we should.'

'You are here because we believe you,' Simon said. 'Look, we do not think you are guilty. It makes no sense for any of you to have slain Sir Jevan, so far as we can see. So we wish to do what we may to have you released. But in order to do that, we have to know if you can tell us any more about what happened, the night Sir Jevan died.'

'We were asleep,' Harry said simply. 'It was his screams that woke us.'

'All we did was go to help a man being attacked,' Senchet agreed.

'What of you, Dolwyn?' Sir Richard asked.

'I was in my bed, same as these. We were all woken by the screams.'

'When you reached the body, then – is there anything more you can tell us?'

'Sir Richard, if there had been anything I could have said to aid my defence, I would have told the coroner at the inquest.'

Sir Richard nodded and looked across at Simon.

1 25 April 1327

Simon shrugged dispiritedly. 'Ach! I wish Baldwin were here,' he said.

Near Stockport

Baldwin rose with the sun. He and Edgar worked in a companionable silence as they saddled and bridled their horses. Both knew their work, and had spent so many years together that there was seldom need for a word to pass between them. Much as John had been with Paul. It made him feel even more lonely to see them – he felt like an intruder.

Yet he had to get back with them to warn the Dunheveds that the plan was already known and risked disaster, were they to continue. The words of Lord Berkeley were not idly spoken; he clearly knew that there was to be an attempt upon the castle. Sir Edward of Caernarfon would be at risk: he could well die.

'Sir Baldwin,' he said as they trotted along the road, 'do you think that Lord Berkeley knows something about the men guarding the old King?'

'Yes,' Baldwin stated. His tone was rough, as though he hated to speak such words.

'Why?'

'If I had to guess, I would think that the castle has a man or men inside it whose task it is to ensure that the good Sir Edward never leaves it alive,' Baldwin said gruffly. 'And if I were to speculate, I would guess that it was not my Lord Berkeley's man, but another's.'

'Whose?'

Sir Baldwin looked at him as if measuring him. Speaking too plainly to someone who was not a close companion was always dangerous. There were men willing to spy for others at all levels in the nation. But Sir Baldwin was not a man to be fearful of speaking what he believed to be the truth.

'At a guess, I would think Sir Roger Mortimer's,' he said. 'No one else would be as easy to command as a man loyal to Sir Roger.'

CHAPTER FORTY-SEVEN

Sir Edward of Caernarfon's chamber
'Bring me wine,' Sir Edward demanded.

The days were inexpressibly tedious. His new books had not arrived, and all his other activities were curtailed, so that his hours were spent staring at the whitewashed walls overwhelmed with self-pity.

One of the few pleasures left to him was wine. At least when he was drunk he was less aware of Sir Ralph's pained expression. He knew that Sir Ralph considered him a spent force. Gilbert was as bad. He sat on a stool near the door with the look of a man who had bitten into an apple to find half a maggot.

His entire life had been spent under the gaze of others. In his role as law-maker and judge, every moment had taken place in public, and even his private existence was observed. He had never known true peace, except those glorious hours spent alone with his closest companions: Sir Hugh le Despenser, and before him Sir Piers Gaveston.

Now, all his friends were gone. In their place were these glum churls.

The sound of a man rapping at his door made him sigh heavily. More fools come to pester him, or insult him, no doubt.

He motioned and the guard nearer the door opened it to show Sir Richard de Welles and Simon Puttock.

'Yes?' Sir Edward demanded.

'We came to ensure you were comfortable, Sir Edward,' Sir Richard rumbled.

Sir Edward waved a hand about him. 'Look at my marvellous accommodation, and the cheery company. Surely I could wish for nothing more.'

The sardonic tone was painful to hear, and Simon looked about him to avoid Sir Edward's gaze, while Sir Richard turned and ordered Gilbert and a steward from the room. They demurred, and it took a threatening glower from Sir Richard to finally get them to leave. Sir Ralph remained.

'Sir Edward,' Sir Richard began, 'we have had a murder in the castle. A knight called Sir Jevan.'

'He broke his oath to me; I will not mourn him.'

'You won't be alone in that. Some believe Master Dolwyn of Guildford killed the fellow.'

'What do *you* think?'

Sir Richard said. 'There are others with more reason to want to kill him.'

'Such as?'

'Benedetto di Bardi,' said Simon, and explained about the murder of the two youngsters, as described by Alured.

'But,' Sir Edward said, 'the Bardis are good, loyal servants of the Crown. They would not seek to support a murderer.'

'Sir Edward,' Simon interposed, 'you know, I think, of the letter that this man Dolwyn carried?'

423

'I do.'

'It was written by the Bardis, but Benedetto was determined to aid the Queen, not you. Through Sir Jevan, he gave her his assurance of money and support. I think Matteo was on your side – which could explain why Sir Jevan may have attempted to kill him.'

'Perhaps,' Sir Edward agreed. 'What of it?'

Simon took a deep breath. 'I have to ask: Sir Jevan was no friend of yours. Did you arrange for him to be slain? If so, we shall drop the matter. But if you did not, we feel bound to enquire into it.'

Sir Edward met his look with a firm determination. 'I have not instructed, asked nor requested that any man should kill Sir Jevan.'

'In that case, we must speak with Alured and the Bardis,' Simon said.

Third Wednesday after Easter[1]

Berkeley Castle

Baldwin saw the castle rising before him at last with a distinct relief. The last days of riding at speed had been hard, and he would be glad indeed of a bed.

He rode in under the gatehouse with Edgar close at his side, Wolf lumbering along behind them. John had been with them until the day before, but then, during the morning, he had told Baldwin that he was unwell. It was true that he looked very pale and jittery, but to Baldwin, it looked as though the man was scared. To put it bluntly: petrified. Of what, Baldwin had

1 29 April 1327

no idea, but he was persuaded that it was something or someone to do with the castle.

Whatever the reason, Baldwin was of no mind to drag him
back to Berkeley if he was unwilling. He was happy to let the
fellow go and continue alone with Edgar.

Simon was in the court with his servant Hugh when Baldwin
clattered into the yard.

'Good God, Baldwin!' Simon exclaimed, his face wiped free
of the look of introspection that had clouded it. 'It is good to
see you, old friend.'

In a short time they were inside the hall with mazers of wine
in their hands.

'So, what brought you back before the muster?' Simon
asked.

Baldwin told him about the fight with the Scots. 'They were
from Donald of Mar. Since they were heading south, Lord Berkeley
felt that they could be gathering in order to try to free Sir Edward.'

Simon nodded doubtfully. 'Rebels made an attempt on
Kenilworth, and were slaughtered. They must be lunatic to try
it here as well.'

'But everyone will know that the garrison here has been
denuded and that Lord Berkeley is away. They may well try
again. So we must improve the defences in the time we have.'

'How long is that, do you think?' Simon asked.

'My friend, I have no idea,' Baldwin said frankly. 'It could be
a week, it could be a month. Not much more, though, I would
think. The Earl of Mar will want the advantage of surprise.'

Simon nodded bleakly.

'Simon, what is it that clouds your face so?' Baldwin asked.
'You looked glum as I rode in.'

'Sir Jevan was slain a little over a week ago,' Simon told
him.

Baldwin gave a frown. 'Do you have any idea who was the killer?'

Simon shook his head. 'There was no witness, no indication as to who could have committed the crime. Only the fact that an axe was used. Perhaps that—'

But Baldwin was ahead of him. 'Any man who sought to show it was the same person as he who killed the carter would do that. The woman and the priest from the vill are both gone, are they not?'

'Yes.'

Baldwin nodded slowly. 'Then I think that for now Dolwyn and his friends cannot be released. But we need not see them languish in the gloom and cold of a dank cell. We should devote our efforts to the protection of this castle, and they can help. Perhaps once that is achieved, we can return to this matter again.'

Willersey

The day was a dull one. There was no rain, but it might as well have been pouring, from the priest's mood.

His garden had been invaded by slugs which had eaten the majority of his lettuces and peas, caterpillars had taken refuge in his cabbages, and before he could deal with any or all of them, he had been called to listen to the last confession of a farmer up in the shadow of the hill. The fool had been trying to separate a calf from its mother, and had been gored by her. Nobody thought he could survive more than a few hours.

Father Luke returned to the vill with a conviction that the world was not functioning as it ought. Only a few days ago he had been a contented man with many blessings to count, and now he felt as though his life was an abject failure. He had lost the King's money, he had lost a pair of good fellows from his

426

flock, and no matter what he tried, he was not able to console Jen.

Only this morning he had seen the poor child looking desolate. Perhaps, he wondered, he ought to speak with Agatha about her? But the widow was already doing all she could, and did not need his interference. No, he was better leaving her and the child alone, surely, and allowing them to find their own way to peace.

At the same time he still had John's confession on his mind. He recalled how he had thought John such a pleasant fellow when he first met him – a cheerful soul with the smile of a rogue, he had thought. Little had he realised that John would become devoted to homicide: to murdering Sir Edward of Caernarfon.

Berkeley Castle

The discussion with Sir Richard and Simon Puttock had been intriguing to Sir Ralph. However, it was a matter of days ago now. They had not succeeded in capturing the murderer, and he wondered whether they ever would.

Sir Jevan had not been a congenial companion, and Sir Ralph did not bemoan his passing, but he took a keen interest in any issues that could lead to danger to his charge. If a murderer stalked the castle, he would wish to see the man apprehended.

Sir Edward himself was difficult in the mornings with a sore head, and grew more amiable as the day progressed. There was, indeed, little to occupy him now that the common pursuits of chivalry were denied him. But no matter what, Sir Ralph did agree with Gilbert that to allow the King to leave the castle to ride would present untold dangers.

For Sir Edward, the incarceration was tedious, but Sir Ralph was beginning to think that if he himself did not escape this chamber soon, he too would become quite mad. Being locked in here was taxing all his reserves of patience.

The only escape was to sit and consider who it was who could have killed Sir Jevan – and imagine how to defend Sir Edward, were the killer to try to assassinate him.

Minchenhamtone[1]

The little vill was peaceful as John rode in.

There was not much to the village – only a small market square, with a modest-sized chapel and a pair of inns and some taverns. It was a place which Stephen and Thomas had once told John was safe. They had relatives who owned the manor nearby and the people of the area were very keen supporters of the Dunheveds and the old King. If he had need, they said, he should make his way here.

He had greater need than ever now. Filled with depression, he felt all the miles he had covered in recent days as he reined in by an ale-house and gazed about him. The illness he had mentioned to Baldwin had not been feigned. It was a fresh manifestation of his inner desperation. If only Paul were still alive, so that he had someone with whom to discuss this whole matter. But Paul was dead, and there was no one else in whom he could confide. His desperation was caused by that very solitude that would, with luck, ensure a measure of success.

It had been hellish to travel with Sir Baldwin. All the way he had felt as though he was being studied, as though Sir Baldwin knew he was a member of the party determined to release the King. In honesty, he was unsure as to whether Sir Baldwin himself was devoted to the incarceration of the old King, or would aid his release. Perhaps he would support those

1 Minchinhampton

determined to free Sir Edward of Caernarfon? Many might. Many would.

'John? What are *you* doing here?'

John's head snapped around and he found himself staring at Sir Edmund Gascelin. 'I am glad to find you. The whole plan has been discovered.'

Sir Edmund swore under his breath. 'How?'

'Men of the Earl of Mar were captured and beaten. It was not their cowardice or treachery that betrayed us; the simple fact that they were men from the Earl was enough to alert Lord Berkeley. He's convinced there's to be an attempt to free Sir Edward.'

'Is he returning?'

'No, he has to attend the Muster, but he has sent a knight to warn the castle,' John said as he swung himself down from the saddle. An ostler came to take his horse from him, and John and Sir Edmund entered the inn. Inside, John found the two Dunheveds, and he repeated his story to them.

Frere Thomas looked at Stephen. 'Does it change anything?'

'We have the men ready. If they aren't going to increase the garrison as John said, we will be safe enough.'

Sir Edmund grinned. 'In that case, the plan will go ahead. Soon we will have rescued our liege-lord from Berkeley, and there'll be nothing anyone can do to stop his return to the throne.'

'There will be war again,' John said.

'Of course there will. How else would he recover his throne?' Sir Edmund had a savage look about him, keenly anticipating the battles to come. 'You must return to the castle now.'

'I can't,' John said dully. 'Sir Jevan is there, and he knows me. If I go back, with so few men in the garrison he will be sure to recognise me.'

'He's no threat to you now,' Stephen said. 'William has sent a message. He's dead.'

'So now we can consider the battle,' Sir Edmund said with a ferocious grin.

John nodded, but inwardly his heart sank. The prospect of thousands of deaths, in order to return the failed King to his throne, had become abhorrent to him.

CHAPTER FORTY-EIGHT

Fourth Wednesday after Easter[1]

Cirencester

The little town was busy even though this was not a market day. Stephen Dunheved walked out into the sunshine with a sense that this was a good place for their efforts to begin.

He had heard that Cirencester had once been a great city, second only to London, but that was a fable to make the peasants here feel more important than they deserved. True, the local farmers had a good stock of sheep; their flocks were huge, and the fleeces they produced were very much in demand. That was the source of the town's wealth: wool.

An apprentice barged into him, hurrying from a tavern, and Stephen swallowed the urge to clout him. He must not draw attention to himself in any way.

1 6 May 1327

The sun was directly overhead when he finally heard what he had been waiting for. Hoofbeats. A cry, then a scream and shouting. He walked away from the roadside and waited near his own horse.

It was here, at the market square, that the riders came at speed. There were seventy of them all told, bold fighters from the Dunheved estates, wiry, tough Scotsmen with Earl Donald, and Welsh knifemen from the Marches, and Stephen's brother at their head with Sir Edmund and John. They rode into the square and Thomas dismounted, walking to the middle.

'Fellow Englishmen!' he shouted. 'Listen to me! They say that we are Godless people because we do not acknowledge the right of any to deprive our King of his crown. Who dares to think that a man should attempt to deny God's own anointing? Who dares to think that God would approve of a man's effort to overrule His judgement? This heretic and false knight, Sir Roger Mortimer, believes he has such a right. Do you?'

There was no sound from the people in the square. For the most part, they were staring about them at the force of men on horseback who stood ringing them, rather than at the Dominican.

Thomas walked in amongst them. 'Listen to me, I say! You are in grave peril, my friends. For while you permit this traitor to rule, you are submitting to the man whom God would see brought down. You flout His laws when you honour this man who has demeaned the throne of your country, who has proved himself a traitor, and who even now commits adultery against God's laws. Sir Roger Mortimer is a loathsome outlaw! You have a duty to rise up and overthrow him!'

Stephen could hear his brother, but it was obvious that his message was failing to attract the crowd. The townspeople here

432

were not interested in an uprising. But no matter. Stephen had spent his money carefully and wisely.

It was as the Dominican was pleading with the town to follow him and march upon the castle, that there came a roar of support.

Stephen grinned. He had bribed with ale a gathering of thirty or more apprentices and labourers at an inn, telling them to come and join him when they had drunk his money if they wanted more. Now they were coming out to partake of more of his largesse, and there was a general movement away from them by the rest of the crowd.

Even then the situation might not have gone the way Stephen and Thomas had hoped, had not the castellan intervened.

A small force of men-at-arms appeared at one end of the square, with a knight at their head. 'What in Christ's name is all this noise about?' he demanded, his horse nudging the men and women out of his way. 'Who are you, Friar? What are these men doing here?'

His horse pushed over a woman, who screamed as she fell. The baby she carried had rolled under the feet of others, and her shrieks rose to Heaven. The noise under his horse's hooves made the beast rear, and his men, thinking he was being attacked, brought their weapons to bear on the people in front of them, their polearms lowered threateningly. A man shouted defiance, which led to the drinkers from Stephen's tavern to shout still louder, and while the knight battled to get his plunging horse under control, someone threw a stone that clashed against the helmet of a man-at-arms. He fell back, reeling, and that seemed to be the signal for others to begin to lift cobbles from the street and hurl them at the party from the castle.

Stephen saw a stone strike a man in the face. Beneath his steel bonnet, his features became awash with blood and he was shoved back out to safety behind his comrades.

'Reject them! These are the same as the heretic criminal who sits behind the throne, and sleeps with the real King's wife! Throw them from your square, people of Cirencester!' Thomas bellowed, and suddenly the crowd began to roar. There was a forward push, and the men with the knight looked about them with fear. It was plain that they were alarmed to see this normally bovine town roused to such fury.

More stones, and then the mob was barging forward in earnest. The knight on his horse drew his sword and began to flail about him, but a rock the size of a man's fist struck his unprotected temple, and he fell. His mount turned and bolted, and tore through the men-at-arms like a rock from a siege engine.

Stephen ran the risk of being drawn along with the people, but he stood his ground. There was a butcher's shop nearby, and he eyed the meats on display. Next to a pair of hanging ducks was some sausage, dried and smoked, which he took. A youth in the shop asked for money, but Stephen struck him back-handed in answer, and left the lad bleeding on the floor as he walked back outside.

A full-scale riot was in progress. Men and women were screaming and baying, demanding that the group from the castle throw down their weapons, while more stones rattled about them. One of the men-at-arms was pulled into the crowd, and while Stephen watched, a maddened peasant with a cleaver took his head off, and then the rest of the men backed away, realising their danger. Stephen was sure that they would all survive – but then he saw more rocks and sticks being flung, and he knew that the men-at-arms stood no chance.

'Brother, we should leave,' Thomas said to him, eyeing the furious mob with a certain trepidation.

'Your sermon appears to have achieved what we hoped.'

'If it helps bring Mortimer to justice, it is worthwhile,' Thomas said, and the two hurried off to their horses.

Fourth Friday after Easter[1]

Berkeley Castle

With the assistance of Sir Richard, Baldwin had managed to instil a sense of urgency into the men in the castle. In place of the leisurely rebuilding works, there was now an atmosphere of febrile activity. The stores had been replenished, and the wall and keep prepared for attack.

'There are plenty more sections of wall that would benefit from repairs,' Sir Richard said. 'Looks like a group of choristers could push it over in places.'

'We shall have to do the best we may,' Baldwin said. He looked about him at the defences and felt a twinge to see so much more that needed to be done.

'We'll be prepared enough,' Sir Richard said.

'Perhaps.'

It was while they were still on the wall, talking about the need for supplies of arrows, that they saw the approaching dust.

Baldwin narrowed his eyes. His sight was not as keen as it once had been. 'Who is that?'

'No idea. Soon find out, though,' Sir Richard said.

They descended the stairs and reached the yard a short while before the rider appeared.

'I must see the castellan,' the lad panted.

Baldwin eyed him. This was no messenger of the King; it

1 8 May 1327

was a youth of perhaps sixteen mounted on a rounsey. 'You can tell us. I am Sir Baldwin, this is Sir Richard de Welles.'

'Sirs, a group of men led by a Dominican Friar and his brother Stephen Dunheved caused a riot in Cirencester the day before yesterday. The whole town's in an uproar, and three were killed. I've been sent to warn you that they may come this way next. They have a large company with them.'

'Aha!' Sir Richard boomed. He looked about at Baldwin. 'Well, maybe we'll get a chance to test our defences sooner than we'd expected, eh?'

Second Tuesday before Ascension[1]

Berkeley Castle

Their efforts were bringing results, Baldwin reckoned. The labourers seemed to appreciate the dangers and were working well. The walls where the worst of the dilapidation had taken its toll were already patched and mended. Enhancements to the defences were being added wherever possible, and there were additional items designed to ensure the King's safety. The smith from the nearby town was commissioned to make new bars and bolts to keep Sir Edward safe in his chamber, and there were new keys for his door, four of them, of which Baldwin took one, and Sir Richard another. Then there were new locks for the door to the Chapel of St John in the tower, and for a postern gate that faced Alkington. After looking about the defences, Baldwin and Sir Richard also agreed to have a new lock and hinges with reinforcing bars fitted to the chamber over the outer gate. This gave them three secure locations in which to hold off attackers.

1 12 May 1327

Baldwin hoped that they would not be necessary, but in these times it was not possible to be sanguine about their chances of keeping the King safe if they did not take all precautions. The rioting in Cirencester showed all too clearly that the Dunheveds were still a force to be feared. There had come reports of the Dunheved gang raiding other places about Berkeley. Wandering men were robbing travellers, while riders were out stealing cattle and sheep to feed their growing numbers. Meanwhile there had been a pair of murders in the last two days, and one hideous rumour of a woman who was raped repeatedly, while her farm was torched with her husband tied up alive inside it, but Baldwin had not been able to substantiate that.

It was in part due to this last story that Baldwin had taken to riding out across the country with Edgar. He had established a perimeter of farmsteads and villas at about a mile and a half distance all around the castle, and he would visit this each morning to ensure that all was secure. If incursions began to affect these places, he would become more concerned and close up the castle. Fortunately, so far there had been no signs of additional violence within his boundary.

However, for the last few days the atmosphere in the castle had grown more tense. All were aware of the potential for disaster, were the Dunheveds and their gang to get inside. While there was no outbreak yet of complete panic, there were some signs of growing alarm. Baldwin recalled that there had been a similar mood within Acre during the siege. His secret fear was that the men within the castle might themselves react by rebelling.

For his part, at least Sir Edward of Caernarfon appeared to be calm enough. Sir Ralph reported that he sat in his chamber: quiet and unemotional, drinking a quart of wine each afternoon. A kind of fatalism had settled upon him.

Baldwin spent as much time as he could with the man who had been his King, relieving Sir Ralph when possible, but it was wearing. It was one thing to sympathise with a man who knew he was soon to be executed, but quite another to sit with a drunken man. A one-night vigil was sad, but this was a vigil without end. Edward had not been openly condemned to death, but he retained the conviction that someone would kill him, and the strain showed. His face, for all its supernatural calmness, was lined and haggard. His appetite was gone, and without exercise his body was losing its fine tone and strength. It was a relief that Sir Ralph was staying with the King every night and much of the day too. Baldwin would have found the duty too onerous.

Today he rode about the circuit with Simon, the two speaking little as they travelled. There was no news from the vills or the farms, to their relief.

'I don't know how much longer I can stand this hanging around,' Simon said as they cantered gently back towards the castle after their last stop.

'I am sure that if you wish to, it would be possible for you to go home,' Baldwin said.

'It's an idea I find appealing,' Simon sighed. 'But I wouldn't leave you here with only Sir Richard to keep you company.'

Baldwin pulled a face. 'The good Sir Richard's appetite for ale, wine and dreadful jokes does create its own strain.'

'And there are dangers from these mad brothers.'

Baldwin nodded. 'The Dunheveds would appear set upon their course. They are determined to enrich themselves, but whether they intend to make a serious attempt upon the castle is a different matter.'

'If they do,' Simon said, 'they will find a warmer welcome in Berkeley than ever they did in Kenilworth.'

'Perhaps so,' Baldwin said.

They rode on in companionable silence. Approaching the castle, Baldwin began casting about for any signs of spies in the land, but as usual there was nothing to give him cause for concern.

'I begin to wonder if they will do anything,' he muttered. 'It is almost a week since their riot in Cirencester; months since they tried to raid Kenilworth. Perhaps they are losing men and cannot make an assault. What do you think, Simon?'

They were riding up the straight road to the gate as Simon shrugged. 'Baldwin, you know the minds of men like them better than I do. If it were me, I would have decided that the old King was a lost cause. It's been months since his capture. Why would anyone fool themselves into thinking that they could liberate him and return him to his throne when there are so many who would do all in their power to prevent that? Too many have their interests bound up with those of Sir Roger. Even if these Dunheveds did succeed in breaking into the castle and freeing Sir Edward – what then? Would they ride to London with a hundred men-at-arms and hope that the city would welcome them? They might get an unpleasant surprise, if they were to try it.'

Riding under the gatehouse, they swung from their saddles and Baldwin stood pulling his gloves off, when he heard a hail from the porter's doorway.

'Sir Baldwin. I am glad to see you again.'

Baldwin gave a slow smile. 'John. I had not thought you would come here.'

'I am recovered now, I thank you. The malady did not last long,' John said.

Baldwin nodded, but could not help thinking that the man

looked more unwell than before. 'It is good to see you once more. You have heard of the threat?'

'Yes, the Dunheveds are a terror to the whole land. But I will do what I can to help,' John said – and he meant it with all his heart.

CHAPTER FORTY-NINE

Thursday before Ascension[1]

Willersey

Father Luke had been at the home of William and Margaret to help them to hold vigil over their son Adam, who had died suddenly yesterday. His mood was sombre as he walked the short way home. They would be bringing the body to the church later, and Luke must have everything ready to honour the poor young man. Only two-and-twenty – a terribly young age to die. For William it was doubly shattering, for he had no other sons, and Adam had not yet married. There was no son or grandson to carry on farming his land; no one to look after him and his wife when they grew old. All their hopes and dreams had shattered.

It was the same each time. Bereavement was always appalling.

1 14 May 1327

For instance, Jen was wasting away by the day. The brightness in her eyes had grown dim, and the intelligence which had been her most obvious attribute, seemed to have been swallowed up by her misery.

She was there now, he saw, a small figure at the door to the church. Taking a deep breath, he steeled himself to meet her. He had so little time to spare now, before the arrival of the funeral party.

'Hello, Jen,' he smiled. 'I am glad to see you.'

'May I come inside for a little?'

'Of course! All are welcome in God's house.' Luke opened the door, walked inside and held it for her. She followed him, and he noticed that her eyes went straight to the cross. It was good to see a child so sure of her faith, he thought. If it were not for the fact that she was still suffering from the loss of her father, he would have wondered whether she might have a vocation; as it was he would not attempt to test her for such a path, but instead would try to aid her to overcome her sadness.

'Come, child, would you like to help me clean the floor? There is a funeral today. Adam Williamson – drowned, you know. Would you help me to prepare the church for him?'

'Yes,' she said. 'I'd like to.'

She was a good helper. While he went about the church preparing the altar, setting out candles, bread, and wine, she took his besom and swept the flagstone floor.

When he cast surreptitious glances at her, Father Luke was pleased to see that she had lost a little of her desolate look. Perhaps he should have her help a little more often. The girl obviously enjoyed being here.

And then the mood was broken. Agatha appeared in the doorway, and her eyes snapped from Jen to him, full of suspicion and doubt.

'It is all right, Agatha. Jen came in to help me,' Father Luke said.

Agatha nodded brusquely, but even as she turned to leave, Father Luke's polite smile stiffened on his lips. Her expression – why so suspicious? And then he threw a glance at Jen, and saw that her eyes were wide with fear.

And suddenly Father Luke was filled with horror as he realised the truth.

Eve of Ascension[1]

Berkeley Castle

Harry and Senchet had taken to sitting apart from Dolwyn. It had been cold down there in their gaol, but since Sir Baldwin had returned, they had been moved to this chamber in the main keep, which was considerably warmer and more pleasant.

Still, if anything, Harry thought that Dolwyn's mood was deteriorating. The days of enforced inactivity, with nothing to break the monotony other than the two meals they were given – one of bread and pottage and one of oaten cakes with a little cheese – was giving him too much opportunity for introspection. He was not coping well.

Senchet yawned and scratched at an armpit where a flea or louse had bitten him the night before. 'How much longer do we remain in here?'

'Until the lord of the castle comes back and holds court,' Harry said.

'Ah. We wait only for his return. And if he dies?'

1 20 May 1327

'I suppose we have a court sooner, with professionals sitting in justice. It depends on the custom of the manor.'

Senchet shook his head and sighed. 'And all because of the cart, and saving our friend here.'

'I am sorry – all right? I wish I'd never taken the blasted cart,' Dolwyn said bitterly.

'Do not be downhearted,' Senchet murmured. 'You gave me a sight of a treasure chest larger than I have ever seen before. It was,' he added, 'a beautiful vision.'

'I wish we'd just knocked you on the head and taken it,' Harry said, only half-joking.

'No, Harry,' Senchet remonstrated. 'You forget yourself. Our friend here saved us from tedium. Besides, if he had not appeared we might have starved. It was his food that kept us alive. Our next action would have been to waylay a traveller and steal from him, which would have led to us being in a gaol in any case.'

'I wonder where that money is now?' Harry said.

'Ah, I expect the good Lord of Berkeley has it with him. He is no fool, after all. Would you trust your money to men such as those who are his guards here at the castle? No – nor I. The money will help pay for the goods and food he will need on his way, assuredly.'

Dolwyn groaned. 'It hurts to think of all that coin going to a lord who already has so much.'

Harry shrugged. 'That's the way of things. There is nothing we can get our hands on that isn't likely to be filched by some baron. That's how they get their money, by stealing it from the likes of you and me.'

Dolwyn grunted. 'I was hoping to be rich. And I would be, if it wasn't for those prickles at Kenilworth. I could have got Sir Edward out, and then I'd have been rolling in gold for the rest of my life. I could have been made sergeant of a nice little manor somewhere – that would have suited me down to the ground. And instead I'm stuck in here, accused of murders I didn't even do.'

Senchet looked at him. 'Well, my friend, for my money, I don't think it matters who did it or why. But unless someone else is found guilty, all three of us could suffer the punishment. And I do not like that idea one bit.'

Ascension Day[1]

Berkeley Castle

Benedetto saw his brother at the other side of the yard and hurried over to see him, his bodyguards about him. 'Matteo, I must talk to you.'

'No. Keep away from me,' Matteo pleaded, and retreated a few paces. Alured was nearby, and now he interposed himself, his hand on his long knife.

'Matteo, please. You haven't spoken to me for days, little brother.'

'You tried to kill me! You had your assassin Jevan stab me, and then you killed him. I know it all.'

Benedetto gaped. 'How can you say these things? You *know* I wouldn't hurt you! I am your own flesh and blood – I could no more harm you than cut off my own arm.'

'I don't trust you!'

Alured was keeping his eyes on Benedetto and his men, and the moment Benedetto tried to step forward, Alured's knife was out. Two henchmen pulled out their own weapons, and

1 21 May 1327

one made a feint at Alured, but he had learned how to fight in the back alleys near the Thames, and he easily blocked the blade with his own, twisting his wrist to hold it. Then leaning forward, he slammed his forehead into the other man's nose. He screamed and fell back, his nose exploding with blood, and Alured kept hold of his knife, flicking it into the air and catching it in his left hand. Quickly, he stepped back and watched Benedetto's other men warily.

'Enough!' Sir Richard roared. He had been at the hall's steps, and had seen the fight.

But Benedetto's second guard was unwilling to give up. He tried to stab Alured's hip. There was a flash of steel, and Alured knocked his sword to the ground. He stood on the point and held out his long knife to the henchman's neck. The man froze.

While Alured's attention was on him, the man on the ground caught hold of Alured's ankle. Giving it a sharp jerk, he saw Alured crash to the ground with an expression of delight on his bloody face. He was on his feet in a moment, and kicked Alured twice in the head.

Alured thought the first must break his neck. It felt like a kick from a destrier, and he could feel the muscle at the side of his skull, behind his ear, rip. Before he could react to it, a second kick caught his cheek.

As the man pulled his leg back to kick one last time, Sir Richard shoved his boot between the man's legs and lifted his knee, hard.

'I SAID,' Sir Richard bellowed, as the man collapsed, eyes bulging, 'ENOUGH!'

Willersey

He stood at the altar with the pride that he felt on this day every year. Ascension Day, the day that Our Lord was taken up to

Heaven to sit at God's right hand. It was one of the principal feasts in the Christian calendar, and in Luke's simple mind, one of the most important. He loved the culmination of Christ's story, with the picture in his mind of the Christ rising to Heaven over the heads of the eleven disciples as they watched, awe-struck and reverential.

But today there was another feeling as he celebrated the Mass and prayed to God. A certainty that in his little church was a murderer.

Jen had said nothing. When he questioned her, she had simply stared at him with those wide, terrified eyes of hers, the fear plain on her face. She knew something. It was there in the way she became calm in the church while alone with Father Luke, but trembled when her mother came into view.

She was there now, he knew, behind him. Jen would be standing like a little sapling, swaying slightly, not glancing once at her mother beside her.

It made his heart want to burst. Perhaps his first inclination had been correct when he looked upon Jen a week ago and wondered whether the child might wish to enter a convent. Father Luke was not entirely certain how to go about this, but surely nuns had a need of lay-sisters to perform menial tasks. Perhaps Jen could be introduced in such a manner as to let her gradually become accustomed to the regime and see if she had a vocation.

The ceremony ended, he turned and gave his parishioners the blessing, and the words almost stuck in his throat. The look Agatha was giving him was one of pure poison. Her husband had been an irritation and annoyance, after all. Perhaps she looked upon Luke too as a blockage in the path to her happiness and would seek to destroy him next.

As the congregation filed out of the church, he hurried to ensure that he was safely amongst others. But it was not only his own safety which he must protect, it was that of Jen as well. Were the woman to try to harm the girl, Luke would never forgive himself. He licked dry lips as he went into the sunlight with the other men. They were looking forward to the feast, laughing and joking about the food and drink waiting for them at the reeve's house, and he was swept along with them.

When he a look over his shoulder, he saw that Agatha's eyes were fixed steadfastly upon him, and he suddenly felt entirely helpless. He had no idea how to protect himself or Jen.

Berkeley Castle

'How are you?' Baldwin asked as Alured's eyes opened.

He looked a mess. The castle's healer had come to see him, but beyond washing the worst of the dirt from his cheek and covering it with a pad smeared in honey, the fellow did not seem to think there was much he need do.

'I've had worse,' Alured said weakly, trying to smile. His head was pounding, his neck twisted, and his cheek as raw as a burn. 'You should see the other man.'

'I have done,' Sir Richard said loudly. 'He will remain in the gaol until I am ready to release him. That will be a long time.'

'Is there anything you need?' Baldwin asked.

'Only sleep, I think. But I thank you. Could you arrange for someone to protect Matteo while I am unwell?'

'You believe him in danger?' Baldwin said.

'*Matteo* firmly believes Benedetto tried to kill him. I thought it was an irrational fancy, but now I'm less sure. If Matteo is right, Benedetto may succeed. Please, don't let him.'

'We will do all we can,' Baldwin promised. 'Now rest. My servant will guard your master. However, we need to protect you as well, I think.'

'Hugh can stay here for now,' Simon suggested. 'He will be adequate against the henchmen of a banker.'

The three men left Alured in his chamber.

'Benedetto must be held until this matter is resolved,' Baldwin said. 'Lord Berkeley would not be happy, were he to learn such a fight took place in his castle. He will be angry enough to hear of Sir Jevan's death.'

'We cannot keep the banker indefinitely,' Sir Richard protested.

'They won't want him until the Scottish campaign is over,' Baldwin said with certainty. 'He can wait until then at least. He should be glad we aren't placing him in the gaol for his men's behaviour tonight.'

CHAPTER FIFTY

Willersey

Father Luke sat at the table beside the reeve and ate, although his appetite was flown.

All he had ever wanted to do was protect the souls of his parish. He had no ambition to become a bishop; for him the greatest pleasure in life was to help to save the eternal sparks of life that existed in the people here. They were an amiable group: kindly, generous, happy. They misbehaved occasionally, but there was no rancour in it. He loved them.

He felt as though Agatha had betrayed him.

She was there at the farther end of the hall, sitting with her girl at her side, eating with gusto, as though there was nothing on her conscience. She had not confessed, and that meant that her soul was in mortal danger. If she were to fall into a well tonight, and die unshriven, she would go straight to Hell, without any possibility of redemption. He must not fail her! And yet if she refused to confess, what could he do?

He remained at the table as others drank themselves silly. There were games afterwards: two youths throwing knives at a target on the wall; three men gambling in a corner; one enterprising woman attempting to ply her trade with some of the unmarried men, while wives watched with tart disapproval and Luke with unseeing eyes.

Rising, he made his way from the room. Outside it was dark, and he looked for the moon. It was a large, silvery shape behind clouds, but there was enough light to show him the way to St Peter's. Inside the church, he used flint and tinder to ignite a scrap or two from which he could light a candle.

'You guessed, didn't you?' came a voice from behind him.

His heart pounded painfully. 'I did, yes, Agatha. I should have realised sooner, I suppose, but I was always an innocent, as you once told me.'

'You don't have to tell anyone.'

That stung. He flung himself around. 'Do you think that is in my mind, woman? Do you think I care about broadcasting your guilt? My fear is for *you*, for you and Jen. If you do nothing, you will burn in Hell.'

'Huh! What do I care of Hell? You tell these stories to make men and women behave, but when have the demons come and taken away a man from the vill? You know of men who have killed, and do they receive punishment? Those men who went with you to Kenilworth, did they get their judgement?'

'It is not punishment here on earth, Agatha – don't you see that? After all this time, surely you realise that God is watching you all the while. No matter what you do, He is up there,' Father Luke said, pointing with a finger. 'Even now, He is up there, looking down upon you and hoping to save you. But you have committed a grievous crime.'

'I've done nothing wrong. I put down a useless wastrel – the same as killing an injured dog. He meant nothing to me,' Agatha declared.

'I don't believe you. You grow pale as you speak. Come, sit here with me now, on the floor, and let me hear your confession, I beg.'

'All I wanted was a better life,' she said, her voice choked. 'My friend managed that with her husband. What was so special about her that she could have that, while I must struggle and scrape?'

'We cannot tell what His purpose is, but be assured that her example was there to—'

'*Alice* isn't an example! She's just luckier, that's all. She wedded a man who became rich, and now she has servants and maids falling over themselves to do her bidding, while I stay here and work my hands to the bones, and then that useless doddypoll Ham went with you to the castle and came back with nothing.'

'How did you know?'

'I didn't. It was the dog. The fool kept up his barking, and I wondered why, and then suddenly Ham was there. He walked in, said he wanted food and told me about the attack about how he'd not been paid – *again* – and that he might be chased. So he said he'd best disappear for a few days. And then he went. And I was in the house, looking round at the little things we had, the goose feather for cleaning, the bed rolls . . . so very little. I couldn't bear it. Got in a red-hot rage. So I followed him. Just walked out and went up after him. When I got there, he was already asleep. So I took his hatchet from beneath the cart's seat, and I hit him until he was still.'

She stood with an expression of confusion and dismay as she spoke, as though recounting a dream.

'Kneel with me,' Father Luke begged.

'And the trouble was, Jen realised at once,' Agatha said dully, not seeming to hear him. 'When she saw the axe in his head the next day, she knew it was me. She'd been awake when Ham came home, and she heard me go after him. So she guessed what had happened. She won't talk to me now. She is too scared. She thinks I'll kill her. Perhaps I will.'

She glanced at Luke, and he gasped to see the torment in her eyes. He should have seen it before!

Without saying another word, Agatha strode from the church.

Luke murmured '*Oh!*' but it was more a sob than an exclamation. He clambered to his feet and hurried after her. She must have gone to her house. He picked up the front of his robe and ran, hammering on her door. There was no answer, and he beat once again, and this time he heard a rattling crash, then a staccato tapping. He sobbed aloud. Then, bellowing and roaring for help, he tried to prise the door open with his bare hands, but there was nothing he could do. When some villagers finally arrived, it took a hefty beam to force the door wide where she had slipped the bar across it.

She was long dead by then. The leather thong about her throat was tied to a beam, and when she kicked away the stool on which she had stood, her feet had just reached the ground to make the tapping noise.

Luke helped them cut her down, and then gave her the *viaticum* while his tears fell unceasingly over her bulging face.

Monday after Ascension Day[1]

Berkeley Castle

Simon was walking about the walls and peering at the works when he saw the lone figure marching towards the castle. He was sure that he recognised the man . . . and soon realised it was Father Luke, the priest who had left only a few days ago.

Walking down the stairs, he passed John, who was chatting to a labourer while leaning against the tower's wall. Both fell silent as he darted past, but he paid them no heed. Only later did he recall that incident and think to himself that he should have paid more attention to it.

'Father!' he called as he reached the courtyard. The priest was at the doors, halted by a pair of guards, and Simon had to convince them that the man was not a threat.

'I had to come,' Father Luke declared on seeing him. 'I hope I am not too late.'

'For what?' Simon asked.

'Dolwyn did not kill the poor fellow Ham from my vill. He is completely innocent. I have learned that it was his wife who murdered him.'

Before long they were sitting at a bench in the hall, Baldwin and Sir Richard with them, a large jug of wine on a table with mazers. Sir Richard had seen that the priest was exhausted, and had called for a large platter of meats to refresh him, but Father Luke eyed the enormous collation with dismay as he spoke.

'It was not your fellow who killed Ham. I realised only a few days ago while with Ham's daughter that she was petrified of her mother. It appears that Ham went to his house on the night he died. He had been a part of the abortive attack on Kenilworth

Castle, and feared that he might be followed home, so dared not stay there. Something must have been said between them, I think, for when he returned to his cart outside the vill, his wife followed him. She it was who beat him to death.'

'With an axe,' Baldwin murmured.

'Yes. She took it from the cart, apparently. So presumably your man's story is true. He came across the cart later, and the horse, and saw nobody about there to rob. So he took what was wandering loose. He should of course have come to the vill and declared his discovery, but he did not steal it. I believe Agatha left it there, hoping to collect it the following day. It was a shock to her to learn that it had gone.'

'Dolwyn is still being held because of the murder of Sir Jevan,' Baldwin said. He looked over at Sir Richard and Simon. 'We have perhaps been too busy with other matters to trouble ourselves about him. Now we should review the matter.'

'Do you wish me to release the men now?' Edgar asked.

Baldwin considered. 'Yes. It would be wrong to keep them locked up if they are innocent. And if the original murder of Ham Carter was not their fault, the worst suspicion that remains against them in the matter of Sir Jevan is that they were First Finders. But it could have been anyone who killed him. Simon, I will want to see this place where Sir Jevan was found. Shall we go there now?'

When he had seen Simon hurrying down to the gates to welcome Father Luke, John had felt his heart sink, for the priest was the confessor to whom he had spoken.

He should never have made his confession! The idea of admitting to a priest that he was going to help Sir Edward of Caernarfon to escape had seemed a sensible precaution when he did it. The priest was duty bound to maintain the bonds of

455

secrecy, and he was leaving in any case. It had appeared the perfect solution to John's predicament, requiring forgiveness as he did. He was only too aware that at any moment he could be killed during the attack on the castle, and he wanted to ensure that his soul was protected. But now Luke was back – why? Did it mean he would break his vow of secrecy? He had given it to John, and if he were to break it now, he would be breaking his oath to God.

John watched the men as they crossed the yard, heading for the hall where the three prisoners were being held. He could scarcely bear to to think that all this effort, all the plans, all the desperate acts of the last six months could be overthrown by his foolish trust of this one priest.

Senchet felt he must soon go completely mad if he didn't see the clear sky again soon. Confinement was torture for him; he who was used to the wide open spaces of Galicia.

The boots hurried down the stairs towards their hall, and he eased himself up from his seat at the wall's base. It was the only moderately dry part of the floor in here. Standing, he nudged Harry and Dolwyn with the toe of his boot. He had an unpleasant suspicion that this would be a short walk. They had been accused of the murder of that arse Sir Jevan, and justice in this land was all too often swift and far from just.

As Dolwyn stirred, the door's bolts were slammed back and the door creaked wide.

'Ah, Sir Baldwin,' Senchet said. 'Are you executioner now?'

'I often sit on the bench as a Justice of Gaol Delivery,' Baldwin said steadily. 'I bring people from their gaols and confirm their sentences. Would you like me to do that?'

'I think I prefer not to die today,' Senchet said with a small bow, keeping his eyes on Baldwin as he did so.

456

'I do not blame you, friend Senchet. Now come, all of you. You need not stay any longer.'

Senchet followed Sir Baldwin with as much alacrity as stiffened muscles and feeble legs would allow. He stood still at the top of the steps and stared about him with real delight, enjoying the sunshine. That it seared his eyes did not matter. It was bliss to be free.

'Senchet, please come and sit, and you too, Dolwyn – and you, Harry.' Baldwin picked up a bench and set it near them. A table was brought, and a large pie set on it, with ale in an immense jug placed at its side by a young maid who, Senchet noticed, only had eyes for the oldest man there, Sir Richard.

Senchet took his seat, and looked across the table without touching the food and drink. 'Is this a ruse? You bring us up here to raise our hopes, so that you can dash them again when you return us to the cell? I do not think I like this behaviour of constant torture, gentles. I prefer to know where I belong. Are we to remain in the world of men, or not?'

'You will remain up here for as long as you are not found guilty of any crimes,' Baldwin said. 'But if you are found to have committed a crime, you will return to the gaol, and you will hang.'

'Very well. Of what are we accused now?'

'Nothing. The original charge against you is shown to be false,' Baldwin said. 'This good priest has returned to tell us that the man you were thought to have killed was actually murdered by his own wife.'

'You have proof?' Senchet asked with some suspicion.

'She hanged herself after she confessed to me,' Luke said sadly. 'She told me how and why she killed her husband. I think she wished to save herself from the stake.'

457

All the men present knew that there was only one punishment for a woman guilty of murdering her husband. Death by burning on a pyre.

'So we are free?' Dolwyn demanded.

'As far as I am concerned, you are free to stay or go,' Baldwin said. 'However, I recommend that you remain here. I appreciate that the castle is not your favourite place, but the countryside is unsafe. There has been a riot in Cirencester, and many gangs of men are roaming about all the lands near here.'

'For my part I am happy to remain, if I can believe that the good Lord Berkeley will consider me as one of his household,' Senchet said.

'And I too,' Harry said.

Dolwyn shook his head. 'I have my master already. I will go to him.'

'Your master is the Bardi?' Baldwin asked.

'Yes. Matteo Bardi,' Dolwyn said.

'He is still here. His other servant is injured,' Simon said.

'All the more reason for me to go to him.'

CHAPTER FIFTY-ONE

Berkeley Castle

Matteo heard the tap at his door and jerked nervously. Since Alured's beating, he had been a very unwilling guest here. Having no servant to protect him from the assaults of his brother and his men made him scared even to leave his room. He remained here, afraid that at any time a fellow paid for by Benedetto could come through and kill him. There were so many men in this castle motivated solely by money.

'Who is it?' he demanded, gripping his sword's hilt as he moved to the side of the door.

'Me – Dolwyn.'

He felt that word, that voice, like a hammer-blow in his belly. Benedetto could have bribed the gaoler to release Dolwyn, perhaps so he could come here and kill him?

To have reached Matteo's door here in the keep, he must have been released with the approval of the steward of the castle.

He pulled at the bolts with a feverish enthusiasm now his

mind was made up, and as the last slid back, he took a pace back into the room.

Dolwyn walked in with a quick look about him. He looked terrible. His clothing was filthy, his hair straggly and verminous, and his skin had a grave-like pallor. 'Apparently they have decided I'm innocent,' he said. 'The carter was killed by his wife. For tonight, at least, I am safe.'

'I am glad you are free,' Matteo said. 'I was worried.'

'Yes. I am sure you were,' Dolwyn said. 'Especially since Alured is injured.'

'They nearly killed him, because he was protecting me! It was not his fault: he was only doing his job. And for that they tried to kick him to death!'

'They won't while I'm here,' Dolwyn said. 'But I hope you can afford my services. I will want good money now. This place is too dangerous.'

Matteo nodded abstractedly. 'Of course. Shall we leave this castle, then?'

'Master, we're safer behind these walls than out there in the open.'

Matteo nodded, but his mind was already back on the former King. If Edward were to be freed, with the help of Matteo, and he recovered his throne, Matteo would become the most valuable ally he had. With the wealth of the Bardis, anything would be possible.

For the first time in days, the Florentine felt more positive about the future.

Alured was sleeping again; he spent a lot of time sleeping. It left Hugh with time to muse, and he didn't mind that. But he was growing fretful at being stuck in here.

When the door opened and Dolwyn peered round it, Hugh grasped his cudgel and snapped, 'What do *you* want?'

'I've been released,' Dolwyn said curtly, and explained about Agatha's confession. 'I wanted to see how Alured was doing.'

'He's all right,' Hugh said, still suspicious. He had learned early on in life never to trust strangers.

'Glad to hear it. I think he's a good man.'

'Is it true you killed your wife?' Hugh asked baldly.

'There was a fire, but I wasn't the cause. It was an accident,' Dolwyn said.

Hugh nodded. The sadness in Dolwyn's tone spoke to his own bereavement. He considered a moment, then said gruffly, 'You want a pot of ale?'

Tuesday after Ascension Day[1]

Berkeley Castle
Baldwin stood at the wall.

All around was the noise of masons and labourers at work: the creaking of hempen rope straining, and timbers complaining as the men on the treadwheel winched the heavy sections of rock up high overhead to the walls. The area they were repairing was where Sir Jevan had been found.

The chamber in which the body had lain was for storage. There were two piles of masonry which had been precut, and were awaiting insertion into the hole in the wall. This comprised part of the actual curtain wall of the castle, and looking through it, Baldwin could see all the way to south and east.

'So, you found him in here?' he asked.

1 26 May 1327

Dolwyn was standing behind him with Harry and Senchet. 'Yes. He was lying between those two piles of rock. You can see his blood still.'

Baldwin turned back from the hole in the wall. 'Why did none of the masons come?'

Simon could answer that. 'They did – but not until all were awake and ready. They were too scared to come alone. Someone said that the Devil was up here, apparently, and that put off the rest.'

'So the killer presumably hurried away through them all,' Baldwin said. 'He must be a cool character, to kill and then escape while the garrison was on its way to capture him.'

'Or insane,' Simon said.

'Such is not the behaviour of a madman,' Baldwin muttered. He stared down at the piles of dressed stone, but then he knelt. The pile of dressed rocks to the left of where the body had lain had a curious formation. 'There is space in here for a man to hide,' Baldwin said, peering over the top. 'The killer could have concealed himself here, after the body was found. Perhaps he felt no need to run down the stairs or along the passageways, Simon.'

'And perhaps he flew, like Hugh said,' Simon smiled.

'Eh?'

'Hugh was prepared to listen to the rumours of a Devil flying past.'

'Who spoke of that?' Baldwin asked.

'A mason.'

Baldwin nodded. It was a sad place to die, he thought. Alone, in the dark, attacked by an unseen assailant. 'Why was he here?'

'We wondered that too,' Simon said. 'It is not on the way to a garderobe or urinal.'

Baldwin looked about him. He crossed the floor to the door in the northernmost wall. This led into a passageway that ran straight to the keep. He stared at that in silence, thinking for a long moment. 'And that is where many others slept?'

'Yes. The Bardis were there, and Alured.'

'Let us meet this mason who spoke of the Devil,' Baldwin said.

Masons' Yard, Berkeley Castle

'Who was it?' Baldwin demanded as they reached the encampment below the tower.

Simon sent Hugh to find the man, and before too long he was back with a grey-haired fellow in his middle years. He had a square, sunburned face, and hands that looked as powerful as the rocks he had spent his life breaking and shaping. Although his eyes were blue and clear, there was an unfocused look about them as he smiled a little blankly at the men ranged about him. 'You wanted me?'

'I hear you said that there was a Devil came to kill the knight in the chamber up there,' Baldwin said.

'No. It was a Devil took his soul away with him,' the man said.

'Why did you think that?'

'Who else would have been there with him in the middle of the night?'

'You saw nothing, though?' Baldwin said. His patience with the overly superstitious was never extensive.

'I saw him, yes.'

'What?' Baldwin said.

Simon peered at him. 'Are you sure? Where?'

'Up there,' the man said, pointing to the roof of the passage that led from the chamber to the keep.

'You didn't tell me this before,' Simon said irritably.

'That's because you didn't ask me. You asked me if I'd heard the noise, and if so, what I thought it was. I told you I thought it was the Devil, but you didn't ask if I saw Him.'

'But you did?'

'Something like. A figure was bounding along up there with a thick, raggedy cloak about him. That's what I think I saw.'

'You aren't more certain?'

'It was the Devil. What does it matter what I think?'

It was cold here in his room. Benedetto Bardi stirred the fire and daydreamed about Florentine sunshine. Here all was perpetually hazy.

The look on Matteo's face had been truly appalling. He had been terrified at the sight of Benedetto, and then for those dull-witted tarses of his to beat up Matteo's man – well, any fears that were already in his younger brother's mind would hardly have been assuaged by that, would they?

Benedetto cursed profusely. Here he was, marooned in this miserable castle, and here he must remain until Lord Berkeley came home.

The quiet tap at his door surprised him. 'Yes?' he snapped, opening it. Then: 'Sir Baldwin, this is a pleasant surprise. Please enter and join me in a cup of wine.'

He was not alone, Benedetto saw. There was Sir Richard, and the man Puttock, too. They all walked in and stood looking at him as though he was some kind of felon.

'Well?' he prompted.

'We have an interesting series of deaths, Master Benedetto,' Baldwin said heavily. 'First one brother dies, and your other brother is almost killed. Two other fellows die near your brother's body, all in the space of a day. And the man responsible, we think, was on his way to your house. He was an ally of yours.

But now, he too is dead. It seems very strange that so much bloodshed should happen in so short a space, so near to you.'

'I agree. It is most peculiar. But on that particular day in London, many people were killed. Even the Bishop of Exeter died about then, and numerous peasants.'

'Did you order Sir Jevan to kill your brothers?' Sir Richard rumbled.

'Did I . . .' Benedetto sighed. 'No. Categorically not. I would never kill my brothers. Look at me, sirs. Do I look like the sort of man who could do such a thing? It would insult my blood, insult my mother's memory, my father's good name.'

'I have heard of men of business who are capable of such dishonour,' Simon said.

'Well, I am not one of them. No, I think it is more likely that the killer of Sir Jevan was Alured, servant to my brother. Look at him: he is irrational. Sir Richard, Master Puttock, you both saw him entering into a fight with my men when all I wished was a word with my brother.'

'But that was only a little after the death of Sir Jevan. Alured was protecting his master. Perhaps Matteo thought you guilty of killing him too?'

'I say again, no.'

Baldwin reached into his purse and pulled out the parchment. He held it up for Benedetto to see. 'Read this.'

'I . . . oh.' Benedetto winced to see it again. It had suffered in the last months since Manuele had signed it. 'I know this letter.'

'It says that the Bardi will support Sir Edward with money and all aid. And yet you supported the Queen against him.'

He shrugged. 'A man of business must sometimes look to both sides.'

'Even when it means seeking the death of your own brothers?' Baldwin asked pointedly.

'Never! I would do anything in my power to protect them.'

'Your protestations are fascinating,' Baldwin said. 'However, if you did not do these things, who did?'

'That madman, Alured.'

'Or could it have been your brother?'

At the thought Benedetto winced, thinking of the conversation when Matteo had accused him of trying to murder him. 'He would be shocked indeed to think anyone could accuse *him* of such a crime.'

'So you believe it can only be Alured?' Baldwin said.

'Who else?' He stared. 'You are asking me to believe that Matteo could have killed our brother Manuele? No. Nothing would make me believe that.'

'And yet your brother is convinced it must be you.'

'He is a frail thing, Matteo. It is his work, sifting information all day. I think it is only natural that he sometimes has these monstrous dreams. He sees plots under every stone, assassins under his bed. Sometimes he doesn't know what is real and what is false.'

'What do you think, Baldwin?' Simon asked as they made their way back down the stairs.

'I do not know what to think,' Baldwin admitted. 'Or rather, I think I shall be glad to be away from here, and gladder still to see the back of Benedetto and Matteo and their men. How can we serve them, while we believe that they could be murderers?'

He had reached the level of the wall now, and he moved to a door. It opened to the walkway, and he stepped out, peering down. 'Ah, if someone were to run across there, over the roof, he would be visible from the ground.'

Simon peered over to look. There was a broad wall rising from the building beneath. It lay just below the walkway, and a man could easily reach it by jumping down. And at this end there was a wide window facing into the court, where an arrow slit had been widened. 'An easy journey,' he agreed, cursing himself for not seeing it before.

Sir Richard nodded. 'But would a Devil try it?'

'I don't think so. But I am perfectly content to believe that a man might dart across there, and when he reached the keep, he could run up here to this door and get in through it.'

Simon smiled sadly. 'Which helps us not at all, because Matteo, Benedetto and Alured were all sleeping in the keep, as were many others. Any one of them could have killed Jevan.'

CHAPTER FIFTY-TWO

Wednesday after Ascension Day[1]

Berkeley Castle

But the next day brought news that made their search for the murderer less important.

Simon was standing guard with Hugh outside the chamber where Sir Edward of Caernarfon was being held, when the men came.

There were four of them, all begrimed and weary, their clothing in tatters, and all with the same look of despair in their eyes.

Simon and Sir Richard strode out to meet them, but Baldwin was already talking to them, asking questions and listening carefully.

'You say there were how many in the party?' he said.

'At least fifty,' one man said. He was the oldest of them, and his eyes were red-rimmed under the thatch of grey hair. 'They got to us about an hour before sunset.'

1 27 May 1327

468

'How many are dead?' Baldwin asked.

'All told, seven. My son, two farmers, a cattleman, the warrener and two women. Both were raped. My son and the cattleman were trying to protect them when they were killed.'

'What has happened?' Sir Richard demanded, standing arms akimbo with his chin jutting pugnaciously.

'Another attack. Not a riot like Cirencester,' Baldwin said, 'but a raid on these men's vill, five leagues north of here.'

'Were they English?' Simon asked.

'No. For the most part these were Scottish.'

'The Earl of Mar's men,' Baldwin said grimly.

He ordered that the men should be given food and drink, then told Edgar to take a horse and ride about the perimeter he had set out before. 'But take care, Edgar. No risks. If you see these devils, come straight back to tell us.'

'Yes, sir,' Edgar said, and was off to the stables in an instant.

'Simon,' Baldwin said, 'I wonder whether we should consider removing Sir Edward from here. I do not like this place: it is too isolated. If we were in Okehampton, or down at Corfe, I would feel more easy in my mind.'

'Corfe is hardly less isolated,' Sir Richard said.

'I suppose not,' Baldwin agreed. 'But at least it is farther from Scotland. I dislike these stories of men from the north attacking farms down here.'

'There is certainly great danger in leaving the castle now,' Sir Richard said. 'I think it would be a mistake. With the men we have here, we should be able to protect the place.'

'I hope so,' Baldwin said, but as he glanced again at the rebuilding works, Simon could see that his concerns were not allayed. 'When those men have been fed,' he said, 'have them work on the walls too. I want this place as secure as the Tower of London.'

Friday before Whit Sunday[1]

Benedetto paced his chamber furiously. He did not want to be here – in fact, he loathed the very sight of the place – and yet he was terrified at the thought of leaving. The land all about had become dangerous: every hedge and ditch could conceal a bowman. There were rumoured to be hundreds in the immediate area, each of them desperate to rescue Edward – or kill him.

The one thing that made him forget this was the expression on Matteo's face when they last met. That look of loathing and terror had struck him to the core. No matter what happened, it was clear Matteo would never trust him.

Benedetto would try to explain, if he got the opportunity. Sir Jevan was a blunt weapon, true, but he had been effective. So often he had worked for the House of Bardi and brought matters to successful conclusions. Still, if he had stabbed Matteo, he most certainly had not been ordered to do so. And those two poor youngsters – that was a shame, too. Benedetto had a heart: he could understand how Alured had been determined to find and punish the man responsible.

The Florentine's thoughts returned once more to his younger brother. Could Matteo not remember all the times when he had been cosseted and spoiled by Benedetto? The latter had, after all, spent much of his youth looking after him.

There was nothing on God's good earth that could make him hurt his little brother. Nothing at all.

1 29 May 1327

Whit Sunday[1]

Berkeley Castle

As they left the little chapel of St Mary next to the hall, Baldwin heard Benedetto Bardi calling after him.

'Sir Baldwin,' he said, and pushed through the men to reach him. 'I would speak with you.'

'Please do.'

'I must leave this place and hurry to the King's side. The Regent is to about to wage war on the Scottish and I should be with them, arranging finances for the King on his first war, not languishing here.'

'When it is clear that Alured will recover fully, you may leave. However, I will expect you to compensate him for the damage you have done to him. And if he were to die within a year and a day of the attack on him, you could be liable with your men for his death.'

'I will do all that is necessary,' Benedetto said. 'But for how much longer will I need to remain here?'

'I would think a week. If Alured is better, then you may go, if you consider it wise.'

'I think nothing about my coming here was wise,' Benedetto said with regret.

'You know how dangerous the roads are just now. There are men all over this county.'

'Yes, I know. But I need to leave as soon as I may.'

Benedetto walked away, over to the keep, and Baldwin heard Sir Richard and Simon approach.

'He is not happy here,' Baldwin said. 'He prefers the dangers of the roads.'

---

1 31 May 1327

'Aye, well, in all truth, the man's probably safe enough. The threat from these Dunhead fellows and the Earl of Mar has not materialised, has it? With every day that they do not attack, their strength weakens,' Sir Richard said comfortably.

'I just wish I knew what they planned,' Baldwin fretted. 'It would be good to be prepared.'

'While it is quiet here, I am content,' Simon said.

But it would not remain quiet for very much longer.

In his chamber, Alured lay trying to rest while Hugh snored over by the door.

Every movement was painful, as it tightened his scabs, and when he shifted his position there was a tearing sensation at his face. But if he did not move, the torn muscles behind his ear would cramp and ache. That was intolerable. Better that he should move his head occasionally.

When the door opened, he glanced up to see a young maid. She smiled down at him as she put the jug of ale and bowl of soup on the low table near his palliasse. There was a small hunk of bread beside them. 'How are you?'

'Better for seeing you, maid,' he croaked. He dared not grin. Over a week, he told himself, and still it hurt too much to smile.

'Here's some food and drink. Do you want me to help you?'

She had been here twice a day since his injuries, at first helping spoon pottage or soup into his mouth, but more recently she had soaked bread in it and pressed it gently between his lips as his mouth began to loosen and he could open it wider.

'I would be glad of your help,' he said.

He was eating, Hugh rubbing his eyes and yawning, as Baldwin and Simon entered.

'Master Alured, how do you feel this fine morning?' Baldwin asked.

Alured swallowed. 'How do I look?' he countered.

'More lively, at least,' Baldwin said with a smile.

'I reckon I shall live,' Alured acknowledged.

'Benedetto has asked to be allowed to leave the castle. Do you object?'

'The sooner the bastard's gone, the happier I'll be,' Alured grunted.

Baldwin nodded. 'We do have an interesting conundrum, you appreciate. Someone killed Sir Jevan. It could have been Benedetto, but the knight appears to have been an ally of his. Why should he seek to murder his own accomplice? But the alternative to his slaying Sir Jevan means it may well be you or your master who was responsible.'

'As to me, why would I bother? I told you of my suspicions. If I was going to act anyway, why should I tell you first? No, it would not make sense for me to kill him.' Alured took another mouthful of soup.

'Your master?'

'Signor Matteo could have wished vengeance on the man who might have stabbed him, but I was asleep before his door all night. He wouldn't have been able to pass by me without my knowing.'

'You sleep lightly?'

'Always.'

'And you remained there on your bench until your master opened his door, you said?'

Alured began to nod; it hurt and he winced. 'Yes. I was there until he came and asked what the noise was all about.'

'So you were asleep until he opened the door?'

'I . . .' Alured was still for a moment as he considered. 'Perhaps. I must have heard the screams and then, when I turned he was there.'

'So he was there in the doorway.'

'Well, I suppose so.' Alured's brow was creased with the effort of recall.

'Was the door actually open?'

Alured's eyes gazed at him blankly.

'You realise what this could mean,' Baldwin said gently.

Alured did not need to nod.

'What was he wearing?' Baldwin asked.

'A loose cloak. It's quite old and tatty.'

'I see. What happened to it?'

'He opened the door and threw it inside.'

Baldwin sighed. 'And that is that,' he said. 'Let us find this man.'

Matteo saw them leaving Benedetto's chamber. Had they accused him? It was as clear as day that he had been the one responsible for all the mayhem and murder. They must remove him.

Matteo decided he would go and check on his brother. The corridor outside Benedetto's room was quiet. There was not even a guard. Matteo tapped lightly upon the door and listened. Hearing his brother invite him in, he froze. Just for an instant, he had thought that the men with the grim faces might have killed Benedetto.

He opened the door and walked in. And Benedetto immediately backed away as though he feared him.

'What is it, brother?' Matteo asked.

'I will not lie, Matteo. I am scared of you. How could you kill so many?'

'Well, how could *you* try to have me murdered in a London street?'

'I swear that was not me. I am innocent. We are brothers!'

'Yes, I believe you,' Matteo lied. It was clear that Benedetto had convinced the others, but Matteo was trained in intelligence. He could see through the falsehoods put forward by others – and today he knew that his brother was desperate to see him killed.

'You always feared me, Benedetto, didn't you? You must have thought I was just a bit too clever for my own good. I was always the bright one in our family. That's why I ended up with the job of intelligencer – sifting all the lies and deceptions to reach the truth. I did it so well, day in, day out, that Manuele was scared of me. And when he died, you realised the only way to keep the power to yourself was to kill me.'

'No. I took over because poor Manuele died. That was all.'

'So you should thank me for that, at least.'

Benedetto's jaw fell open. 'You couldn't have! Not Manuele! Why? All he ever did was try to help you, Matteo!'

'He would have ruined the bank – I couldn't allow that. And you were little better. The pair of you, niggling at each other, while the bank was collapsing! You two could not see further than your own ridiculous ambitions. The House of Bardi needs a stronger man in control of it. Someone who can demonstrate good leadership.'

'Why did you kill Sir Jevan?'

'You used him to assassinate me. He tried to kill me.'

'No! Look, Matteo, that day in London there were rifflers all over the city. It was one of them who caught you and stabbed you.'

'No, brother,' Matteo said, and in his face there was a sad understanding.

For a split second Benedetto saw his childhood in that face – those happier times when they were all young – and he saw the tear that formed in Matteo's eye as he held out a hand to him. Benedetto felt a surge of relief to see his brother returned to him. He moved forward, and too late saw the blade that flashed to his chest.

CHAPTER FIFTY-THREE

Berkeley Castle

Matteo was out at the bench by the buttery wall when Baldwin, Simon and Sir Richard left Alured's chamber. His pale features were warmed a little by a flush when he saw the men cross the yard towards him. 'Sir Baldwin, Sir Richard. Have you any news?'

'We have news, aye,' said Sir Richard heavily. 'We have discovered how Sir Jevan was murdered.'

'I am glad to hear it. Have you arrested him yet?'

'We are about to,' Baldwin said. 'Matteo Bardi, I accuse you of murdering Sir Jevan. Do you have anything you wish to say?'

'*Me*?' Matteo's colour drained from his face. 'But you know I couldn't have. Alured was outside my door all the while.'

'He was, yes. But he thinks that you were in the doorway when he woke, and you opened the door to throw your cloak inside. I suppose it was besmottered with blood after you hacked at Sir Jevan.'

'I didn't . . . No, it was Benedetto.'

'Matteo, you killed him because you thought he had tried to kill *you* – and because you thought he had murdered Manuele, didn't you?' Baldwin challenged him.

'No – it was Benedetto. It must have been him! *He* slipped out from his room and killed Sir Jevan. You should arrest him, have him put to the *peine forte et dure* and see how he squeals!'

'You thought it was intolerable that Sir Jevan should live on after killing your brother and stabbing you.'

'He didn't kill Manuele!'

Baldwin leaned closer. 'What was that?'

'Nothing. No, it was the mob killed Manuele, I meant. Not Sir Jevan.'

'What were you about to say about your brother's death, Matteo?' Baldwin demanded. 'Did *you* kill him?'

'I was nowhere near him,' Matteo said with a sly look. 'And then I was attacked. You cannot accuse me of any of those murders.'

'I think you had him attacked too. In fact, I think you had your brother killed . . . that was what you were about to say,' Baldwin said. He was a good manager of the bank, wasn't he? 'Why kill him?'

His words stung Matteo to a response. 'He was pathetic, that's why! You didn't know him. He was a fool, with the brain of a servant. He couldn't see the truth when it was sat on his lap! He wanted to carry on funding that buffoon up there in the chamber,' he said, throwing an arm extravagantly towards Sir Edward of Caernarfon's room in the keep behind them. 'It was obvious to all that the old King must fail, but no, Manuele wanted to keep on paying him more and more, bleeding us dry. He refused to let us support the Queen when she was in France, and when she invaded, he was still determined to back King Edward against her. Well, I couldn't allow that. I could not let him ruin us all. I would have been far better as the controller of the bank. I know how it works, how people look on us. I have all the information at my fingertips! I will be a better master of the business than Manuele or Benedetto could ever be.'

'You will manage nothing. As a murderer, you will be hanged,' Sir Richard said.

'You think so?' Matteo gave a hoarse chuckle. 'You will hold me, perhaps, until Lord Berkeley returns to his castle. Perhaps you will even hold me until the Queen demands to speak with me. And then I will buy a pardon. I can, because I have the intelligence and the money to do what I need to. There is nothing you can do to stop me.'

Baldwin glanced at Simon. 'Master Matteo Bardi, you will—'

'Hold him – he has killed me too!'

Baldwin turned to see Benedetto, pale and stumbling, a hand to his chest through which the blood seeped, standing at the top of the steps to the hall. 'Hold him before he can kill another,' Benedetto choked out, and sank to his knees.

Matteo had reached for his dagger as soon as Benedetto began to speak, but Sir Richard's hand flashed out and caught his wrist. When Benedetto was finished, Sir Richard reached down and gently removed Matteo's dagger.

'You won't be needing this for a while, Signor Bardi.'

Benedetto was utterly crushed by his brother's crimes. Baldwin and Sir Richard went to visit him in his room when his wound had been tended by a physician, an old nervous fellow with cold, shaking hands.

'He said he had Manuele killed? How?' he asked now, taking a sip of spiced wine.

'I think the important thing is, he was trying to have you hanged for Sir Jevan's death,' Baldwin said. 'He wanted you suspected, and then he was going to take over the bank and become the head of the House of Bardi. It is clear that in his mind, he thought he could run it more effectively.'

'I see.'

'You do not seem surprised,' Sir Richard remarked.

'I am not. It seems obvious that Matteo must be responsible for Sir Jevan's death, but to think that he could arrange the killing of Manuele . . . Dear God, that is shocking.'

Baldwin said quietly, 'I am sad to bring such news to you.'

'What will you do?'

'He will remain here as a prisoner until the Lord of the Manor returns and hears his case. And then, perhaps, a fine and a Royal Pardon may save him, if you deem it worthwhile. But if you do decide to have him released, bear in mind that your life will always be in danger. Matteo considers your job to be his by right.'

'If I had guessed this, I would have given it to him and returned to Florence,' Benedetto said. 'I have no need of this job. There are many others things I can do. To think that he worked so unceasingly to destroy us all. His own blood . . .'

They left him dozing in his bed, and made their way down to the buttery.

'I wonder how Matteo thought he had arranged for Manuele's death,' Baldwin said.

'He must have paid someone,' Simon considered. 'Oh well, he may be released when the Regent or Queen hear of his imprisonment, but for now he can remain locked. up. In the meantime, I need a drink.'

'Excellent idea!' Sir Richard agreed before bellowing for a servant to fetch wine.

Tuesday after Whit Sunday[1]

Chester

The group rode into the city over the great bridge, the mass of the old castle rising up on their left as they passed under the sandstone gatehouse at the northern bank.

Stephen Dunheved whistled as he took in the city. 'This is richer than London.'

'Perhaps so,' Thomas said. He was casting about him as he jogged along on his horse. 'They say it's the richest port in the west after Bristol. But their money comes from their access to Wales, I think.'

'What of the castle?'

'The main forces have already marched to York,' the Dominican said smugly. 'The few that are left won't dare come to trade blows with us. They'll stay put and hope we soon go away.'

'And so we shall.' Stephen grinned at his brother. 'Are you ready?'

In answer Thomas glanced over his shoulder and waved to the men on the bridge and at the bridge gates, before laughing aloud for the joy of action, and clapping spurs to his horse.

They rode up the bridge street, all the way to St Olave's, and then on, past St Bridget's and St Michael's, and up to the old market. There, by the pillories, Stephen stopped and gazed about him. 'This will do,' he said.

Thomas dropped from his horse and reached for his sword. The ringing slither of steel seemed unduly harsh here in the

1 2 June 1327

481

street, but before anyone could remonstrate with the Dominican for drawing a blade, the streets were loud with the bellowing of men and the clatter of their horses' iron-shod hooves. A group of men was being gathered up to the north, and herded by the Dunheved men towards the market square, and at the same time more men were being brought from about the great abbey.

'Men of Chester, are you sick of being farmed like sheep, and shorn for your money?' Thomas bellowed. 'The abbot here is a thief. He would have the clothes from your backs! Look at him over there, his belly gross from the food he steals from you, his purse enormous from the tithes he squeezes from you, his mind as full of evil, greed and wantonness as the worst whore! Do you want this man to rule your lives? Do you want him to continue to take lands from you, to demand ever more money from you? I say he is a thief, and thieves should be forced to pay for their crimes!'

He held his sword aloft.

'Men of Chester, come with me. Let us break down the gates and take back what is yours!'

The mass of the crowd was unimpressed by his demand, but in amongst the people were some of the Dunheved men. Seeing the sword raised high, these began to cheer and bellow. Thin and unimpressive they sounded, but then a few more took up their call, for the abbot was unpopular here in the city, and in a short space, the majority of the mob realised that there could be possibilities for rich plunder if they helped, and began to bay for the abbot on their own.

'Come! Follow me!' Thomas roared again, and he began to push through the crowds. Soon he was in the midst of a tide of men that ebbed from the marketplace and washed up at the abbey's great gatehouse.

Foolishly, the gatekeeper had not thought to shut and lock his gates in time. He was attempting to do so now, but it was too late. Men were pouring in, and a fellow with a long knife saw to the gatekeeper. He slumped to the ground, blood staining his robes, as a pair of lay-brothers came running. These too were soon despatched, and then the mob moved into the abbey itself, pillaging in an orgy of destruction and thievery.

Stephen and the rest of the men were with them as the mob roved over the close. Stephen it was who battered the monk at the door to the abbot's chambers; Stephen it was who pulled the confessor from the hall where he had been hiding, and who slammed his war-axe into the man's face, striking him to the ground. It was a miracle that he did not die, but the wound marked him hideously for the rest of his life.

The abbot's lodging was torn apart as the men snatched at hallings, tapestries, his clothes, knives, spoons, his boots – everything. All his belongings were strewn about the floor or stolen. Nothing of any value was left behind.

'Brother, I think we are done,' Stephen said with a broad smile. He wiped his cheek and brow with a sleeve, smearing a little of the blood.

'Yes, we must return now.' Thomas was standing gazing with a small smile of approval at the rampaging crowds. 'This is glorious work, Stephen. Glorious.'

Monday before Corpus Christi[1]

Berkeley Castle

Since the capture of Matteo Bardi, the castle had lost much of the febrile atmosphere that had so characterised the last weeks. The resolution of the murders of Sir Jevan and the others had

1 8 June 1327

brought a cloak of calmness over the whole of the castle. Simon found himself whistling as he walked about the yard, that morning. There appeared no reason to think that the place was under threat any more. The garrison certainly appeared to believe that any risk posed by the rioting in Cirencester was long since dissipated.

Under Baldwin's incessant demands, however, the majority of the rebuilding works had been completed. The labourers and masons were working with less urgency now that the main weaknesses were restored to their earlier strength.

'Look at it,' Baldwin had said to Simon the day before. 'I would almost wish that they *would* try to storm the castle now. Never was a fortress so quickly renewed to its former power. Those masons deserve a good portion of the money held here for their efforts.'

Simon could not dispute his words. The men had worked really hard. Even those who were unused to stone workings, such as the four who had arrived from the vill to the north, had slaved with the rest.

He saw Senchet and Harry over towards the keep's main entrance, and was idly wondering about going to talk to them, when he heard hoofbeats outside. They were galloping wildly, and now a guard on the ramparts was calling down to the gate-keeper, and the three men with polearms at the gate walked out to intercept the rider. There was still a strict control on any new people coming into the castle.

Soon there was an excited babbling at the gate, and Simon hurried over to learn what he could.

There was a young man of perhaps four-and-twenty, lolling in his saddle with exhaustion. His horse was all but blown, and it was clear that they had ridden for miles.

'What is it?' Simon demanded, looking up at the fellow.

'This man says that the Dunheved brothers and their gang have been causing more riots,' the gatekeeper explained, 'but this time in Chester!'

Simon, who had at best only a rudimentary understanding of the realm, asked, 'Where is that?'

'Sir, it must be fifty leagues from here. About a hundred and fifty miles.'

'Yes?'

His incomprehension only served to delight the happy gate-keeper. 'Sir, if the gang is raising Cain a hundred and fifty miles away, they aren't down here readying themselves to attack us, are they?'

CHAPTER FIFTY-FOUR

The Feast of Corpus Christi[1]

Berkeley Castle

It was happy, that feast day. Father Luke joined in the festivities, Simon was glad to see, and even the grim-faced Benedetto unbent a little and managed to smile as the minstrels entered and began to play for the company's pleasure.

'It does me heart good to hear music,' Sir Richard said, leaning back in his seat with a contented sigh. The little maid was a short distance away, and she moved nearer to serve him with more wine whenever he held his mazer out. Simon shook his head once more in honest bemusement at the effect the hoary old warrior had upon even the prettiest young maids. It was, as other members of the garrison were fond of repeating, 'Not fair.'

But for now, no one cared. All had taken the feast day to heart, especially since the messengers Baldwin had sent to

1 11 June 1327

Gloucester, to Tewkesbury and farther afield, had started to return with the news that there was no longer any signs of the Dunheved brothers in the vicinity. Their murderous plundering appeared to have ceased, and all the lands about seemed empty. King's Wood, Michael Wood, the Heath, and even Berkeley Vale were searched and the local villeins interrogated about any gangs of wild men in the area, but all the answers came back that the whole of the lands about Berkeley were clear. The gangs had disappeared as completely as a summer's mist.

The men in the garrison were celebrating; even now they were close to cheerful rioting. It was best, Baldwin said, to allow them to let off a little steam after the last tense weeks. Now that there was no apparent danger, tonight the men-at-arms were permitted more licence than usual, and Sir Richard was keeping his maid close at hand to protect her from drunken fumblings or worse.

'Master Puttock,' Benedetto said, leaning towards Simon. It was fortunate that his wound was only shallow. Matteo's blade had missed its target, and Benedetto's rib had been scored, instead of his heart. Now, although sore and in some pain, he had begun to recover: his eye was clear and his manner sober, for all that he had drunk more than a pint of wine already. 'Do you think it would be safe for me to leave the castle? Would I be able to make my way to Oxford and thence to London, do you think?'

'I would think so, yes,' Simon said. He looked further along the tables until he saw the man with the bandage about his face. 'Why do you not take Alured with you? He is a loyal and resourceful fellow, from all I have heard. And Dolwyn, of course. Both would help you on your way.'

'Perhaps so. Yes, I shall think of that. They are both good fighters, and that is what I need now.'

'You should have less need of their fighting skills, but it is always best to plan for the worst,' Simon agreed. 'But you must

487

wait here and rest. You cannot ride with that wound.'

'It is little more than a scratch.'

'A tiny scratch can kill if the pus grows,' Simon said firmly. 'You must wait until the scab is healed and the wound can be shown to be clean. That will take at least a week.'

'I should leave soon,' Benedetto fretted. The minstrels were playing a merry tune, but Simon saw that the music did not lift Benedetto's mood. 'I will have much to do to catch up after being here so long. But I confess, I find it difficult to go. Once I have departed from Berkeley, I will have lost both brothers for ever. At least when I arrived here I had one still, but leaving here will mean Matteo will be irrevocably lost to me as well.'

'Have you spoken to him since?'

'He will not see me or talk to me.'

Simon could see how moved Benedetto was. He put his hand out and rested it on the Florentine's wrist, gripping it with enough pressure to convey sympathy.

'Why not wait until the Feast of Saint John,' he suggested. 'That will give you and Alured another two weeks to heal, but it will also give us time to ensure that the land all about here is safe, and that the men in the gangs are not merely hiding. There should be no need to worry if they remain quiet until then.'

Benedetto nodded. 'Very well. Thank you, Bailiff. Let us pray for peace.'

Feast Day of St John the Baptist[1]

It was to be his last day here. Benedetto looked around his chamber in the castle. He had little idea what to do with Matteo.

1 24 June 1327

Part of him felt it would be best for his brother to remain here, incarcerated. But it was a shameful way to treat a brother. Better, perhaps, to have him taken to Florence and held there.

Matteo still refused to see him. There had been a day, almost a week ago now, when he had seemed eager to speak to Benedetto, but it was only to plead that he was actually innocent. When Benedetto reminded him that he had confessed while trying to kill him, Matteo had thrown a fit of rage so explosive, Benedetto feared his mind could actually break. Men could die of brain fever.

It was the castle chaplain, for Luke had left for Willersey some days before, who had explained to him that the cause of his illness was undoubtedly demon who had taken control of his mind. The only possible cure was to cast out the demon, but although the chaplain had done his best, there was no change in Matteo's behaviour. He was grown quite violent.

Benedetto made the decision to leave him alone. He did not believe there was a demon in Matteo's mind. It seemed more like jealousy of his older brothers and naked ambition, nothing more. Matteo would not hang, for certain, because he was not in his right mind. A King's Pardon would be obtained – costly, but better that than the shame of seeing a Bardi hanged. There must be another route, he thought. But although he had racked his brains for two weeks, no remedy suggested itself.

He made his way to the great hall, and sat at the massive table on the dais with the other guests. Sir Baldwin looked disappointed at the procession of colourful dishes being paraded: he was always happier with simpler fare, Benedetto had noticed. Not so the Bailiff and Sir Richard. They were hearty eaters, content to feed on anything and everything.

Benedetto picked at the dish before him, missing the food of his natural home. In fact, just now he missed everything about

489

Florence. The sunshine on the flat fields, the tall trees, the sights and sounds, the wines . . . all of them called him home.

Thanks be to God, his wound was recovered cleanly. Alured too had healed, although he still held his head at a curious angle, and his nose and cheek were badly scarred. Dolwyn would be there as a bodyguard – so his journeying should be secure.

Senchet was in no mood to enjoy the festivities. He wandered disconsolately about the upper battlements on the walkways, brooding. He did not like this castle.

However, if he and Harry awaited the return of Lord Berkeley, he might hire them and pay them well. A man-at-arms was not expensive in comparison with a knight, but men with the skills and abilities of Senchet and Harry did not come cheap. He had already asked that Florentine if he could join his party, but the banker had looked askance at him, as though he was some kind of felon trying to inveigle his way into an easy gull's party so he could rob him.

While he was on the battlements, he saw a man surreptitiously cross the yard, and head towards a little low building near a tower. Senchet himself had developed an interest in that particular building, because the little chest from the back of the cart had been stored there. It was a small building, but constructed all of stone, and the roof was strong, too. He had considered, and rejected, the idea of breaking in as impractical. There were too many men here who would come running to investigate – and it was but a short step from being investigated to hanging from a tree.

This man, however, slipped past the door to the building, and disappeared in the shadows. That was interesting to Senchet, and he stepped silently down the staircase to the yard, leaned against a dark wall, and waited.

Sure enough, a few minutes later the same figure returned. He stood in the shadows, his head moving from side to side, and then he hurried away back to the feast.

Senchet watched him go, and then went the same way. He wondered if that other man might have essayed a hole in the building's wall, in order to get in and filch the chest of coins. Not that he could do anything with it: he could hardly take the chest to his sleeping chamber and conceal it as a pillow!

But there was no hole in the wall. When Senchet walked along the way, he found only a postern door set into the wall. He touched the lock and felt the coolness of fresh oil, but that was all.

Why was the man coming here and making sure that the lock was oiled? Senchet wondered to himself. He frowned at it, trying to think of any reason other than the obvious one.

None occurred to him.

'Who was he?' Harry asked as Senchet spoke of the man at the postern gate.

Senchet had gone to the hall and attracted Harry's attention by the simple expedient of pulling him from his seat.

'One of the labourers, I think.'

'A labourer going to oil the locks on a postern . . .'

'At night. When all others are in the hall feasting.'

'It does seem a little odd.'

Senchet sighed with extravagant emphasis. 'Odd, you think? Why should a man do such a thing?'

'All locks need oiling,' Harry protested.

'In the dark?'

'Yes, that was curious. But perhaps he was supposed to do it during the day, and this was the first opportunity.'

Senchet looked at him.

'Oh, all right. Come on.'

Sir Richard saw the two approaching. 'Hey, Sir Baldwin, what d'you think of those fellows? Coming to beg alms or more ale?'

Baldwin glanced towards them, still smiling at a jocular comment from Benedetto, but his smile froze when he had heard what Senchet and Harry had to say.

A short time later, he and Simon had joined Sir Richard at the postern. All three studied it with interest. Baldwin touched the oil, feeling it slick between thumb and forefinger. 'It is good that the gate's lock is eased.'

'Not the time o' day for doin' that sort of work,' Sir Richard commented.

'No. I agree,' Baldwin said. 'But the fellow did not unlock or unbolt the postern. It is still secure, so it is not the work of a man who is set upon allowing strangers in immediately.'

'But could be sometime soon, was what we thought,' Harry said. 'If you're seeing parties leaving the castle, the garrison will be reduced. And now it'll take little time for a man to open the gate.'

'Very true,' Sir Richard said. 'What d'you think, Simon? You have a good mind for subterfuge.'

'I think we should mount a permanent guard here,' Simon said. 'Whoever did this could be opening the castle.'

'Would you recognise the man again?' Sir Richard demanded.

'Yes. Without a doubt,' Senchet said.

Sir Richard looked at Baldwin. 'I think we ought to have all the masons and labourers stand in front of this good fellow and see if he can identify him.'

'Absolutely,' Baldwin agreed. 'Let us go to their camp and do that straight away.'

The labourers had moved from directly below the tower in the north-east corner of the yard, and were a little further towards the southern wall because the tower had been one of the last sections to be completed and the tents were blocking the area the masons needed for their workings.

In the chill evening air, all the labourers and workers were made to stand and Senchet viewed each carefully before shaking his head. 'No, it is not one of these here.'

Baldwin thanked the master mason responsible for the works and asked, 'Is there any man missing?'

'How would I know?' he snapped. 'I'm not responsible for them. My own fellows are here, and that's all I care about.'

Baldwin and the others left him still fuming, and returned to the hall and their food. But at the doorway, Baldwin looked back. 'I want a guard on the wall over the postern and another down by the gate itself. They will be relieved, but I want men there all through the night.'

'Yes,' Sir Richard said, and belched. 'Damn nuisance.'

It was a tight fit in here, but William atte Hull was glad that he had spent time constructing this little hideaway.

The fact that the knights had gone to check where he had oiled the locks on the postern showed that someone had seen him. It was Art who saw the man walk in after William had left the dark alley. Art was a good, loyal servant of the King, and as soon as he saw Senchet down there, he had gone to warn William. And now here he was, hidden in what appeared to be a loose pile of rocks beside the southern wall. But it was not solid. He had carefully built a chamber in the heart of this pile, and now he lay in the makeshift shelter and considered what he could do to facilitate the attack.

One thing was certain, if he was seen by that foreign scrote, he would be captured as a traitor.

CHAPTER FIFTY-FIVE

Morrow of the Feast of St John the Baptist[1]

Berkeley Castle

The castle was quiet this morning, after the festivities of the night before, and Baldwin was up and on the castle's walls before any other than a pale-faced sentry or two. One leaned on his polearm as if it was the only thing holding him upright.

Simon was asleep still. Baldwin had left him on his bench snoring fit to crack the walls. He had kept Sir Richard company until the very early hours, and Baldwin suspected that his head would be exceedingly painful when he did wake. Which was a source of pleasure to Baldwin, bearing in mind that Simon's snores had kept him awake for much of the night.

From here on the walls he could see over the acres of boggy marshland. The land all about here was wild, untamed and dangerous. North was the Severn Estuary, where Baldwin

1 25 June 1327

could see occasional ships moving sluggishly on the water between clouds of mist. Nearer, lay the main Gloucester to Bristol road, and it was always busy. It was the reason for the castle's construction, after all.

Baldwin looked around one last time in the grey pre-dawn light: there was nothing to be seen yet, but he knew that the fog could conceal hundreds of men, and here in the castle they would have no idea of their presence until the enemy launched an assault.

He passed the guard on the wall over the postern gate. The man had been up late, to judge from the look of his bleary eyes. He leaned against the battlements, casually watching the swirling mists, and Baldwin was content that at least he was awake, if not as alert as he could have been. Below, when Baldwin glanced into the court, he saw another man at the alleyway, picking his nose assiduously.

There was nothing more he could do, he thought. He turned and was about to walk down the stairs when he heard something.

It was faint – a metallic 'snick' from outside the castle. On the misty air, the sound was leaden. There was no perception of direction, not with his deaf right ear, and Baldwin turned his head so that his left ear was projected towards the noise. Nothing. It could have been his imagination, but he didn't think so. Baldwin turned his head again so that he faced the wild heath once more. His eyes studied the mists as though he could penetrate them with his fierce glare.

And then there was a swirl as a breeze moved them, and he saw through the mists a column of men.

'Guards! Guards! Alarm!' he bellowed at the top of his voice, even as the mists began to clear and he saw the massed men outside the castle.

*   *   *

Simon heard the roar of his friend's voice through the blanket of sleep that had so fully bound him. He tried to leap from his bench, only to stumble over his clothes on the floor. Quickly pulling on his chemise and tugging on his hosen, tying them quickly, he shrugged himself into his aketon, and thrust his feet into boots before buckling his sword about his waist.

Outside, the shouts were increasing, and he stood taking stock. The guards and men-at-arms were already pelting over the court to their allocated places, most of them looking the worse for wear after the feast last night. One youngster was throwing up at the corner of a wall. Simon gave him a buffet over the back of the head. 'Get to your place, boy!' he snarled. The sight and stench of vomit made him want to puke too. He had drunk far too much last night. His head was thudding painfully, and the thought of fighting in this condition did not fill him with confidence.

The men on the wall were already hurling abuse at the men below, one or two throwing rocks. There was a supply of stones left over from the mason's works, and these were employed to good effect. Three men had crossbows, and they were calling down for more bolts to shoot. Simon was about to bellow for men to fetch them, when he saw two of the labourers grab bags of rocks and some staffs, and hurry up to the wall.

Simon had enough to think of. He was crossing the yard when he glanced up at the wall. To his astonishment, he saw fighting. Then, 'Watch out! We have them inside already!' he shouted as he ran to the wall himself. Some of the labourers had taken their sticks and knocked down the men from the walls. One crossbowman was thrown to the court, landing on his head. He didn't move again.

Now Simon looked about him, he saw other little groups fighting, and he stood in the midst of the mayhem, sword in hand, trying to see which men were fighting for the castle, which were against it. It was almost impossible. Then he saw a man dart down that alley towards the postern, and felt his scalp crawl at the thought of more men entering.

He ran without thinking, and was at the alley as the man reached the gate. He had already shoved the key in the lock, and Simon gave a hoarse cry and threw himself forwards. The fellow darted to one side, but then he had a knife out. He had the look of a fighter, and Simon was wary, aware of his own slowness this morning. His sword-tip did not waver, and he thrust quickly, only to see his blade miss the mark. Back to circling. Simon panted slightly, his mouth open as he kept his eyes firmly fixed on the fellow.

There was a crunch on his head, and he slumped in the same moment, falling to his knees. Behind him, he heard a man cry to the other to open the postern, and Simon fell, rolling over, recognising John standing over him, a great truncheon in his fist. It was fortunate he had not grabbed for a sword, Simon thought as he succumbed to the blow and felt the waves of nausea washing through his body. They seemed to rise from his feet with a tingling, pins-and-needles sensation until it reached his belly. He rolled over again, to the base of the wall, and was heartily sick even as he heard the postern flung wide and the triumphant roar of the enemy's troops as they poured in.

On the walls, Baldwin had no idea what had happened to Simon, but when he saw the labourers attack the crossbowmen, he realised the danger posed by the masons and labourers, and shouted to Edgar, who was even now running up the stairs to the wall.

'No! Edgar, watch the stone workers! There are traitors among them. Stop them!'

Edgar said nothing, but lightly sprang down to the ground again. There was a mason with a sword beating at a man-at-arms, and as Edgar passed him, he casually rammed the pommel of his sword into the man's head. The mason collapsed.

Baldwin saw his sergeant walk to the masons' area, and on his way, he collected Senchet and Harry and a bemused Hugh to join him. They seemed keen to help, and Baldwin hoped that they would not show themselves traitors too. He heard a loud roaring, and realised too late that it must be the exultation of men entering the castle. Peering over the wall's edge, he saw that already thirty or more men were inside, and he swore with bitter futility at the sight. He was the wrong side of the castle to get to Sir Edward. The great keep was across from him here, and he would not reach it before the men below, no matter how fast he ran.

He must do *something*!

Harry stood nervously with Senchet as the masons glowered back at them. Edgar appeared unconcerned by their anger, and eyed them with an easy nonchalance, his sword swinging lazily in his hand, but to Harry the sight of twenty or more strongly built men who were used to handling large rocks and heavy hammers was deeply troubling.

When the rush came from the postern gate, all changed in an instant. Edgar heard the pounding of feet, and was immediately off towards the tumult. Harry and Senchet took a look at each other, and then back at the masons.

'What now?' Harry said.

One mason pointed at the fighting at the gate. 'Fellows, if those bastards get in here, they will undo all our work. Who's with me to protect the castle?'

Senchet grabbed a hammer, and weighed it meaningfully in his hand. 'Friends, I think you should stay here.'

The mason who had spoken looked at him contemptuously. 'You aren't going to stop me protecting my works, boy. Out of my way.'

And behind him the other labourers grabbed weapons and rushed towards the gate. Soon Senchet could see them grabbing at the men attacking, hurling them to the ground and beating them with hammers.

'My friend,' he said to Harry, 'I think soon we shall have a chance to help ourselves.'

Sir Richard had been at the hall seeing whether the little serving wench could rustle up some breakfast when the first roars came from the yard, and he stood, torn between hunger and duty, before sighing sadly and turning from the room.

At the stairs he saw the fight degenerate into a number of smaller battles. There were the small clusters on the battlements, and he saw Baldwin opposite, fighting like a berserker, while there were groups of men-at-arms brawling and bellowing in front of the gates, and then he saw the masons and labourers slam into the side of the fellows who had entered by the postern, led by Edgar, and nodded approvingly.

His maid appeared beside him with a platter. She almost dropped it as she took in the scene outside, and he caught the cold chicken leg before it could fall. 'Careful,' he admonished.

'They're storming the castle!'

'Aye,' he agreed pensively. 'Think they are, at that.'

He gave her a quick kiss. 'Lock the door, little flower. I'll be back in a while,' he said, gently pushing her inside and closing the door. He waited until he had heard the bar fall into place at the other side, and gave it an experimental push to make sure it was secure, before descending the stairs, sucking the meat from the bones. His sword was still in his hand, and as he passed a pair of fighting men, he peered into their faces. One was recognisable, the other unfamiliar, so he waited until there was a suitable moment, and brought his gloved fist round to the man's face. He felt bones snap and shatter, and looked down with wistful irritation at the mangled chicken in his fist. 'Bugger.'

Continuing to the keep, he had to pause while three men passed in front of him, herded by the grinning Edgar. All were armed, but none dared confront the man-at-arms. It was apparent that Edgar needed no aid. He was happily slashing and thrusting with speed and agility. There was a shriek, then a whimper, and one fell. Edgar advanced on the other two with renewed vigour, and as Sir Richard watched, a second collapsed with a sigh as Edgar's blade punctured his breast. The last man dropped to his knees and threw his sword away, and Edgar tutted then smashed his pommel into the man's skull before going in search of fresh targets.

Sir Richard found a group of four at the keep's door. They were all unknown to him, so he wandered over to them. 'Tryin' to get inside?' he enquired.

There was no word from them. All turned to him and he found himself faced by three swords and a war-hammer. His sword was already up, and the third man to spin spitted himself on the point. Sir Richard pulled it free as the fellow tumbled, sobbing, hands to his belly, and knocked the second sword away, slashing back to cut off the man's hand with the sword still gripped tightly in his fist. The man with the hammer sprang away, and Sir Richard lifted his brows enquiringly at the remaining swordsman. He looked at Sir Richard with the terror making his face clench, and then he dropped the sword and slid slowly to the ground.

Sir Richard stared down at him in bafflement. 'Fellow's

fainted,' he muttered, and pushed him aside with his boot. Then he lifted his fist and beat on the timbers. 'Hoi! It's me, Sir Richard de Welles. You all right in there? Eh? Speak up, man? Are you all right, I say?'

There was a muttered response, and Sir Richard glanced around. 'Open up. There's no danger for a while.'

He heard a thud or two as the heavy bolts were pulled aside, and then the door opened and he slipped inside. 'Lock it again,' he ordered. 'How's Sir Edward?'

The three men at the door gazed at him uncomprehendingly and he grunted to himself before striding off to see for himself.

Sir Edward of Caernarfon had heard the noise of battle from the first, and now he stood in his chamber with a feeling of panic. Sir Ralph was with him, and Gilbert, and the two stood resolutely at his side.

There was a loud rapping at the door, and he felt his heart leap into his throat, but then he heard the welcome bellow of Sir Richard. 'Sir Edward, you all right in there?'

'Yes,' he cried. 'Sir Richard, what is happening?'

'A force come to break into the castle,' Sir Richard shouted. 'Don't know why.'

Sir Edward felt a chill at those words. Sir Richard no fool, was reminding him that there was no guarantee that this attack was destined to save him. It could be for another reason entirely – to kill him. It was certainly not past Sir Roger Mortimer to arrange for his death by sending men to sack the castle. He would not care about the loss of life that ensued.

'What should I do?'

'Stay where you are,' Sir Richard said. 'With luck we'll hold 'em off.'

*   *   *

When Sir Richard had finished speaking, he went to a window that gave a view of the courtyard, and the scene that met his eyes was a shock. The main gates were wide, and there was a rabble of men outside, some on horseback, milling about. He heard a crashing thunder, and knew that already some men were attacking the door to the keep. With all the masons' tools, he knew it would not take too long before the door gave way.

He scowled at the thought, then strode to a door which led to the spiral staircase in the wall. Climbing quickly for a man of his build, he went to the topmost wall and stared about, trying to assess possible methods of concealment or escape, but could see nothing.

Baldwin, he saw, was still on the battlements. His companions had almost all fallen, and only two survived with him of all the garrison and labourers who had joined him. As he watched, three lunged forward, and Baldwin stepped back, feinted, and stabbed. One of the attackers gave a shrill scream, dropped his sword and clutched his throat.

'Good man,' Sir Richard said approvingly, but his eyes were already studying the rest of the battle, and it was quickly apparent that there was little hope of escape. The courtyard was held by the enemy, and there was no sign of Edgar or the others fighting to defend the castle.

Then he saw Edgar, a dark, rushing figure carrying a ladder; he set it against the battlements and then swarmed up it, to run at the men holding Baldwin at bay. He gave a cry Sir Richard could hear distinctly from the top of the tower, and soon Baldwin was relieved. The last attackers were driven off. Sir Richard saw Baldwin pointing and staring down into the yard, and when their eyes met, he waved. Baldwin waved back.

In the castle there was the sound of breaking timbers as doors were smashed open, and a few wisps of smoke showed where some men had broken tables and stools just for the pleasure of destruction. A bellow of delight told that one man had discovered the undercroft where the wines were stored. Sir Richard returned to the door to Sir Edward's chamber and stood outside.

He had enjoyed his life. It had been moderately long, and he was happy enough. If he could serve Sir Edward now by dying in his service, it would be no bad thing. He was ready enough to die. Since the death of his wife many years ago, raped and killed by a servant he had trusted, he had felt as if he had lived on too long. And to die in the service of a fellow's liege lord was always good. Better than living as a coward.

So he gripped his sword more firmly and waited.

The men were already turning to looting as Stephen Dunheved knocked on the doors to the keep.

'There is no need for more blood to be shed,' he shouted. 'We want our King, that is all. Let him out, and you can all live.'

The negotiations took a little while, but it was not long before a sulky face appeared in the doorway and Stephen and Thomas walked inside. Their men were behind, and they took the weapons from the guards before herding them outside, while the brothers took one to lead them to Sir Edward's chamber.

'I will prevent you,' Sir Richard said as they ascended the stairs.

He was a great bear of a man, and he balanced on the balls of his feet, readying himself to launch at them.

Stephen held up his hands in a placatory manner. 'Sir Richard, do you remember me?'

'Eh?'

'I used to serve your King, just as you did. Sir Richard, would it not be arrant nonsense for us to battle – you to hold him, I to free him? Ask him what he wishes. Do not listen to those who demand you keep him here. If it is against our King's wishes, who are we to argue?'

'Our King wishes to keep Sir Edward here,' Sir Richard said.

'Ask Sir Edward, then,' Stephen Dunheved said. 'Look through the window at how many men I have with me, Sir Richard. If you wish, I can have an archer come here and fill you with arrows. It would change nothing. Your death would alter nothing. Sir Edward will still be released.'

'If I die defending him . . .'

'But you aren't. You are fighting to protect Sir Roger Mortimer's plan to hold him here. Do you want that?'

Sir Richard gripped his sword tighter. 'No. But it is my duty,' he said.

Stephen was about to order a general charge at Sir Richard when Sir Ranulf pushed past him.

Sir Richard's face was pale with shock to see him. 'You? Coroner, you are with them too?'

'Of course,' Sir Ranulf said. 'And Rodney, too. We want the real King on his throne. Think of the rewards for the bold ones who reinstal him!'

Sir Richard shook his head. 'This is treachery!' He lifted his sword and was about to leap on them, when the sound of the door unlocking behind him made him pause.

Sir Ralph walked out and put his hand on Sir Richard's shoulder. 'Sir Richard, I think there have been enough dead, my friend. It is time to end it.'

'Aye, perhaps,' Sir Richard said, but his eyes were on Sir Edward.

Sir Edward of Caernarfon slowly walked from the room like one in a dream. He stared at Sir Richard with an expression of blank uncertainty, as though he had no idea whether he was being rescued or captured.

CHAPTER FIFTY-SIX

Berkeley Castle

It was obvious that the castle was lost. Where there were one or two men left standing, they were collected by the attackers in dribs and drabs, and led to a wall where they were watched.

Senchet eyed the men with interest. Beside him, Harry was binding a cut over his knuckles where a sword had caught him, swearing quietly to himself.

'There!' Senchet hissed, and pointed. There, with the men being held, was the Keeper of the gate. Senchet remembered him from the day of their capture. 'He had the keys.'

'What?'

'The room over there, where our chest has been stored. That man locked the door.'

'What of it?'

Senchet licked his lips. The gatekeeper's room was a little chamber in the gatehouse, and from here Senchet could see the open door. There was no one inside.

'Come with me,' he said.

Carefully they made their way past bodies, past piles of rock, and in at the chamber. Nobody challenged them; nobody paid them any heed. And inside, there on the floor, they saw the little bunch of keys. Senchet took them up reverentially and thrust them into his shirt, turning a look of simple happiness to Harry.

'We'll wait here until they have gone, and then . . . We'll be rich!'

The noise was infuriating! Matteo wanted to know what was happening, but when he beat at his door, early on, he was told to belt up and be quiet, and now, there was nothing. It was clear enough that there was a battle going on, and he wanted to know who was attacking. With luck, his brother and the snakes who had thrown him in here would die, and then he would be able to take over the bank as he had intended for the last few months. That would be good, he thought with a smile.

There was a clattering in the corridor, like men running and dropping weapons, but then there was silence again.

He jerked and pulled at the door, but it was firmly locked. If only he could have escaped this chamber, he could have climbed through the little window that gave access to the roof, along which he had fled that evening when he killed Sir Jevan.

It had been shocking how the man writhed and shrieked. Matteo had intended to just hack once and leave him for dead. It had been easy enough to plan. He had merely left a piece of parchment in Jevan's room telling him to meet Benedetto in the tower before dawn because of a new threat to the Queen's finances. It was all he needed write. He knew that Sir Jevan would be unable to ignore the summons. And Sir Jevan was punctual. All Matteo need do was step up close and strike with his axe.

The axe had seemed such a clever idea. A weapon that could implicate Dolwyn, and thus remove the two threats to Matteo's stability and comfort. He wished he had an axe here now. That would be good.

He had no weapon. The only tool he had in the chamber was a large steel poker. Perhaps with that he could break through the door? It was worth trying, he thought, and he took it up – but just as he was about to begin, he heard voices outside.

'Help me! Help!' he shouted, and to his relief he heard the key turn in the lock. As the door was thrown wide, he dashed forward to thank his rescuers.

It was his misfortune that the three men outside had reason to fear all those held in the castle. They knew that this was not their King, for he was already saved. But seeing a man armed, so they thought, with a sword, rush at them, they all took the precaution of cutting at him before he could hurt any of them.

Matteo fell screaming at the agony of the blows, and was still shrieking as he died.

Up on the battlements, for a moment Baldwin thought that there might have been a victory in the keep, but then he saw the men cheering, lifting their hats and waving them as the slim, elegant, fair-haired figure stood in the doorway at the top of the stairs.

'What was it all for, Edgar?' he said tiredly.

'I think we may be heading for another war, Sir Baldwin.'

'Sweet Mother of God, preserve us from that,' the knight breathed. He set his blue sword blade against a fold of his tunic and wiped it clean. The blood, mingled with the oil used to preserve it, stained the material, but he was past caring. Looking about him, he could see the bodies of four men he had killed, and seven more lay dead or squirming. One man had crawled to the corner and lay there now, shivering with shock and cold as his lifeblood drained and drenched his clothes.

Baldwin shoved his sword into its scabbard and leaned against the battlements. All these dead . . . and if Sir Edward were to escape, more would die in the continual struggle for power. This time the battles could range over the whole nation, if the King were to gather enough support.

But there was nothing he could do to stop it. He had done his best.

John stood in the court looking on while all around him men cheered and shouted as the King appeared at the top of the stairs, a hand raised tentatively, as though not quite sure whether these men actually planned to support him or kill him. He had the look of a man who receives a pardon while standing on the ladder, the noose already about his neck, unsure whether the ladder will be taken away before he can have the rope removed.

John moved forward, one man among all the forces brought to this place to release their King.

In his mind John saw Paul's face, the happy, smiling companion whom he had loved closer than a brother. And he saw again that same Paul, choking as he drowned in blood.

This King, this Edward, would raise a host of men to march on his son to take back his authority. His host would attack the castles owned by Sir Roger Mortimer, and slaughter all those inside. The desire for revenge would be all-consuming. After the last civil war, six years ago, the King's rage had resulted in his cousin being executed, and then hundreds of knights up and down the country had been ritually slain, their bodies carved up and tarred to hang from hooks outside the city walls of the realm. Two years later they were still there.

How many more. *How many more must die?*

He looked up and saw Sir Edward in front of him.

'Edgar!' Baldwin exclaimed. 'That man there – it's John of Shulton, isn't it? What's he doing?'

Edgar looked down at the men below and spotted the fellow in question pushing through the crowds towards Sir Edward. Edgar ran to the crossbows. One was spanned and loaded still. He took it up.

John saw the face smile. Sir Edward – King Edward – was smiling at him with gratitude.

The irony was appalling, he thought. He had his sword in his hand still, and he glanced down at it. When he returned his gaze to Sir Edward, he saw that the King's eyes too were fixed on the sword – but not with terror nor even surprise, just a kind of acceptance. He did not try to hide or cower, nor plead to save his life. He merely stood, waiting for the blow.

John mouthed, *'I am sorry!'* before moving to plunge the sword into Sir Edward's body.

But before he could do so there was an explosion of pain that ran from his shoulder all the way down to his bowels. He went down, his left knee slamming into the ground, as though he had been punched by someone behind him. There was a searing heat through the whole of his body, and as he turned his head, his chin hit something. The object was red and raw, like a bone freshly butchered – and then he realised it was a bone – *his* bone. And then the knives and swords came battering and butchering him, and he fell again, staring up at the sky as his heart stopped beating.

CHAPTER FIFTY-SEVEN

Friday after the Nativity of St John the Baptist[1]

Berkeley Castle

Sir Richard de Welles sat at the table with a grunt of satisfaction. The maid was there already, a hunk of bread ready and waiting for him, and he smiled at her a little wearily as he took it and bit off a piece.

Baldwin walked in a short while later, and Sir Richard said nothing, merely pushed his jug of ale towards him.

'Thank you, Sir Richard,' Baldwin said as he sat.

'How are you?' the other man asked.

'Sore, mainly,' Baldwin answered with a grin. 'My arms are aching. It reminds me that I am no longer as young as I once was.'

'Simon?'

'He'll recover. He has a hard pate,' Baldwin said unsympathetically. 'There are many others who will not wake this morning.'

1 26 June 1327

512

'It was a fierce battle,' Sir Richard said quietly.

He could see those men again, staring at him as he prepared himself for death before Sir Edward's chamber. In truth, he felt as though he had endured it. Strange, but it was an uplifting experience, not a shameful one, as though passing so near to dying was almost the same as dying in reality.

'We lost a lot of the garrison,' Baldwin said.

'Aye – and Sir Edward.' Sir Ralph was morosely sipping at a mazer of wine.

'The posse of the county must search for him,' Baldwin said.

'You yourself will not?'

'No. I never wanted to be his gaoler and I would not see him imprisoned again. Let him find what peace he may, while he may.'

'Aye. I can understand that,' Sir Richard said. He was still unnaturally pensive. 'Your man – a good shot, that.'

'I was just sorry that John had to die. I rather liked him.' Baldwin shook his head. 'He appeared to be with those who wanted to free Sir Edward. I was astonished to see him try to stab him.'

'We'll never know why,' Sir Richard said.

Gradually people began to enter to break their fast after yesterday's efforts.

Baldwin walked outside. The yard was a mess still. The fires started by the men in the assault were more or less out now, but all about the ward was a fine layer of ash and some thick clots of soot. Baldwin and Sir Richard had caused the bodies to be taken to one side of the yard near the chapel. There were more than thirty men lying there, Baldwin counted. It was enough to spoil his appetite, and he threw his crust away. Wolf snatched it up and bolted it in a moment, and Baldwin put his hand on his dog's head and ruffled his coat, taking comfort from the animal.

There was no telling, he thought, just what the outcome of this attack would be. Perhaps the old King would fight for his throne again and oust his own son.

But even as he wondered, he saw again the look on the man's face as John stood before him with his sword unsheathed. Sir Edward had looked almost as though he welcomed the killing blow. To feel like that, Baldwin thought, a man must have travelled through Hell already. Sir Edward had lost wife, friends, throne, authority, wealth – everything. Would it be a surprise if he would be glad of an end to his suffering?

He had survived because of Edgar's crossbow bolt . . .

Baldwin wondered now whether he was, or was not, grateful for that shot.

Willersey

Father Luke smiled at Jen as she swept out his church.

What a year this had been! He was glad to be away from the castle. Berkeley had only miserable memories for him, which all merged in Luke's mind to form a mosaic of horror.

Not that it was all that much better here, he thought. There were too many memories of Agatha and Ham for his entire comfort. Still, he must forget that in the interests of Jen. She needed all the help she could get.

Her face was a little rounder, he was sure, and she had lost the look of bewildered terror that had so characterised her until her mother's death. He wished – he *prayed* – that she would find some comfort from the fact that she had the support of the entire vill. The reeve had made it plain that he would look with disfavour upon any man who refused to help the child. But for her part, although it was highly unorthodox, she insisted that she could cope with her father's farm. She would not tolerate another man taking it on, even though Will Sharp and Dan

Bakere both offered to take her in and work her lands for her. She gratefully accepted their offers of aid but refused to leave her house, and there was nothing anyone could do to persuade her otherwise.

They could have forced her, perhaps, but as Luke said to them, what was the point? She could feed herself, she could see to her own animals – she had done so, much of the time already in her short life – and it was surely better that when she truly needed help, the vill would support her.

He would always be there for her, in any case.

Oxford Road

Benedetto was glad to have left the charnelhouse that was Berkeley Castle behind him. He had managed to pack his belongings, and with his guards about him, had been pleased to ride away.

The journey was to be a lengthy one, but it was good to be moving at last. His horse had a comforting gait, rolling gently from side to side as Benedetto recalled the horrors of the last weeks. His own injury was nothing compared with those of Alured and others, and yet it did not prevent him from missing his younger brother. If only there had been something he could have done for poor Matteo.

Still, there was one good thing about Matteo's death yester-day. Benedetto had been able to bring his brother's body with him. He would ensure that Matteo was given a good funeral at Oxford.

And it did save the family's honour. Matteo had died, so all would hear, from wounds earned while trying to protect Berkeley Castle from attackers. Benedetto would make sure that Queen Isabella and the Regent heard that story, he promised himself.

It should help the bank. And Matteo would be glad to know that his death had helped it.

Dolwyn too was relieved to be away from the castle.

He found it hard to believe how drastically his life had changed in recent weeks. From being a loyal servant of Matteo, he had managed to risk his all to take a message to Sir Edward at Kenilworth, and then there had been all the deaths, the fighting, and the ignominy of arrest and the gaols.

Never again, he swore, would he spend time in a gaol. If there was any risk, he would prefer to fight to the death. He had seen too much of Newgate and Berkeley's prisons in the last year.

Matteo had lost his mind – a fortunate development. Dolwyn wouldn't have wanted people to hear about his own part in Matteo's affairs. Benedetto would disembowel him alive if he learned that Dolwyn had been responsible for Manuele's death. Dolwyn had gone to the mob and given them the money Matteo had paid so that Manuele should be killed. It had been Dolwyn's task to pay and point out their man, and he had done so without trouble. But then, when they had pulled Manuele from his horse and cut off his head, many of them, drunk with bloodlust, had run on and grabbed Matteo.

There was nothing underhand about his stabbing. It was just the London mob acting in character. Dolwyn had tried to make him see that, but Matteo was always busy looking for secrets, assuming that there was an undercurrent to everything. He just could not believe that his own injury could have been committed on the whim of a crowd.

Road to Gloucester

They rode side by side, and every so often Senchet turned and gazed behind him at the road going back towards Berkeley Castle.

'Is anyone there?' Harry said.

'No. No one.'

'Oh.'

They rode on again in silence.

Then Senchet said, 'It wasn't really theirs.'

'You tell that to the men with the swords.'

'They took it.'

'Aha.'

'It was Despenser's, really.'

'Aye.'

'And he's dead.'

Harry made no comment.

Senchet looked down at the bag that hung over his belly. Inside it were a number of little leather pouches. In each, fistfuls of gold coins. He looked across at Harry. Harry had a similar bag at his stomach. Senchet looked up into Harry's face, and Harry looked back at him.

Their laughter could be heard by a peasant called Martin at the farm a half-mile from the road.

His wife came out and gestured towards the roadway. 'What's so funny, you reckon?'

'God knows,' he muttered dourly. But his eyes were on the two riders as they continued on their way, laughing uproariously as they increased the distance between themselves and the castle.